WOOL

WOOL

HUGH
HOWEY

arrow books

Published by Arrow Books 2013

21

Copyright © Hugh Howey 2013

Hugh Howey has asserted his right under the Copyright, Designs
and Patents Act 1988 to be identified as the author of this work

First published in Great Britain in 2013 by Century

Arrow Books
Random House, 20 Vauxhall Bridge Road,
London SW1V 2SA

www.randomhouse.co.uk

Addresses for companies within The Random House Group Limited
can be found at: www.randomhouse.co.uk/offices.htm

The Random House Group Limited Reg. No. 954009

A CIP catalogue record for this book
is available from the British Library

ISBN 9780099580485

The Random House Group Limited supports The Forest Stewardship Council®
(FSC®), the leading international forest-certification organisation. Our books carrying
the FSC label are printed on FSC®-certified paper. FSC is the only forest certification
scheme supported by the leading environmental organisations, including Greenpeace.
Our paper procurement policy can be found at: www.randomhouse.co.uk/environment

Typeset in Adobe Caslon by Palimpsest Book Production Limited,
Falkirk, Stirlingshire
Printed in Great Britain by Clays Ltd, St Ives plc

For those who dare to hope

PART 1 – HOLSTON

PART I—HOUSES

The children were playing while Holston climbed to his death; he could hear them squealing as only happy children do. While they thundered about frantically above, Holston took his time, each step methodical and ponderous, as he wound his way around and around the spiral staircase, old boots ringing out on metal treads.

The treads, like his father's boots, showed signs of wear. Paint clung to them in feeble chips, mostly in the corners and undersides, where they were safe. Traffic elsewhere on the staircase sent dust shivering off in small clouds. Holston could feel the vibrations in the railing, which was worn down to the gleaming metal. That always amazed him: how centuries of bare palms and shuffling feet could wear down solid steel. One molecule at a time, he supposed. Each life might wear away a single layer, even as the silo wore away that life.

Each step was slightly bowed from generations of traffic, the edge rounded down like a pouting lip. In the centre, there was almost no trace of the small diamonds that once gave the treads their grip. Their absence could only be inferred from the pattern to either side, the small pyramidal bumps rising from the flat steel with their crisp edges and flecks of paint.

Holston lifted an old boot to an old step, pressed down, and did it again. He lost himself in what the untold years had done, the ablation of molecules and lives, layers and layers ground to fine dust. And he thought, not for the first time, that neither life nor staircase had been meant for such an existence. The tight confines of that long spiral, threading through the buried silo like a straw in a glass, had not been built for such abuse. Like much of their cylindrical home, it seemed to have been made for other purposes, for functions long since forgotten. What was now used as a thoroughfare for thousands of people, moving up and down in repetitious daily cycles, seemed more apt in Holston's view to be used only in emergencies and perhaps by mere dozens.

Another floor went by – a pie-shaped division of dormitories. As Holston ascended the last few levels, this last climb he would ever take, the sounds of childlike delight rained down even louder from above. This was the laughter of youth, of souls who had not yet come to grips with where they lived, who did not yet feel the press of the earth on all sides, who in their minds were not buried at all, but *alive*. Alive and unworn, dripping happy sounds down the stairwell, trills that were incongruous with Holston's actions, his decision and determination to go *outside*.

As he neared the upper level, one young voice rang out above the others, and Holston remembered being a child in the silo – all the schooling and the games. Back then, the stuffy concrete cylinder had felt, with its floors and floors of apartments and work-shops and hydroponic gardens and purification rooms with their tangles of pipes, like a vast universe, a wide expanse one could never fully explore, a labyrinth he and his friends could get lost in for ever.

But those days were more than thirty years distant. Holston's childhood now felt like something two or three lifetimes ago, something someone else had enjoyed. Not him. He had an entire lifetime as sheriff weighing heavy, blocking off that past. And more recently, there was this third stage of his life – a secret life beyond childhood and being sheriff. It was the last layers of himself ground to dust; three years spent silently waiting for what would never come, each day longer than any month from his happier lifetimes.

At the top of the spiral stairway, Holston's hand ran out of railing. The curvy bar of worn steel ended as the stairwell emptied into the widest rooms of the entire silo complex: the cafeteria and the adjoining lounge. The playful squeals were level with him now. Darting bright shapes zagged between scattered chairs, playing chase. A handful of adults tried to contain the chaos. Holston saw Donna picking up scattered chalk and crayon from the stained tiles. Her husband Clarke sat behind a table arranged with cups of juice and bowls of cornflour cookies. He waved at Holston from across the room.

Holston didn't think to wave back, didn't have the energy or the desire. He looked past the adults and playing children to the blurry view beyond, projected on the cafeteria wall. It was the largest uninterrupted vista of their inhospitable world. A morning scene. Dawn's dim light coated lifeless hills that had hardly changed since Holston was a boy. They sat, just as they always had, while he had gone from playing chase among the cafeteria tables to whatever empty thing he was now. And beyond the stately rolling crests of these hills, the top of a familiar and rotting skyline caught the morning rays in feeble glints. Ancient glass and steel stood distantly where people, it was suspected, had once lived aboveground.

A child, ejected from the group like a comet, bumped into Holston's knees. He looked down and moved to touch the kid – Susan's boy – but just like a comet the child was gone again, pulled back into the orbit of the others.

Holston thought suddenly of the lottery he and Allison had won the year of her death. He still had the ticket; he carried it everywhere. One of these kids – maybe he or she would be two by now and tottering after the older children – could've been theirs. They had dreamed, like all parents do, of the double fortune of twins. They had tried, of course. After her implant was removed, they had spent night after glorious night trying to redeem that ticket, other parents wishing them luck, other lottery hopefuls silently praying for an empty year to pass.

Knowing they only had a year, he and Allison had invited superstition into their lives, looking to anything for help. Tricks like hanging garlic over the bed that supposedly increased fertility, two dimes under the mattress for twins, a pink ribbon in Allison's hair, smudges of blue dye under Holston's eyes – all of it ridiculous and desperate and fun. The only thing crazier would have been to *not* try everything, to leave some silly seance or tale untested.

But it wasn't to be. Before their year was even out, the lottery had passed to another couple. It hadn't been for a lack of trying; it had been a lack of time. A sudden lack of *wife*.

Holston turned away from the games and the blurry view and walked towards his office, situated between the cafeteria and the silo's airlock. As he covered that ground, his thoughts went to the struggle that once took place there, a struggle of ghosts he'd had to walk through every day for the last three years. And he knew, if he turned and hunted that expansive view on the wall, if he squinted past the ever-worsening blur of cloudy camera lenses and airborne grime, if he followed that dark crease up the hill, that wrinkle that worked its way over the muddy dune towards the city beyond, he could pick out her quiet form. There, on that hill, his wife could be seen. She lay like a sleeping boulder, the air and toxins wearing away at her, her arms curled under her head.

Maybe.

It was difficult to see, hard to make out clearly even back before the blurring had begun anew. And besides, there was little to trust in that sight. There was much, in fact, to doubt. So Holston simply chose not to look. He walked through that place of his wife's ghostly struggle, where bad memories lay eternal, that scene of her sudden madness, and entered his office.

'Well, look who's up early,' Marnes said, smiling.

Holston's deputy closed a metal drawer on the filing cabinet, a lifeless cry singing from its ancient joints. He picked up a steaming mug, then noted Holston's solemn demeanour. 'You feeling okay, boss?'

Holston nodded. He pointed to the rack of keys behind the desk. 'Holding cell,' he said.

The deputy's smile drooped into a confused frown. He set down the mug and turned to retrieve the key. While his back was turned, Holston rubbed the sharp, cool steel in his palm one last time, then placed the star flat on the desk. Marnes turned and held out the key. Holston took it.

'You need me to grab the mop?' Deputy Marnes jabbed a thumb back towards the cafeteria. Unless someone was in cuffs, they only went into the cell to clean it.

'No,' Holston said. He jerked his head towards the holding cell, beckoning his deputy to follow.

He turned, the chair behind the desk squeaking as Marnes rose to join him, and Holston completed his march. The key slid in with ease. There was a sharp clack from the well-built and well-maintained inner organs of the door. The barest squeak from the hinges, a determined step, a shove and a clank, and the ordeal was over.

'Boss?'

Holston held the key between the bars. Marnes looked down at them, unsure, but his palm came up to accept it.

'What's going on, boss?'

'Get the mayor,' Holston said. He let out a sigh, that heavy breath he'd been holding for three years.

'Tell her I want to go outside.'

2

The view from the holding cell wasn't as blurry as it had been in the cafeteria, and Holston spent his final day in the silo puzzling over this. Could it be that the camera on that side was shielded against the toxic wind? Did each cleaner, condemned to death, put more care in preserving the view they'd enjoyed on their last day? Or was the extra effort a gift to the *next* cleaner, who would spend their final day in that same cell?

Holston preferred this last explanation. It made him think longingly of his wife. It reminded him why he was there, on the wrong side of those bars, and willingly.

As his thoughts drifted to Allison, he sat and stared out at the dead world some ancient peoples had left behind. It wasn't the best view of the landscape around their buried bunker, but it wasn't the worst, either. In the distance, low rolling hills stood a pretty shade of brown, like coffee mash with just the right amount of pig's milk in it. The sky above the hills was the same dull grey of his childhood and his father's childhood and his grandfather's childhood. The only moving feature on the landscape was the clouds. They hung full and dark over the hills. They roamed free like the herded beasts from the picture books.

The view of the dead world filled up the entire wall of his cell, just like all the walls on the silo's upper level, each one full of a different slice of the blurry and ever-blurrier wasteland beyond. Holston's little piece of that view reached from the corner by his cot, up to the ceiling, to the other wall, and down to the toilet. And despite the soft blur – like oil rubbed on a lens – it looked like a scene one could stroll out into, like a gaping and inviting hole oddly positioned across from forbidding prison bars.

The illusion, however, convinced only from a distance. Leaning closer, Holston could see a handful of dead pixels on the massive display. They stood stark white against all the brown and grey hues. Shining with ferocious intensity, each pixel (Allison had called them 'stuck' pixels) was like a square window to some brighter place, a hole the width of a human hair that seemed to beckon towards some better reality. There were dozens of them, now that he looked closer. Holston wondered if anyone in the silo knew how to fix them, or if they had the tools required for such a delicate job. Were they dead for ever, like Allison? Would all of the pixels be dead eventually? Holston imagined a day when half of the pixels were stark white, and then generations later when only a few grey and brown ones remained, then a mere dozen, the world having flipped to a new state, the people of the silo thinking the outside world was on fire, the only *true* pixels now mistaken for malfunctioning ones.

Or was that what Holston and his people were doing even now?

Someone cleared their throat behind him. Holston turned and saw Mayor Jahns standing on the other side of the bars, her hands resting in the belly of her overalls. She nodded gravely towards the cot.

'When the cell's empty, at night when you and Deputy Marnes are off duty, I sometimes sit right there and enjoy that very view.'

Holston turned back to survey the muddy, lifeless landscape. It only looked depressing compared to scenes from the children's books – the only books to survive the uprising. Most people doubted those colours in the books, just as they doubted purple elephants and pink birds ever existed, but Holston felt that they were truer than the scene before him. He, like some others, felt something primal and deep when he looked at those worn pages splashed green and blue. Even so, when compared to the stifling silo, that muddy grey view outside looked like some kind of salvation, just the sort of open air men were born to breathe.

'Always seems a little clearer in here,' Jahns said. 'The view, I mean.'

Holston remained silent. He watched a curling piece of cloud break off and move in a new direction, blacks and greys swirling together.

'You get your pick for dinner,' the mayor said. 'It's tradition—'

'You don't need to tell me how this works,' Holston said, cutting Jahns off. 'It's only been three years since I served Allison her last meal right here.' He reached to spin the copper ring on his finger out of habit, forgetting he had left it on his dresser hours ago.

'Can't believe it's been that long,' Jahns murmured to herself. Holston turned to see her squinting at the clouds displayed on the wall.

'Do you miss her?' Holston asked venomously. 'Or do you just hate that the blur has had so much time to build?'

Jahns's eyes flashed his way a moment, then dropped to the floor. 'You know I don't want this, not for any view. But rules are the rules—'

'It's not to be blamed,' Holston said, trying to let the anger go. 'I know the rules better than most.' His hand moved, just a little, towards the missing badge, left behind like his ring. 'Hell, I enforced those rules for most my life, even after I realised they were bullshit.'

Jahns cleared her throat. 'Well, I won't ask why you chose this. I'll just assume it's because you'd be unhappier here.'

Holston met her gaze, saw the film on her eyes before she was able to blink it away. Jahns looked thinner than usual, comical in her gaping overalls. The lines in her neck and radiating from her eyes were deeper than he remembered. Darker. And he thought the crack in her voice was genuine regret, not just age or her ration of tobacco.

Suddenly, Holston saw himself through Jahns's eyes, a broken man sitting on a worn bench, his skin grey from the pale glow of the dead world beyond, and the sight made him dizzy. His head spun as it groped for something reasonable to latch on to, something that made sense. It seemed a dream, the predicament his life had become. None of the last three years seemed true. Nothing seemed true any more.

He turned back to the tan hills. In the corner of his eye, he thought he saw another pixel die, turning stark white. Another tiny window had opened, another clear view through an illusion he had grown to doubt.

Tomorrow will be my salvation, Holston thought savagely, even if I die out there.

'I've been mayor too long,' Jahns said.

Holston glanced back and saw that her wrinkled hands were wrapped around the cold steel bars.

'Our records don't go back to the beginning, you know. They don't go back before the uprising a century and a half ago, but since then no mayor has sent more people to cleaning than I have.'

'I'm sorry to burden you,' Holston said dryly.

'I take no pleasure in it. That's all I'm saying. No pleasure at all.'

Holston swept his hand at the massive screen. 'But you'll be the first to watch a clear sunset tomorrow night, won't you?' He hated the way he sounded. Holston wasn't angry for his death, or life, or whatever came after tomorrow, but resentment over Allison's fate still lingered. He continued to see inevitable events from the past as avoidable, long after they'd taken their course. 'You'll all love the view tomorrow,' he said, more to himself than the mayor.

'That's not fair at all,' Jahns said. 'The law is the law. You broke it. You knew you were breaking it.'

Holston looked at his feet. The two of them allowed a silence to form. Mayor Jahns was the one who eventually spoke.

'You haven't threatened yet to *not* go through with it. Some of the others are nervous that you might not do the cleaning because you aren't saying you won't.'

Holston laughed. 'They'd feel better if I said I *wouldn't* clean the sensors?' He shook his head at the mad logic.

'Everyone who sits there says they aren't gonna do it,' Jahns told him, 'but then they do. It's what we've all come to expect—'

'Allison never threatened that she wouldn't do it,' Holston

reminded her, but he knew what Jahns meant. He himself had been sure Allison wouldn't wipe the lenses. And now he thought he understood what she'd been going through as she sat on that very bench. There were larger things to consider than the act of cleaning. Most who were sent outside were caught at something, were surprised to find themselves in that cell, their fate mere hours away. Revenge was on their mind when they said they wouldn't do it. But Allison and now Holston had bigger worries. Whether or not they'd clean was inconsequential; they had arrived here because they wanted, on some insane level, to *be* here. All that remained was the curiosity of it all. The wonder of the outside world beyond the projected veil of the wall screens.

'So, are you planning on going through with it or not?' Jahns asked directly, her desperation evident.

'You said it yourself.' Holston shrugged. 'Everyone does it. There must be some reason, right?'

He pretended not to care, to be disinterested in the *why* of the cleaning, but he had spent most of his life, the past three years especially, agonising over the why. The question drove him nuts. And if his refusing to answer Jahns caused pain to those who had murdered his wife, he wouldn't be upset.

Jahns rubbed her hands up and down the bars, anxious. 'Can I tell them you'll do it?' she asked.

'Or tell them I won't. I don't care. It sounds like either answer will mean the same to them.'

Jahns didn't reply. Holston looked up at her, and the mayor nodded.

'If you change your mind about the meal, let Deputy Marnes know. He'll be at the desk all night, as is tradition . . .'

She didn't need to say. Tears came to Holston's eyes as he remembered that part of his former duties. He had manned that desk twelve years ago when Donna Parkins was put to cleaning, eight years ago when it was Jack Brent's time. And he had spent a night clinging to the bars, lying on the floor, a complete wreck, three years ago when it was his wife's turn.

Mayor Jahns turned to go.

'Sheriff,' Holston muttered before she got out of earshot.

'I'm sorry?' Jahns lingered on the other side of the bars, her grey, bushy brows hanging over her eyes.

'It's Sheriff Marnes now,' Holston reminded her. 'Not Deputy.'

Jahns rapped a steel bar with her knuckles. 'Eat something,' she said. 'And I won't insult you by suggesting you get some sleep.'

Three Years Earlier

'Y'ou've gotta be *kidding* me,' Allison said. 'Honey, listen to this. You won't believe this. Did you know there was more than *one* uprising?'

Holston looked up from the folder spread across his lap. Around him, scattered piles of paper covered the bed like a quilt – stacks and stacks of old files to sort through and new complaints to manage. Allison sat at her small desk at the foot of the bed. The two of them lived in one of the silo condos that had been subdivided only twice over the decades. It left room for luxuries like desks and wide non-bunk beds.

'And how would I have known about that?' he asked her. His wife turned and tucked a strand of hair behind her ear. Holston jabbed a folder at her computer screen. 'All day long you're unlocking secrets hundreds of years old, and I'm supposed to know about them before *you* do?'

She stuck out her tongue. 'It's an expression. It's my way of informing you. And why don't you seem more curious? Did you hear what I just said?'

Holston shrugged. 'I never would've assumed the one uprising we know about was the first – just that it was the most recent. If I've learned one thing from my job, it's that no crime or crazy mob is ever all that original.' He picked up a folder by his knee. 'You think this is the first water thief the silo's known? Or that it'll be the last?'

Allison's chair squealed on the tile as she turned to face him. The monitor on the desk behind her blinked with the scraps and fragments of data she had pulled from the silo's old servers, the remnants of information long ago deleted and overwritten count-less times. Holston still didn't understand how the retrieval process worked, or why someone smart enough to come up with it was dumb enough to love him, but he accepted both as truth.

'I'm piecing together a series of old reports,' she said. 'If true, they mean something like our old uprising used to take place regularly. Like once every generation or so.'

'There's a lot we don't know about the old times,' Holston said. He rubbed his eyes and thought about all the paperwork he wasn't getting done. 'Maybe they didn't have a system for cleaning the sensors, you know? I'll bet back then, the view upstairs just got blurrier and blurrier until people went crazy, there'd be a revolt or something, and then they'd finally exile a few people to set things straight. Or maybe it was just natural population control, you know, before the lottery.'

Allison shook her head. 'I don't think so. I'm starting to think . . .' She paused and glanced down at the spread of paperwork around Holston. The sight of all the logged transgressions seemed to make her consider carefully what she was about to say. 'I'm not passing judgement, not saying anyone was right or wrong or anything like that. I'm just suggesting that maybe the servers weren't wiped out by the rebels during the uprising. Not like we've always been told, anyway.'

That got Holston's attention. The mystery of the blank servers, the empty past of the silo's ancestors, haunted them all. The erasure was nothing more than fuzzy legend. He closed the folder he was working on and set it aside. 'What do you think caused it?' he asked his wife. 'Do you think it was an accident? A fire or a power outage?' He listed the common theories.

Allison frowned. 'No,' she said. She lowered her voice and looked around anxiously. 'I think *we* wiped the hard drives. Our ancestors, I mean, *not* the rebels.' She turned and leaned towards the monitor, running her finger down a set of figures Holston couldn't discern from the bed. 'Twenty years,' she said. 'Eighteen. Twenty-four.' Her finger slid down the screen with a squeak. 'Twenty-eight. Sixteen. Fifteen.'

Holston ploughed a path through the paperwork at his feet,

putting the files back in stacks as he worked his way towards the desk. He sat on the foot of the bed, put a hand on his wife's neck, and peered over her shoulder at the monitor.

'Are those dates?' he asked.

She nodded. 'Just about every two decades, there's a major revolt. This report catalogued them. It was one of the files deleted during the most recent uprising. *Our* uprising.'

She said 'our' like either of them or any of their friends had been alive at the time. Holston knew what she meant, though. It was the uprising they had been raised in the shadow of, the one that seemed to have spawned them – the great conflict that hung over their childhoods, over their parents and grandparents. It was the uprising that filled whispers and occupied sideways glances.

'And what makes you think it was us, that it was the good guys who wiped the servers?'

She half turned and smiled grimly. 'Who says we are the good guys?'

Holston stiffened. He pulled his hand away from Allison's neck. 'Don't start. Don't say anything that might—'

'I'm kidding,' she said, but it wasn't a thing to kid about. It was two steps from traitorous, from *cleaning*. 'My theory is this,' she said quickly, stressing the word *theory*. 'There's generational upheaval, right? I mean for over a hundred years, maybe longer. It's like clockwork.' She pointed at the dates. 'But then, during the great uprising – the only one we've known about till now – someone wiped the servers. Which, I'll tell you, isn't as easy as pressing a few buttons or starting a fire. There's redundancies on top of redundancies. It would take a concerted effort, not an accident or any sort of rushed job or mere sabotage—'

'That doesn't tell you who's responsible,' Holston pointed out. His wife was a wizard with computers, no doubt, but sleuthing was not her bag, it was his.

'What tells me something,' she continued, 'is that there were uprisings every generation for all this time, but there hasn't been an uprising *since*.' Allison bit her lip.

Holston sat up straight. He glanced around the room and allowed her observation to sink in. He had a sudden vision of his wife yanking his sleuthing bag out of his hands and making off with it.

'So you're saying . . .' He rubbed his chin and thought this through. 'You're saying that someone wiped out our history to stop us from repeating it?'

'Or worse.' She reached out and held his hand with both of hers. Her face had deepened from seriousness to something more severe. 'What if the reason for the revolts was right there on the hard drives? What if some part of our known history, or some data from the outside, or maybe the knowledge of whatever it was that made people move in here long, long ago – what if that information built up some kind of pressure that made people lose their marbles, or go stir crazy, or just want *out*?'

Holston shook his head. 'I don't want you thinking that way,' he cautioned her.

'I'm not saying they were right to go nuts,' she told him, back to being careful. 'But from what I've pieced together so far, this is my theory.'

Holston gave the monitor an untrusting glance. 'Maybe you shouldn't be doing this,' he said. 'I'm not even sure *how* you're doing it, and maybe you shouldn't be.'

'Honey, the information is there. If I don't piece it together now, somebody else will at some point. You can't put the genie back in the bottle.'

'What do you mean?'

'I've already published a white paper on how to retrieve deleted and overwritten files. The rest of the IT department is spreading it around to help people who've unwittingly flushed something they needed.'

'I still think you should stop,' he said. 'This isn't the best idea. I can't see any good coming of it—'

'No good coming from the truth? Knowing the truth is always good. And better that it's us discovering it than someone else, right?'

Holston looked at his files. It'd been five years since the last person was sent to cleaning. The view of the outside was getting worse every day, and he could feel the pressure, as sheriff, to find someone. It was growing, like steam building up in the silo, ready to launch something out. People got nervous when they thought the time was near. It was like one of those self-fulfilling prophecies where the nerves finally made someone twitch, then lash out or say something regretful, and then they'd find themselves in a cell, watching their last blurry sunset.

Holston sorted through the files all around him, wishing there was something in them. He would put a man to his death tomorrow if it meant releasing that steam. His wife was poking some great, overly full balloon with a needle, and Holston wanted to get that air out of it before she poked too far.

4

Present Time

Holston sat on the lone steel bench in the airlock, his brain numb from lack of sleep and the surety of what lay before him. Nelson, the head of the cleaning lab, knelt in front of him and worked a leg of the white hazard suit over Holston's foot.

'We've played around with the joint seals and added a second spray-on lining,' Nelson was saying. 'It should give you more time out there than anyone has had before.'

This registered with Holston, and he remembered watching his wife go about her cleaning. The top floor of the silo with its great screens showing the outside world was usually empty for cleanings. The people inside couldn't bear to watch what they'd done – or maybe they wanted to come up and enjoy a nice view without seeing what it took to get it. But Holston had watched; there was never any doubt that he would. He couldn't see Allison's face through her silver-masked helmet, couldn't see her thin arms through the bulky suit as she scrubbed and scrubbed with her wool pads, but he knew her walk, her mannerisms. He had watched her finish the job, taking her time and doing it well, and then she had stepped back, looked in the camera one last time, waved at him, then turned to walk away. Like others before her, she had lumbered towards a nearby hill and had begun climbing up, trudging towards the dilapidated spires of that ancient and crumbling city just visible over the horizon. Holston hadn't moved the entire time. Even as she fell on the side of the hill, clutching her helmet, writhing while the toxins first ate away the spray-on linings, then the suit and finally his wife, he hadn't moved.

'Other foot.'

Nelson slapped his ankle. Holston lifted his foot and allowed the tech to bunch the rest of the suit around his shins. Looking at his hands, at the black carbon undersuit he wore against his skin, Holston pictured it all dissolving off his body, sloughing away like flakes of dried grease from a generator's pipe while the blood burst from his pores and pooled up in his lifeless suit.

'If you'll grab the bar and stand—'

Nelson was walking him through a routine he'd seen twice before. Once with Jack Brent, who had been belligerent and hostile right up to the end, forcing him as sheriff to stand guard by the bench. And once with his wife, whom he had watched get ready through the airlock's small porthole. Holston knew what to do from watching these others, but he still needed to be told. His thoughts were elsewhere. Reaching up, he grabbed the trapeze-like bar hanging above him and pulled himself upright. Nelson grabbed the sides of the suit and yanked them up to Holston's waist. Two empty arms flapped at either side.

'Left hand here.'

Holston numbly obeyed. It was surreal to be on the other side of this – this mechanical death-walk of the condemned. Holston had often wondered why people complied, why they just went along. Even Jack Brent had done what he was told, as foul-mouthed and verbally abusive as he'd been. Allison had done it quietly, just like this, Holston thought as he inserted one hand and then the other. The suit came up, and Holston thought that maybe people went along with it because they couldn't believe it was happening. None of it was real enough to rebel against. The animal part of his mind wasn't made for this, to be calmly ushered to a death it was perfectly aware of.

'Turn.'

He did.

There was a tug at the small of his back, and then a noisy zipping sound up to his neck. Another tug, another zip. Two layers of futility. The crunch of industrial Velcro over the top. Pats and double-checks. Holston heard the hollow helmet slide off its shelf;

he flexed his fingers inside the puffy gloves while Nelson checked over the dome's innards.

'Let's go over the procedure one more time.'

'It's not necessary,' Holston said quietly.

Nelson glanced towards the airlock door leading back to the silo. Holston didn't need to look to know someone was likely watching. 'Bear with me,' Nelson said. 'I have to do it by the book.'

Holston nodded, but he knew there wasn't any 'book'. Of all the mystic oral traditions passed through silo generations, none matched the cult-like intensity of the suit makers and the cleaning techs. Everyone gave them their space. The cleaners might perform the physical act, but the techs were the people who made it possible. These were the men and women who maintained the view to that wider world beyond the silo's stifling confines.

Nelson placed the helmet on the bench. 'You got your scrubbers here.' He patted the wool pads stuck to the front of the suit.

Holston pulled one off with a ripping sound, studied the whorls and curls of the rough material, then stuck it back on.

'Two squirts from the cleaning bottle before you scrub with the wool, then dry with this towel, then put the ablating films on last.' He patted the pockets in order, even though they were clearly labelled and numbered – upside down so Holston could read them – and colour-coded.

Holston nodded and met the tech's eyes for the first time. He was surprised to see fear there, fear he had learned well to notice in his profession. He almost asked Nelson what was wrong before it occurred to him: the man was worried all these instructions were for naught, that Holston would walk out – like everyone in the silo feared all cleaners would – and not do his duty. Not clean up for the people whose rules, rules against dreaming of a better place, had doomed him. Or was Nelson worried that the expensive and laborious gear he and his colleagues had built, using those secrets and techniques handed down from well before the uprising, would leave the silo and rot to no purpose?

'You okay?' Nelson asked. 'Anything too tight?'

Holston glanced around the airlock. My life is too tight, he wanted to say. My skin is too tight. The walls are too tight.

He just shook his head.

'I'm ready,' he whispered.

It was the truth. Holston was oddly and truly very much ready to go.

And he remembered, suddenly, how ready his wife had been as well.

5

Three Years Earlier

'I want to go out. I want to go out. Iwanttogoout.'

Holston arrived at the cafeteria in a sprint. His radio was still squawking, Deputy Marnes yelling something about Allison. Holston hadn't even taken the time to respond, had just bolted up three flights of stairs towards the scene.

'What's going on?' he asked. He swam through the crowd by the door and found his wife writhing on the cafeteria floor, held down by Connor and two other food staff employees. 'Let her go!' He slapped their hands off his wife's shins and was nearly rewarded by one of her boots to his chin. 'Settle down,' he said. He reached for her wrists, which were twisting this way and that to get out of the desperate grips of grown men. 'Baby, what the *hell* is going on?'

'She was running for the airlock,' Connor said through grunts of exertion. Percy corralled her kicking feet, and Holston didn't stop him. He saw now why three men were needed. He leaned close to Allison, making sure she saw him. Her eyes were wild, peeking through a curtain of dishevelled hair.

'Allison, baby, you've gotta settle down.'

'I want to go out. I want to go out.' Her voice had quietened, but the words kept tumbling out.

'Don't say that,' Holston told her. Chills ran through his body at the sound of the grave utterances. He held her cheeks. 'Baby, don't say that!'

But some part of him knew, in a jolting flash, what it meant. He knew it was too late. The others had heard. Everyone had heard. His wife had signed her own death certificate.

The room spun around Holston as he begged Allison to be quiet. It was like he had arrived at the scene of some horrible accident – some mishap in the machine shop – to find a person he loved wounded. Arrived to find them alive and kicking, but knowing at a glance that the injury was fatal.

Holston felt warm tears streak down his cheeks as he tried to wipe the hair from her face. Her eyes finally met his, stopped their fevered swirling and locked on to his with awareness. And for a moment, just a second, before he could wonder if she'd been drugged or abused in any way, a spark of calm clarity registered there, a flash of sanity, of cool calculation. And then it was blinked away and her eyes went wild again as she begged to be let out, over and over.

'Lift her up,' Holston said. His husband eyes swam behind tears while he allowed his dutiful sheriff-self to intervene. There was nothing for it but to lock her up, even as he wanted no more than room enough to scream. 'That way,' he told Connor, who had both hands under her twisting shoulders. He nodded towards his office and the holding cell beyond. Just past that, down at the end of the hall, the bright yellow paint on the great airlock door stood out, serene and menacing, silent and waiting.

Once in the holding cell, Allison immediately calmed. She sat on the bench, no longer struggling or blabbering, as if she'd only stopped by to rest and enjoy the view. Holston was now the writhing wreck. He paced outside the bars and blubbered un-answered questions while Deputy Marnes and the mayor handled his procedural work. The two of them were treating Holston and his wife *both* like patients. And even as Holston's mind spun with the horror of the past half-hour, in the back of his sheriff brain, where he was always alert for the rising tensions in the silo, he was dimly aware of the shock and rumours trembling through walls of concrete and rebar. The enormous pent-up pressure of the place was now hissing through the seams in whispers.

'Sweetheart, you've gotta talk to me,' he pleaded again and again. He stopped his pacing and twisted the bars in his hands. Allison kept her back to him. She gazed at the wall screen, at the brown hills and grey sky and dark clouds. Now and then a hand came up to brush hair out of her face, but otherwise she didn't move or speak. Only when Holston's key had gone into the lock, not long after they had wrestled her in and shut the door, did she utter a single *'don't'* that had convinced him to remove it.

While he pleaded and she ignored, the machinations of the looming cleaning gyred through the silo. Techs rumbled down the hallway as a suit was sized and readied. Cleaning tools were prepped in the airlock. A canister hissed somewhere as argon was loaded into the flushing chambers. The commotion of it sporadically rumbled past the holding cell where Holston stood gazing at his wife. Chattering techs went dreadfully silent as they squeezed past; they didn't even seem to *breathe* in his presence.

Hours passed and Allison refused to talk – behaviour that created its own stir in the silo. Holston spent the entire day blubbering through the bars, his brain on fire with confusion and agony. It had happened in a single moment, the destruction of all that he knew. He tried to wrap his brain around it while Allison sat in the cell, gazing out at the dismal land, seemingly pleased with her far worse status as a cleaner.

It was after dark when she finally spoke, after her last meal had been silently refused for the final time, after the techs had finished in the airlock, closing the yellow door and retiring for a sleepless night. It was after his deputy had gone for the night, patting Holston on the shoulder twice. What felt like many hours after that, when Holston was near to passing out in fatigue from his crying and hoarse remonstrations, long after the hazy sun had settled over the hills visible from the cafeteria and lounge – the hills that hid the rest of that distant, crumbling city. In the near-dark left in the holding cell, Allison whispered something almost inaudible: 'It's not real.'

That's what Holston *thought* he heard. He stirred.

'Baby?' He gripped the bars and pulled himself up to his knees. 'Honey,' he whispered, wiping the crust from his cheeks.

She turned. It was like the sun changing its mind and rising back over the hills. To acknowledge him gave him hope. It choked him up, causing him to think this had all been a sickness, a fever, something they could have Doc write up to excuse her for everything she'd uttered. She'd never meant it. She was saved just by snapping out of it, and Holston was saved just by seeing her turn to him.

'Nothing you see is real,' she said quietly. She seemed calm of body even as her craziness continued, condemning her with forbidden words.

'Come talk to me,' Holston said. He waved her to the bars.

Allison shook her head. She patted the cot's thin mattress beside her.

Holston checked the time. It was long past visiting hours. He could be sent to cleaning just for doing what he was about to do.

The key went into the lock without hesitation.

A metallic click rang out impossibly loud.

Holston stepped inside with his wife and sat beside her. It killed him to not touch her, to not wrap her up or drag her out to some safe place, back to their bed where they could pretend it had all been a bad dream.

But he didn't dare move. He sat and twisted his hands together while she whispered:

'It doesn't have to be real. Any of this. None of this.' She looked to the screen.

Holston leaned so close he could smell the dried sweat from the day's struggle. 'Baby, what's going on?'

Her hair stirred with the breath from his words. She reached out and rubbed the darkening display, feeling the pixels.

'It could be morning right now and we'd never know. There could be people outside.' She turned and looked at him. 'They could be watching us,' she said with a sinister grin.

Holston held her gaze. She didn't seem crazy at all, not like earlier. Her *words* were crazy, but she didn't seem to be. 'Where did you get that idea?' he asked. He thought he knew, but he asked anyway. 'Did you find something on the hard drives?' He'd heard that she had run straight from her lab towards the airlock, already barking her madness. Something had happened while she was at work. 'What did you find?'

'There's more deleted than just from the uprising,' she

whispered. 'Of course there would be. Everything is deleted. All the recent stuff, too.' She laughed. Her voice got suddenly loud and her eyes lost focus. 'Emails you never sent me, I bet!'

'Honey.' Holston dared to reach for her hands, and she didn't pull away. He held them. 'What did you find? Was it an email? Who was it from?'

She shook her head. 'No. I found the programs they use. The ones that make pictures on the screens that look so *real*.' She looked back to the quickening dusk. 'IT,' she said. 'Eye. Tee. They're the ones. They *know*. It's a secret that only they know.' She shook her head.

'What secret?' Holston couldn't tell if this was nonsense or important. He only knew that she was talking.

'But now I know. And you will too. I'll come back for you, I swear. This'll be different. We'll break the cycle, you and me. I'll come back and we'll go over that hill together.' She laughed. 'If it's there,' she said loudly. 'If that hill is there and it's green, we'll go over it together.'

She turned to him.

'There is no uprising, not really, there's just a gradual leak. Just the people who know, who want out.' She smiled. 'They get to go out,' she said. 'They get just what they ask for. I know why they clean, why they say they won't but why they do. I know. I know. And they never come back, they wait and wait and wait, but I won't. I'll come right back. This'll be different.'

Holston squeezed her hands. Tears were dripping off his cheeks. 'Baby, why are you doing this?' He felt like she wanted to explain herself now that the silo was dark and they were all alone.

'I know about the uprisings,' she said.

Holston nodded. 'I know. You told me. There were others—'

'No.' Allison pulled away from him, but it was only to make space so she could look him in the eyes. Hers were no longer wild, as before.

'Holston, I know why the uprisings took place. I know *why*.'

Allison bit her lower lip. Holston waited, his body tense.

'It was always over the doubt, the suspicion, that things weren't as bad out there as they seemed. You've felt that, right? That we could be *anywhere*, living a lie?'

Holston knew better than to answer, to even twitch. Broaching this subject led to cleaning. He sat frozen and waited.

'It was probably the younger generations,' Allison said. 'Every twenty years or so. They wanted to push further, to explore, I think. Don't you ever feel that urge? Didn't you when you were younger?' Her eyes lost focus. 'Or maybe it was the couples, newly married, who were driven to madness when they were told they couldn't have kids in this damned, limited world of ours. Maybe they were willing to risk everything for that chance . . .'

Her eyes focused on something far away. Perhaps she was seeing that lottery ticket they had yet to redeem and now never would. She looked back at Holston. He wondered if he could be sent to cleaning even for his silence, for not yelling her down as she uttered every one of the great forbidden words.

'It could even have been the elderly residents,' she said, 'cooped up too long, no longer afraid in their final years, maybe wanting to move out and make room for the others, for the few precious grandchildren. Whoever it was, whoever, every uprising took place because of this doubt, this feeling, that *we're* in the bad place right *here*.' She looked around the cell.

'You can't say that,' Holston whispered. 'That's the great offence . . .'

Allison nodded. 'Expressing any desire to leave. Yes. The great offence. Don't you see why? Why is that so forbidden? Because all the uprisings started with that desire, that's why.'

'You get what you ask for,' Holston recited, those words drilled into his head since youth. His parents had warned him – their only precious child – never to want out of the silo. Never even to *think* it. Don't let it cross your mind. It was instant death, that thought, and it would be the destruction of their one and only.

He looked back at his wife. He still didn't understand her madness, this decision. So she had found deleted programs that could make worlds on computer screens look real. What did that mean? Why do this?

'Why?' he asked her. 'Why do it this way? Why didn't you

come to me? There has to be a better way to find out what's going on. We could start by telling people what you're finding on those drives—'

'And be the ones who start the next great uprising?' Allison laughed. Some of the madness was still there, or maybe it was just an intense frustration and boiling anger. Perhaps a great, multi-generational betrayal had pushed her to the edge. 'No thanks,' she said, her laughter subsiding. 'I wiped everything I found. I don't want them to know. Damn them if they stay here. I'm only coming back for *you.*'

'You don't come *back* from this,' Holston said angrily. 'You think the banished are still out there? You think they choose not to come back because they feel betrayed by us?'

'Why do you think they do the cleaning?' Allison asked. 'Why do they pick up their wool and set to work without hesitation?'

Holston sighed. He felt the anger in him draining away. 'No one knows why,' he said.

'But why do you *think*?'

'We've talked about this,' he said. 'How many times have we discussed this?' He was sure all couples whispered their theories when they were alone. He looked past Allison as he remembered those times. He looked to the wall and saw the moon's position and read in it the night's hour. Their time was limited. His wife would be gone tomorrow. That simple thought came often, like lightning from stormy clouds.

'Everyone has theories,' he said. 'We've shared ours countless times. Let's just—'

'But now you know something new,' Allison told him. She let go of his hand and brushed the hair from her face. 'You and I know something new, and now it all makes sense. It makes perfect sense. And tomorrow I'll know for sure.' Allison smiled. She patted Holston's hand as if he were a child. 'And one day, my love, you will know it, too.'

The first year without her, Holston had waited, buying into her insanity, distrusting the sight of her on that hill, hoping she'd come back. He'd spent the first anniversary of her death scrubbing the holding cell clean, washing the yellow airlock door, straining for some sound, some knock, that would mean the ghost of his wife was back to set him free.

When it didn't happen, he began to consider the alternative: going out after her. He had spent enough days, weeks, months going through her computer files, reading some of what she had pieced together, making sense of half of it, to become half mad himself. His world was a lie, he came to believe, and without Allison in it he had nothing to live for even if it were truth.

The second anniversary of her departure was his year of cowardice. He had walked to work, the poisonous words in his mouth – his desire to go out – but he had choked them down at the last second. He and Deputy Marnes had gone on patrol that day with the secret of how near he'd come to death burning inside of him. That was a long year of cowardice, of letting Allison down. The first year had been her failure; last year had been his. But no more.

Now, one more year later, he was alone in the airlock, wearing a cleaning suit, full of doubts and convictions. The silo was sealed off behind him, that thick yellow door bolted tight, and Holston thought that this was *not* how he'd thought he'd die, or what he had hoped would become of him. He had thought he would remain in the silo for ever, his nutrients going as the nutrients of his parents had: into the soil of the eighth-floor dirt farm. It seemed a lifetime ago that he had dreamed of a family, of his own child, a fantasy of twins or another lottery win, a wife to grow old with—

A klaxon sounded on the other side of the yellow doors, warning everyone but him away. He was to stay. There was nowhere else for him to go.

The argon chambers hissed, pumping the room full of the inert gas. After a minute of this, Holston could feel the pressure of the air as it crinkled the cleaning suit tight around his joints. He breathed the oxygen circulating inside his helmet and stood before the other door, the forbidden door, the one to the awful outside world, and waited.

There was a metal groan from pistons deep within the walls. The sacrificial plastic curtains covering the interior of the airlock wrinkled from the pressure of the built-up argon. These curtains would be incinerated inside the airlock while Holston cleaned. The area would be scrubbed before nightfall, made ready for the next cleaning.

The great metal doors before him shuddered, and then a shaft of incredible space appeared at their joint, widening as the doors withdrew into the jamb. They wouldn't open all the way, not like they were once designed to – the risk of invading air had to be minimised.

An argon torrent hissed through the gap, dulling to a roar as the space grew. Holston pressed close, as horrified at himself for not resisting as he'd previously been perplexed by the actions of others. Better to go out, to see the world one time with his own eyes, than to be burned alive with the plastic curtains. Better to survive a few moments more.

As soon as the opening was wide enough, Holston squeezed through, his suit catching and rubbing at the doors. There was a veil of fog all around him as the argon condensed in the less pressurised air. He stumbled forward blindly, pawing through the soft cloud.

While still in that mist, the outer doors groaned and began closing. The klaxon howls behind were swallowed by the press of thick steel against thick steel, locking him and the toxins out while cleansing fires began to rage inside the airlock, destroying any contamination that leaked its way inside.

Holston found himself at the bottom of a concrete ramp, a ramp that led *up*. His time felt short – there was a constant reminder thrumming in the back of his skull – *hurry! Hurry!* His life was ticking away. He lumbered up the ramp, confused that he wasn't already aboveground, so used as he was to seeing the world and the horizon from the cafeteria and lounge, which were on the same level as the airlock.

He shuffled up the narrow ramp, walls of chipped concrete to either side, his visor full of a confusing, brilliant light. At the top of the ramp, Holston saw the heaven into which he'd been condemned for his simple sin of hope. He whirled around, scanning the horizon, his head dizzy from the sight of so much green!

Green hills, green grass, green carpet beneath his feet. Holston whooped in his helmet. His mind buzzed with the sight. Hanging over all the green, there was the exact hue of blue from the children's books, the white clouds untainted, the movement of living things flapping in the air.

Holston turned around and around, taking it in. He had a sudden memory of his wife doing the same; he had watched her awkwardly, slowly turning, almost as if she were lost or confused or considering whether to do the cleaning at all.

The cleaning!

Holston reached down and pulled a wool pad from his chest. The cleaning! He knew, in a dizzying rush, a torrent of awareness, why, why. *Why!*

He looked where he always assumed the tall circular wall of the uppermost silo floor would be, but of course that wall was buried. All that stood behind him was a small mound of concrete, a tower no more than eight or nine feet tall. A metal ladder ran up one side; antennae bristled from the top. And on the side facing him – on all the sides he saw as he approached – were the wide, curving, fisheye lenses of the silo's powerful cameras.

Holston held out his wool and approached the first. He imagined the view of himself from inside the cafeteria, staggering forward, becoming impossibly large. He had watched his wife do the same thing three years ago. He remembered her waving, he had thought at the time for balance, but had she been telling him something? Had she been grinning like a fool, as wide as he was grinning now, while she remained hidden behind that silver visor? Had her heart been pounding with foolish hope while she sprayed, scrubbed, wiped, applied? Holston knew the cafeteria would be empty; there was no one left who loved him enough to watch, but he waved anyway. And for him, it wasn't the raw anger he imagined many might have cleaned with. It wasn't the knowledge that they in the silo were condemned and the condemned set free; it wasn't the feeling of betrayal that guided the wool in his hand in small, circular motions. It was pity. It was raw pity and unconstrained joy.

The world blurred, but in a good way, as tears came to Holston's eyes. His wife had been right: the view from inside was a lie. The hills were the same – he'd recognise them at a glance after so many years of living with them – but the colours were all wrong. The screens inside the silo, the programs his wife had found, they somehow made the vibrant greens look grey, they somehow removed all signs of life. Extraordinary life!

Holston polished the grime off the camera lens and wondered if the gradual blurring was even real. The grime certainly was. He saw it as he rubbed it away. But was it simple dirt, rather than some toxic, airborne grime? Could the program Allison discovered modify only what was already seen? Holston's mind spun with so many new facts and ideas. He was like an adult child, borne into a wide world, so much to piece together all at once that his head throbbed.

The blur is real, he decided, as he cleaned the last of the smear from the second lens. It was an overlay, like the false greys and browns the program must use to hide that green field and this blue sky dotted with puffy white. They were hiding from them a world so beautiful, Holston had to concentrate not to just stand still and gape at it.

He worked on the second of the four cameras and thought about those untrue walls beneath him, taking what they saw and modifying it. He wondered how many people in the silo knew.

Any of them? What kind of fanatical devotion would it take to maintain this depressing illusion? Or was this a secret from *before* the last uprising? Was it an unknown lie perpetuated through the generations – a fibbing set of programs that continued to hum away on the silo computers with nobody aware? Because if someone knew, if they could show anything, why not something nice?

The uprisings! Maybe it was just to prevent them from happening over and over again. Holston applied an ablative film to the second sensor and wondered if the ugly lie of an unpleasant outside world was some misguided attempt to keep people from *wanting* out. Could someone have decided that the truth was worse than a loss of power, of control? Or was it something deeper and more sinister? A fear of unabashed, free, many-as-you-like children? So many horrible possibilities.

And what of Allison? Where was she? Holston shuffled around the corner of the concrete tower towards the third lens, and the familiar but strange skyscrapers in the distant city came into view. Only, there were more buildings than usual there. Some stood to either side, and an unfamiliar one loomed in the foreground. The others, the ones he knew by heart, were whole and shining, not twisted and jagged. Holston gazed over the crest of the verdant hills and imagined Allison walking over them at any minute. But that was ridiculous. How would she know he'd been expelled on this day? Would she remember the anniversary? Even after he'd missed the last two? Holston cursed his former cowardice, the years wasted. He would have to go to *her*, he decided.

He had a sudden impulse to do just that, to tear off his helmet and bulky suit and scamper up the hill in nothing but his carbon undersuit, breathing in deep gulps of crisp air and laughing all the way to his waiting wife in some vast, unfathomable city full of people and squealing children.

But no, there were appearances to keep, illusions to maintain. He wasn't sure why, but it was what his wife had done, what all the other cleaners before him had done. Holston was now a member of that club, a member of the *out* group. There was a press of history, of *precedent*, to obey. They had known best. He would complete his performance for the *in* group he had just joined. He wasn't sure why he was doing it, only that everyone before him had, and look at the secret they all shared. That secret was a powerful drug. He knew only to do what he had been told, to follow the numbers on the pockets, to clean mechanically while he considered the awesome implications of an outside world so big one couldn't live to see it all, couldn't breathe all the air, drink all the water, eat all the food.

Holston dreamed of such things while he dutifully scrubbed the third lens, wiped, applied, sprayed, then moved to the last. His pulse was audible in his ears; his chest pounded in that constricting suit. Soon, soon, he told himself. He used the second wool pad and polished the grime off the final lens. He wiped and applied and sprayed a final time, then put everything back in its place, back in the numbered pouches, not wanting to bespoil the gorgeous and healthy ground beneath his feet. Done, Holston stepped back, took one last look at the nobodies not watching from the cafeteria and lounge, then turned his back on those who had turned their backs on Allison and all the others before her. There was a reason nobody came back for the people inside, Holston thought, just as there was a reason everyone cleaned, even when they said they wouldn't. He was free; he was to join the others, and so he strolled towards that dark crease that ran up the hill, following in his wife's footsteps, aware that some familiar boulder, long-sleeping, no longer lay there. That, too, Holston decided, had been nothing more than another awful pixelated lie.

7

Holston was a dozen paces up the hill, still marvelling at the bright grass at his feet and the brilliant sky above, when the first pang lurched in his stomach. It was a writhing cramp, something like intense hunger. At first, he worried he was going too fast, first with the cleaning and now with his impatient shuffling in that cumbersome suit. He didn't want to take it off until he was over the hill, out of sight, maintaining whatever illusion the walls in the cafeteria held. He focused on the tops of the skyscrapers and resigned himself to slowing down, to calming down. One step at a time. Years and years of running up and down thirty flights of stairs should make this nothing.

Another cramp, stronger this time. Holston winced and stopped walking, waiting for it to pass. When did he eat last? Not at all yesterday. Stupid. When did he last use the bathroom? Again, he couldn't remember. He might need to get the suit off earlier than he'd hoped. Once the wave of nausea passed, he took a few more steps, hoping to reach the top of the hill before the next bout of pain. He only got another dozen steps in before it hit him, more severe this time, worse than anything he'd ever felt. Holston retched from the intensity of it, and now his dry stomach was a blessing. He clutched his abdomen as his knees gave out in a shiver of weakness. He crashed to the ground and groaned. His stomach was burning, his chest on fire. He managed to crawl forward a few feet, sweat dripping from his forehead and splashing on the inside of his helmet. He saw sparks in his vision; the entire world went bright white, several times, like lightning strikes. Confused and senseless, he crawled ever upward, moving laboriously, his startled mind still focused on his last, clear goal: cresting that hill.

Again and again, his view shimmered, his visor letting in a solid bright light before it flickered away. It became difficult to see. Holston ran into something before him, and his arm folded, his shoulder crashing to the ground. He blinked and gazed forward, up the hill, waiting for a clear sight of what lay ahead, but saw only infrequent strobes of green grass.

And then his vision completely disappeared. All was black. Holston clawed at his face, even as his stomach tangled in a new torturous knot. There was a glow, a blinking in his vision, so he knew he wasn't blind. But the blinking seemed to be coming from *inside* his helmet. It was his *visor* that had become suddenly blind, not him.

Holston felt for the latches on the back of the helmet. He wondered if he'd used up all his air. Was he asphyxiating? Being poisoned by his own exhalations? Of course! Why would they give him more air than he needed for the cleaning? He fumbled for the latches with his bulky gloves. They weren't meant for this. The gloves were part of his suit, his suit a single piece zipped up twice at the back and Velcroed over. It wasn't meant to come off, not without help. Holston was going to die in it, poison himself, choke on his own gases, and now he knew true fear of containment, a true sense of being closed in. The silo was nothing to this as he scrambled for release, as he writhed in pain inside his tailored coffin. He squirmed and pounded at the latches, but his padded fingers were too big. And the blindness made it worse, made him feel smothered and trapped. Holston wretched again in pain. He bent at the waist, hands spread in the dirt, and felt something sharp through his glove.

He fumbled for the object and found it: a jagged rock. A tool. Holston tried to calm himself. His years of enforcing calm, of soothing others, of bringing stability to chaos, came back to him. He gripped the rock carefully, terrified of losing it to his blindness, and brought it up to his helmet. There was a brief thought of cutting away his gloves with the rock, but he wasn't sure his sanity or air would last that long. He jabbed the point of the rock at his armoured neck, right where the latch should be. He heard the crack as it landed. *Crack. Crack.* Pausing to probe with his padded finger, retching again, Holston took more careful aim. There was a click instead of a crack. A sliver of light intruded as one side of the helmet came free. Holston was choking on his exhalations, on the stale and used air around him. He moved the rock to his other hand and aimed for the second latch. Two more cracks before it landed, and the helmet popped free.

Holston could *see*. His eyes burned from the effort, from not being able to breathe, but he could see. He blinked the tears away and tried to suck in a deep, crisp, revitalising lungful of blue air.

What he got instead was like a punch to the chest. Holston gagged. He threw up spittle and stomach acid, the very lining of him trying to flee. The world around him had gone brown. Brown grass and grey skies. No green. No blue. No life.

He collapsed to one side, landing on his shoulder. His helmet lay open before him, the visor black and lifeless. There was no looking through the visor. Holston reached for it, confused. The outside of the visor was coated silver, the other side was nothing. No glass. A rough surface. Wires leading in and out of it. A display gone dark. Dead pixels.

He threw up again. Wiping his mouth feebly, looking down the hill, he saw the world with his naked eyes as it *was*, as he'd always known it to be. Desolate and bleak. He let go of the helmet, dropping the lie he had carried out of the silo with him. He was dying. The toxins were eating him from the inside. He blinked up at the black clouds overhead, roaming like beasts. He turned to see how far he had got, how far it was to the crest of the hill, and he saw the thing he had stumbled into while crawling. A boulder, sleeping. It hadn't been there in his visor, hadn't been a part of the lie on that little screen, running one of the programs Allison had discovered.

Holston reached out and touched the object before him, the white suit flaking away like brittle rock, and he could no longer support his head. He curled up in pain from the slow death overtaking him, holding what remained of his wife, and thought, with his last agonising breath, what this death of his must look like to those who could see, this curling and dying in the black crack of a lifeless brown hill, a rotting city standing silent and forlorn over him.

What would they see, anyone who had chosen to watch?

Part 2 – Proper Gauge

8

Her knitting needles rested in a leather pouch in pairs, two matching sticks of wood, side by side like the delicate bones of the wrist wrapped in dried and ancient flesh. Wood and leather. Artefacts like clues handed down from generation to generation, innocuous winks from her ancestors, harmless things like children's books and wood carvings that managed to survive the uprising and the purge. Each clue stood as a small hint of a world beyond their own, a world where buildings stood aboveground like the crumbling ruins visible over the grey and lifeless hills.

After much deliberation, Mayor Jahns selected a pair of needles. She always chose carefully, for proper gauge was critical. Too small a needle, and the knitting would prove difficult, the resulting sweater too tight and constricting. Too large a needle, on the other hand, would create a garment full of large holes. The knitting would remain loose. One would be able to see straight through it.

Her choice made, the wooden bones removed from their leather wrist, Jahns reached for the large ball of cotton yarn. It was hard to believe, weighing that knot of twisted fibres, that her hands could make of it something ordered, something useful. She fished for the end of the yarn, dwelling on how things came to be. Right now, her sweater was little more than a tangle and a thought. Going back, it had once been bright fibres of cotton blooming in the dirt farms, pulled, cleaned, and twisted into long strands. Even further, and the very substance of the cotton plant itself could be traced to those souls who had been laid to rest in its soil, feeding the roots with their own leather while the air above baked under the full glory of powerful grow lights.

Jahns shook her head at her own morbidity. The older she got, the quicker her mind went to death. Always, in the end, the thoughts of death.

With practised care, she looped the end of the yarn around the point of one needle and crafted a triangle-shaped web with her fingers. The tip of the needle danced through this triangle, casting the yarn on. This was her favourite part, casting on. She liked beginnings. The first row. Out of nothing comes something. Since her hands knew what to do, she was free to glance up and watch a gust of morning wind chase pockets of dust down the slope of the hill. The clouds were low and ominous today. They loomed like worried parents over these smaller darting eddies of windswept soil, which tumbled like laughing children, twirling and spilling, following the dips and valleys as they flowed towards a great crease where two hills collided to become one. Here, Jahns watched as the puffs of dust splashed against a pair of dead bodies, the frolicking twins of dirt evaporating into ghosts, solid playful children returning once more to dreams and scattered mist.

Mayor Jahns settled back in her faded plastic chair and watched the fickle winds play across the forbidding world outside. Her hands worked the yarn into rows, requiring only occasional glances to keep her place. Often, the dust flew towards the silo's sensors in sheets, each wave causing her to cringe as if a physical blow were about to land. This assault of blurring grime was difficult to watch at any time, but especially brutal the day after a cleaning. Each touch of dust on the clouding lenses was a violation, a dirty man touching something pure. Jahns remembered what that felt like. And sixty years later, she sometimes wondered if the misting of grime on those lenses, if the bodily sacrifice needed to keep them clean, wasn't even more painful for her to abide.

'Ma'am?'

Mayor Jahns turned away from the sight of the dead hills cradling her recently deceased sheriff. She turned to find Deputy Marnes standing by her side.

'Yes, Marnes?'

'You asked for these.'

Marnes placed three manilla folders on the cafeteria table and slid them towards her through the scattered crumbs and juice stains of last night's cleaning celebration. Jahns set her knitting aside and reluctantly reached for the folders. What she really wanted was to be left alone a little longer to watch rows of knots become something. She wanted to enjoy the peace and quiet of this unspoiled sunrise before the grime and the years dulled it, before the rest of the upper silo awoke, rubbed the sleep from their eyes and the stains from their consciences, and came up to crowd around her in their own plastic chairs and take it all in.

But duty beckoned: she was mayor by choice, and the silo needed a sheriff. So Jahns put aside her own wants and desires and weighed the folders in her lap. Caressing the cover of the first one, she looked down at her hands with something between pain and acceptance. The backs of them appeared as dry and crinkled as the pulp paper hanging out of the folders. She glanced over at Deputy Marnes, whose white moustache was flecked with the occasional black. She remembered when the colours were the other way around, when his tall, thin frame was a mark of vigour and youth rather than gaunt fragility. He was handsome still, but only because she knew him from long ago, only because her old eyes still remembered.

'You know,' she told Marnes, 'we could do this different this time. You could let me promote you to sheriff, hire yourself a deputy, and do this proper.'

Marnes laughed. 'I've been deputy almost as long as you've been mayor, ma'am. Don't figure on being nothing else but dead one day.'

Jahns nodded. One of the things she loved about having Marnes around was that his thoughts could be so black as to make hers shine grey. 'I fear that day is rapidly approaching for us both,' she said.

'Truer than true, I reckon. Never figured to outlive so many. Sure as sin don't see me outliving you.' Marnes rubbed his moustache and studied the view of the outside. Jahns smiled at him, opened the folder on top, and studied the first bio.

'That's three decent candidates,' Marnes said. 'Just like you asked for. Be happy to work with any of them. Juliette, I think she's in the middle there, would be my first pick. Works down in Mechanical. Don't come up much, but me and Holston . . .' Marnes paused and cleared his throat.

Jahns glanced over and saw that her deputy's gaze had crept towards that dark crook in the hill. He covered his mouth with a fist of sharp knuckles and faked a cough.

'Excuse me,' he said. 'As I was sayin', the sheriff and me worked a death down there a few years back. This Juliette – I think she prefers Jules, come to think of it – was a right shiner. Sharp as a tack. Big help on this case, good at spotting details, handling people, being diplomatic but firm, all that. I don't think she comes up past the eighties much. A down-deeper for sure, which we ain't had in a while.'

Jahns sorted through Juliette's folder, checking her family tree, her voucher history, her current pay in chits. She was listed as a shift foreman with good marks. No history in the lottery.

'Never married?' Jahns asked.

'Nope. Something of a johnboy. A wrencher, you know? We were down there a week, saw how the guys took to her. Now, she could have her pick of them boys but chooses not to. Kind of person who leaves an impression but prefers to go it alone.'

'Sure seems like she left an impression on you,' Jahns said, regretting it immediately. She hated the jealous tone in her own voice.

Marnes shifted his weight to his other foot. 'Well, you know me, Mayor. I'm always sizing up candidates. Anything to keep from bein' promoted.'

Jahns smiled. 'What about the other two?' She checked the names, wondering if a down-deeper was a good idea. Or possibly worried about Marnes having a crush. She recognised the name on the top folder. Peter Billings. He worked a few floors down in Judicial, as a clerk or a judge's shadow.

'Honestly, ma'am? They're filler to make it seem fair. Like I said, I'd work with them, but I think Jules is your girl. Been a long time since we had a lass for a sheriff. Be a popular choice with an election comin' up.'

'That won't be why we choose,' Jahns said. 'Whoever we decide on will probably be here long after we're gone—' She stopped herself as she recalled having said the same thing about Holston, back when he'd been chosen.

Jahns closed the folder and returned her attention to the wall screen. A small tornado had formed at the base of the hill, the gathering dust whipped into an organised frenzy. It built some steam, this small wisp, as it swelled into a larger cone, spinning and spinning on a wavering tip like a child's top as it raced towards sensors that fairly sparkled in the wan rays of a clear sunrise.

'I think we should go see her,' Jahns finally said. She kept the folders in her lap, fingers like rolled parchment toying with the rough edges of handmade paper.

'Ma'am? I'd rather us fetch her up here. Do the interview in your office like we've always done. It's a long way down to her and an even longer way back up.'

'I appreciate the concern, Deputy, I do. But it's been a long while since I've been much past the fortieth. My knees are no excuse not to see my people—' The mayor stopped. The tornado of dust wavered, turned, and headed straight for them. It grew and grew – the wide angle of the lens distorting it into a monster much larger and more fierce than she knew it to actually be – and then it blew over the sensor array, the entire cafeteria descending into a brief darkness until the zephyr caromed past, retreating across the screen in the lounge and leaving behind it a view of the world now tainted with a slight, dingy film.

'Damn those things,' Deputy Marnes said through gritted teeth. The aged leather of his holster squeaked as he rested his hand on the butt of his gun, and Jahns imagined the old deputy out on that landscape, chasing the wind on thin legs while pumping bullets into a cloud of fading dust.

The two of them sat silent a moment, surveying the damage. Finally, Jahns spoke.

'This trip won't be about the election, Marnes. It won't be

for votes, either. For all I know, I'll run again unopposed. So we won't make a deal of it, and we'll travel light and quiet. I want to *see* my people, not be seen by them.' She looked over at him, found that he was watching her. 'It'll be for me, Marnes. A getaway.'

She turned back to the view.

'Sometimes . . . sometimes I just think I've been up here too long. The both of us. I think we've been *anywhere* too long . . .'

The ringing of morning footsteps on the spiral staircase gave her pause, and they both turned towards the sound of life, the sound of a waking day. And she knew it was time to start getting the images of dead things out of her mind. Or at least to bury them for a while.

'We'll go down and get us a proper gauge of this Juliette, you and me. Because sometimes, sitting here, looking out on what the world makes us do – it needles me deep, Marnes. It needles me straight through.'

They met after breakfast in Holston's old office. Jahns still thought of it as his, a day later. It was too early for her to think of the room as anything else. She stood beyond the twin desks and old filing cabinets and peered into the empty holding cell while Deputy Marnes gave last-minute instructions to Terry, a burly security worker from IT who often held down the fort while Marnes and Holston were away on a case. Standing dutifully behind Terry was a teenager named Marcha, a young girl with dark hair and bright eyes who was apprenticing for work in IT. She was Terry's shadow; just about half of the workers in the silo had one. They ranged in age from twelve to twenty, these ever-present sponges absorbing the lessons and techniques for keeping the silo operational for at least one generation more.

Deputy Marnes reminded Terry how rowdy people got after a cleaning. Once the tension was released, people tended to live it up a little. They thought, for a few months at least, that anything went.

The warning hardly needed saying – the revelry in the next room could be heard through the shut door. Most residents from the top forty were already packed into the cafeteria and lounge. Hundreds more from the mids and the down deep would trickle up throughout the day, asking for time off work and turning in holiday chits just to see the mostly clear view of the world outside. It was a pilgrimage for many. Some came up only once every few years, stood around for an hour muttering that it looked the same as they remembered, then shooed their children down the stairs ahead of them, fighting the upward-surging crowds.

Terry was left with the keys and a temporary badge. Marnes checked the batteries in his wireless, made sure the volume on the office unit was up, and inspected his gun. He shook Terry's hand and wished him luck. Jahns sensed it was almost time for them to go and turned away from the empty cell. She said goodbye to Terry, gave Marcha a nod, and followed Marnes out the door.

'You feel okay leaving right after a cleaning?' she asked as they stepped out into the cafeteria. She knew how rowdy it would get later that night, and how testy the crowd would become. It seemed an awful time to drag him away on a mostly selfish errand.

'Are you kidding? I need this. I need to get away.' He glanced towards the wall screen, which was obscured by the crowds. 'I still can't figure what Holston was thinking, can't reckon why he never talked to me about all that was going on in that head of his. Maybe by the time we get back, I won't feel him in the office any more, 'cause right now I can't hardly breathe in there.'

Jahns thought about this as they fought through the crowded cafeteria. Plastic cups sloshed with a mix of fruit juices, and she smelled the sting of tub-brewed alcohol in the air, but ignored it. People were wishing her well, asking her to be careful, promising to vote. News of their trip had leaked out faster than the spiked punch, despite hardly telling anyone. Most were under the impression that it was a goodwill trip. A re-election campaign. The younger silo residents, who only remembered Holston as sheriff, were already saluting Marnes and giving him that honorific title. Anyone with wrinkles in their eyes knew better. They nodded to the duo as they passed through the cafeteria and wished them a different sort of unspoken luck. *Keep us going*, their eyes said. *Make it so my kids live as long as me. Don't let it unravel, not just yet.*

Jahns lived under the weight of this pressure, a burden brutal on more than knees. She kept quiet as they made their way to the central stairwell. A handful called for her to make a speech, but the lone voices did not gain traction. No chant formed, much to her relief. What would she say? That she didn't know why it all held together? That she didn't even understand her own knitting, how if you made knots, and if you did it right, things just worked out? Would she tell them it took only one snip for it all to unravel? One cut, and you could pull and pull and turn that garment into a pile. Did they really expect her to understand, when all she did was follow the rules, and somehow it kept working out, year after year after year?

Because she didn't understand what held it together. And she didn't understand their mood, this celebration. Were they drinking and shouting because they were safe? Because they'd been spared by fate, passed over for cleaning? Her people cheered while a good man, her friend, her partner in keeping them alive and well, lay dead on a hill next to his wife. If she gave a speech, if it weren't full of the forbidden, it would be this: that no two better people had ever gone to cleaning of their own free will, and what did that say about the lot of them who remained?

Now was not the time for speeches. Or for drinking. Or for being merry. Now was the hour of quiet contemplation, which was one of the reasons Jahns knew she needed to get away. Things had changed. Not just by the day, but by the long years. She knew better than most. Maybe old lady McNeil down in Supply knew, could see it coming. One had to live a long time to be sure, but now she was. And as time marched on, carrying her world faster and faster than her feet could catch up, Mayor Jahns knew that it would soon leave her completely behind. And her great fear, unspoken but daily felt, was that this world of theirs probably wouldn't stagger very far along without her.

9

Jahns's walking stick made a conspicuous ring as it impacted each metal step. It soon became a metronome for their descent, timing the music of the stairwell, which was crowded and vibrating with the energy of a recent cleaning. All the traffic seemed to be heading upward, save for the two of them. They jostled against the flow, elbows brushing, cries of 'Hey, Mayor!' followed by nods to Marnes. And Jahns saw it on their faces: the temptation to call him sheriff tempered by their respect for the awful nature of his assumed promotion.

'How many floors you up for?' Marnes asked.

'Why, you tired already?' Jahns glanced over her shoulder to smirk at him, saw his bushy moustache twisted up in a smile of his own.

'Going down ain't a problem for me. It's the going back up I can't stand.'

Their hands briefly collided on the twisted railing of the spiral staircase, Jahns's hand trailing behind her, Marnes's reaching ahead. She felt like telling him she wasn't tired at all, but she did feel a sudden weariness, an exhaustion more mental than physical. She had a childish vision of more youthful times and pictured Marnes scooping her up and carrying her down the staircase in his arms. There would be a sweet release of strength and responsibility, a sinking into another's power, no need to feign her own. This was not a remembrance of the past; it was a future that had never happened. And Jahns felt guilty for even thinking it. She felt her husband beside her, his ghost perturbed by her thoughts—

'Mayor? How many you thinking?'

The two of them stopped and hugged the rail as a porter trudged up the stairs. Jahns recognised the boy, Connor, still in his teens but already with a strong back and steady stride. He had an array of bundles strapped together and balanced on his shoulders. The sneer on his face was not from exhaustion or pain, but annoyance. Who were all these people suddenly on his stairwell? These tourists? Jahns thought of something encouraging to say, some small verbal reward for these people who did a job her knees never could, but he was already gone on his strong young feet, carrying food and supplies up from the down deep, slowed only by the crush of traffic attempting to worm up through the silo for a peek of the clear and wide outside.

She and Marnes caught their breath for a moment between flights. Marnes handed her his canteen, and she took a polite sip before passing it back.

'I'd like to do half today,' she finally answered. 'But I want to make a few stops on the way.'

Marnes took a swig of water and began twisting the cap back on. 'House calls?'

'Something like that. I want to stop at the nursery on twenty.'

Marnes laughed. 'Kissin' babies? Mayor, ain't nobody gonna vote you out. Not at your age.'

Jahns didn't laugh. 'Thanks,' she said, with a mask of false pain. 'But no, not to kiss babies.' She turned her back and resumed walking; Marnes followed. 'It's not that I don't trust your professional opinion about this Jules lady. You haven't picked anything but a winner since I've been mayor.'

'Even . . . ?' Marnes interrupted.

'Especially him,' Jahns said, knowing what he was thinking. 'He was a good man, but he had a broken heart. That'll take even the best of them down.'

Marnes grunted his agreement. 'So what're we checkin' at the nursery? This Juliette weren't born on the twentieth, not if I recall—'

'No, but her father works there now. I thought, since we were passing by, that we'd get a feel for the man, get some insight on his daughter.'

'A father for a character witness?' Marnes laughed. 'Don't reckon you'll get much of an impartial there.'

'I think you'll be surprised,' Jahns said. 'I had Alice do some digging while I was packing. She found something interesting.'

'Yeah?'

'This Juliette character still has every vacation chit she's ever earned.'

'That ain't rare for Mechanical,' Marnes said. 'They do a lot of overtime.'

'Not only does she not get out, she doesn't have visitors.'

'I still don't see where you're going with this.'

Jahns waited while a family passed. A young boy, six or seven probably, rode on his father's shoulders with his head ducked to avoid the undersides of the stairs above. The mother brought up the rear, an overnight bag draped over her shoulder, a swaddled infant cradled in her arms. It was the perfect family, Jahns thought. Replacing what they took. Two for two. Just what the lottery aimed for and sometimes provided.

'Well then, let me tell you where I'm going with this,' she told Marnes. 'I want to find this girl's father, look him in the eyes, and ask him why, in the nearly twenty years since his daughter moved to Mechanical, he hasn't visited her. Not once.'

She looked back at Marnes, saw him frowning at her beneath his moustache. 'And why she hasn't once made her way up to see him,' she added.

The traffic thinned as they made their way into the teens and past the upper apartments. With each step down, Jahns dreaded having to reclaim those lost inches on the way back up. This was the easy part, she reminded herself. The descent was like the uncoiling of a steel spring, pushing her down. It reminded Jahns of nightmares she'd had of drowning. Silly nightmares, considering she'd never seen enough water to submerge herself in, much less enough that she couldn't stand up to breathe. But they were like the occasional dreams of falling from great heights, some legacy of another time, broken fragments unearthed in each of their sleeping minds that suggested: *We weren't supposed to live like this.*

And so the descent, this spiralling downward, was much like the drowning that swallowed her at night. It felt inexorable and inextricable. Like a weight pulling her down combined with the knowledge that she'd never be able to claw her way back up. They passed the garment district next, the land of multi-coloured overalls and the place her balls of yarn came from. The smell of the dyes and other chemicals drifted over the landing. A window cut into the curving breeze blocks looked through to a small food shop at the edge of the district. It had been ransacked by the crowds, shelves emptied by the crushing demand of exhausted hikers and the extra post-cleaning traffic. Several porters crowded up the stairs with heavy loads, trying their best to satisfy demand, and Jahns recognised an awful truth about yesterday's cleaning: the barbaric practice brought more than psychological relief, more than just a clear view of the outside: it also buttressed the silo's economy. There was suddenly an excuse to travel. An excuse to trade. And as gossip flowed, and family and old friends met again for the first time in months or perhaps years, there was a vitality injected into the entire silo. It was like an old body stretching and loosening its joints, blood flowing to the extremities. A decrepit thing was becoming *alive* again.

'Mayor!'

She turned to find Marnes almost out of sight around the spiral above her. She paused while he caught up, watching his feet as he hurried.

'Easy,' he said. 'I can't keep up if you take off like that.'

Jahns apologised. She hadn't been aware of any change in her pace. As they entered the second tier of apartments, down below the sixteenth floor, Jahns realised she was already in territory she hadn't seen in almost a year. There was the rattle here of younger legs chasing along the stairwell, getting tangled up in the slow climbers. The grade school for the upper third was just above the nursery. From the sound of all the traffic and voices, school had been cancelled. Jahns imagined it was a combination of knowing how few would turn up for class (with parents taking their kids up to the view) plus how many teachers would want to do the same. They passed the landing for the school, where chalk games of Hop and Square-Four were blurred from the day's traffic, where kids sat hugging the rails, skinned knees poking out, feet swinging below the jutting landings, and where catcalls and eager shouts faded to secret whispers in the presence of adults.

'Glad we're almost there, I need a rest,' Marnes said, as they spiralled down one more flight to the nursery. 'I just hope this feller is available to see us.'

'He will be,' Jahns said. 'Alice wired him from my office that we were coming.'

They crossed traffic at the nursery landing and caught their breath. When Marnes passed his canteen, Jahns took a long pull and then checked her hair in its curved and dented surface.

'You look fine,' he said.

'Mayoral?'

He laughed. 'And then some.'

Jahns thought she saw a twinkle in his old brown eyes when he said this, but it was probably the light bouncing off the canteen as he brought it to his lips.

'Twenty floors in just over two hours. Don't recommend the pace, but I'm glad we're this far already.' He wiped his moustache and reached around to try and slip the canteen back into his pack.

'Here,' Jahns said. She took the canteen from him and slid it into the webbed pouch on the rear of his pack. 'And let me do the talking in here,' she reminded him. Marnes lifted his hands and showed his palms, as if no other thought had ever crossed his mind. He stepped past her and pulled one of the heavy metal doors open, the customary squeal of rusted hinges not coming as expected. The silence startled Jahns. She was used to hearing the chirp of old doors up and down the staircase as they opened and closed. They were the stairwell's version of the wildlife found in the farms, ever present and always singing. But these hinges were coated in oil, rigorously maintained. The signs on the walls of the waiting room reinforced the observation. They demanded silence in bold letters, accompanied by pictures of fingers over lips and circles with slashes through open mouths. The nursery evidently took their quietude seriously.

'Don't remember so many signs last time I was here,' Marnes whispered.

'Maybe you were too busy yapping to notice,' Jahns replied.

A nurse glared at them through a glass window, and Jahns elbowed Marnes.

'Mayor Jahns to see Peter Nichols,' she told the woman.

The nurse behind the window didn't blink. 'I know who you are. I voted for you.'

'Oh, of course. Well, thank you.'

'If you'll come around.' The woman hit a button on her desk and the door beside her buzzed faintly. Marnes pushed on the door, and Jahns followed him through.

'If you'll don these.'

The nurse – Margaret, according to the hand-drawn tag on her collar – held out two neatly folded white cloth robes. Jahns accepted them both and handed one to Marnes.

'You can leave your bags with me.'

There was no refusing Margaret. Jahns felt at once that she was in this much younger woman's world, that she had become her inferior when she passed through that softly buzzing door. She leaned her walking stick against the wall, took her pack off and lowered it to the ground, then shrugged on the robe. Marnes struggled with his until Margaret helped, holding the sleeve in place. He wrestled the robe over his denim shirt and held the loose ends of the long fabric waist tie as if its working was beyond his abilities. He watched Jahns knot hers, and finally made enough of a mess of it for the robe to hold fairly together.

'What?' he asked, noticing the way Jahns was watching him. 'This is what I've got cuffs for. So I never learned to tie a knot, so what?'

'In sixty years,' Jahns said.

Margaret pressed another button on her desk and pointed down the hall. 'Dr Nichols is in the nursery. I'll let him know you're coming.'

Jahns led the way. Marnes followed, asking her, 'Why is that so hard to believe?'

'I think it's cute, actually.'

Marnes snorted. 'That's an awful word to use on a man my age.'

Jahns smiled to herself. At the end of the hall, she paused at a set of double doors before pushing them open a crack. The light in the room beyond was dim. She opened the door further, and they entered a sparse but clean waiting room. She remembered a similar one from the mid levels where she had waited with a friend to be reunited with her child. A glass wall looked into a room that held a handful of cribs and bassinets. Jahns's hand dropped to her hip. She rubbed the hard nub of her now-useless implant, inserted at birth and never removed, not once. Being in that nursery reminded her of all she had lost, all she had given up for her work. For her ghosts.

It was too dark inside the nursery to see if any of the small beds stirred with newborns. She was notified of every birth, of course. As mayor, she signed a letter of congratulations and a birth certificate for each one, but the names ran together with the days. She could rarely remember what level the parents lived on, if it was their first or second. It made her sad to admit it, but those certificates had become just more paperwork, another rote duty.

The shadowy outline of an adult moved among the small cribs, the shiny clamp of a clipboard and the flash of a metal pen winking from the light of the observation room. The dark shape was obviously tall, with the gait and build of an older man. He took his time, noting something as he hovered over a crib, the two shimmers of metal uniting to jot a note. When he was done, he crossed the room and passed through a wide door to join Marnes and Jahns in the waiting room.

Peter Nichols was an imposing figure, Jahns saw. Tall and lean, but not like Marnes, who seemed to fold and unfold unsure limbs to move about. Peter was lean like a habitual exerciser, like a few porters Jahns knew who could take the stairs two at a time and make it look like they'd been expressly designed for such a pace. It was height that lent confidence. Jahns could feel it as she took Peter's outstretched hand and let him pump it firmly.

'You came,' Dr Nichols said simply. It was a cold observation. There was only a hint of surprise. He shook Marnes's hand, but his eyes returned to Jahns. 'I explained to your secretary that I wouldn't be much help. I'm afraid I haven't seen Juliette since she became a shadow twenty years ago.'

'Well, that's actually what I wanted to talk to you about.' Jahns glanced at the cushioned benches where she imagined anxious grandparents, aunts, and uncles waited while parents were united with their newborns. 'Could we sit?'

Dr Nichols nodded and waved them over.

'I take each of my appointments for office very seriously,' Jahns explained, sitting across from the doctor. 'At my age, I expect most judges and lawmen I install to outlive me, so I choose carefully.'

'But they don't always, do they?' Dr Nichols tilted his head, no expression on his lean and carefully shaven face. 'Outlive you, I mean.'

Jahns swallowed. Marnes stirred on the bench beside her.

'You must value family,' Jahns said, changing the subject, realising this was just another observation, no harm meant. 'To have shadowed so long and to choose such a demanding line of work.'

Nichols nodded.

'Why do you and Juliette never visit? I mean, not once in almost twenty years. She's your only child.'

Nichols turned his head slightly, his eyes drifting to the wall. Jahns was momentarily distracted by the sight of another form moving behind the glass, a nurse making the rounds. Another set of doors led off to what she assumed were the delivery rooms, where right now a convalescing new mother was probably waiting to be handed her most precious possession.

'I had a son as well,' Dr Nichols said.

Jahns felt herself reaching for her bag to procure the folders within, but it wasn't by her side. This was a detail she had missed, a brother.

'You couldn't have known,' Nichols said, correctly reading the shock on Mayor Jahns's face. 'He didn't survive. Technically, he wasn't born. The lottery moved on.'

'I'm sorry . . .'

She fought the urge to reach over and hold Marnes's hand. It had been decades since the two of them had purposefully touched, even innocently, but the sudden sadness in the room punctured that intervening time.

'His name was going to be Nicholas, my father's father's name. He was born prematurely. One pound eight ounces.'

The clinical precision in his voice was somehow sadder than an outpouring of emotion might have been.

'They intubated, moved him into an incubator, but there were . . . complications.' Dr Nichols looked down at the backs of his hands. 'Juliette was thirteen at the time. She was as excited as we were, if you can imagine, to have a baby brother on the way. She was one year out from shadowing her mother, who was a delivery nurse.' Nichols glanced up. 'Not here in this nursery, mind you, but in the old mid-level nursery, where we both worked. I was still an intern then.'

'And Juliette?' Mayor Jahns still didn't understand the connection.

'There was a failure with the incubator. When Nicholas—' The doctor turned his head to the side and brought his hand halfway to his eyes, but was able to compose himself. 'I'm sorry. I still call him that.'

'It's okay.'

Mayor Jahns was holding Deputy Marnes's hand. She wasn't sure when or how that had happened. The doctor didn't seem to notice or, more likely, care.

'Poor Juliette.' He shook his head. 'She was distraught. She blamed Rhoda at first, an experienced delivery nurse who had done nothing but work a miracle to give our boy the slim chance he had. I explained this. I think Juliette knew. She just needed someone to hate.' He nodded to Jahns. 'Girls that age, you know?'

'Believe it or not, I remember.' Jahns forced a smile and Dr Nichols returned it. She felt Marnes squeeze her hand.

'It wasn't until her mother died that she took to blaming the incubator that had failed. Well, not the incubator, but the poor condition it was in. The general state of rot all things become.'

'Your wife died from the complications?' It was another detail Jahns felt she must have missed from the file.

'My wife killed herself a week later.'

Again, the clinical detachment. Jahns wondered if this was a survival mechanism that had kicked in after these events, or a personality trait already in place.

'Seems like I would remember that,' Deputy Marnes said, the first words he'd uttered since introducing himself to the doctor.

'Well, I wrote the certificate myself. So I could put whatever cause I wanted—'

'And you admit to this?' Marnes seemed ready to leap off the bench. To do what, Jahns could hardly guess. She held his arm to keep him in place.

'Beyond the statute of limitations? Of course. I admit it. It was a worthless lie, anyway. Juliette was smart, even at that age. She knew. And this is what drove her—' He stopped himself.

'Drove her what?' Mayor Jahns asked. 'Crazy?'

'No.' Dr Nichols shook his head. 'I wasn't going to say that. It's what drove her away. She applied for a change in casters. Demanded to move down to Mechanical, to enter the shop as a shadow. She was a year too young for that sort of placement, but I agreed. I signed off on it. I thought she'd go, get some deep air, come back. I was naive. I thought the freedom would be good for her.'

'And you haven't seen her since?'

'Once. For her mother's funeral, just a few days later. She marched up on her own, attended the burial, gave me a hug, then marched back down. All without rest, from what I've heard. I try to keep up with her. I have a colleague in the deep nursery who will wire now and then with a bit of news. It's all focus, focus, focus with her.'

Nichols paused and laughed.

'You know, when she was young, all I saw was her mother in her. But she grew up to be more like me.'

'Is there anything you know that would preclude her from or make her ill-suited for the job of silo sheriff? You do understand what's involved with the job, right?'

'I understand.' Nichols looked over at Marnes, his eye drifting to the copper badge visible through the open, shoddily tied robe, down to the bulge of a pistol at his side. 'All the little lawmen throughout the silo have to have someone up top, giving commands, is that it?'

'More or less,' Jahns said.

'Why her?'

Marnes cleared his throat. 'She helped us with an investigation once—'

'Jules? She was up here?'

'No. We were down there.'

'She has no training.'

'None of us have,' Marnes said. 'It's more of a . . . political office. A citizen's post.'

'She won't agree to it.'

'Why not?' Jahns asked.

Nichols shrugged. 'You'll see for yourself, I suppose.' He stood. 'I wish I could give you more time, but I really should get back.' He glanced at the set of double doors. 'We'll be bringing a family in soon—'

'I understand.' Jahns rose and shook his hand. 'I appreciate you seeing us.'

He laughed. 'Did I have a choice?'

'Of course.'

'Well, I wish I'd known that sooner.'

He smiled, and Jahns saw that he was joking, or attempting to. As they parted company and walked back down the hallway to collect their things and return the robes, Jahns found herself more and more intrigued by this nomination of Marnes's. It wasn't his style, a woman from the down deep. A person with baggage. She wondered if his judgement was perhaps clouded by *other* factors. And as he held the door for her, leading out to the main waiting room, Mayor Jahns wondered if she was going along with him because *her* judgement was clouded as well.

10

It was lunchtime, but neither of them was powerfully hungry. Jahns nibbled on a cornbar while she walked, priding herself on 'eating on the climb' like a porter. They continued to pass these tradesmen, and Jahns's esteem of their profession grew and grew. She had a strange pang of guilt to be heading down under such a light load while these men and women trudged up carrying so much. And they moved so *fast*. She and Marnes pressed themselves against the rail as a downward porter apologetically stomped past. His shadow, a girl of fifteen or sixteen, was right behind him, loaded down with what looked to be sacks of garbage for the recycling centre. Jahns watched the young girl spiral out of sight, her sinewy and smooth legs hanging miles out of her shorts, and suddenly felt very old and very tired.

The two of them fell into a rhythmic pace, the reach of each foot hovering over the next tread, a sort of collapsing of the bones, a resignation to gravity, falling to that foot, sliding the hand, extending the walking stick forward, repeat. Doubt crept into Jahns around the thirtieth floor. What seemed a fine adventure at sunrise now seemed a mighty undertaking. Each step was performed reluctantly, knowing how gruelling it would be to win that elevation back.

They passed the upper water treatment plant on thirty-two, and Jahns realised she was seeing portions of the silo that were practically new to her. It had been a lifetime ago that she'd been this deep, a shameful thing to admit. And in that time, changes had been made. Construction and repairs were ongoing. Walls were a different colour than she remembered. But then, it was hard to trust one's memory. The traffic on the stairs lightened as they neared the IT floors. Here were the most sparsely populated levels of the silo, where less than two dozen men and women – but mostly men – operated within their own little kingdom. The silo servers took up almost an entire floor, the machines slowly reloading with recent history, having been wiped completely during the uprising. Access to them was now severely restricted, and as Jahns passed the landing on the thirty-third, she swore she could hear the mighty thrumming of all the electricity they consumed. Whatever the silo had been, or had been originally designed for, she knew without asking or being told that these strange machines were some organ of primacy. Their power draw was a constant source of contention during budget meetings. But the necessity of the cleaning, the fear of even talking about the outside and all the dangerous taboos that went with it, gave IT incredible leeway. They housed the labs that made the suits, each one tailored to the person waiting in the holding cell, and this alone set them apart from all else.

No, Jahns told herself, it wasn't simply the taboo of the cleaning, the fear of the outside. It was the hope. There was this unspoken, deadly hope in every member of the silo. A ridiculous, fantastical hope. That maybe not for them, but perhaps for their children, or their children's children, life on the outside would be possible once again, and that it would be the work of IT and the bulky suits that emerged from their labs that would make it all possible.

Jahns felt a shiver even to think it. Living outside. The child-hood conditioning was that strong. Maybe God would hear her thoughts and rat her out. She imagined herself in a cleaning suit, a far too common thought, placing herself into the flexible coffin into which she had condemned so many.

On the thirty-fourth, she slipped off onto the landing. Marnes joined her, his canteen in hand. Jahns realised she'd been drinking out of his all day while hers had stayed strapped to her back. There was something childlike and romantic about this, but also something practical. It was more difficult to reach one's own water than it was to grab that of the other from their pack.

'You need a break?' He passed the canteen, which had two swallows left in it. Jahns took one of them.

'This is our next stop,' she said.

Marnes looked up at the faded number stencilled over the doorway. He had to know what floor they were on, but it was as if he needed to double-check.

Jahns returned his canteen. 'In the past, I've always wired them to get the okay on my nominations. It was something Mayor Humphries did before me, and Mayor Jeffers before him.' She shrugged. 'Way of the world.'

'I didn't know they had to approve.' He took the last swallow and patted Jahns on the back, twirled his finger for her to turn around.

'Well, they've never rejected any of my nominations.' Jahns felt her canteen tugged out of her pouch, Marnes's canteen shoved in its place. Her pack felt a smidgen lighter. She realised Marnes wanted to carry her water and share it until it too was empty. 'I think the unwritten rule is there just so we'll carefully consider every judge and lawman, knowing there's some informal oversight.'

'So this time you're doing it in person.'

She turned back around to face her deputy. 'I figured we were passing this way . . .' She paused while a young couple hurried up the stairs behind Marnes, holding hands and taking the treads two at a time. 'And that it might feel even more conspicuous *not* to stop and check in.'

'Check in,' Marnes said. Jahns half expected him to spit over the railing; the tone seemed to require such punctuation. She suddenly felt another of her weaknesses exposed.

'Think of it as a goodwill mission,' she said, turning towards the door.

'I'm gonna think of it as a fact-finding raid,' Marnes muttered, following her.

Jahns could tell that, unlike at the nursery, they would not be buzzed through and sent back into the mysterious depths of IT. While they waited to be seen, she watched as even a member of the staff, identifiable from their red overalls, was patted down and searched just to *leave* the wing and exit towards the stairs. A man with a wand – a member of IT's own internal security detail – seemed to have the job of checking everyone who passed through the metal gates. The receptionist on the outside of the gates was deferential enough, however, and seemed pleased to have the mayor for a visit. She expressed her condolences for the recent cleaning, an odd thing to say but something Jahns wished she heard more often. They were shown to a small conference room attached to the main foyer, a place, she supposed, for meeting with various departments without putting them through the hassle of passing through security.

'Look at all this space,' Marnes whispered, once they were alone in the room together. 'Did you see the size of that entrance hall?'

Jahns nodded. She looked around the ceiling and walls for some peephole, something to confirm the creepy sensation that she was being watched. She set her bag and walking stick down and collapsed wearily into one of the plush chairs. When it moved, she realised the thing was on wheels. Nicely oiled wheels.

'Always wanted to check this place out,' Marnes said. He peered through the glass window that looked back into the wide foyer. 'Every time I've passed this place – and it's only been a dozen times or so – I've been curious to see what's inside.'

Jahns nearly asked him to stop talking, but worried that it would hurt his feelings.

'Boy, he's coming in a hurry. Must be because of you.'

Jahns turned and looked out the window to see Bernard Holland heading their way. He disappeared from view as he approached the door, the handle flicked down, and the small man whose job it was to keep IT running smoothly strode into the room.

'Mayor.'

Bernard was all teeth, the front ones crooked. He had a wispy moustache that hung down in a weak attempt to hide this flaw. Short, portly, and with a pair of glasses perched on his small nose, he looked every bit the technical expert. Above all, to Jahns at least, he looked *smart*.

He reached for Jahns's hand as she rose from the chair, the blasted thing nearly scooting out from underneath her as she pressed down on the arm rests.

'Careful,' Bernard said, grabbing her elbow to steady her. 'Deputy.' He nodded towards Marnes while Jahns regained her balance. 'It's an honour to have you down. I know you don't take these trips often.'

'Thanks for seeing us on short notice,' Jahns said.

'Of course. Please, make yourselves comfortable.' He swept his hand over the lacquered conference table. It was nicer than the one in the mayor's office, though Jahns assuaged herself by assuming it was shiny from being less frequently employed. She sat in the chair warily, then reached into her bag and produced the set of files. 'Straight to business, as always,' Bernard said, sitting beside her. He pushed his small round spectacles up his nose and glided forward on the chair until his plump belly met the desk. 'Always appreciated that about you. We are, as you can imagine with yesterday's unfortunate events, as busy as ever. Lots of data to go through.'

'How's that going?' Jahns asked, while she arranged the material in front of her.

'Some positives and negatives, as always. Readouts from some of the seal sensors showed improvement. Atmospheric levels of eight of the known toxins have declined, though not by much. Two have risen. Most have remained unchanged.' He waved his hand. 'It's a lot of boring technical stuff, but it'll all be in my report. I should have it ported up before you get back to your office.'

'That'll be fine,' Jahns said. She wanted to say something else, to acknowledge his department's hard work, to let him know that another cleaning had been successful, God knew why. But it was Holston out there, the closest thing she'd ever had to a shadow, the only man she'd ever seen running for her office when she was dead and feeding the roots of the fruit trees. It was too soon to mention it, much less applaud it.

'I normally wire this sort of thing to you,' she said, 'but since we were passing by, and you won't be up for the next committee meeting for, what, another three months?'

'The years go fast,' Bernard said.

'I just figured we could informally agree to this now, so I could offer our best candidate the job.' She glanced up at Marnes. 'Once she accepts, we can finish the paperwork on our way back up, if you don't mind.' She slid the folder towards Bernard, and was surprised when he produced one of his own, rather than accept hers.

'Well, let's go over this,' Bernard said. He opened his folder, licked his thumb, and flipped through a few pieces of high-quality paper. 'We were wired about your visit, but your list of candidates didn't hit my desk until this morning. Otherwise, I would have tried to save you the trip down and back up.' He pulled out a piece of paper devoid of creases. It didn't even look bleached. Jahns wondered where IT got such things while her office was held together with cornflour paste. 'I'm thinking, of the three names listed here, that Billings is our man.'

'We may consider him next—' Deputy Marnes started to say.

'I think we should consider him now.' He slid the paper towards Jahns. It was an acceptance contract. There were signatures at the bottom. One line was left blank, the mayor's name neatly printed underneath.

She had to catch her breath.

'You've already contacted Peter Billings about this?'

'He accepted. The judge's robe was going to be a little stifling for him, being so young and full of energy. I thought he was a fine choice for that role, but I think he's an even better one now for the job of sheriff.'

Jahns remembered Peter's judicial nomination process. It had been one of the times she'd gone along with Bernard's suggestion, seeing it as a trade for a future pick of her own. She studied the signature, Peter's hand familiar from his various notes sent up on behalf of Judge Wilson, under whom he currently shadowed. She imagined one of the porters who had flown past them on the steps that day, apologising as they went, rushing this very piece of paper down.

'I'm afraid Peter is currently third on our list,' Mayor Jahns finally said. Her voice suddenly felt tired. It sounded frail and weak in the cavernous and wasteful space of that underused and outsized conference room. She looked up at Marnes, who was glaring at the contract, his jaw clenching and unclenching.

'Well, I think we both know Murphy's name is on this list for flattery. He's too old for the job—'

'Younger than me,' Marnes interrupted. 'I hold up just fine.'

Bernard tilted his head. 'Yes, well, your first choice simply won't do, I'm afraid.'

'And why is that?' Jahns asked.

'I'm not sure how . . . *thorough* your background check has been, but we've had enough problems with this candidate that I recognised her name. Even though she's from Maintenance.'

Bernard said this last word like it was full of nails and might gut him to spit it out.

'What kinda problems?' Marnes demanded to know.

Jahns shot the deputy a look of warning.

'Nothing we would have wanted to report, mind you.' Bernard turned to Marnes. There was venom in the small man's eyes, a raw hatred for the deputy, or perhaps for the star on his chest. 'Nothing worth involving the *law*. But there have been some . . . creative requisitions from her office, items rerouted from our use, improper claims of priority and the like.' Bernard took a deep breath and folded his hands together on top of the folder in front of him. 'I wouldn't go as far as calling it *stealing*, per se, but we have filed complaints with Deagan Knox as head of Mechanical to inform him of these . . . irregularities.'

'That's it?' Marnes growled. 'Requisitions?'

Bernard frowned. He spread his hands on the folder. 'That's it? Have you been listening? The woman has practically stolen goods, has had items rerouted from *my* department. It's not clear if these are even for silo use. They could be for personal gain. God knows, the woman uses more than her allowance of electricity. Maybe she trades for chits—'

'Is this a formal accusation?' Marnes asked. He made a show of pulling his pad from his pocket and clicking his mechanical pen.

'Ah, no. As I said, we would not want to trouble your office. But, as you can see, this is not the sort of person to enter a career in high law. It's what I expect of a mechanic, to be honest, which is where, I'm afraid, this candidate should stay.' He patted the folder as if putting the issue to rest.

'That's your suggestion,' Mayor Jahns said.

'Why, yes. And I think since we have such a fine candidate ready and willing to serve and already living in the up top—'

'I'll take your *suggestion* into account.' Jahns took the crisp contract from the table and deliberately folded it in half, pinching the crease with her fingernails as she slid them down its length. She stuck the piece of paper in one of her folders while Bernard watched, horrified.

'And since you have no *formal* complaints about our first candidate, I will take this as tacit approval to speak with her about the job.' Jahns stood and grabbed her bag. She slid the folders into the outside pouch and secured the flap, then grabbed her walking stick from where it leaned against the conference table. 'Thank you for seeing us.'

'Yes, but—' Bernard scooted away from the table and hurried after her as Jahns made for the door. Marnes got up and followed, smiling.

'What should I tell Peter? He's of the assumption that he starts any time!'

'You should never have told him anything,' Jahns said. She stopped in the foyer and glared at Bernard. 'I gave you my list in confidence. You betrayed that. Now, I appreciate all you do for the silo. You and I have a long and peaceable history working together, overseeing what might be the most prosperous age our people have known—'

'Which is why—' Bernard began.

'Which is why I'm forgiving this trespass,' Mayor Jahns said. 'This is *my* job. My people. They elected me to make these kinds of decisions. So my deputy and I will be on our way. We will give our top choice a fair interview. And I will be sure to stop by on my way up in case there is anything to sign.'

Bernard spread his hands in defeat. 'Very well,' he said. 'I apologise. I only hoped to expedite the process. Now please, rest a little, you are our guests. Let me get you some food, maybe some fruit?'

'We'll be on our way,' Jahns said.

'Fine.' He nodded. 'But at least some water? Top up your canteens?'

Jahns remembered one of them was already empty, and they had a few more flights to go.

'That would be a kind gesture,' she said. She signalled to Marnes, who turned so she could grab his canteen from his pack. Then she turned her back so he could grab hers as well. Bernard waved to one of his workers to come fetch them and fill them up, but the entire time he kept his eyes on this curious and intimate exchange.

11

They were almost down to the fifties before Jahns could think straight. She imagined she could feel the weight of Peter Billings's contract in her pack. Marnes muttered his own complaints from a few steps behind, bitching about Bernard and trying to keep up, and Jahns realised she was fixated now. The weariness in her thighs and calves had become compounded by the growing sense that this trip was more than a mistake: it was probably futile. A father who warns her that his daughter won't accept. Pressure from IT to choose another. Now, each step of their descent was taken with dread. Dread and yet a new certainty that Juliette was the person for the job. They would have to convince this woman from Mechanical to take the post, if only to show Bernard, if only to keep this arduous journey from becoming a total waste.

Jahns was old, had been mayor a long time, partly because she got things done, partly because she prevented worse things from happening, but mostly because she rarely made a ruckus. She felt like it was about time – now, while she was old enough for the consequences not to matter. She glanced back at Marnes and knew the same went for him. Their time was almost up. The best, the most important thing they could do for the silo was to make sure their legacy endured. No uprisings. No abuses of power. It was why she had run unopposed the last few elections. But now she could sense that she was gliding to the finish while stronger and younger runners were preparing to overtake her. How many judges had she signed off on at Bernard's request? And now the sheriff, too? How long before Bernard was mayor?

Or worse: a puppet master with strings interwoven throughout the silo.

'Take it easy,' Marnes huffed.

Jahns realised she was going too fast. She slowed her pace.

'That bastard's got you riled up,' he said.

'And you better be as well,' she hissed back at him.

'You're passing the gardens.'

Jahns checked the landing number and saw that he was right. If she'd been paying attention, she would've noticed the smell. When the doors on the next landing flew open, a porter bearing sacks of fruit on each shoulder strode out, the scent of lush and wet vegetation accompanying him and overpowering her.

It was past dinner time, and the smell was intoxicating. The porter, even though overburdened, saw that they were leaving the stairwell for the landing and held the door open with a planted foot as his arms bulged around the weight of the large sacks.

'Mayor,' he said, bowing his head and then nodding to Marnes as well.

Jahns thanked him. Most of the porters looked familiar to her: she'd seen them over and over as they delivered throughout the silo. But they never stayed in one place long enough for her to catch and remember a name, a normally keen skill of hers. She wondered, as she and Marnes entered the hydroponic farms, if the porters made it home every night to be with their families. Or did they even have families? Were they like the priests? She was too old and too curious not to know these things. But then, maybe it took a day on the stairwell to appreciate their job, to notice them fully. The porters were like the air she breathed, always there, always serving, so necessary as to be ubiquitous and taken for granted. But now the weariness of the descent had opened her senses completely to them. It was like a sudden drop in the oxygen, triggering her appreciation.

'Smell those oranges,' Marnes said, snapping Jahns out of her thoughts. He sniffed the air as they passed through the low garden gates. A staff member in green overalls waved them through. 'Bags here, Mayor,' he said, gesturing to a wall of cubbies sporadically filled with shoulder bags and bundles.

Jahns complied, leaving her kit in one of the cubbies. Marnes pushed hers to the back and added his to the same one. Whether it was to save space or merely his habitual protectiveness, Jahns found the act as sweet as the air inside the gardens.

'We have reservations for the evening,' Jahns told the worker.

He nodded. 'One flight down for the rooms. I believe they're still getting yours ready. Are you here just for a visit or to eat?'

'A little of both.'

The young man smiled. 'Well, by the time you've had a bite, your rooms should be available.'

Rooms, Jahns thought. She thanked the young man and followed Marnes into the garden network.

'How long since you were here?' she asked the deputy.

'Wow. A while back. Four years or so?'

'That's right.' Jahns laughed. 'How could I forget? The heist of the century.'

'I'm glad you think it's funny,' Marnes said.

At the end of the hallway, the twisting spiral of the hydroponic gardens diverted off both ways. This main tunnel snaked through two levels of the silo, curving maze-like all the way to the edges of the distant concrete walls. The constant sound of water dripping from the pipes was oddly soothing, the splatters echoing off the low ceiling. The tunnel was open on either side, revealing the bushy green of plants, vegetables, and small trees growing amid the lattice of white plastic pipes, twine strung everywhere to give the creeping vines and stems something to hold. Men and women with their young shadows tended to the plants, all in green overalls. Sacks hung around their necks bulged with the day's harvest, and the cutters in their hands clacked like little claws that were a biological part of them. The pruning was mesmerisingly adroit and effortless, the sort of ability that came only from day after week after year of practice and repetition.

'Weren't you the first one to suggest the thievery was an inside job?' Jahns asked, still laughing to herself. She and Marnes followed the signs pointing towards the tasting and dining halls.

'Are we really going to talk about this?'

'I don't know why it's embarrassing. You've got to laugh about it.'

'With time.' He stopped and gazed through the mesh fencing at a stand of tomatoes. The powerful odour of their ripeness made Jahns's stomach grumble.

'We were really hyped up to make a bust at the time,' Marnes said quietly. 'Holston was a mess during all of this. He was wiring me every night for an update. I've never seen him want to take someone down so bad. Like he really needed it, you know?' He wrapped his fingers in the protective grate and stared past the vegetables as if into the years gone by. 'Looking back, it's almost like he knew something was up with Allison. Like he saw the madness coming.' Marnes turned to Jahns. 'Do you remember what it was like before she cleaned? It had been so long. Everyone was on edge.'

Jahns had long since stopped smiling. She stood close to Marnes. He turned back to the plants, watched a worker snip off a red ripe tomato and place it in her basket.

'I think Holston wanted to let the air out of the silo, you know? I think he wanted to come down and investigate the thefts himself. Kept wiring me every day for reports like a life depended on it.'

'I'm sorry to bring it up,' Jahns said, resting a hand on his shoulder.

Marnes turned and looked at the back of her hand. His bottom lip was visible below his moustache. Jahns could picture him kissing her hand. She pulled it away.

'It's fine,' he said. 'Without all that baggage, I guess it is pretty funny.' He turned and continued down the hallway.

'Did they ever figure out how it got in here?'

'Up the stairwell,' Marnes said. 'Had to be. Though I heard one person suggest that a child could've stolen one to keep as a pet and then released it up here.'

Jahns laughed. She couldn't help herself. 'One rabbit,' she said, 'confounding the greatest lawman of our time and making off with a year's salary of greens.'

Marnes shook his head and chuckled a little. 'Not the greatest,' he said. 'That was never me.' He peered down the hallway and cleared his throat, and Jahns knew perfectly well who he was thinking of.

After a large and satisfying dinner, they retired a level down to the guest rooms. Jahns had a suspicion that extra pains had been taken to accommodate them. Every room was packed, many of them double- and triple-booked. And since the cleaning had been scheduled well before this last-minute interview adventure of theirs, she suspected rooms had been bumped around to make space. The fact that they had been given separate rooms, the mayor's with two beds, made it worse. It wasn't just the waste, it was the arrangement. Jahns was hoping to be more . . . inconvenienced.

And Marnes must've felt the same way. Since it was still hours before bedtime, and they were both buzzing from a fine meal and strong wine, he asked her to his small room so they could chat while the gardens settled down.

His room was tastefully cosy, with only a single twin bed, but nicely appointed. The upper gardens were one of just a dozen large private enterprises. All the expenses for their stay would be covered by her office's travel budget, and that money as well as the fares of the other travellers helped the establishment afford finer things, like nice sheets from the looms and a mattress that didn't squeak.

Jahns sat on the foot of the bed. Marnes took off his holster, placed it on the dresser and plopped onto a changing bench just a few feet away. While she kicked off her boots and rubbed her sore feet, he went on and on about the food, the waste of separate rooms, brushing his moustache down with his hand as he spoke.

Jahns worked her thumbs into the soreness in her heels. 'I feel like I'm going to need a week of rest at the bottom before we start the climb up,' she said during a pause.

'It's not all that bad,' Marnes told her. 'You watch. You'll be sore in the morning, but once you start moving, you'll find that you're stronger than you were today. And it's the same on the way up. You just lean into each step, and before you know it, you're home.'

'I hope you're right.'

'Besides, we'll do it in four days instead of two. Just think of it as an adventure.'

'Trust me,' Jahns said. 'I already am.'

They sat quietly for a while, Jahns resting back on the pillows, Marnes staring off into space. She was surprised to find how calming and natural it was, just being in a room, alone, with him. The talk wasn't necessary. They could just *be*. No badge, no office. Two people.

'You don't take a priest, do you?' Marnes finally asked.

'No.' She shook her head. 'Do you?'

'I haven't. But I've been thinking about it.'

'Holston?'

'Partly.' He leaned forward and rubbed his hands down his thighs like he was squeezing the soreness out of them. 'I'd like to hear where they think his soul has gone.'

'It's still with us,' Jahns said. 'That's what they'd say, anyway.'

'What do you believe?'

'Me?' She pushed herself up from the pillows and rested on one elbow, watching him watch her. 'I don't know, really. I keep too busy to think about it.'

'Do you think Donald's soul is still here with us?'

Jahns felt a shiver. She couldn't remember the last time someone had uttered his name.

'He's been gone more years than he was ever my husband,' she said. 'I've been married more to his ghost than to him.'

'That don't seem like the right thing to say.'

Jahns looked down at the bed, the world a little blurry. 'I don't think he'd mind. And yes, he's still with me. He motivates me every day to be a good person. I feel him watching me all the time.'

'Me too,' Marnes said.

Jahns looked up and saw that he was staring at her.

'Do you think he'd want you to be happy? In all things, I mean?' He stopped rubbing his legs and sat there, hands on his knees, until he had to look away.

'You were his best friend,' Jahns said. 'What do you think he'd want?'

He rubbed his face, glanced towards the closed door as a laughing child thundered down the hallway. 'I reckon he only ever wanted you to be happy. That's why he was the man for you.'

Jahns wiped her eyes while he wasn't looking and peered curiously down at her wet fingers.

'It's getting late,' she said. She slid to the edge of the small bed and reached down for her boots. Her bag and stick were waiting for her by the door. 'And I think you're right. I think I'll be a little sore in the morning, but I think I'll feel stronger, eventually.'

12

On the second and final day of their descent into the down deep, the novel gradually became the habitual. The clank and thrum of the great spiral staircase found a rhythm. Jahns was able to lose herself in her thoughts, daydreaming so serenely that she would glance up at the floor number – seventy-two, eighty-four – and wonder where a dozen landings went. The kink in her left knee was even soothed away, whether by the numbness of fatigue or an actual return to health, she didn't know. She took to using the walking stick less, finding it only held up her pace as it often slipped between the treads and got caught there. With it tucked under her arm, it felt more useful. Like another bone in her skeleton, holding her together.

When they passed the ninetieth floor, with the stench of fertiliser and the pigs and other animals that produced this useful waste, Jahns pressed on, skipping the tour and lunch she'd planned, thinking only briefly of the small rabbit that somehow had escaped from another farm, made it twenty floors up without being spotted, and ate its fill for three weeks while it confounded half a silo.

Technically, they were already in the down deep when they reached ninety-seven. The bottom third. But even though the silo was mathematically divided into three sections of forty-eight floors each, her brain didn't work that way. Floor one hundred was a better demarcation. It was a milestone. She counted the floors down until they reached the first landing with three digits, and stopped for a break.

Marnes was breathing deeply, she noticed. But she felt great. Alive and renewed in the way she had hoped the trip would make her. The futility, dread, and exhaustion from the day before were gone. All that remained was a small twinge of fear that these dour feelings could return, that this exuberant elation was a temporary high, that if she stopped, if she thought on it too long, it would spiral away and leave her dark and moody once more.

They split a small loaf of bread between them, sitting on the metal grating of the wide landing with their elbows propped up on the railings, their feet swinging over empty space, like two kids cutting class. Level one hundred teemed with people coming and going. The entire floor was a bazaar, a place for exchanging goods, for cashing in work chits for whatever was needed or merely coveted. Workers with their trailing shadows came and went, families yelled for one another among the dizzying crowds, merchants barked their best deals. The doors remained propped open for the traffic, letting the smells and sounds drift out onto the double-wide landing, the grating shivering with excitement.

Jahns revelled in the anonymity of the passing crowd. She bit into her half of the loaf, savouring the fresh yeastiness of bread baked that morning, and felt like just another person. A younger person. Marnes cut her a piece of cheese and a slice of apple and sandwiched them together. His hand touched hers as he passed it to her. Even the breadcrumbs in his moustache were part of the moment's perfection.

'We're way ahead of schedule,' Marnes said before taking a bite of fruit. It was just a pleasant observation. A pat on their elderly backs. 'I figure we'll hit one-forty by dinner.'

'Right now, I'm not even dreading the climb out,' Jahns said. She finished the cheese and apple and chewed contentedly. Everything tasted better while climbing, she decided. Or in pleasant company, or amid the music leaking out of the bazaar, some beggar strumming his uke over the noise of the crowd.

'Why don't we come down here more often?' she asked.

Marnes grunted. 'Because it's a hundred flights down? Besides, we've got the view, the lounge, the bar at Kipper's. How many of these people come up to any of that more than once every few years?'

Jahns chewed on that and on her last bite of bread.

'Do you think it's natural? Not wandering too far from where we live?'

'Don't follow,' Marnes said around a bite of food.

'Pretend, just as a hypothetical, mind you, that people lived in those ancient aboveground silos poking up over the hillside. You don't think they would move around so little, do you? Like stay in the same silo? Never wander over here or up and down a hundred flights of stairs?'

'I don't think on those things,' Marnes said. Jahns took it as a hint that she shouldn't, either. It was impossible sometimes to know what could and couldn't be said about the outside. Those were discussions for spouses, and maybe the walk and the day together yesterday had got to her. Or maybe she was as susceptible to the post-cleaning high as anyone else: the sense that some rules could be relaxed, a few temptations courted, the release of pressure in the silo giving excuse for a month of jubilant wiggling in one's own skin.

'Should we get going?' Jahns asked, as Marnes finished his bread.

He nodded, and they stood and collected their things. A woman walking by turned and stared, a flash of recognition on her face, gone as she hurried to catch up with her children.

It was like another world down here, Jahns thought to herself. She had gone too long without a visit. And even as she promised herself not to let that happen again, some part of her knew, like a rusting machine that could feel its age, that this journey would be her last.

Floors drifted in and out of sight. The lower gardens, the larger farm on the one-thirties, the pungent water treatment plant below that. Jahns found herself lost in thought, remembering her conversation with Marnes the night before, the idea of Donald living with her more in memory than reality, when she came to the gate at one-forty.

She hadn't even noticed the change in the traffic, the preponderance of blue denim overalls, the porters with more satchels of parts and tools than clothes, food, or personal deliveries. But the crowd at the gate showed her that she'd arrived at the upper levels of Mechanical. Gathered at the entrance were workers in loose blue overalls spotted with age-old stains. Jahns could nearly peg their professions by the tools they carried. It was late in the day, and she assumed most were returning home from repairs made throughout the silo. The thought of climbing so many flights of stairs and *then* having to work boggled her mind. And then she remembered she was about to do that very thing.

Rather than abuse her station or Marnes's power, they waited in line while the workers checked through the gate. As these tired men and women signed back in and logged their travel and hours, Jahns thought of the time she had wasted ruminating about her own life during the long descent, time she should've spent polishing her appeal to this Juliette. Rare nerves twisted her gut as the line shuffled forward. The worker ahead of them showed his ID, the card coloured blue for Mechanical. He scratched his information on a dusty slate. When it was their turn, they pushed through the outer gate and showed their golden IDs. The station guard raised his eyebrows, then seemed to recognise the mayor.

'Your Honour,' he said, and Jahns didn't correct him. 'Weren't expecting you this shift.' He waved their IDs away and reached for a nub of chalk. 'Let me.'

Jahns watched as he spun the board around and wrote their names in neat print, the side of his palm collecting dust from the old film of chalk below. For Marnes, he simply wrote 'Sheriff', and again, Jahns didn't correct him.

'I know she wasn't expecting us until later,' Jahns said, 'but I wonder if we could meet with Juliette Nichols now.'

The station guard turned and looked behind him at the digital clock that recorded the proper time. 'She won't be off the generator for another hour. Maybe two, knowing her. You could hit the mess hall and wait.'

Jahns looked at Marnes, who shrugged. 'Not entirely hungry yet,' he said. 'What about seeing her at work? It would be nice to see what she does. We'd try our best to stay out of the way.'

The guard lifted his shoulders. 'You're the mayor. I can't say no.' He jabbed the nub of chalk down the hall, the people lined up outside the gate shifting impatiently as they waited. 'See Knox. He'll get someone to run you down.'

The head of Mechanical was a man hard to miss. Knox amply filled the largest set of overalls Jahns had ever seen. She wondered if the extra denim cost him more chits, and how a man managed to keep such a belly full. A thick beard added to his scope. If he smiled or frowned at their approach, it was impossible to know. He was as unmoved as a wall of concrete.

Jahns explained what they were after. Marnes said hello, and she realised they must've met the last time he was down. Knox listened, nodded, and then bellowed in a voice so gruff, the words were indistinguishable from one another. But they meant something to someone, as a young boy materialised from behind him, a waif of a kid with unusually bright orange hair.

'Gitemoffandowntojules,' Knox growled, the space between the words as slender as the gap in his beard where a mouth should have been.

The young boy, young even for a shadow, waved his hand and darted away. Marnes thanked Knox, who didn't budge, and they followed after the boy.

The corridors in Mechanical, Jahns saw, were even tighter than elsewhere in the silo. They squeezed through the end-of-shift traffic, the concrete blocks on either side primed but not painted, and rough where they brushed against her shoulder. Overhead, parallel and twisting runs of pipe and wire conduit hung exposed. Jahns felt the urge to duck, despite the half foot of clearance; she noticed many of the taller workers walking with a stoop. The lights overhead were dim and spaced well apart, making the sensation of tunnelling deeper and deeper into the earth overwhelming.

The young shadow with the orange hair led them around several turns, his confidence in the route seemingly habitual. They came to a flight of stairs, the square kind that made right turns, and went down two more levels. Jahns heard a rumbling grow louder as they descended. When they left the stairwell on one-forty-two, they passed an odd contraption in a wide-open room just off the hallway. A steel arm the size of several people end to end was moving up and down, driving a piston through the concrete floor. Jahns slowed to watch its rhythmic gyrations. The air smelled of something chemical, something rotten. She couldn't place it.

'Is this the generator?'

Marnes laughed in a patronising, uniquely manly way.

'That's a pump,' he said. 'Oil well. It's how you read at night.'

He squeezed her shoulder as he walked past, and Jahns forgave him instantly for laughing at her. She hurried after him and Knox's young shadow.

'The generator is that thrumming you hear,' Marnes said. 'The pump brings up oil, they do something to it in a plant a few floors down, and then it's ready to burn.'

Jahns vaguely knew some of this, possibly from a committee meeting. She was amazed, once again, at how much of the silo was alien to even her, she who was supposed to be – nominally at least – running things.

The persistent grumbling in the walls grew louder as they neared the end of the hall. When the boy with the orange hair pulled open the doors, the sound was deafening. Jahns felt wary about approaching further, and even Marnes seemed to stall. The kid waved them forward with frantic gestures, and Jahns found herself willing her feet to carry her towards the noise. She wondered, suddenly, if they were being led *outside*. It was an illogical, senseless idea, born of imagining the most dangerous threat she could possibly summon.

As she broke the plane of the door, cowering behind Marnes, the boy let the door slam shut, trapping them inside with the onslaught. He pulled headphones – no wires dangling from them – from a rack by the wall. Jahns followed his lead and put a pair over her own ears. The noise was deadened, remaining only in her chest and nerve endings. She wondered why, for what cause, this rack of ear protection would be located *inside* the room rather than outside.

The boy waved and said something, but it was just moving lips. They followed him along a narrow passageway of steel grating, a floor much like the landings on each silo floor. When the hallway turned, one wall fell away and was replaced with a railing of three horizontal bars. A machine beyond reckoning loomed on the other side. It was the size of her entire apartment and office put together. Nothing seemed to be moving at first, nothing to justify the pounding she could feel in her chest and across her skin. It wasn't until they fully rounded the machine that she saw the steel rod sticking out of the back of the unit, spinning ferociously, and disappearing into another massive metal machine which had cables as thick as a man's waist rising up towards the ceiling.

The power and energy in the room were palpable. As they reached the end of the second machine, Jahns finally saw a solitary figure working beside it. A young-looking woman in overalls, a hard hat on, brown braided hair hanging out the back, was leaning into a wrench nearly as long as she was tall. Her presence gave the machines a terrifying sense of scale, but she didn't seem to fear them. She threw herself into her wrench, her body frightfully close to the roaring unit, reminding Jahns of an old children's tale where a mouse pulled a barb out of an imaginary beast called an elephant. The idea of a woman this size fixing a machine of such ferocity seemed absurd. But she watched the woman work while the young shadow slipped through a gate and ran up to tug on her overalls.

The woman turned, not startled, and squinted at Jahns and Marnes. She wiped her forehead with the back of one hand, her other hand swinging the wrench around to rest on her shoulder. She patted the young shadow on the head and walked out to meet them. Jahns saw that the woman's arms were lean and well defined with muscle. She wore no undershirt, just blue overalls cut high up over her chest, exposing a bit of olive skin that gleamed with sweat. She had the same dark complexion as the farmers who worked under grow lights, but it could have been as much from the grease and grime if her denims were any indication.

She stopped short of Jahns and Marnes, and nodded at them. She smiled at Marnes with a hint of recognition. She didn't offer a hand, for which Jahns was grateful. Instead, she pointed towards a door by a glass partition, and then headed that way herself.

Marnes followed on her heels like a puppy, Jahns close behind. She turned to make sure the shadow wasn't underfoot, only to see him scurrying off the way he had come, his hair glowing in the wan overhead lights of the generator room. His duty, as far as he was concerned, was done.

Inside the small control room, the noise lessened. It dropped almost to nothing as the thick door was shut tight. Juliette pulled off her hard hat and earmuffs and dropped them on a shelf. Jahns took hers away from her head tentatively, heard the noise reduced to a distant hum, and removed them all the way. The room was tight and crowded with metal surfaces and winking lights unlike anything she had ever seen. It was strange to her that she was mayor of this room as well, a thing she hardly knew existed and certainly couldn't operate.

While the ringing in Jahns's ears subsided, Juliette adjusted some spinning knobs, watching little arms waver under glass shields. 'I thought we were doing this tomorrow morning,' she said, concentrating intently on her work.

'We made better time than I'd hoped.'

Jahns looked to Marnes, who was holding his ear protection in both hands, shifting uncomfortably.

'Good to see you again, Jules,' he said.

She nodded and leaned down to peer through the thick glass window at the gargantuan machines outside, her hands darting over the large control board without needing to look, adjusting large black dials with faded white markings.

'Sorry about your partner,' she said, glancing down at a bank of readouts. She turned and studied Marnes, and Jahns saw that this woman, beneath the sweat and grime, was beautiful. Her face was hard and lean, her eyes bright. She had a fierce intelligence you could measure from a distance. And she peered at Marnes with utmost sympathy, visible in the furrow of her brows. 'Really,' she said. 'I'm terribly sorry. He seemed like a good man.'

'The best,' Marnes sputtered, his voice cracking.

Juliette nodded as if that was all that needed saying. She turned to Jahns.

'That vibration you feel in the floor, Mayor? That's a coupling when it's barely two millimetres off. If you think it feels bad in here, you should go put your hands on the casing. It'll jiggle your fingers numb immediately. Hold it long enough, and your bones will rattle like you're coming apart.'

She turned and reached between Jahns and Marnes to throw a massive switch, then turned back to the control board. 'Now imagine what that generator is going through, shaking itself to pieces like that. Teeth start grinding together in the transmission, small bits of metal shavings cycle through the oil like sandpaper grit. Next thing you know, there's an explosion of steel and we've got no power but whatever the backup can spit out.'

Jahns held her breath.

'You need us to get someone?' Marnes asked.

Juliette laughed. 'None of this is news or different from any other shift. If the backup unit wasn't being torn down for new gaskets, and we could go to half power for a week, I could pull that coupler, adjust the mounts, and have her spinning like a top.' She shot a look at Jahns. 'But since we have a mandate for full power, no interruptions, that's not happening. So I'm going to keep tightening bolts while they keep trying to shake loose, and try and find the right revolutions in here to keep her fairly singing.'

'I had no idea, when I signed that mandate—'

'And here I thought I'd dumbed down my report enough to make it clear,' Juliette said.

'How long before this failure happens?'

Jahns suddenly realised she wasn't here interviewing this woman. The demands were heading in the opposite direction.

'How long?' Juliette laughed and shook her head. She finished a final adjustment and turned to face them with her arms crossed. 'It could happen right now. It could happen a hundred years from now. The point is: it's *going* to happen, and it's entirely preventable. The goal shouldn't be to keep this place humming along for our lifetimes' – she looked pointedly at Jahns – 'or our current term. If the goal ain't for ever, we should pack our bags right now.'

Jahns saw Marnes stiffen at this. She felt her own body react, a chill coursing across her skin. This last line was dangerously close to treason. The metaphor only half saved it.

'I could declare a power holiday,' Jahns suggested. 'We could stage it in memory of those who clean.' She thought more about this. 'It could be an excuse to service more than your machine here. We could—'

'Good luck getting IT to power down shit,' Juliette said. She wiped her chin with the back of her wrist, then wiped this on her overalls. She looked down at the grease transferred to the denim. 'Pardon my language, Mayor.'

Jahns wanted to tell her it was quite all right, but the woman's attitude, her power, reminded her too much of a former self that she could just barely recall. A younger woman who dispensed with niceties and got what she wanted. She found herself glancing over at Marnes. 'Why do you single out their department? For the power, I mean.'

Juliette laughed and uncrossed her arms. She tossed her hands towards the ceiling. 'Why? Because IT has, what, three floors out of one-forty-four? And yet they use up over a quarter of all the power we produce. I can do the maths for you—'

'That's quite all right.'

'And I don't remember a server ever feeding someone or saving someone's life or stitching up a hole in their britches.'

Jahns smiled. She suddenly saw what Marnes liked about this woman. She also saw what he had once seen in her younger self, before she married his best friend.

'What if we had IT ratchet down for some maintenance of their own for a week? Would that work?'

'I thought we came down here to recruit her *away* from all this,' Marnes grumbled.

Juliette shot him a look. 'And I thought I told you – or your secretary – not to bother. Not that I've got anything against what you do, but I'm needed down here.' She raised her arm and checked something dangling from her wrist. It was a timepiece. But she was studying it as if it still worked.

'Look, I'd love to chat more.' She looked up at Jahns. 'Especially if you can guarantee a holiday from the juice, but I've got a few more adjustments to make and I'm already into my overtime. Knox gets pissed if I push into too many extra shifts.'

'We'll get out of your hair,' Jahns said. 'We haven't had dinner yet, so maybe we can see you after? Once you punch out and get cleaned up?'

Juliette looked down at herself, as if to confirm she even needed cleaning.

'Yeah, sure,' she said. 'They've got you in the bunkhouse?'

Marnes nodded.

'All right. I'll find you later. And don't forget your muffs.' She pointed to her ears, looked Marnes in the eye, nodded, then returned to her work, letting them know the conversation, for now, was over.

13

Marnes and Jahns were guided to the mess hall by Marck, a mechanic just getting off second shift. Marnes seemed to take umbrage at needing a tour guide. The deputy possessed that distinctly male quality of pretending to know where he was, even when he didn't. Walking slightly ahead in an attempt to prove this, he would pause at some intersection, point questioningly in one direction, only to have Marck laugh and correct him.

'But it all looks the same,' he grumbled as he continued to forge ahead.

Jahns laughed at the manly display and hung back to bend the young mechanic's ear, recognising that he worked on Juliette's shift. He smelled of the down deep, that odour that wafted in whenever a mechanic came up to repair something in her offices. It was the blend born of their work, a mix of perspiration, grease, and vague chemicals. But Jahns was learning to ignore that. She saw that Marck was a kind and gentle man, a man who took her by the arm when a trolley of rattling parts was hurried past, a man who acknowledged every single person they passed in those dim corridors of jutting pipes and drooping wires. He lived and breathed well above his lot in life, Jahns thought. He radiated confidence. Even in the darkness, his smile threw shadows.

'How well do you know Juliette?' she asked him, once the noisy cart rattled out of earshot.

'Jules? I know her like a sister. We're all family down here.'

He said this as though he assumed the rest of the silo operated differently. Ahead of them, Marnes scratched his head at the next intersection before guessing correctly. A pair of mechanics crowded around the corner from the other direction, laughing. They and Marck exchanged a snippet of conversation that sounded to Jahns like a foreign language. She suspected Marck was right, that perhaps things did work differently in the deepest depths of the silo. People down there seemed to wear their thoughts and feelings on the outside, seemed to say exactly what they meant, much as the pipes and wires of the place lay exposed and bare.

'Through here,' Marck said, pointing across a wide hall towards the sound of overlapping conversations and the tinkling of knives and forks on metal plates.

'So, is there anything you can tell us about Jules?' Jahns asked. She smiled at Marck as he held the door for her. 'Anything you think we should know?' The two of them followed Marnes to a handful of empty seats. The kitchen staff bustled among the tables, actually serving the food rather than having the mechanics line up for it. Before they'd even situated themselves on the dented aluminium benches, bowls of soup were being set out, glasses of water with lime slices bobbing on top, and hunks of bread torn from loaves and placed directly on the beaten-up surface of the table.

'Are you asking me to vouch for her?' Marck sat down and thanked the large man who portioned out their food and spoons. Jahns looked around for a napkin and saw most of the men and women using the greasy rags that dangled from their back or breast pockets.

'Just anything we should know,' she said.

Marnes studied his bread, sniffed it, then dunked one corner into his soup. A neighbouring table erupted with laughter at the conclusion of some story or joke being told.

'I know she can do any job thrown at her. Always could. But I figure you don't need me to talk you into something you've already walked this far to get. I'd imagine your minds are already made up.'

He sipped on a spoonful of soup. Jahns picked up her utensil and saw that it was chipped and twisted, the butt of the spoon scratched like it'd been used to gouge at something.

'How long have you known her?' Marnes asked. The deputy

chewed on his soggy bread and was doing a heroic job of blending in with his surroundings, of looking like he belonged.

'I was born down here,' Marck told them, raising his voice over the din-filled room. 'I was shadowing in Electrical when Jules showed up. She was a year younger than me. I gave her two weeks before I figured she'd be kicking and screaming to get out of here. We've had our share of runaways and transfers, kids from the mids thinking their problems wouldn't dare follow them—'

He left the sentence short, his eyes lighting up as a demure woman squeezed in next to Marnes on the other side of the table. This new arrival wiped her hands with her rag, stuffed it into her breast pocket, and leaned over the table to kiss Marck on the cheek.

'Honey, you remember Deputy Marnes.' Marck gestured to Marnes, who was wiping his moustache with the palm of his hand. 'This is my wife, Shirly.' They shook hands. The dark stains on Shirly's knuckles seemed permanent, a tattoo from her work.

'And your mayor. This is Jahns.' The two women shook hands as well. Jahns was proud of herself for accepting the firm grip without caring about the grease.

'Pleased,' Shirly said. She sat. Her food had somehow materialised during the introductions, the surface of her soup undulating and throwing off steam.

'Has there been a crime, Officer?' Shirly smiled at Marnes as she tore off a piece of her bread, letting him know it was a joke.

'They came to harangue Jules into moving up top with them,' Marck said, and Jahns caught him lifting an eyebrow at his wife.

'Good luck,' she said. 'If that girl moves a level, it'll be down from here and into the mines.'

Jahns wanted to ask what she meant, but Marck turned and continued where he'd left off.

'So I was working in Electrical when she showed up—'

'You boring them with your shadow days?' Shirly asked.

'I'm tellin' them about when Jules arrived.'

His wife smiled.

'I was studying under old Walk at the time. This was back when he was still moving around, getting out and about now and then—'

'Oh yeah, Walker.' Marnes jabbed a spoon at Jahns. 'Crafty fellow. Never leaves his workshop.'

Jahns nodded, trying to follow. Several of the revellers at the neighbouring table got up to leave. Shirly and Marck waved goodbye and exchanged words with several of them, before turning their attention back to the table.

'Where was I?' Marck asked. 'Oh, so the first time I met Jules was when she arrived at Walk's shop with this pump.' Marck took a sip of his water. 'One of the first things they have her doing, now keep in mind this is just a waif of a girl, right? Twelve years old. Skinny as a pipe. Fresh from the mids or somewhere up there.' He waved his hand like it was all the same. 'They've got her hauling these massive pumps up to Walk's to have him re-spool the motors, basically unwrap a mile of wire and lay it back in place.' Marck paused and laughed. 'Well, to have Walk make *me* do all the work. Anyway, it's like this initiation, you know? You all do that sort of thing to your shadows, right? Just to break 'em down a little?'

Neither Jahns nor Marnes moved. Marck shrugged and continued. 'Anyway, these pumps are heavy, okay? They had to weigh more than she did. Maybe double. And she's supposed to wrestle these things onto carts by herself and get them up four flights of stairs—'

'Wait. How?' Jahns asked, trying to imagine a girl that age moving a hunk of metal twice her weight.

'Doesn't matter. Pulleys, ropes, bribery, whatever she likes. That's the point, right? And they've got ten of these things set aside for her to deliver—'

'Ten of them,' Jahns repeated.

'Yeah, and probably *two* of them actually needed re-spooling,' Shirly added.

'Oh, if that.' Mark laughed. 'So Walk and I are taking bets on how long before she cuts and runs back to her old man.'

'I gave her a week,' Shirly said.

Marck stirred his soup and shook his head. 'The thing was, after she pulled it off, none of us had any idea how she'd done it. It was years later that she finally told us.'

'We were sitting over at that table.' Shirly pointed. 'I'd never laughed so hard in my life.'

'Told you what?' Jahns asked. She had forgotten her soup. The steam had long stopped swirling from its surface.

'Well, sure enough, I wound the coils on ten pumps that week. The whole time, I'm waiting for her to break. Hoping for it. My fingers were sore. No way she could move all of them.' Marck shook his head. 'No way. But I kept winding them, she kept hauling them off, and a while later she'd bring another. Got all ten of them done in six days. The little snot went to Knox, who was just a shift manager back then, and asked if she could take a day off.'

Shirly laughed and peered into her soup.

'So she got someone to help her,' Marnes said. 'Somebody probably just felt sorry for her.'

Marck wiped his eyes and shook his head. 'Aw, hell, no. Somebody would've seen, would've said something. Especially when Knox demanded to know. Old man nearly blew a fuse asking her what she'd done. Jules just stands there, calm as a dead battery, shrugging.'

'How did she do it?' Jahns asked. Now she was dying to know.

Marck smiled. 'She only moved the one pump. Nearly broke her back getting it up here, but only moved the one.'

'Yeah, and you rewound that thing ten times,' Shirly said.

'Hey, you don't have to tell me.'

'Wait.' Jahns held up her hand. 'But what about the others?'

'Done them herself. I blame Walk, talking his head off while she swept the shop that first night. She was asking questions, badgering me, watching me work on that first pump. When I got done, she pushed the pump down the hall, didn't bother with the stairs, and stowed it in the paint shop right on the trolley. Then she went downstairs, got the next pump, and hauled it around the corner into the tool lock-up. Spent the entire night in there teaching herself how to rewire a motor.'

'Ah,' Jahns said, seeing where this was going. 'And the next morning she brought you the same pump from the day before, from just around the corner.'

'Right. Then she went and wound copper four levels below while I was doing the same thing up here.'

Marnes erupted with laughter and slapped the table, bowls and bread hopping.

'I averaged two motors a day that week, a brutal pace.'

'Technically, it was only one motor,' Shirly pointed out, laughing.

'Yeah. And she kept up with me. Had them all back to her caster with a day to spare, a day she asked to take off.'

'A day she got off, if I remember right,' Shirly added. She shook her head. 'A shadow with a day off. The damnedest thing.'

'The point is, she wasn't ever supposed to get the task done in the first place.'

'Smart girl,' Jahns said, smiling.

'Too smart,' Marck said.

'So what did she do with her day off?' Marnes asked.

Marck pushed his lime down beneath the surface of his water with his finger and held it there a moment.

'She spent the day with me and Walk, sweeping the shop, asking how things worked, where these wires went to, how to loosen a bolt and dig inside something, that kind of stuff.' He took a sip of water. 'I guess what I'm sayin' is that if you want to give Jules a job, be very careful.'

'Why be careful?' Marnes asked.

Marck gazed up at the confusion of pipes and wires overhead.

''Cause she'll damn well do it. Even if you don't really expect her to.'

14

After their meal, Shirly and Marck gave them directions to the bunk room. Jahns watched as the young married couple exchanged kisses. Marck was coming off his shift while Shirly was going onto hers. The shared meal was breakfast for one and supper for the other. Jahns thanked them both for their time and complimented the food, then she and Marnes left a mess hall nearly as noisy as the generator room had been, and followed the winding corridors towards their beds for the night.

Marnes would be staying in the communal bunk room used by junior first-shift mechanics. A small cot had been made up for him that Jahns gauged to be half a foot too short. Down the hall from the bunk room, a small apartment had been reserved for Jahns. The two of them decided to wait there, biding their time in private, rubbing the aches in their legs, talking about how different everything in the down deep was, until there was a knock on their door. Juliette pushed it open and stepped inside.

'They got you both in one room?' Juliette asked, surprised.

Jahns laughed. 'No, they've got the deputy in the bunk room. And I would've been happy staying out there with the others.'

'Forget it,' Juliette said. 'They put up recruits and visiting families in here all the time. It's nothing.'

Jahns watched as Juliette placed a length of string in her mouth, then gathered her hair, still wet from a shower, and tied it up in a tail. She had changed into another pair of overalls, and Jahns guessed the stains in them were permanent, that the fabric was actually laundered and ready for another shift.

'So how soon could we announce this power holiday?' Juliette asked. She finished her knot and crossed her arms, leaning back against the wall beside the door. 'I would think you'd wanna take advantage of the post-cleaning mood, right?'

'How soon can *you* start?' Jahns asked. She realised, suddenly, that part of the reason she wanted this woman as her sheriff was that she felt unattainable. Jahns glanced over at Marnes and wondered how much of his attraction to her, all those many years ago when she was young and with Donald, had been as simply motivated.

'I can start tomorrow,' Juliette said. 'We could have the backup generator online by morning. I could work another shift tonight to make sure the gaskets and seals—'

'No,' Jahns said, raising her hand. 'How soon can you start as sheriff?' She dug through her open bag, sorting folders across the bed, looking for the contract.

'I'm – I thought we discussed this. I have no interest in being—'

'They make the best ones,' Marnes said. 'The ones who have no interest in it.' He stood across from Juliette, his thumbs tucked into his overalls, leaning against one of the small apartment's walls.

'I'm sorry, but there's no one down here who can just slip into my boots,' Juliette said, shaking her head. 'I don't think you two understand all that we do—'

'I don't think you understand what we do up top,' Jahns said. 'Or why we need you.'

Juliette tossed her head and laughed. 'Look, I've got machines down here that you can't possibly—'

'And what good are they?' Jahns asked. 'What do these machines do?'

'They keep this whole goddamned place running!' Juliette declared. 'The oxygen you breathe? We recycle that down here. The toxins you exhale? We pump them back into the earth. You want me to write up a list of everything oil makes? Every piece of plastic, every ounce of rubber, all the solvents and cleaners, and I'm not talking about the power it generates, but everything else!'

'And yet it was all here before you were born,' Jahns pointed out.

'Well, it wouldn't have lasted my lifetime, I'll tell you that. Not in the state it was in.' She crossed her arms again and leaned back against the wall. 'I don't think you get what mess we'd be in without these machines.'

'And I don't think you get how pointless these machines are going to become without all these people.'

Juliette looked away. It was the first time Jahns had seen her flinch.

'Why don't you ever visit your father?'

Juliette snapped her head around and looked at the other wall. She wiped some loose hair back from her forehead. 'Go look at my work log,' she said. 'Tell me when I'd fit it in.'

Before Jahns could reply, could say that it was family, that there's always time, Juliette turned to face her. 'Do you think I don't care about people? Is that it? Because you'd be wrong. I care about every person in this silo. And the men and women down here, the forgotten floors of Mechanical, *this* is my family. I visit with them every day. I break bread with them several times a day. We work, live, and die alongside one another.' She looked to Marnes. 'Isn't that right? You've seen it.'

Marnes didn't say anything. Jahns wondered if she was referring specifically to the 'dying' part.

'Did you ask him why he never comes to see me? Because he has all the time in the world. He has *nothing* up there.'

'Yes, we met with him. Your father seemed like a very busy man. As determined as you.'

Juliette looked away.

'And as stubborn.' Jahns left the paperwork on the bed and went to stand by the door, just a pace away from Juliette. She could smell the soap in the younger woman's hair. Could see her nostrils flare with her rapid, heavy breathing.

'The days pile up and weigh small decisions down, don't they? That decision not to visit. The first few days slide by easy enough, anger and youth power them along. But then they pile up like unrecycled trash. Isn't that right?'

Juliette waved her hand. 'I don't know what you're talking about.'

'I'm talking about days becoming weeks becoming months becoming years.' She almost said that she'd been through the same exact thing, was still piling them up, but Marnes was in the room, listening. 'After a while, you're staying mad just to justify an old mistake. Then it's just a game. Two people staring away, refusing to look back over their shoulders, afraid to be the first one to take that chance—'

'It wasn't like that,' Juliette said. 'I don't want your job. I'm sure you've got plenty of others who do.'

'If it's not you, it's someone I'm not sure I can trust. Not any more.'

'Then give it to the next girl.' She smiled.

'It's you or him. And I think he'll be getting more guidance from the thirties than he will from me, or from the Pact.'

Juliette seemed to react to this. Her arms loosened across her chest. She turned and met Jahns's gaze. Marnes was studying all this from across the room.

'The last sheriff, Holston, what happened to him?'

'He went to cleaning,' Jahns said.

'He volunteered,' Marnes added gruffly.

'I know, but why?' She frowned. 'I heard it was his wife.'

'There's all kinds of speculation—'

'I remember him talking about her, when you two came down to look into George's death. I thought, at first, that he was flirting with me, but all he could talk about was this wife of his.'

'They were in the lottery while we were down here,' Marnes reminded her.

'Yeah. That's right.' She studied the bed for a while. Paperwork was spread across it. 'I wouldn't know how to do this job. I only know how to fix things.'

'It's the same thing,' Marnes told her. 'You were a big help with our case down here. You see how things work. How they fit together. Little clues that other people miss.'

'You're talking about *machines*,' she said.

'People aren't much different,' Marnes told her.

'I think you already know this,' Jahns said. 'I think you have the right attitude, actually. The right disposition. This is only slightly a political office. Distance is good.'

Juliette shook her head and looked back to Marnes. 'So you nominated me for this, is that it? I wondered how this came up. Seemed like something right out of the ground.'

'You'd be good at it,' Marnes told her. 'I think you'd be damned good at anything you set your mind to. And this is more important work than you think.'

'And I'd live up top?'

'Your office is on level one. Near the airlock.'

Juliette seemed to mull this over. Jahns was excited that she was even asking questions.

'The pay is more than you're making now, even with the extra shifts.'

'You checked?'

Jahns nodded. 'I took some liberties before we came down.'

'Like talking to my father.'

'That's right. He would love to see you, you know. If you came with us.'

Juliette looked down at her boots. 'Not sure about that.'

'There's one other thing,' Marnes said, catching Jahns's eye. He glanced at the paperwork on the bed. The crisply folded contract for Peter Billings was on top. 'IT,' he reminded her.

Jahns caught his drift.

'There's one matter to clear up, before you accept.'

'I'm not sure I'm accepting. I'd want to hear more about this power holiday, organise the work shifts down here—'

'According to tradition, IT signs off on all nominated positions.'

Juliette rolled her eyes and blew out her breath. 'IT.'

'Yes, and we checked in with them on the way down as well, just to smooth things over.'

'I'm sure,' Juliette said.

'It's about these requisitions,' Marnes interjected.

Juliette turned to him.

'We know it probably ain't nothing, but it's gonna come up—'

'Wait, is this about the heat tape?'

'Heat tape?'

'Yeah.' Juliette frowned and shook her head. 'Those bastards.'

Jahns mimed pinching two inches of air. 'They had a folder on you this thick. Said you were skimming supplies meant for them.'

'No they didn't. Are you kidding?' She pointed towards the door. 'We can't get any of the supplies we need because of them. When I needed heat tape – we had a leak in a heat exchanger a few months back – we couldn't get any because Supply tells us the backing material for the tape is all spoken for. Now, we had that order in a while back, and then I find out from one of our porters that the tape is going to IT, that they've got miles of the stuff for the skins of all their test suits.'

Juliette took a deep breath.

'So I had some intercepted.' She looked to Marnes as she admitted this. 'Look, I'm keeping the power on so they can do whatever it is they do up there, and I can't get basic supplies. And even when I do, the quality is complete crap, probably because of unrealistic quotas, rushing the manufacturing chain—'

'If these are items you really needed,' Jahns interrupted, 'then I understand.' She looked to Marnes, who smiled and dipped his chin as if to say he'd *told* her this was the right woman for the job.

Jahns ignored him. 'I'm actually glad to hear your side of this,' she told Juliette. 'And I wish I made this trip more often, as sore as my legs are. There are things we take for granted up top, mostly because they aren't well understood. I can see now that our offices need to be in better communication, have more of the constant contact I have with IT.'

'I've been saying that for just about twenty years,' Juliette said. 'Down here, we joke that this place was laid out to keep us well out of the way. And that's how it feels, sometimes.'

'Well, if you come up top, if you take this job, people will hear you. You could be the first link in that chain of command.'

'Where would IT fall?'

'There will be resistance, but that's normal with them. I've handled it before. I'll wire my office for some emergency waivers. We'll make them retroactive, get these acquisitions above board.' Jahns studied the younger woman. 'As long as I have your assurance that every one of those diverted supplies were absolutely necessary.'

Juliette did not flinch away from the challenge. 'They were,' she said. 'Not that it mattered. The stuff we got from them was crap. Couldn't have fallen apart better if it'd been designed to. I'll tell you what, we finally got our shipment from Supply and have extra tape. I'd love to drop off a peace offering on our way up. Our design is so much better—'

'Our way up?' Jahns asked, making sure she understood what Juliette was saying, what she was agreeing to.

Juliette looked them both over. She nodded. 'You'll have to give me a week to sort out the generator. I'm holding you to that power holiday. And just so you understand, I'll always consider myself Mechanical, and I'll be doing this partly because I see what happens when problems are ignored. My big push down here has been preventive maintenance. No more waiting for things to break before we fix them, but to go around and make them hum while they're still working. Too many issues have been ignored, let degrade. And I think, if the silo can be thought of as one big engine, we are like the dirty oil pan down here that needs some people's attention.' She reached her hand out to Jahns. 'Get me that power holiday, and I'm your man.'

Jahns smiled and took her hand, admired the warmth and power in her confident handshake.

'I'll get on it first thing in the morning,' she said. 'And thank you. Welcome aboard.'

Marnes crossed the room to shake Juliette's hand as well. 'Nice to have you on, boss.'

Juliette smirked as she took his hand. 'Well now, let's not get ahead of ourselves. I think I'll have a lot to learn before you go calling me that.'

15

It felt appropriate that their climb back to the up top would occur during a power holiday. Jahns could feel her own energy complying with the new decree, draining away with each laborious step. The agony of the descent had been a tease, the discomfort of constant movement disguising itself as the fatigue of exercise. But now her frail muscles were really put to work. Each step was something to be conquered. She would lift a boot to the next tread, place a hand on her knee, and push herself another ten inches up what felt like a million feet of spiral staircase.

The landing to her right displayed the number fifty-eight. Each landing seemed to be in view for ever. Not like the trip down, where she could daydream and skip right past several floors. Now they loomed in sight gradually beyond the outer railing and held there, taunting in the dim green glow of the emergency lights, as she struggled upward, one plodding and wavering step at a time.

Marnes walked beside her, his hand on the inner rail, hers on the outer, the walking stick clanging on the lonely treads between them. Occasionally, their arms brushed against one another. It felt as though they'd been away for months, away from their offices, their duties, their cold familiarity. The adventure down to wrangle a new sheriff had played out differently than Jahns had imagined it would. She had dreamed of a return to her youth and had instead found herself haunted by old ghosts. She had hoped to find a renewed vigour and instead felt the years of wear in her knees and back. What was to be a grand tour of her silo was instead trudged in relative anonymity, and now she wondered if its operation and upkeep even needed her. The world around her was stratified. She saw that ever more clearly. The up top concerned itself with a blurring view, taking for granted the squeezed juice enjoyed with breakfast. The people who lived below and worked the gardens or cleaned animal cages orbited their own world of soil, greenery, and fertiliser. To them, the outside view was peripheral, ignored until there was a cleaning. And then there was the down deep, the machine shops and chemistry labs, the pumping oil and grinding gears, the hands-on world of grease-limned fingernails and the musk of toil. To these people, the outside world and the food that trickled down were mere rumours and bodily sustenance. The point of the silo was for the people to keep the machines running, when Jahns had always, her entire long life, seen it the other way around.

Landing fifty-seven appeared through the fog of darkness. A young girl sat on the steel grate, her feet tucked up against herself, arms wrapped around her knees, a children's book in its protective plastic cover held out into the feeble light spilling from an over-head bulb. Jahns watched the girl, who was unmoved save her eyes as they darted over the colourful pages. The girl never looked up to see who was passing the apartment's landing. They left her behind, and she gradually faded in the darkness as Jahns and Marnes struggled ever upward, exhausted from their third day of climbing, no vibrations or ringing footsteps above or below them, the silo quiet and eerily devoid of life, room enough for two old friends, two comrades, to walk side by side on the steps of chipping paint, their arms swinging and every now and then, and very occasionally, brushing together.

They stayed that night at the mid-level deputy station, the officer of the mids insisting they take his hospitality and Jahns eager to buttress support for yet another sheriff nominated from outside the profession. After a cold dinner in near darkness and enough idle banter to satisfy their host and his wife, Jahns retired to the main office where a convertible couch had been made as comfortable as possible, the linens borrowed from a nicer elsewhere and smelling of two-chit soap. Marnes had been set up on a cot in the holding cell, which still smelled of tub-gin and a drunk who had got too carried away after the cleaning.

It was impossible to notice when the lights went out, they were so dim already. Jahns rested on the cot in the darkness, her muscles throbbing and luxuriating in her body's stillness, her feet cramped and feeling like solid bone, her back tender and in need of stretching. Her mind, however, continued to move. It drifted back to the weary conversations that had passed the time on their most recent day of climbing.

She and Marnes seemed to be spiralling around one another, testing the memory of old attractions, probing the tenderness of ancient scars, looking for some soft spot that remained among brittle and broken bodies, across wrinkled and dried-paper skin, and within hearts calloused by law and politics.

Donald's name came up often and tentatively, like a child sneaking into an adult bed, forcing wary lovers to make room in the middle. Jahns grieved anew for her long-lost husband. For the first time in her life, she grieved for the subsequent decades of solitude. What she had always seen as her calling – this living apart and serving the greater good – now felt more like a curse. Her life had been taken from her. Squeezed into pulp. The juice of her efforts and sacrificed years had dripped down through a silo that, just forty levels below her, hardly knew and barely cared.

The saddest part of this journey had been this understanding she'd come to with Holston's ghost. She could admit it now: a great reason for her hike, perhaps even the reason for wanting Juliette as sheriff, was to fall all the way to the down deep, away from the sad sight of two lovers nestled together in the crook of a hill as the wind etched away all their wasted youth. She had set out to escape Holston, and had instead found him. Now she knew, if not the mystery of why all those sent out to clean actually did so, why a sad few would dare to volunteer for the duty. Better to join a ghost than to be haunted by them. Better no life than an empty one—

The door to the deputy's office squeaked on a hinge long worn beyond the repair of grease. Jahns tried to sit up, to see in the dark, but her muscles were too sore, her eyes too old. She wanted to call out, to let her hosts know that she was okay, in need of nothing, but she listened instead.

Footsteps came to her, nearly invisible in the worn carpet. There were no words, just the creaking of old joints as they approached the bed, the lifting of expensive and fragrant sheets, and an understanding between two living ghosts.

Jahns's breath caught in her chest. Her hand groped for a wrist as it clutched her sheets. She slid over on the small convertible bed to make room, and pulled him down beside her.

Marnes wrapped his arms around her back, wiggled beneath her until she was lying on his side, a leg draped over his, her hands on his neck. She felt his moustache brush against her cheek, heard his lips purse and peck the corner of hers.

Jahns held his cheeks and burrowed her face into his shoulder. She cried, like a schoolchild, like a new shadow who felt lost and afraid in the wilderness of a strange and terrifying job. She cried with fear, but that soon drained away. It drained like the soreness in her back as his hands rubbed her there. It drained until numbness found its place, and then, after what felt like a forever of shuddering sobs, *sensation* took over.

Jahns felt alive in her skin. She felt the tingle of flesh touching flesh, of just her forearm against his hard ribs, her hands on his shoulder, his hands on her hips. And then the tears were some joyous release, some mourning of the lost time, some welcomed sadness of a moment long delayed and finally there, arms wrapped around it and holding tight.

She fell asleep like that, exhausted from far more than the climb, nothing more than a few trembling kisses, hands interlocking, a whispered word of tenderness and appreciation, and then the depths of sleep pulling her down, the weariness in her joints and bones succumbing to a slumber she didn't want but sorely needed. She slept with a man in her arms for the first time in decades, and woke to a bed familiarly empty, but a heart strangely full.

In the middle of their fourth and final day of climbing, they approached the mid-thirties of IT. Jahns had found herself taking more breaks for water and to rub her muscles along the way, not for the exhaustion she feigned, but the dread of this stopover and seeing Bernard, the fear of their trip ever coming to an end.

The dark and deep shadows cast by the power holiday followed them up, the traffic sparse as most merchants had closed for the silo-wide brownout. Juliette, who had stayed behind to oversee the repairs, had warned Jahns of the flickering lights from the backup generator. Still, the effect of the shimmering illumination had worn on her nerves during the long climb. The steady pulsing reminded her of a bad light bulb she'd unhappily endured for the better part of her first term. Two different techs from Electrical had come to inspect the bulb. Both had deemed it too operational to replace. It had taken an appeal to McLain, the head of Supply even back then, to score her a replacement.

Jahns remembered McLain delivering the bulb herself. She hadn't been head of Supply for long, and had fairly smuggled the thing up those many flights of stairs. Even then, Jahns had looked up to her, this woman with so much power and responsibility. She remembered McLain asking her why Jahns didn't just do what everyone else did – simply break the bulb the rest of the way.

The fact that this had never occurred to Jahns used to bother her – until she began to take pride in this failing; until she got to know McLain well enough to understand the question was a compliment, the hand delivery her reward.

When they reached the thirty-fourth, Jahns felt like they were, in a sense, home again: back in the realm of the familiar, at the main landing for IT. She waited by the railing, leaning on it and her walking stick, while Marnes got the door. As it was cracked open, the pale glow of diminished power was swept off the stairwell by the bright lights blooming inside. It hadn't been widely publicised, but the reason for the severe power restrictions on other levels was largely due to the exemptions IT possessed. Bernard had been quick to point out various clauses in the Pact to support this. Juliette had bitched that servers shouldn't get priority over grow lights, but resigned herself to getting the main generator realigned, and taking what she could. Jahns told Juliette to view this as her first lesson in political compromise. Juliette said she saw it as a display of weakness.

Inside, Jahns found Bernard waiting for them, a look on his face like he'd swallowed sour fruit juice. A conversation between several IT workers standing off to the side quickly silenced with their entry, leaving Jahns little doubt that they'd been spotted on the way up and expected.

'Bernard,' she said, trying to keep her breathing steady. She didn't want him to know how tired she was. Let him think she was strolling by on her way up from the down deep, like it was no big deal.

'Marie.'

It was a deliberate slight. He didn't even look Marnes's way or acknowledge that the deputy was in the room.

'Would you like to sign these here? Or in the conference room?' She dug into her bag for the contract with Juliette's name on it.

'What games are you playing at, Marie?'

Jahns felt her temperature rise. The cluster of workers in silver IT jumpsuits were following the exchange. 'Playing at?' she asked.

'You think this *power holiday* of yours is cute? Your way of getting back at me?'

'Getting back—?'

'I've got servers, Marie—'

'Your servers have their full allocation of power,' Jahns reminded him, her voice rising.

'But their cooling comes ducted from Mechanical, and if temps get any higher, we'll be ramping down, which we've *never* had to do!'

Marnes stepped between the two of them, his hands raised. 'Easy,' he said coolly, his gaze on Bernard.

'Call off your little shadow here,' Bernard said.

Jahns placed a hand on Marnes's arm.

'The Pact is clear, Bernard. It's my choice. My nomination. You and I have a nice history of signing off on each other's—'

'And I told you this girl from the pits will not do—'

'She's got the job,' Marnes said, interrupting. Jahns noticed his hand had fallen to the butt of his gun. She wasn't sure if Bernard had noticed or not, but he fell silent. His eyes, however, did not leave Jahns's.

'I won't sign it.'

'Then next time, I won't ask.'

Bernard smiled. 'You think you'll outlive another sheriff?' He turned towards the workers in the corner and waved one of them over. 'Why do I somehow doubt that?'

One of the technicians removed himself from the whispering group and approached. Jahns recognised the young man from the cafeteria, had seen him up top on nights she worked late. Lukas, if she remembered correctly. He shook her hand and smiled an awkward *hello*.

Bernard twirled his own hand, stirring the air with his impatience. 'Sign whatever she needs. I refuse to. Make copies. Take care of the rest.' He waved dismissively, turned and looked Marnes and Jahns up and down one final time as if disgusted with their condition, their age, their positions, *something*. 'Oh, and have Sims top up their canteens. See that they have food enough to stagger to their homes. Whatever it takes to power their decrepit legs out of here and back to wherever it is they belong.'

And with that, Bernard strode off towards the barred gates that led into the heart of IT, back to his brightly lit offices where servers hummed happily, the temperature rising in the slow-moving air like the heat of angered flesh as capillaries squeezed, the blood in them rising to a boil.

16

The floors flew by faster as they approached home. In the darkest sections of the staircase, between quiet floors of people hunkered down and awaiting a return to normality, old hands wrapped around each other and swung between two climbers, brazenly and open, grasping each other while their other hands slid up the cool steel of the rails.

Jahns let go sporadically only to check that her walking stick was secure against her back, or to grab Marnes's canteen from his pack and take a sip. They had taken to drinking each other's water, it being easier to reach across than around one's own back. There was a sweetness to it as well, carrying the sustenance another needed and being able to provide and reciprocate in a perfectly equitable relationship. It was a thing worth dropping hands for. Momentarily, at least.

Jahns finished a sip, screwed on the metal cap with its dangling chain, and replaced it in his outer pouch. She was dying to know if things would be different once they got back. They were only twenty floors away. An impossible distance yesterday now seemed like something that could slip away without noticing. And as they arrived, would familiar surroundings bring familiar roles? Would last night feel more and more like a dream? Or would old ghosts return to haunt them both? She wanted to ask these things, but talked of trivialities instead. When would Jules, as she insisted they call her, be ready for duty? What case files did he and Holston have open that needed tending to first? What concession would they make to keep IT happy, to calm down Bernard? And how would they handle Peter Billings's disappointment? What impact would this have on hearings he might one day preside over as judge?

Jahns felt butterflies in her stomach as they discussed these things. Or perhaps it was the nerves of all she wanted to say, but couldn't. These topics were as numerous as grains of dust in the outside air, and just as likely to dry her mouth and still her tongue. She found herself drinking more and more from his canteen, her own water making noises at her back, her stomach lurching with every landing, each number counting down towards the conclusion of their journey, an adventure that had been a complete success in so many ways.

To start with, they had their sheriff: a fiery girl from the down deep who seemed every bit as confident and inspiring as Marnes had intimated. Jahns saw her kind as the future of the silo. People who thought long term, who planned, who got things done. There was a precedent of sheriffs running for mayor. She thought Juliette would eventually make a fine choice.

And speaking of running, the trip had fired up her own goals and ambitions. She was excited about the upcoming elections, however unopposed she might be, and had even dreamed up dozens of short speeches during the climb. She saw how things could run better, how she could perform her duties more diligently, and how the silo could have new life breathed into old bones.

But the biggest change was whatever had grown between herself and Marnes. She had even begun to suspect, just in the last hours, that the real reason for him never taking a promotion was because of her. As deputy, there was enough space between them to contain his hope, his impossible dream of holding her. As sheriff, it couldn't happen: too much conflict of interest, too much his immediate superior. This theory of hers contained a powerful sadness and an awe-inspiring sweetness. She squeezed his hand as she thought about this theory, and it filled her with a deep hollowness, a cramp in her gut at all he had silently sacrificed, a massive debt to live up to no matter what happened next.

They approached the landing to the nursery, and had no plans for stopping to see Juliette's father, to urge him to receive his daughter on the way up, but Jahns changed her mind as she felt her bladder beg for release.

'I've got to go pretty bad,' she told Marnes, embarrassed like a child to admit she couldn't hold it. Her mouth was dry and her stomach churning from so much fluid, and maybe from the fear of getting home. 'I wouldn't mind seeing Juliette's father, either,' she added.

Marnes's moustache bent up at the corners with the excuse. 'Then we should stop,' he said.

The waiting room was empty, the signs reminding them to be quiet. Jahns peered through the glass partition and saw a nurse padding through the dark corridor towards her, a frown becoming a slight smile of recognition.

'Mayor,' she whispered.

'I'm sorry not to have wired ahead, but I was hoping to see Dr Nichols. And possibly use your restroom?'

'Of course.' She buzzed the door and waved them through. 'We've had two deliveries since you last stopped by. Things have been crazy with this generator mess—'

'Power holiday,' Marnes corrected, his voice gruff and louder than theirs.

The nurse shot him a look, but nodded as if duly noted. She took two robes from the racks and held them out, told them to leave their stuff by her desk.

In the waiting room, she waved towards the benches and said she would find the doctor. 'The bathrooms are through there.' She pointed at a door, the old sign painted on its surface nearly worn clean away.

'I'll be right back,' Jahns told Marnes. She fought the urge to reach out and squeeze his hand, as normal as that dark and hidden habit had lately become.

The bathroom was almost completely devoid of light. Jahns fumbled with an unfamiliar lock on the stall door, cursed under her breath as her stomach churned noisily, then finally threw the stall open and hurried to sit down. Her stomach felt like it was on fire as she relieved herself. The mixture of welcomed release and the burn of having held it too long left her unable to breathe. She went for what felt like for ever, remained sitting as her legs shook uncontrollably, and realised she had pushed herself too hard on the climb up. The thought of another twenty levels mortified her, made her insides feel hollow with dread. She finished and moved over to the adjoining toilet to splash herself clean, then dried herself with one of the towels. She flushed both units to cycle the water. It all required fumbling in the darkness, unfamiliar as she was with the spacing and location that were second nature in her apartment and office.

She staggered out of the bathroom on weak legs, wondering if she might need to stay one more night, sleep in a delivery bed, wait until the morning to make the climb to her office. She could barely feel her legs as she pulled open the door and returned to Marnes in the waiting room.

'Better?' he asked. He sat on one of the family benches, a space left conspicuously beside him. Jahns nodded and sat heavily. She was breathing in shallow pants and wondered if he'd find her weak to admit she couldn't go any further that day.

'Jahns? You okay?'

Marnes leaned forward. He wasn't looking at her, he was looking towards the ground. 'Jahns. What the hell just happened?'

'Lower your voice,' she whispered.

He screamed, instead.

'Doctor!' he yelled. 'Nurse!'

A form moved beyond the dusky glass of the nursery. Jahns laid her head back against the seat cushion, trying to form the words on her lips, to tell him to keep it down.

'Jahns, sweetheart, what did you do?'

He was holding her hand, patting the back of it. He shook her arm. Jahns just wanted to sleep. There was the slapping of footsteps running their way. Lights turned up forbiddingly bright. A nurse yelled something. There was the familiar voice of Juliette's father, a doctor. He would give her a bed. He would understand this exhaustion . . .

There was talk of blood. Someone was examining her legs. Marnes was crying, tears falling into his white moustache, peppered with black. He was shaking her shoulders, looking her in the eye.

'I'm okay,' Jahns tried to say.

She licked her lips. So dry. Mouth so damned dry. She asked for water. Marnes fumbled for his canteen, brought it to her lips, splashing water against and into her mouth.

She tried to swallow, but couldn't. They were stretching her out on the bench, the doctor touching her ribs, shining a light in her eyes. But things were getting darker anyway.

Marnes clutched the canteen in one hand, smoothed her hair back with the other. He was blubbering. So sad for some reason. So much more energy than her. She smiled at him and reached for his hand, a miraculous effort. She held his wrist and told him that she loved him. That she had for as long as she could remember. Her mind was tired, loosening its grip on her secrets, mouthing them to him as tears flowed down his face.

She saw his eyes, bright and wrinkled, peering down at her, then turning to the canteen in his hand.

The canteen that he had carried.

The water, she realised, the poison meant for him.

17

The generator room was unusually crowded and eerily silent. Mechanics in worn overalls stood three deep behind the railing and watched the first-shift crew work. Juliette was only dimly aware of them; she was more keenly aware of the silence.

She leaned over a device of her own making, a tall platform welded to the metal floor and arrayed with mirrors and tiny slits that bounced light across the room. This light shined on mirrors attached to the generator and its large dynamo, helping her get them in perfect alignment. It was the shaft between the two of them that she cared about, that long steel rod the size of a man's waist where the power of combusting fuel was transformed into the spark of electricity. She was hoping to have the machines on either end of this rod aligned to within a thousandth of an inch. But everything they were doing was without precedent. The procedures had been hurriedly planned in all-night sessions while the backup generator was put online. Now, she could only concentrate, could only hope the eighteen-hour shifts had been good for something, and trust in plans made back when she'd had some decent rest and could think soundly.

While she guided the final placement, the chamber around her stood deathly quiet. She gave a sign, and Marck and his team tightened several of the massive bolts on the new rubber floor mounts. They were four days into the power holiday. The generator needed to be up and running by morning and at full power that next evening. With so much done to it – the new gaskets and seals, the polishing of cylinder shafts that had required young shadows to crawl down into the heart of the beast – Juliette was worried about it even starting up. The generator had never been fully powered down during her lifetime. Old Knox could remember it shutting itself down in an emergency once, back when he was a mere shadow, but for everyone else the rumble had been as constant and close as their own heartbeats. Juliette felt inordinate pressure for everything to work. She was the one who had come up with the idea to do a refit. She calmed herself with reassurances that it was the right thing to do, and that the worst that could happen now was that the holiday would be extended until they sorted out all the kinks. That was much better than a catastrophic failure years from now.

Marck signalled that the bolts were secure, the lock nuts tightened down. Juliette jumped off her home-made platform and strolled over to the generator to join him. It was difficult to walk casually with so many eyes on her. She couldn't believe this rowdy crew, this extended and dysfunctional family of hers, could be so perfectly silent. It was like they were all holding their breath, wondering if the crushing schedule of the last few days was going to be for naught.

'You ready?' she asked Marck.

He nodded, wiping his hands on a filthy rag that always seemed to be draped over his shoulder. Juliette checked her watch. The sight of its second hand ticking around in its constant path comforted her. Whenever she had doubts about something working, she looked at her wrist. Not to see the time, but to see a thing she had fixed. A repair so intricate and impossible – one that had taken years of cleaning and setting parts almost too small to see – that it made her current task, whatever it was, feel small by comparison.

'We on schedule?' Marck asked, grinning.

'We're doing fine.' She nodded to the control room. Whispers began to stir through the crowd as they realised the restart was imminent. Dozens of them pulled sound protection from their necks and settled the muffs over their ears. Juliette and Marck joined Shirly in the control room.

'How's it going?' Juliette asked the second-shift foreman, a young woman, small and spirited.

'Golden,' Shirly said as she continued to make adjustments, zeroing out all the corrections that had built up over the years. They were starting from the ground up, none of the patches and fixes of old to disguise any new symptoms. A fresh start. 'We're good to go,' she said.

She backed away from the controls and moved to stand near her husband. The gesture was transparent: this was Juliette's project, perhaps the last thing she would ever try to fix in the down deep of Mechanical. She would have the honour, and the full responsibility, of firing the generator up.

Juliette stood over the control board, looking down at knobs and dials that she could locate in utter darkness. It was hard to believe that this phase of her life was over, that some new one was about to begin. The thought of travelling to the up top frightened her more than this project could. The idea of leaving her friends and family, of dealing with politics, did not taste as sweet to her as the sweat and grease on her lips. But at least she had allies up there. If people like Jahns and Marnes were able to get by, to survive, she figured she'd be okay.

With a trembling hand, more from exhaustion than nerves, Juliette engaged the starter motor. There was a loud whine as a small electrical engine tried to get the massive diesel generator moving. It seemed to be taking for ever, but Juliette had no idea what normal sounded like. Marck stood by the door, propping it open so they could better hear any shouts to abort. He glanced over at Juliette as she continued to hold the ignition, creases of worry in his brow as the starter whined and groaned in the next room.

Someone outside waved both arms, trying to signal her through the glass.

'Shut it off, shut it off,' Marck said. Shirly hurried towards the control panel to help.

Juliette let go of the ignition and reached for the kill switch, but she stopped herself from pressing it. There was a noise outside. A powerful hum. She thought she could feel it through the floor, but not like the vibration of old.

'It's already running!' someone yelled.

'It was already running,' Marck said, laughing.

The mechanics outside were cheering. Someone pulled off their ear protection and hurled the muffs up into the air. Juliette realised the starter motor was louder than the rebuilt generator, that she'd been holding the ignition even as it had already started and continued to run.

Shirly and Marck hugged one another. Juliette checked the temps and pressures on all the zeroed gauges and saw little to adjust, but she wouldn't be sure until it warmed up. Her throat constricted with emotion, the release of so much pressure. Work crews were leaping over the railing to crowd around the rebuilt beast. Some who rarely visited the generator room were reaching out to touch it, almost with reverent awe.

Juliette left the control room to watch them, to listen to the sound of a perfectly working machine, of gears in alignment. She stood behind the railing, hands on a steel bar that used to rattle and dance while the generator laboured, and watched an unlikely celebration take place in a normally avoided workspace. The hum was magnificent. Power without dread, the culmination of so much hurried labour and planning.

The success gave her a new confidence for what lay ahead, for what lay above. She was in such fine spirits and so fixated on the powerful and improved machines that she didn't notice the young porter hurry into the room, his face ashen, his chest swelling with the deep gulps of a long and frantic run. She barely noticed the way the news travelled from mouth to mouth throughout the room, spreading among the mechanics until fear and sadness registered in their eyes. It wasn't until the celebration died completely, the room falling into a different sort of quiet, one studded with sobs and gasps of disbelief, of grown men wailing, that Juliette knew something was amiss.

Something had happened. A great and powerful thing had fallen out of alignment.

And it had nothing to do with her generator.

PART 3 – CASTING OFF

18

There were numbers on each of the pockets. Juliette could look down at her chest and read them, and so it occurred to her that they must be printed upside down. They were there for her to read, and for no one else. She numbly stared at them through her helmet visor while the door behind her was sealed. There was another door, a forbidden one, looming in front of her. It stood silently as it waited to be opened.

Juliette felt lost in this void between the two doors, trapped in this airlock full of brightly coloured pipes jutting from the walls and ceiling, everything shimmering behind plastic-wrapped shrouds.

The hiss of argon being pumped into the room sounded distant through her helmet. It let her know the end was near. Pressure built against the plastic, crinkling it across the bench and walls, wrapping it tightly around the pipes. She could feel the pressure against her suit, like an invisible hand gently squeezing.

She knew what was to happen next – and part of her wondered how she had got here, a girl from Mechanical who had never cared one whit about the outside, who had only ever broken minor laws, and who would've been content for the rest of her life to live in the deepest bowels of the earth, covered in grease and fixing the broken things, little concern for the wider world of the dead that surrounded her . . .

19

Days Earlier

Juliette sat on the floor of the holding cell, her back against the tall rows of steel bars, a mean world displayed on the wall screen before her. For the past three days, while she had attempted to teach herself how to be silo sheriff, she had studied this view of the outside and wondered what the fuss was all about.

All she saw out there were dull slopes of ground, these grey hills rising up towards greyer clouds, dappled sunlight straining to illuminate the land with little success. Across it all were the terrible winds, the frenzied gusts that whipped small clouds of soil into curls and whorls that chased one another across a landscape meant only for them.

For Juliette, there was nothing inspiring about the view, nothing that aroused her curiosity. It was an uninhabitable wasteland devoid of anything useful. There were no resources beyond the tainted steel of crumbling towers visible over the hills, steel it would no doubt cost more to reclaim, transport, smelt, and purify than it would to simply pull new ore from the mines beneath the silo.

The forbidden dreams of the outside world, she saw, were sad and empty. They were dead dreams. The people of the up top who worshipped this view had it all backwards – the future was *below*. That's where the oil came from that provided their power, the minerals that became anything useful, the nitrogen that renewed the soil in the farms. Any who shadowed in the footsteps of chemistry and metallurgy knew this. Those who read children's books, those who tried to piece together the mystery of a forgotten and unknowable past, remained deluded.

The only sense she could make of their obsession was the open space itself, a feature of the landscape that frankly terrified her. Perhaps it was something wrong with *her* that she loved the walls of the silo, loved the dark confines of the down deep. Was everyone else crazy to harbour thoughts of escape? Or was it something about her?

Juliette looked from the dry hills and the fog of soil to the scattered folders around her. It was her predecessor's unfinished work. A shiny star sat balanced on one of her knees, not yet worn. There was a canteen sitting on one of the folders, safe inside a plastic reusable evidence bag. It looked innocent enough lying there, having already done its deadly deed. Several numbers written with black ink on the bag had been crossed out, cases long since solved or abandoned. A new number stood to one side, a case number matching a folder not present, a folder filled with page after page of testimony and notes dealing with the death of a mayor whom everyone had loved – but whom someone had killed.

Juliette had seen some of those notes, but only from a distance. They were written in Deputy Marnes's hand, hands that would not relinquish the folder, hands that clutched it madly. She had taken peeks at the folder from across his desk and had seen the spattered tears that smeared occasional words and caused the paper to pucker. The writing amid those drying tears was a scrawl, not as neat as his notes in the other folders. What she could see seemed to crawl angrily across the page, words slashed out violently and replaced. It was the same ferocity Deputy Marnes displayed all the time now, the boiling anger that had driven Juliette away from her desk and into the holding cell to work. She had found it impossible to sit across from such a broken soul and be expected to think. The view of the outside world that loomed before her, however sad, cast a far less depressing shadow.

It was in the holding cell that she killed time between the static-filled calls on her radio and the jaunts down to some disturbance. Often, she would simply sit and sort and re-sort her folders according to perceived severity. She was sheriff of all the silo, a job she had not shadowed for, but one she was beginning to understand. One of the last things Mayor Jahns had told her had proved truer than she could imagine: people were like machines. They broke down. They rattled. They could burn you or maim you if you weren't careful. Her job was not only to figure out why this happened and who was to blame, but also to listen for the signs of it coming. Being sheriff, like being a mechanic, was as much the fine art of preventive maintenance as it was the cleaning up after a breakdown.

The folders scattered on the floor were sad cases of the latter: complaints between neighbours that got out of hand; reported thefts; the source of a poisonous batch of amateur tub-gin; several more cases stemming from the trouble this gin had caused. Each folder awaited more findings, more legwork, more hikes down the twisting stairs to engage in twisted dialogue, sorting lies from truth.

Juliette had read the Law portion of the Pact twice in preparation for the job. Lying in her bed in the down deep, her body exhausted from the work of aligning the primary generator, she had studied the proper way to file case folders, the danger of disturbing evidence, all of it logical and analogous to some part of her old job as mechanic. Approaching the scene of a crime or an active dispute was no different from walking into a pump room where something was broken. Someone or something was always at fault. She knew to listen, to observe, to ask questions of anyone who could have had anything to do with the faulty equipment or the tools they had used, following a chain of events all the way down to the bedrock itself. There were always confounding variables – you couldn't adjust one dial without sending something else a-kilter – but Juliette had a skill, a talent, for knowing what was important and what could be ignored.

She assumed it was this talent that Deputy Marnes had originally seen in her, this patience and scepticism she employed to ask one more stupid question and stumble eventually onto the answer. It was a boost to her confidence that she had helped solve a case before. She hadn't known it then, had been more concerned with simple justice and her private grief, but that case had been an interview and job training all in one.

She picked up that very folder from years gone by, a pale red stamp on its cover reading 'CLOSED' in bold block letters. She peeled the tape holding its edges together and flipped through the notes. Many of them were in Holston's neat hand, a forward-slanting print she recognised from just about everything on and inside her desk, a desk that had once been his. She read his notes about her, refamiliarised herself with a case that had seemed an obvious murder but had actually been a series of unlikely events. Going back through it, something she had avoided until now, gave birth to old pains. And yet she could also recall how comforting it had been to distract herself with the clues. She could remember the rush of a problem solved, the satisfaction of having answers to offset the hollowness left by her lover's death. The process had been similar to fixing a machine on extra shifts. There was the pain in her body from the effort and exhaustion, offset slightly by the knowledge that a rattle had been wrenched away.

She set the folder aside, not yet ready to relive it all. She picked up another and placed it in her lap, one hand falling to the brass star on her knee.

A shadow danced across the wall screen, distracting her. Juliette looked up and saw a low wall of dirt spill down the hill. This layer of soot seemed to shiver in the wind as it travelled towards sensors she had been trained to think of as important, sensors that gave her a view of the outside world she had been frightened as a child into believing was worth seeing.

But she wasn't so sure, now that she was old enough to think for herself and near enough to observe it first-hand. This up top's obsession with cleaning barely trickled its way to the down deep where *true* cleaning kept the silo humming and everyone alive. But even down there, her friends in Mechanical had been told since birth not to speak of the outside. It was an easy enough task when you never saw it, but now, walking by it to work, sitting before this view of a vastness one's brain could not comprehend, she saw how the inevitable questions must surface. She saw why it might be important to squelch certain ideas before a stampede to the exits formed, before questions foamed on people's mad lips and brought an end to them all.

She flipped opened Holston's folder. Behind the bio tab was

a thick stack of notes about his last days as sheriff. The portion relating to his actual crime was barely half a page long, the rest of the piece of paper blank and wasted. A single paragraph simply explained that he had reported to the up-top holding cell and had expressed an interest in the outside. That was it. A few lines to spell a man's doom. Juliette read the words several times before flipping the page over.

Underneath was a note from Mayor Jahns asking that Holston be remembered for his service to the silo and not as just another cleaner. Juliette read this letter, written in the hand of someone who was also recently deceased. It was strange to think of people she knew that she could never see again. Part of the reason she had avoided her father all these years was because he was, simply put, *still there*. There was never the threat of her not being able to change her mind. But it was different with Holston and Jahns: they were gone for ever. And Juliette was so used to rebuilding devices thought beyond repair that she felt if she concentrated enough, or performed the correct series of tasks in the right order, she should be able to bring the deceased back, be able to recreate their wasted forms. But she knew that wasn't the case.

She flipped through Holston's folder and asked herself forbidden questions, some for the very first time. What had seemed trivial when she lived in the down deep, where exhaust leaks could asphyxiate and broken flood pumps could drown everyone she knew, now loomed large before her. What was it all about, this life they lived in underground confines? What was out there, over those hills? Why were they here, and for what purpose? Had her kind built those tall silos crumbling in the distance? What for? And most vexing of all: what had Holston, a reasonable man – or his wife for that matter – been thinking to want to leave?

Two folders to keep her company, both marked 'CLOSED'. Both belonging in the mayor's office, where they should be sealed up and filed away. But Juliette kept finding herself returning to them rather than the more pressing cases in front of her. One of these folders held the life of a man she had loved, whose death she had helped unravel in the down deep. In the other lived a man she had respected whose job she now held. She didn't know why she obsessed over the two folders, especially since she couldn't stomach seeing Marnes peer forlornly down at his own loss, studying the details of Mayor Jahns's death, going over the depositions, convinced he had a killer but with no evidence to corner the man.

Someone knocked on the bars above Juliette's head. She looked up, expecting to find Deputy Marnes telling her it was time to call it a day, but saw a strange man peering down at her instead.

'Sheriff?' he said.

Juliette set the folders aside and palmed the star off her knee. She stood up and turned around, facing this small man with a protruding gut, glasses perched at the end of his nose, his silver IT overalls snugly tailored and freshly pressed.

'Can I help you?' she asked.

The man stuck his hand between the bars. Juliette moved the star from one palm to the other and reached out to accept it.

'Sorry I'm late getting up here,' he said. 'There's been a lot going on, what with the ceremonies, that generator nonsense, and all the legal wrangling. I'm Bernard, Bernard Holland.'

Juliette felt her blood run cold. The man's hand was so small, it felt like it was missing a finger. Despite this, his grip was solid. She tried to pull back, but he refused to let go.

'As sheriff, I'm sure you already know the Pact inside and out, so you know that I'll be acting mayor, at least until we can arrange a vote.'

'I'd heard,' Juliette said coolly. She wondered how this man had got past Marnes's desk without some sort of violence. Here was their prime suspect in Jahns's death – only he was on the wrong side of the bars.

'Doing some filing, are you?' He relinquished his grip, and Juliette pulled her hand away. He peered down at the paperwork strewn across the floor, his eyes seeming to settle on the canteen in its plastic bag, but Juliette couldn't be sure.

'Just familiarising myself with our ongoing cases,' she said. 'There's a little more room in here to . . . well, think.'

'Oh, I'm sure a lot of deep thought has taken place in this room.' Bernard smiled, and Juliette noticed his front teeth were crooked, one of them overlapping the other. It made him look like the stray mice she used to trap in the pump rooms.

'Yes, well, I've found the space conducive to sorting my thoughts out, so maybe there's something to that. And besides,' she levelled her eyes at him, 'I don't expect it to remain empty for long. And once it's occupied, I'll be able to take leave of all this deep thought for a day or two while someone is put to cleaning—'

'I wouldn't count too much on that,' Bernard said. He flashed his crooked teeth again. 'The word down below is that the poor mayor, rest her soul, plumb wore herself out with that crazy climb of hers. I believe she was hiking down to see *you*, isn't that right?'

Juliette felt a sharp sting in her palm. She loosened her grip on the brass star, the knuckles on both hands white from making fists.

Bernard adjusted his glasses. 'But now I hear you're investigating for foul play?'

Juliette continued to level her eyes at him, trying not to be distracted by the reflection of the dull hills visible in his spectacles. 'I suppose you should know, as *acting* mayor, that we're treating this very much as a murder,' she said.

'Oh my.' His eyes widened over a limp smile. 'So the rumours are true. Who would do such a thing?' The smile grew, and Juliette realised she was dealing with a man who felt himself invulnerable. It wasn't the first time she'd encountered a dirty and outsized ego such as his. Her time as a shadow in the down deep had been spent surrounded by them.

'I believe we'll find the party responsible was the one with the most to gain,' she said dryly. After a pause, she added: '*Mayor.*'

The crooked smile faded. Bernard let go of the bars and stepped back, his hands tucking into his overalls. 'Well, it's nice to finally put a face to the name. I'm aware that you haven't spent much time out of the down deep – and to be honest I've stayed much too insulated in my own office – but things are changing around here. As mayor and sheriff, we will be working together a lot, you and me.' He glanced down at the files at her feet. 'So I expect you to keep me posted. About everything.'

With that, Bernard turned and left, and it required a concerted effort for Juliette to relax her fists. When she finally peeled her fingers away from the star, she found its sharp edges had gouged into her palm, cutting her and drawing blood. A few drops caught the light on the edge of the brass, looking like wet rust. Juliette wiped the star clean on her new overalls, a habit born of her previous life among the sludge and grease. She cursed herself when she saw the dark spot the blood had left on her new clothes. Turning the star over, she peered at the stamped insignia on its face. There were the three triangles of the silo and the word 'Sheriff' arched over the top of them. She turned it over again and fingered the clasp that held the sharp spike of the pin. She opened the clasp and let the pin hinge free. The stiff needle had been bent and straightened in several places over the years, giving it a hand-forged look. It wobbled on its hinge – much like her hesitation to wear the thing.

But as Bernard's footsteps receded, as she heard him say something indecipherable to Deputy Marnes, she felt a new resolve steel her nerves. It was like encountering a rusted bolt that refused to budge. Something about that intolerable stiffness, that reluctance to move, set Juliette's teeth on edge. She had come to believe that there were no fasteners she couldn't unstick, had learned to attack them with grease and with fire, with penetrating oil and with brute strength. With enough planning and persistence, they always gave. Eventually.

She forced the wavy needle through the breast of her overalls and clasped the catch on the back. Looking down at the star was a little surreal. There were a dozen folders at her feet demanding her attention, and Juliette felt, for the first time since arriving at the up top, that this was her job. Her work at Mechanical was behind her. She had left that place in far better condition than she'd found it, had stayed long enough to hear the near-silent hum of a repaired generator, to see a shaft spin in such perfect alignment that one couldn't tell if it was moving at all. And now she had travelled to the up top to find here the rattle and squelch and grind of a different set of gears, a misalignment that was eating away at the true engine of the silo, just as Jahns had forewarned.

Leaving most of the folders where they were, she picked up Holston's, a folder she shouldn't even be looking at but couldn't be without, and pulled the cell door open. Rather than turn to her office, she first walked the other way towards the yellow steel entrance to the airlock. Peering through the triple-paned glass for the dozenth time in several days, she imagined the man she had replaced standing inside, wearing one of those ridiculously bulky suits, waiting for those far doors to open. What goes through a man's thoughts as he waits there alone to be cast off? It couldn't be mere fear, for Juliette had tasted that well enough. It had to be something beyond that, a wholly unique sensation, the calm beyond the pain, or the numbness past the terror. Imagination, she figured, just wasn't up to the task of understanding unique and foreign sensations. It knew only how to dampen or augment what it already knew. It would be like telling someone what sex felt like, or an orgasm. Impossible. But once you felt it yourself, you could then imagine varying degrees of this new sensation.

It was the same as colour. You could describe a new colour only in terms of hues previously seen. You could mix the known, but you couldn't create the strange out of nothing. So maybe it was only the cleaners who understood what it felt like to stand there, trembling – or perhaps not afraid one bit – as they waited for their death.

The obsession with *why* played out in whispers through the silo – people wanting to know why they did what they did, why they left a shiny and polished gift to those who had exiled them – but that did not interest Juliette at all. She figured they were seeing new colours, feeling the indescribable, perhaps having a religious experience that occurred only in the face of the reaper. Wasn't it enough to know that it happened without fail? Problem solved. Take it as an axiom. Move on to a real issue, like what it must *feel* like to be the one going through it. *That* was the real shame of the taboos: not that people couldn't pine for the outside world, but that they weren't even allowed to commiserate with the cleaners during the weeks after, to wonder what they had suffered, to properly express their thanks or regrets.

Juliette tapped the yellow door with the corner of Holston's folder, remembering the man in better times, back when he was in love, a lottery winner, telling her about his wife. She nodded to his ghost and stepped away from the imposing metal door with its small panes of thick glass. There was a kinship she felt from working in his post, now wearing his star, even sitting in his cell. She had loved a man once, and knew what that felt like. She had loved in secret, not involving the silo in their relationship, ignoring the Pact. And so she also knew what it meant to lose something so precious. She could imagine, if her old lover was out there on that hill – wasting away in plain sight rather than feeding the roots – that she could be driven to cleaning, to wanting to see those new colours for herself.

She opened Holston's file again as she wandered back towards her desk. *His* desk. Here was one man who knew of her secret love. She had told him, once the case was settled in the down deep, that the man who had died, whose case she had helped solve, had been her lover. Maybe it was how he had gone on and on about his wife the days before. Maybe it was his trustworthy smile that made him such a good sheriff, engendering this baffling urge to divulge secrets. Whatever the cause, she had admitted something to a man of the law that could have got her in trouble, an affair completely off the books, a wanton disregard for the Pact; and all he had said, this man entrusted with upholding those laws, was: 'I'm sorry.'

Sorry for her loss. And he had hugged her. Like he knew what she was holding inside, this secret grief that had hardened where her hidden love once lay.

And she had respected him for that.

Now she sat at his desk, in his chair, across from his old deputy, who held his head in his hands and peered down, unmoving, at an open folder dotted with tears. All it took was a glance for Juliette to suspect that some forbidden love lay between him and the contents of that folder as well.

'It's five o'clock,' Juliette said as quietly and gently as she could.

Marnes lifted his face out of his hands. His forehead was red from resting it there so long. His eyes were bloodshot, his grey moustache shimmering with fresh tears. He looked so much older than he had a week ago in the down deep, when he had come to recruit her. Swivelling in his old wooden chair, the legs squeaking as if startled by the sudden movement, he glanced at the clock on the wall behind him and surveyed the time imprisoned behind its yellowed and aged plastic dome. He nodded silently at the ticking of the hand, stood up, his back stooping for a moment as he fought to straighten it. He ran his hands down his overalls, reached to the folder, closed it tenderly, and tucked it under his arm.

'Tomorrow,' he whispered, nodding to Juliette.

'See you in the morning,' she said, as he staggered out towards the cafeteria.

Juliette watched him go, feeling sorry for him. She recognised the love behind his loss. It was painful to imagine him back in his small apartment, sitting on a cot wide enough for one, sobbing over that folder until he finally collapsed into his fitful dreams.

Once alone, she placed Holston's folder on her desk and slid her keyboard closer. The keys had been worn bare long ago, but someone in recent years had neatly reprinted the letters in black ink. Now even these handwritten faces were fading and would soon need another coat. Juliette would have to see to that – she couldn't type without looking at her keyboard like all these office workers could.

She slowly pecked out a request to wire down to Mechanical. After another day of getting little done, of being distracted by the mystery of Holston's decision, she had come to a realisation: there was no way she could perform this man's job until she first understood why he had turned his back on it, and on the silo itself. It was a nagging rattle keeping her from other problems. So instead of kidding herself, she was going to embrace the challenge. Which meant that she needed to know more than his folder contained.

She wasn't sure how to get the things she needed, how to even access them, but she knew people who might. This was what she missed most about the down deep. They were family there, all with useful skills that overlapped and covered one another.

Anything she could do for any of them, she would. And she knew they would do the same, even be an army for her. This was a comfort she sorely missed, a safety net that felt all too far away.

After sending the request, she sat back with Holston's folder. Here was a man, a good man, who had known her deepest secrets. He was the only one who ever had. And soon, God willing, Juliette would uncover his.

20

I t was well after ten by the time Juliette pushed herself away from her desk. Her eyes had become too sore to stare at her monitor any longer, too tired to read one more case note. She powered down her computer, filed the folders away, killed the overhead lights, and locked the office door from the outside.

As she pocketed her keys, her stomach grumbled, and the fading odour of a rabbit stew reminded her that she'd missed yet another dinner. That made it three nights in a row. Three nights of focusing so hard on a job she barely knew how to perform, a job she had no one to guide her through, that she'd neglected to eat. If her office didn't abut a noisy, aroma-filled cafeteria, she might be able to forgive herself.

She pulled her keys back out and crossed the dimly lit room, weaving around nearly invisible chairs left scattered between the tables. A teenage couple was just leaving, having stolen a few dark moments in the wall screen's twilight before curfew. Juliette called out for them to descend safely, mostly because it felt like the sheriff thing to do, and they giggled at her as they disappeared into the stairwell. She imagined they were already holding hands and would steal a few kisses before they got to their apartments. Adults knew of these illicit things but let them slide, a gift each generation bestowed on the next. For Juliette, however, it was different. She had made the same choices as an adult, to love without sanction, and so her hypocrisy was more keenly felt.

As she approached the kitchen, she noticed the cafeteria wasn't quite empty. A lone figure sat in the deep shadows by the wall screen, staring at the inky blackness of night-time clouds hanging over darkened hills.

It appeared to be the same figure as the night before, the one who had watched the sunlight gradually fade while Juliette worked alone in her office. She adjusted her route to the kitchen in order to pass behind the man. Staring all day at folders full of bad intentions had made her a budding paranoid. She used to admire people who stood out, but now she could feel herself wary of them.

She moved between the wall screen and the nearest table, pausing to push chairs back into place, their metal feet scraping on the tile. She kept an eye on the seated man, but he never once turned towards the noise. He just stared up at the clouds, something in his lap, a hand held up by his chin.

Juliette walked right behind him, stepping between the table and his chair, which had been moved strangely close to the wall screen. She fought the urge to clear her throat or ask him a question. Instead, she passed on by, jangling her master key from the crowded ring that had come with her new job.

Twice, she glanced back over her shoulder before she reached the kitchen door. The man did not move.

She let herself inside the kitchen and hit one of the light switches. After a genial flicker, the overhead bulbs popped on and shattered her night vision. She pulled a gallon of juice from one of the walk-in refrigerators and grabbed a clean glass from the drying rack. Back in the walk-in, she found the stew – covered and already cold – and brought it out as well. She ladled two scoops into a bowl and rattled around in a drawer for a spoon. She only briefly considered heating up the stew as she returned the large pot to its frosted shelf.

With her juice and bowl in hand, she returned to the cafeteria, knocking the lights off with her elbow and pushing the door shut with her foot. She sat down in the shadows at the end of one of the long tables and slurped on her meal, keeping an eye on this strange man who seemed to peer into the darkness as if something could be seen out there.

Her spoon eventually scraped the bottom of her empty bowl,

and she finished the last of her juice. Not once through the meal had the man turned away from the wall screen. She pushed the dishes away from herself, insanely curious. The figure reacted to this, unless it was mere coincidence. He leaned forward and held his outstretched hand out at the screen. Juliette thought she could make out a rod or stick in his grasp – but it was too dark to tell. After a moment, he leaned over his lap, and Juliette heard the squeak of charcoal on expensive-sounding paper. She got up, taking this movement as an opening, and strolled closer to where he was sitting.

'Raiding the larder, are we?' he asked.

His voice startled her.

'Worked through dinner,' she stammered, as if *she* needed to explain herself.

'Must be nice to have the keys.'

He still didn't turn away from the screen, and Juliette reminded herself to lock the kitchen door before she left.

'What're you doing?' she asked.

The man reached behind himself and grabbed a nearby chair, slid it around to face the screen. 'You wanna see?'

Juliette approached warily, grabbed the backrest, and deliberately slid the chair a few inches further from the man. It was too dark in the room to make out his features, but his voice sounded young. She chastised herself for not committing him to memory the night before when there'd been more light. She would need to become more observant if she was going to be any good at her job.

'What're we looking at, exactly?' she asked. She stole a glance at his lap, where a large piece of white paper glowed faintly in the wan light leaking from the stairwell. It was spread flat across his thighs as if a board or something hard rested beneath it.

'I think those two are going to part. Look there.'

The man pointed at the wall screen and into a mix of blacks so rich and so deep as to appear as one. The contours and shadowy hues Juliette could make out almost seemed to be a trick played by her eyes – as real as ghosts. But she followed his finger, wondering if he were mad or drunk, and tolerated the exhausting silence that followed.

'There,' he whispered, excitement on his breath.

Juliette saw a flash. A spot of light. Like someone flicking on a torch far across a dark generator room. And then it was gone.

She bolted out of her chair and stood near to the wall screen, wondering what was out there.

The man's charcoal squeaked on his paper.

'What the hell was *that*?' Juliette asked.

The man laughed. 'A star,' he said. 'If you wait, you might see it again. We've got thin clouds tonight and high winds. That one there is getting ready to pass.'

Juliette turned to find her chair and saw that he was holding his charcoal at arm's length, staring up at the spot where the light had flashed, one eye winked shut.

'How can you see anything out there?' she asked, settling back into her plastic chair.

'The longer you do this, the better you see at night.' He leaned over his paper and scribbled some more. 'And I've been doing this a long time.'

'Doing what, exactly? Just staring at the clouds?'

He laughed. 'Mostly, yeah. Unfortunately. But what I'm trying to do is see past them. Watch, we might get another glance.'

She peered up in the general area of the last flash. Suddenly, it popped back into view, a pinprick of light like a signal from high over the hill.

'How many did you see?' he asked.

'One,' she told him. She was almost breathless from the newness of the sight. She knew what stars were – they were a part of her vocabulary – but she'd never seen one before.

'There was a faint one just to the side of it as well. Let me show you.'

There was a soft click, and a red glow spilled over the man's lap. Juliette saw that he had a flashlight hanging around his neck, a film of red plastic wrapped around the end. It made the lens look like it was on fire, but it emanated a gentle glow that didn't barrage her eyes the way the kitchen lights had.

Spread across his lap, she saw a large piece of paper covered with dots. They were arranged haphazardly, a few perfectly straight lines running in a grid around them. Tiny notes were scattered everywhere.

'The problem is that they move,' he told her. 'If I see that one here tonight' – he tapped one of the dots with his finger; there was a smaller dot beside it – 'at the same exact time tomorrow, it'll be a little over here.' As he turned to Juliette, she saw that the man was young, probably in his late twenties, and quite handsome in that clean, office-like way. He smiled and added, 'It took me a long time to figure that out.'

Juliette wanted to tell him that he hadn't been *alive* a long time, but remembered what it had felt like as a shadow when people dismissed her the same way.

'What's the point?' she asked, and saw his smile fade.

'What's the point of anything?' He returned his gaze to the wall and doused the flashlight. Juliette realised she'd asked the wrong question, had upset him. And then she wondered if there was anything illicit in this activity of his, anything that defied the taboos. Was collecting data on the outside any different from the people who sat and stared at the hills? She made a mental note to ask Marnes about this, when the man turned to her again in the darkness.

'My name's Lukas,' he said. Her eyes had adjusted well enough to see his hand stretched out towards her.

'Juliette,' she replied, grabbing and squeezing his palm.

'The new sheriff.'

It wasn't a question, and of course he knew who she was. Everyone up top seemed to.

'What do you do when you're not up here?' she asked. She was pretty sure this wasn't his job. Nobody should get chits for staring up at the clouds.

'I live in the upper mids,' Lukas said. 'I work on computers during the day. I only come up when the viewing's good.' He switched the light back on and turned towards her in a way that suggested the stars weren't the most important thing on his mind any more. 'There's a guy on my level who works up here on dinner shift. When he gets home, he lets me know what the clouds were like during the day. If he gives me the thumbs-up, I come take my chances.'

'And so you're making a schematic of them?' Juliette gestured towards the large sheet of paper.

'Trying to. It'll probably take a few lifetimes.' He tucked his charcoal behind his ear, pulled a rag from his overalls, and wiped his fingers clean of black residue.

'And then what?' Juliette asked.

'Well, hopefully I'll infect some shadow with my sickness and they'll pick up wherever I leave off.'

'So literally, like, several lifetimes.'

He laughed, and Juliette realised it was a pleasant one. 'At least,' he said.

'Well, I'll leave you to it,' she said, suddenly feeling guilty for talking to him. She stood and reached out her hand, and he took it warmly. He pressed his other palm to the back of her hand and held it a moment longer than she would have expected.

'Pleasure to meet you, Sheriff.'

He smiled up at her. And Juliette didn't understand a word of what she muttered in return.

21

The next morning, Juliette arrived early at her desk having stolen little more than four hours of sleep. Beside her computer, she saw a package waiting for her: a small bundle wrapped in recycled pulp paper and encircled with white electrical ties. She smiled at this last touch and reached into her overalls for her multi-tool. Pulling out the smallest pick from the tool, she stuck it into the clasp of one of the electrical ties and slowly pulled the ratcheting device apart, keeping it intact for future use. She remembered the trouble she'd got into as a mechanic's shadow the day she'd been caught cutting a plastic tie from an electrical board. Walker, already an old crank those decades ago, had yelled at her for the waste and then shown her how to tease the little clasp loose to preserve the tie for later use.

Years had passed, and when she was much older, she had found herself passing this lesson on to another shadow named Scottie. He had been a young lad at the time, but she had had a go at him when he had made the same careless mistake she once had. She remembered frightening the poor boy white as a breeze block, and he had remained nervous around her for months after. Maybe because of that outburst, she had paid him more attention as he continued his training, and eventually the two had grown close. He quickly grew up to become a capable young man, a whiz with electronics, able to program a pump's timing chip in less time than it took her to break one down and put it back together.

She loosened the other tie crossing the package, and knew the bundle was from him. Several years ago, Scottie had been recruited by IT and had moved up to the thirties. He had become 'too smart for Mechanical', as Knox had put it. Juliette set the two electrical straps aside and pictured the young man preparing this package for her. The request she'd wired down to Mechanical the night before must've bounced back up to him, and he had spent the night dutifully doing this favour for her.

She pried the paper apart carefully. Both it and the plastic ties would need to be returned; they were both too dear for her to keep and light enough to porter on the cheap. As the package came apart, she noticed that Scottie had crimped the edges and had folded these tabs under each other, a trick children learned so they could wrap notes without the expense of glue or tape. She disassembled his meticulous work with care, and the paper finally came loose. Inside, she found a plastic box like the kind used to sort nuts and bolts for small projects down in Mechanical.

She opened the lid and saw that the package wasn't just from Scottie — it must've been hurried up to him along with a copy of her request. Tears came to her eyes as the smell of Mama Jean's oatmeal and cornflour cookies drifted out. She plucked one, held it to her nose, and breathed deeply. Maybe she imagined it, but she swore she noted a hint of oil or grease emanating from the old box — the smells of home.

Juliette folded the wrapping paper carefully and placed the cookies on top. She thought of the people she would have to share them with. Marnes, of course, but also Pam in the cafeteria, who had been so nice in helping her settle into her new apartment. And Alice, Jahns's young secretary, whose eyes had been red with grief for over a week. She pulled the last cookie out and finally spotted the small data drive rattling around in the bottom of the container, a little morsel baked special by Scottie and hidden among the crumbs.

Juliette grabbed it and set the plastic case aside. She blew into the little metal end of the drive, getting any debris out, before slotting it into the front of her computer. She wasn't great with computers, but she could navigate them. You couldn't do anything in Mechanical without submitting a claim, a report, a request, or some other piece of nonsense. And they were handy for logging into pumps and relays remotely to shut them on or off, see their diagnostics, all of that.

Once the light on the drive winked on, she navigated to it on her screen. Inside, she found a host of folders and files; the little drive must've been stuffed to the brim with them. She wondered if Scottie had got any sleep at all the night before.

At the top of a list of primary folders was a file named 'Jules'. She clicked this one, and up popped a short text file obviously from Scottie, but noticeably unsigned:

J--

Don't get caught with this, okay? This is everything from Mr Lawman's computers, work and home, the last five years. A ton of stuff, but wasn't sure what you needed and this was easier to automate.

Keep the ties -- I got plenty.

(And I took a cookie. Hope you don't mind)

Juliette smiled. She felt like reaching out and brushing her fingers across the words, but it wasn't paper and wouldn't be the same. She closed the note and deleted it, then cleared out her trash. Even the first letter of her name up there felt like too much information.

She leaned away from her desk and peered into the cafeteria, which appeared dark and empty. It was not yet five in the morning, and she would have the upper floor to herself for a while. She first took a moment to browse through the directory structure to see what kind of data she was dealing with. Each folder was neatly labelled. It appeared she had an operating history of Holston's two computers, every keystroke, every day, going back a little more than five years, all organised by date and time. Juliette felt overwhelmed by the sheer *amount* of information – it was far more than she could hope to weed through in a lifetime.

But at least she had it. The answers she needed were in there, somewhere, among all those files. And somehow it felt better, *she* felt better, just knowing that the solution to this riddle, to Holston's decision to go to cleaning, could now fit in the palm of her hand.

She was several hours into sifting through the data when the cafeteria crew staggered in to clean up last night's mess and prepare for breakfast. One of the most difficult things to get used to about the up top was the exacting schedule everyone kept. There was no third shift. There was barely a second shift, except for the dinner staff. In the down deep, the machines didn't sleep, and so the workers barely did either. Work crews often stayed on into extra shifts, and Juliette had got used to surviving on a handful of hours of rest a night. The trick was to pass out now and then from sheer exhaustion, to just rest against a wall with one's eyes closed for fifteen minutes, long enough to hold the tiredness at bay.

But what had once been survival was now luxury. The ability to forego sleep gave her time in the morning and at night to herself, time to invest in frivolous pursuits on top of the cases she was supposed to be working. It also gave her the opportunity to teach herself how to do the blasted job, since Marnes had become too depressed to help get her up to speed.

Marnes—

She looked at the clock over his desk. It was ten minutes after eight, and the vats of warm oatmeal and corn grits were already filling the cafeteria with the smells of breakfast. Marnes was late. She'd been around him less than a week, but she had yet to see him late to anything, ever. This break in the routine was like a timing belt stretching out of shape, a piston developing a knock. Juliette turned her monitor off and pushed away from her desk. Outside, first-shift breakfast was beginning to file in, food tokens clinking in the large bucket by the old turnstiles. She left her office and passed through the traffic spilling from the stairwell. In the line, a young girl tugged on her mother's overalls and pointed to Juliette as she passed. Juliette heard the mother scolding her child for being rude.

There had been quite a bit of chatter the past few days over her appointment, this woman who had disappeared into Mechanical as a child and who had suddenly re-emerged to take over from one of the more popular sheriffs in memory. Juliette cringed from the attention and hurried into the stairwell. She wound her way down the steps as fast as a lightly loaded porter, her feet bouncing off each tread, faster and faster in what felt like an unsafe pace. Four flights down, after squeezing around a slow couple and between a family heading up for breakfast, she hit the apartment landing just below her own and passed through the double doors.

The hallway beyond was busy with morning sights and sounds: a squealing teapot, the shrill voices of children, the thunder of feet overhead, shadows hurrying to meet their casters before trailing behind them to work. Younger children were lumbering reluctantly off to school; husbands and wives kissed in doorways while toddlers tugged at their overalls and dropped toys and plastic cups.

Juliette took several turns, winding through the hallways and around the central staircase to the other side of the level. The deputy's apartment was on the far side, way in the back. She surmised that Marnes had qualified for several upgrades over the years, but had passed on them. The one time she had asked Alice, Mayor Jahns's old secretary, about Marnes, she had shrugged and told Juliette that he had never wanted or expected anything more than second fiddle. Juliette assumed she meant that he never wanted to be sheriff, but she had begun to wonder in how many other areas of his life that philosophy applied.

As she reached his hall, two kids ran by holding hands, late for school. They giggled and squealed around the corner, leaving Juliette alone in the hallway. She wondered what she would say to Marnes to justify coming down, to explain her worry. Maybe now was a good time to ask for the folder that he couldn't seem to be without. She could tell him to take the day off, let her handle the office while he got some rest, or maybe fib a little and say she was already in the area for a case.

She stopped outside his door and lifted her hand to knock. Hopefully he wouldn't see this as her projecting authority. She was just concerned for him. That was all.

She rapped on the steel door and waited for him to call her

inside – and maybe he did. His voice over the last few days had eroded into a dull and thin rasp. She knocked again, louder this time.

'Deputy?' she called. 'Everything okay in there?'

A woman popped her head out of a door down the hallway. Juliette recognised her from school recess time in the cafeteria, was pretty sure her name was Gloria.

'Hey, Sheriff.'

'Hey, Gloria, you haven't seen Deputy Marnes this morning, have you?'

She shook her head, placed a metal rod in her mouth and started wrapping her long hair into a bun. 'I haben't,' she mumbled. She shrugged her shoulders and jabbed the rod through her bun, locking her hair into place. 'He was on the landing last night, looking as whipped as ever.' She frowned. 'He not show up for work?'

Juliette turned back to the door and tried the handle. It clicked open with the feel of a well-maintained lock. She pushed the door in. 'Deputy? It's Jules. Just checkin' in on ya.'

The door swung open into the darkness. The only light spilling in was from the hallway, but it was enough.

Juliette turned to Gloria. 'Call Doc Hicks— No, shit . . .' She was still thinking down deep. 'Who's the closest doctor up here? Call him!'

She ran into the room, not waiting for a reply. There wasn't much space to hang oneself in the small apartment, but Marnes had figured out how. His belt was cinched around his neck, the buckle lodged into the top of the bathroom door. His feet were on the bed, but at a right angle, not enough to support his weight. His butt drooped below his feet, his face no longer red, the belt biting deep into his neck.

Juliette hugged Marnes's waist and lifted him up. He was heavier than he looked. She kicked his feet off the bed, and they flopped to the floor, making it easier to hold him. There was a curse at the door. Gloria's husband ran in and helped Juliette support the deputy's weight. Both of them fumbled for the belt, trying to dislodge it from the door. Juliette finally tugged the door open, freeing him.

'On the bed,' she huffed.

They lifted him to the bed and laid him out flat.

Gloria's husband rested his hands on his knees and took deep breaths. 'Gloria ran for Doctor O'Neil.'

Juliette nodded and loosened the belt from around Marnes's neck. The flesh was purple beneath it. She felt for a pulse, remembering George looking just like this when she'd found him down in Mechanical, completely still and unresponsive. It took her a moment to be sure that she was looking at the second dead body she had ever seen.

And then she wondered, as she sat back, sweating, waiting for the doctor to arrive, whether this job she had taken would ensure it wasn't the last.

22

After filling out reports, discovering Marnes had no next of kin, speaking with the coroner at the dirt farm, and answering questions from nosy neighbours, Juliette finally took a long and lonely walk up eight flights of stairs, back to her empty office. She spent the rest of the day getting little work done, the door to the cafeteria open, the small room much too crowded with ghosts. She tried repeatedly to lose herself in the files from Holston's computers, but Marnes's absence was incredibly sadder than his moping presence had been. She couldn't believe he was gone. It almost felt like an affront, to bring her here and then leave her so suddenly. And she knew this was a horrible and selfish thing to feel and even worse to admit.

As her mind roamed, she glanced occasionally out the door, watching the clouds slide across the distant wall screen. She debated with herself on whether they appeared light or dense, if tonight would be a good one for viewing stars. It was another guilt-ridden thought, but she felt powerfully alone, a woman who prided herself on needing no one.

She played some more with the maze of files as the light of an unseen sun diminished in the cafeteria, as two shifts of lunch and two shifts of dinner vibrated and then subsided around her, all the while watching the roiling sky and hoping, for no real logical reason, for another chance encounter with the strange star-hunter from the night before.

And even sitting there, with the sounds and scents of everyone on the upper forty-eight eating, Juliette forgot to grab a bite for herself. It wasn't until the second-shift staff was leaving, the lights cut down to quarter power, that Pam came in with a bowl of soup and a biscuit. Juliette thanked her and reached into her overalls for a few chits, but Pam refused. The young woman's eyes – red from crying – drifted to Marnes's empty chair, and Juliette realised the cafeteria staff had probably been as close to the deputy as anyone.

Pam left without a word, and Juliette ate with what little appetite she could manage. She eventually thought of one more search she could try on Holston's data, a global spellcheck to look for names that might offer clues, and eventually figured out how to run it. Meanwhile, her soup grew cold. While her computer began to churn through the hills of data, she took her bowl and a few folders and left her office to sit at one of the cafeteria tables near the wall screen.

She was looking for stars on her own when Lukas appeared silently at her side. He didn't say anything, just pulled up a chair, sat down with his board and paper, and peered up at the expansive view of the darkened outside.

Juliette couldn't tell if he was being polite to honour her silence, or if he was being rude not to say hello. She finally settled on the former, and eventually the quiet felt normal. Shared. A peace at the end of a horrible day.

Several minutes passed. A dozen. There were no stars and nothing was said. Juliette held a folder in her lap, just to give her fingers something to do. There was a sound from the stairwell, a laughing group moving between the apartment levels below, and then a return to the quiet.

'I'm sorry about your partner,' Lukas finally said. His hands smoothed the paper on the board. He had yet to make a single mark or note.

'I appreciate that,' Juliette said. She wasn't sure what the appropriate response was, but this seemed the least wrong.

'I've been looking for stars, but haven't seen any,' she added.

'You won't. Not tonight.' He waved his hand at the wall screen. 'These are the worst kinds of clouds.'

Juliette studied them, barely able to make them out with the last of the twilight's distant glow. They looked no different to her than any others.

Lukas turned almost imperceptibly in his seat. 'I have a confession, since you're the law and all.'

Juliette's hand groped for the star on her chest. She was often in danger of forgetting what she was.

'Yeah?'

'I knew the clouds were gonna be bad tonight. But I came up anyway.'

Juliette trusted the darkness to conceal her smile.

'I'm not sure the Pact has much to say on such duplicity,' she told him.

Lukas laughed. It was strange how familiar it already sounded, and how badly she needed to hear it. Juliette had a sudden urge to grab him, to tuck her chin into his neck, and to cry. She could almost feel her body begin to piece the moves together – even though her skin would not budge. It could never happen. She knew this, even as the sensation vibrated within her. It was just the loneliness, the horror of holding Marnes in her arms, of feeling that lifeless heft of a body that has lost whatever animates it. She was desperate for contact, and this stranger was the only person she knew little enough to want it from.

'What happens now?' he asked, his laughter fading.

Juliette almost blurted out, inanely, *Between* us? but Lukas saved her.

'Do you know when the funeral will be? And where?' he asked.

She nodded in the darkness.

'Tomorrow. There's no family to travel up, no investigation to make.' Juliette choked back the tears. 'He didn't leave a will, so they left it up to me to make arrangements. I decided to lay him to rest near the mayor.'

Lukas looked to the wall screen. It was dark enough that the bodies of the cleaners couldn't be seen, a welcome relief. 'As he should be,' he said.

'I think they were lovers in secret,' Juliette blurted out. 'If not lovers, then just as close.'

'There's been talk,' he agreed. 'What I don't get is why keep it a secret. Nobody would've cared.'

Somehow, sitting in the darkness with a complete stranger, these things were more easily aired than in the down deep among friends.

'Maybe *they* would have minded people knowing,' she thought out loud. 'Jahns was married before. I suspect they chose to respect that.'

'Yeah?' Lukas scratched something on his paper. Juliette looked up, but was sure there hadn't been a star. 'I can't imagine loving in secret like that,' he said.

'I can't imagine needing someone's permission, like the Pact or a girl's father, to be in love in the first place,' she replied.

'No? How else would it work? Just any two people any time they liked?'

She didn't say.

'How would anyone ever enter the lottery?' he asked, persisting in the line of thought. 'I can't imagine it not being out in the open. It's a celebration, don't you think? There's this ritual, a man asks a girl's father for permission—'

'Well, aren't you with anyone?' Juliette asked, cutting him off. 'I mean . . . I'm just asking because it sounds like, like you have strong opinions but maybe haven't—'

'Not yet,' he said, rescuing her again. 'I have a little strength left yet for enduring my mom's guilt. She likes to remind me every year how many lotteries I've missed out on, and what this has done to her overall chances for a bevy of grandchildren. As if I don't know my statistics. But hey, I'm only twenty-five.'

'That's all,' Juliette said.

'What about you?'

She nearly told him straight away. Nearly blurted out her secret with almost no prompting. As if this man, this boy, a stranger to her, could be trusted.

'Never found the right one,' she lied.

Lukas laughed his youthful laugh. 'No, I mean, how old are you? Or is that impolite?'

She felt a wave of relief. She thought he'd been asking her about being with anyone.

'Thirty-four,' she said. 'And I'm told it's impolite to ask, but I've never been one for rules.'

'Says our sheriff,' Lukas said, laughing at his own joke.

Juliette smiled. 'I guess I'm still getting used to that.'

She turned back to the wall screen, and they both enjoyed the silence that formed. It was strange, sitting with this man. She felt younger and somehow more secure in his presence. Less lonely, at least. She pegged him as a loner as well, an odd-sized washer that didn't fit any standard bolt. And here he had been, at the extreme other end of the silo, searching for stars, while she'd been spending what spare time she could down in the mines, as far away as possible, hunting for pretty rocks.

'It's not going to be a very productive night for either of us, looks like,' she eventually said, ending the silence, rubbing the unopened folder in her lap.

'Oh, I don't know,' Lukas told her. 'That depends on what you came up here for.'

Juliette smiled. And across the wide room, barely audible, the computer on her desk beeped, a search routine having finally pawed through Holston's data before spitting out its results.

23

The next morning, instead of climbing to her office, Juliette descended five flights to the upper dirt farm for Marnes's funeral. There would be no folder for her deputy, no investigation, just the lowering of his old and tired body into the deep soil where it would decompose and feed the roots. It was a strange thought, to stand in that crowd and think of him as a folder or not. Less than a week on the job, and she already saw the manila jackets as places where ghosts reside. Names and case numbers. Lives distilled onto twenty or so sheets of recycled pulp paper, bits of string and darts of random colour woven beneath the black ink that jotted their sad tale.

The ceremony was long, but didn't feel so. The earth nearby was still mounded where Jahns had been buried. Soon, the two of them would intermingle inside the plants, and these plants would nourish the occupants of the silo.

Juliette accepted a ripe tomato as the priest and his shadow cycled among the thick crowd. The two of them, draped in red fabric, chanted as they went, their voices sonorous and complementing one another. Juliette bit into her fruit, allowing a polite amount of juice to spatter her overalls, chewed and swallowed. She could tell the tomato was delicious, but only in a mechanical way. It was hard to truly enjoy it.

When it became time for the soil to be shovelled back into the hole, Juliette watched the crowd. Two people dead from the up top in less than a week. There had been two other deaths elsewhere in the silo, making it a very bad week.

Or good, depending on who you were. She noticed childless

couples biting vigorously into their fruit, their hands intertwined, silently doing the maths. Lotteries followed too closely after deaths for Juliette's tastes. She always thought they should fall on the same dates in the year, just to look as though they were going to happen anyway, whether anyone died or not.

But then, the lowering of the body and the plucking of ripe fruit just above the graves was meant to hammer this home: the cycle of life is here; it is inescapable; it is to be embraced, cherished, appreciated. One departs and leaves behind the gift of sustenance, of life. They make room for the next generation. We are born, we are shadows, we cast shadows of our own, and then we are gone. All anyone can hope for is to be remembered two shadows deep.

Before the hole was completely filled, members of the feast stepped up to the edge of the farm's soil and tossed what remained of their fruit into the hole. Juliette stepped forward and added the rest of her tomato to the colourful hail of rind and pulp. An acolyte leaned on his too-large shovel and watched the last of the fruit fly. Those that missed, he knocked in with scoops of dark, rich soil, leaving a mound that would, in time and with a few waterings, settle.

After the funeral, Juliette began the climb back to her office. She could feel the flights of stairs in her legs, even though she prided herself on being in shape. But walking and climbing were different sorts of exercise. It wasn't turning wrenches or loosening stubborn bolts, and the endurance was of a different kind than merely staying up and alert for an extra shift. She decided it was unnatural, this climbing. Humans weren't meant for it. She doubted they were engineered to travel much beyond a single level of a silo. But then another porter flew down the steps past her, a smile of quick greeting on his fresh face, his feet dancing across steel treads, and she wondered if perhaps it was something that just took practice.

When she finally made it back to the cafeteria, it was lunchtime, and the room was buzzing with noisy chatter and the clinking of metal forks on metal plates. The pile of folded notes outside her office door had grown. There was a plant in a plastic bucket, a pair of shoes, a small sculpture made of colourful wire. Juliette paused over the collection. As Marnes didn't have any family, she supposed it would be up to her to go through it all, to make sure the items went to those who would use them best. She bent down and picked up one of the cards. The writing was in unsure print, scrawled with crayon. She imagined the upper-grade school had spent craft time that day making cards for Deputy Marnes. This saddened Juliette more than any of the ceremonies. She wiped tears out of her eyes and damned the teachers who thought to get the kids involved in the nastiness of it all.

'Leave them out of it,' she whispered to herself.

She replaced the card and composed herself. Deputy Marnes would have liked to have seen this, she decided. He was an easy man to figure, one of those who had grown old everywhere but in his heart, that one organ he had never worn out because he'd never dared to use it.

Inside her office, she was surprised to find she had company. A stranger sat at Deputy Marnes's desk. He looked up from the computer and smiled at her. She was about to ask who he was when Bernard – she refused to think of him as even *interim* mayor – stepped out of the holding cell, a folder in hand, smiling at Juliette.

'How were the services?' he asked.

Juliette crossed the office and snatched the folder out of his hand. 'Please don't tamper with anything,' she said.

'Tamper?' Bernard laughed and adjusted his glasses. 'That's a closed case. I was going to take it back to my offices and refile it.'

Juliette checked the folder and saw that it was Holston's.

'You do know that you report to me, right? You were supposed to have at least glanced over the Pact before Jahns swore you in.'

'I'll hold on to this, thanks.' Juliette left him by the open cell and went to her desk. She shoved the folder in the top drawer, checked that the data drive was still jutting out from her computer, and looked up at the guy across from her.

'And you are?'

He stood, and Deputy Marnes's chair let out its customary

squeak. Juliette tried to force herself not to think of it as his any more.

'Peter Billings, ma'am.' He held out his hand. Juliette accepted it. 'I was just sworn in myself.' He pinched the corner of his star and held it away from his overalls for her to see.

'Peter here was actually up for *your* job,' Bernard said.

Juliette wondered what he meant by that, or what the point was to even mention it. 'Did you need something?' she asked Bernard. She waved at her desk, which had piled up the day before as she had spent most of her time managing Marnes's affairs. 'Because anything you need doing, I can add it to the bottom of one of these piles, here.'

'Anything I give you goes on *top*,' Bernard said. He slapped his hand down on the folder with Jahns's name on it. 'And I'm doing you a favour by coming up and having this meeting here rather than have you come down to *my* office.'

'What meeting is this?' Juliette asked. She didn't look up at him, but busied herself sorting papers. Hopefully he would see how busy she was and leave, and she could start getting Peter up to speed on what little she herself had figured out.

'As you know, there's been quite a bit of . . . *turnover* these past weeks. Unprecedented, really, at least since the uprising. And that's the danger, I'm afraid, if we aren't all on the same page.' He pressed his finger onto the folder Juliette was trying to move, pinning it in place. She glanced up at him.

'People want continuity. They want to know tomorrow will be a lot like yesterday. They want reassurances. Now, we've just had a cleaning, and we've suffered some losses, so the mood is naturally a bit raucous.' He waved at the folders and piles of pulp paper spilling from Juliette's desk and onto Marnes's. The young man across from her seemed to eye the mound warily, like more of the pile could shift towards him, giving him more of it to work through. 'Which is why I am going to announce a forgiveness moratorium. Not only to strengthen the spirits of the entire silo, but to help you two clear the slate so you don't get overwhelmed while you're getting up to speed on your duties.'

'Clear the slate?' Juliette asked.

'That's right. All these drunken misdemeanours. What's this one for?' He picked up a folder and studied the name on the label. 'Oh, now what's Pickens done this time?'

'He ate a neighbour's rat,' Juliette said. 'Family pet.'

Peter Billings chuckled. Juliette squinted at him, wondering why his name seemed familiar. Then she placed it, recalling a memo he had written in one of the folders. This kid, practically a boy, had been shadowing a silo judge, she remembered. She had a difficult time imagining that, looking at him. He seemed more the IT type.

'I thought owning rats as pets was illegal,' Bernard said.

'It is. He's the claimant. It's a counter-suit in retaliation' – she sorted through her folders – 'for this one right here.'

'Let's see,' Bernard said. He grabbed the other folder, held the two of them together, and then dropped them both into her recycle bin, all the carefully organised papers and notes spilling out and intermingling in a jumbled pile on top of other scraps of paper to be re-pulped.

'Forgive and forget,' he said, wiping his palms together. 'That's going to be my election motto. The people need this. This is about new beginnings, forgetting the past during these tumultuous times, looking to the *future*!' He slapped her on the back, hard, nodded to Peter, and headed for the door.

'Election motto?' she asked before he could get away. And it occurred to her that one of the folders he was suggesting could be forgiven was the one wherein *he* was the prime suspect.

'Oh yes,' Bernard called over his shoulder. He grabbed the jamb and looked back at her. 'I've decided, after much deliberation, that there is no one better qualified for this job than me. I don't see any problem with continuing my duties in IT while performing the role as mayor. In fact, I already am!' He winked. 'Continuity, you know.' And then he was gone.

Juliette spent the rest of that afternoon, well past what Peter Billings considered 'sensible working hours', getting him up to speed. What she needed most of all was someone to field complaints and to respond to the radio. This was Holston's old job, ranging the top forty-eight and calling on any disturbance. Deputy Marnes had hoped to see Juliette fill that role with her younger, fresher legs. He also had said that a pretty female might 'do the public will some good'. Juliette had other ideas about his intentions. She suspected Marnes had wanted her away so he could spend time alone with his folder and its ghost. And she well understood that urge. So as she sent Peter Billings home with a list of apartments and merchants to call on the next day, she finally had time to sit down at her computer and see the results from the previous night's search.

The spellchecker had turned up interesting results. Not so much the names she had hoped for, but rather these large blocks of what looked like coded text: gibberish with strange punctuation, indentation, and embedded words she recognised but that seemed out of place. These massive paragraphs were spread throughout Holston's home computer, first showing up just over three years ago. That made it fit the timeline, but what really caught Juliette's eye was how often the data appeared in nested directories, some- times a dozen or more folders deep. It was as if someone had taken pains to keep them hidden, but had wanted multiple copies stashed away, terrified of losing them.

She assumed it was encoded, whatever it was, and important. She tore off bites of a small loaf of bread and dipped these in corn spread while she gathered a full copy of this gibberish to send down to Mechanical. There were a few guys perhaps smart enough to make some sense of the code, starting with Walker. She chewed her food and spent the next hours going back over the trail she had managed to tease out of Holston's final years on the job. It had been difficult to narrow his activities down, to figure out what was important and what was noise, but she had approached it as logically as any other breakdown. Because that's what she was dealing with, she decided. A breakdown. Gradual and interminable. Almost inevitable. Losing his wife had been like a seal or a gasket cracking. Everything that had rattled out of control for Holston could be traced back, almost mechanically, to her death.

One of the first things she'd realised was that his activity on the work computer held no secrets. Holston had obviously become a night rat, just like her, staying up for hours in his apartment. It was yet another commonality she felt between them, further strengthening her obsession with the man. Sticking to his home computer meant she could ignore over half the data. It also became apparent that he had spent most of his time investigating his wife, just as Juliette was now prying into *him*. This was their deepest shared bond, Juliette's and Holston's. Here she was, looking into the last voluntary cleaner as he had looked into his wife, hoping to discover what torturous cause might lead a person to choose the forbidden outside.

And it was here that Juliette began to find clues almost eerie in their connection. Allison, Holston's wife, seemed to be the one who had unlocked the mysteries of the old servers. The very method that had made Holston's data available to Juliette had at some point brought some secret to Allison, and then to Holston. By focusing on deleted emails between the couple, and noting the explosion of communication around the time she had published a document detailing some un-deletion method, Juliette stumbled onto what she felt was a valid trail. She became more certain that Allison had found something on the servers. The trouble was determining what it was – and whether she'd recognise it herself even if she found it.

She toyed with several ideas, even the chance that Allison had been driven to rage by infidelity, but Juliette had enough of a feel for Holston to know that this wasn't the case. And then she noticed each trail of activity seemed to lead back to the paragraphs of gibberish, an answer Juliette kept looking for any excuse to reject because she couldn't make sense of it. Why would Holston, and Allison especially, spend so much time looking at all that nonsense? The activity logs showed her keeping them open for hours at a time, as if the scrambled letters and symbols could be read. To Juliette, it looked like a wholly new language.

So what was it that had sent Holston and his wife to cleaning? The common assumption around the silo was that Allison had got the stirs, had gone crazy for the out-of-doors, and that Holston eventually succumbed to his grief. But Juliette had never bought that. She didn't like coincidences. When she tore a machine down to repair it, and a new problem surfaced a few days later, all she usually had to do was go back through the steps from the last repair. The answer was always there. She saw this riddle the same way: it was a much simpler diagnosis if both of them were driven out by the *same thing*.

She just couldn't see what it might be. And part of her feared that finding it could drive her crazy as well.

Juliette rubbed her eyes. When she looked at her desk again, Jahns's folder caught her attention. On top of her folder sat the doctor's report for Marnes. She moved the report aside and reached for the note underneath, the one Marnes had written and left on his small bedside table:

'It should have been me.'

So few words, Juliette thought. But then, who remained in the silo for him to speak to? She studied the handful of words, but there was little to squeeze from them. It was *his* canteen that had been poisoned, not Jahns's. It actually made her death a case of manslaughter, a new term for Juliette. Marnes had explained something else about the law: the worst offence they could hope to pin on anyone was the *attempted* and unsuccessful murder of *him*, rather than the botched accident that had claimed the mayor. Which meant, if they could nail the act on a guilty party, that person could be put to cleaning for what they had *failed* to accomplish with Marnes, while only getting five years' probation and silo service for what had *accidentally* happened to Jahns. Juliette thought it was this crooked sense of fairness as much as anything else that had worn down poor Marnes. There was never any hope for true justice, a life for a life. These strange laws, coupled with the agonising knowledge that he had carried the poison on his own back, had gravely wounded him. He had to live with being the poison's porter, with the hurtful knowledge that a good deed, a shared walk, had been his love's death.

Juliette held the suicide note and cursed herself for not seeing it coming. It should have been a foreseeable breakdown, a problem solved by a little preventive maintenance. She could have said more, reached out somehow. But she had been too busy trying to stay afloat those first few days to see that the man who had brought her to the up top was slowly unravelling right before her eyes.

The flash of her inbox icon interrupted these disturbing thoughts. She reached for the mouse and cursed herself. The large chunk of data she had sent down to Mechanical some hours earlier must've been rejected. Maybe it was too much to send at once. But then she saw that it was a message from Scottie, her friend in IT who had supplied the data drive.

'Come now,' it read.

It was an odd request. Vague and yet dire, especially given the lateness of the hour. Juliette powered down her monitor, grabbed the drive from the computer in case she had more visitors, and briefly considered strapping Marnes's ancient gun around her waist. She stood, went to the key locker, and ran her hand down the soft belt, feeling the indention where the buckle had, for decades, worn into the same spot on the old leather. She thought again of Marnes's terse note and looked at his empty chair. She decided in the end to leave the gun hanging where it was. She nodded to his desk, made sure she had her keys, and hurried out the door.

24

It was thirty-four levels down to IT. Juliette skipped down the steps so swiftly, she had to keep a hand on the inner railing to keep from flying outward into the occasional upbound traffic. She overtook a porter near six, who was startled from being passed. By the tenth floor, she was beginning to feel dizzy from the round and round. She wondered how Holston and Marnes had ever responded to trouble with any degree of urgency. The other two deputy stations, the one in the mids and the one in the down deep, were nicely situated near the dead centre of their forty-eight floors, a far superior arrangement. She passed into the twenties thinking about this: that her office was not ideally positioned to respond to the far edge of her precinct. Instead, it had been located by the airlock and the holding cell, close to the highest form of the silo's capital punishment. She cursed this decision as she considered the long slog back up.

In the high twenties, she practically bowled a man over who wasn't watching where he was going. She wrapped one arm around him and gripped the railing, keeping them both from a nasty tumble. He apologised while she swallowed a curse. And then she saw it was Lukas, his lapboard strapped to his back, nubs of charcoal sticking out of his overalls.

'Oh,' he said. 'Hello.'

He smiled at seeing her, but his lips drooped into a frown when he realised she'd been hurrying in the opposite direction.

'I'm sorry,' she said. 'I've got to go.'

'Of course.'

He stood out of the way, and Juliette finally took her hand

off his ribs. She nodded, not sure what to say, her thoughts only on Scottie, and then she continued her run down, moving too fast to chance a glance back.

When she finally got to thirty-four, she paused on the landing to catch her breath and let the dizziness fade. Checking her overalls – that her star was in place and the flash drive still in her pocket – she pulled open the main doors to IT and tried to stroll in as if she belonged there.

She sized up the entrance room quickly. To her right, a glass window looked into a conference room. The light was on, even though it was now the middle of the night. A handful of heads were visible through the glass, a meeting taking place. She thought she heard Bernard's voice, loud and nasal, leaching through the door.

Ahead of her stood the low security gates leading back to IT's labyrinth of apartments, offices, and workshops. Juliette could imagine the floor plan; she'd heard the three levels shared much in common with Mechanical, only without the fun.

'Can I help you?' a young man in silver overalls asked from behind the gates.

She approached.

'Sheriff Nichols,' she said. She waved her ID at him, then passed it under the gate's laser scanner. The light turned red and the gate let out an angry buzz. It did not open. 'I'm here to see Scottie, one of your techs.' She tried the card again, with the same result.

'Do you have an appointment?' the man asked.

Juliette narrowed her eyes at the man.

'I'm the sheriff. Since when do I need appointments?' Again with the card, and again the gate buzzed at her. The young man did not move to help.

'Please do not do that,' he said.

'Look, son, I'm in the middle of an investigation here. And you're impeding my progress.'

He smiled at her. 'I'm sure you're familiar with the unique position we maintain here and that your powers are—'

Juliette put her ID away and reached over the gate to grab

the straps of his overalls with both hands. She pulled him almost clear over the gates, her arms bulging with the sinewy muscles that had freed countless bolts.

'Listen here, you blasted runt, I'm coming *through* these gates or I'm coming over them and then through *you*. I'll have you know that I report directly to Bernard Holland, acting mayor, and your goddamned boss. Do I make myself clear?'

The kid's eyes were wide and all-pupil. He jerked his chin up and down.

'Then move it,' she said, letting go of his overalls with a shove.

He fumbled for his ID – swiped it through the scanner.

Juliette pushed through the spinning arms of the turnstile and past him. Then stopped.

'Uh, which way, exactly?'

The boy was still trying to get his ID back into his chest pocket, his hand trembling. 'Th-thataway, ma'am.' He pointed to the right. 'Second hall, take a left. Last office.'

'Good man,' she said. She turned and smiled to herself. It seemed that the same tone that got bickering mechanics to snap-to back home worked here just as well. And she laughed to herself to think of the argument she had used: your boss is also my boss, so open up. But then, with eyes that wide and that much fear in his veins, she could've read him Mama Jean's bread recipe in the same tone and got through the gates.

She took the second hallway, passing by a man and woman in IT silver as they walked the other way. They turned to watch her pass. At the end of the hall, she found offices on both sides and didn't know which one was Scottie's. She peeked first into the one with the open door, but the lights were off. She turned to the other one and knocked.

There was no answer at first, but the light at the bottom of the door dimmed, as if someone had walked across it.

'Who's there?' a familiar voice whispered through the door.

'Open this damn thing,' Juliette said. 'You know who this is.'

The lever dipped, the door clicking open. Juliette pushed her way inside, and Scottie shoved the door closed behind her, engaging the lock.

'Were you seen?' he asked.

She looked at him incredulously. 'Was I seen? Of *course* I was seen. How do you think I got in? There're people everywhere.'

'But did they see you come in *here*?' he whispered.

'Scottie, what the hell is going on?' Juliette was beginning to suspect she had hurried all this way for nothing. 'You sent me a wire, which already seemed desperate enough, but you told me to come now. So here I am.'

'Where did you get this stuff?' he asked. Scottie grabbed a spool of printout from his desk and held it in trembling hands.

Juliette stepped beside him. She placed a hand on his arm and looked at the paper. 'Just calm down,' she said quietly. She tried to read a few lines and immediately recognised the gibberish she had sent to Mechanical earlier that day.

'How did you get this?' she asked. 'I just wired this to Knox a few hours ago.'

Scottie nodded. 'And he wired it to me. But he shouldn't have. I can get into a lot of trouble for this.'

Juliette laughed. 'You're kidding, right?'

She saw that he wasn't.

'Scottie, you're the one who pulled all this stuff for me in the first place.' She stepped back and looked hard at him. 'Wait, you know what this nonsense is, right? You can read it?'

He bobbed his head. 'Jules, I didn't know what I was grabbing for you at the time. It was gigs of crap. I didn't look at it. I just grabbed it and passed it on—'

'Why is this so dangerous?' she asked.

'I can't even talk about it,' Scottie said. 'I'm not cleaning material, Jules. I'm not.' He held out the scroll. 'Here. I shouldn't have even printed it, but I wanted to delete the wire. You've got to take it. Get it out of here. I can't be caught with it.'

Juliette took the scroll, but just to calm him down. 'Scottie, sit down. Please. Look, I know you're scared, but I need you to sit and talk to me about this. It's very important.'

He shook his head.

'Scottie, sit the hell down right now.' She pointed at the chair, and Scottie numbly obeyed. Juliette sat on the corner of his desk and noted that the cot at the back of the room had been recently slept on, and felt pity for the young man.

'Whatever this is' – she shook the roll of paper – 'it's what caused the last two cleanings.'

She told him this like it was more than a rapidly forming theory, like it was something she knew. Maybe it was the fear in his eyes that cemented the idea, or the need to act strong and sure to help calm him. 'Scottie, I need to know what it is. Look at me.'

He did.

'Do you see this star?' She flicked it with her finger, causing a dull ring.

He nodded.

'I'm not your shift foreman any more, lad. I'm the law, and this is very important. Now, I don't know if you're aware of this, but you can't get into any trouble for answering my questions. In fact, you're obliged to answer them.'

He looked up at her with a twinge of hope. He obviously didn't know that she was making this up. Not lying – she would never turn Scottie in for all the silo – but she was pretty sure there was no such thing as immunity, not for anyone.

'What am I holding?' she asked, waving the scroll of printout.

'It's a program,' he whispered.

'You mean like a timing circuit? Like a—'

'No, for a computer. A programming language. It's a . . .' He looked away. 'I don't want to say. Oh, Jules, I just want to go back to Mechanical. I want none of this to have happened.'

These words were like a splash of cold water. Scottie was more than frightened – he was terrified. For his *life*. Juliette got off the desk and crouched beside him, placed her hand on the back of his hand, which rested on his anxiously bouncing knee.

'What does the program do?' she asked.

He bit his lip and shook his head.

'It's okay. We're safe here. Tell me what it does.'

'It's for a display,' he finally said. 'But not for like a readout, or an LED, or a dot matrix. There are algorithms in here I recognise. Anyone would . . .'

He paused.

'Sixty-four-bit colour,' he whispered, staring at her. 'Sixty-four-bit. Why would anyone need that much *colour*?'

'Dumb it down for me,' Juliette said. Scottie seemed on the verge of going mad.

'You've seen it, right? The view up top?'

She dipped her head. 'You know where I work.'

'Well, I've seen it too, back before I started eating every meal in here, working my fingers to the bone.' He rubbed his hands up through his shaggy, sandy-brown hair. 'This program, Jules – what you've got, it could make something like that wall screen look *real*.'

Juliette digested this, then laughed. 'But wait, isn't that what it does? Scottie, there are sensors out there. They just take the images they see, and then the screen has to display the view, right? I mean, you've got me confused, here.' She shook the printed scroll of gibberish. 'Doesn't this just do what I think it does? Put that image on the display?'

Scottie wrung his hands together. 'You wouldn't need anything like this. You're talking about passing an image *through*. I could write a dozen lines of code to do that. No, this, this is about *making* images. It's more complex.'

He grabbed Juliette's arm.

'Jules, this thing can make brand-new views. It can show you anything you *like*.'

He sucked in his breath, and a slice of time hung in the air between them, a pause where hearts did not beat and eyes did not blink.

Juliette sat back on her haunches, balancing on the toes of her old boots. She finally settled her butt on the floor and leaned back against the metal panelling of his office wall.

'So now you see—' Scottie started to say, but Juliette held up her hand, hushing him. It never occurred to her that the view could be fabricated. But why not? And what would be the point?

She imagined Holston's wife discovering this. She must've been at least as smart as Scottie – she was the one who came up with the technique he had used to find this in the first place, right? What would she have done with this discovery? Say something out loud and cause a riot? Tell her husband, the sheriff? What?

Juliette could know only what she herself would do in that position, if she were almost convinced. She was by nature too curious a person to doubt what she might do. It would gnaw at her, like the rattling innards of a sealed machine, or the secret workings of an unopened device. She would have to grab a screwdriver and a wrench and have a peek . . .

'Jules—'

She waved him off. Details from Holston's folder flooded back. Notes about Allison, how she suddenly went crazy, almost out of nowhere. Her curiosity must have driven her there. Unless – unless Holston didn't know. Unless it was all an act. Unless Allison had been shielding her husband from some horror with a mock veil of insanity.

But would it have taken Holston three years to piece together what she had figured out in a *week*? Or did he already know and it just took three years to summon the courage to go after her? Or did Juliette have an advantage he didn't? She had Scottie. And she was, after all, following the breadcrumbs of someone else following more breadcrumbs, a much easier and more obvious trail.

She looked up at her young friend, who was peering worriedly down at her.

'You have to get those out of here,' he said, glancing at the printouts.

Juliette nodded. She pushed up from the floor and tucked the scroll into the breast of her overalls. It would have to be destroyed; she just wasn't sure how.

'I deleted my copies of everything I got for you,' he said. 'I'm done looking at them. And you should do the same.'

Juliette tapped her chest pocket, felt the hard bulge of the flash drive there.

'And Jules, can you do me a favour?'

'Anything.'

'See if there's any way I can transfer back to Mechanical, will you? I don't want to be up here any more.'

She nodded and squeezed his shoulder. 'I'll see what I can do,' she promised, feeling a knot in her gut for getting the poor kid involved at all.

25

The next morning, exhausted, Juliette arrived late at her desk, her legs and back sore from the late climb down to IT and from not getting an ounce of sleep. She had spent the entire night tossing and turning, wondering if she'd discovered a box that was better left unopened, worried she might be raising questions that promised nothing but bad answers. If she went out into the cafeteria and looked in a direction she normally avoided, she would be able to see the last two cleaners lying in the crook of a hill, almost as if in one another's arms. Did those two lovers throw themselves into the rotting wind over the very thing Juliette was now chasing? The fear she'd seen in Scottie's eyes made her wonder if she wasn't being careful enough. She looked across her desk at her new deputy, greener even at this job than she, as he transcribed data from one of the folders.

'Hey, Peter?'

He looked up from his keyboard. 'Yeah?'

'You were in Justice before this, right? Shadowing a judge?'

He tilted his head to the side. 'No, I was a court assistant. I actually shadowed in the mids' deputy office until a few years ago. I wanted that job, but none came up.'

'Did you grow up there? Or the up top?'

'The mids.' His hands fell away from his keyboard to his lap. He smiled. 'My dad was a plumber in the hydroponics. He passed away a few years ago. My mom, she works in the nursery.'

'Really? What's her name?'

'Rebecca. She's one of the—'

'I know her. She was shadowing when I was a kid. My father—'

'He works in the upper nursery, I know. I didn't want to say anything—'

'Why not? Hey, if you're worried about me playing favourites, I'm guilty. You're my deputy now, and I'll have your back.'

'No, it's not that. I just didn't want you to hold anything against me. I know you and your father don't—'

Juliette waved him off. 'He's still my father. We just grew apart. Tell your mom I said hi.'

'I will.' Peter smiled and bent over his keyboard.

'Hey. I've got a question for you. Something I can't figure.'

'Sure,' he said, looking up. 'Go ahead.'

'Can you think of why it's cheaper to porter a paper note to someone than it is to just wire them from a computer?'

'Oh, sure.' He nodded. 'It's a quarter chit per character to wire someone. That adds up!'

Juliette laughed. 'No, I know what it costs. But paper isn't cheap, either. And neither is porting. But it seems like sending a wire would be practically free, you know? It's just information. It weighs nothing.'

He shrugged. 'It's been a quarter chit a character since I've been alive. I dunno. Besides, we've got a fifty-chit-per-day allowance from here, plus unlimited emergencies. I wouldn't stress.'

'I'm not stressed, just confused. I mean, I understand why everyone can't have radios like we carry, because only one person can transmit at a time, so we need the air open for emergencies, but you'd think we could all send and receive as many wires as we wanted.'

Peter propped his elbows up and rested his chin on his fists. 'Well, think about the cost of the servers, the electricity. That means oil to burn and all the maintenance of the wires and cooling and what-not. Especially if you have a ton of traffic. Factor that against pressing pulp on a rack, letting it dry, scratching some ink on it, and then having a person who's already heading that way walk it up or down for you. No wonder it's cheaper!'

Juliette nodded, but mostly for his benefit. She wasn't so sure. She hated to voice why, but she couldn't help herself.

'But what if it's for a different reason? What if someone made it expensive on *purpose?*'

'What? To make money?' Peter snapped his fingers. 'To keep the porters employed with running notes!'

Juliette shook her head. 'No, what if it's to make conversing with each other more difficult? Or at least costly. You know, separate us, make us keep our thoughts to ourselves.'

Peter frowned. 'Why would anyone want to do that?'

Shrugging, Juliette looked back at her computer screen, her hand creeping to the scroll hidden in her lap. She reminded herself that she no longer lived among people she could implicitly trust. 'I don't know,' she said. 'Forget about it. It's just a silly thought.'

She pulled her keyboard towards her and was just glancing up at her screen when Peter saw the emergency icon first.

'Wow. Another alert,' he said.

She started to click on the flashing icon, heard Peter blow out his breath.

'What the hell's going on around here?' he asked.

She pulled the message up on her screen and read it quickly, disbelieving what she was seeing. Surely this wasn't the way of the job. Surely people didn't die this often. Had she simply not heard about it before, with her nose always buried in some crankcase or under an oil pan?

The blinking number code above the message was one she recognised without even needing her cheat sheet. It was becoming sadly familiar. Another suicide. They didn't give the victim's name, but there was an office number. And she knew the floor and address. Her legs were still sore from her trip down there.

'No—' she said, gripping the edge of her desk.

'You want me to—?' Peter reached for his radio.

'No, dammit, no.' Juliette shook her head. She pushed herself away from her desk, knocking over the recycling bin, which spilled all the pardoned folders across the floor. The scroll from her lap rolled into them.

'I can—' Peter began.

'I got this,' she said, waving him away. 'Dammit.' She shook her head. The office was spinning around her head, the world getting blurry. She staggered for the door, arms wide for balance, when Peter snapped back to his computer screen, dragging his mouse with its little cord behind, clicking something.

'Uh, Juliette—?'

But she was already stumbling out the door, bracing herself for the long and painful descent.

'Juliette!'

She turned to find Peter running behind her, his hand steadying the radio attached to his hip.

'What?' she asked.

'I'm sorry . . . It's . . . I don't know how to do this—'

'Spit it out,' she said impatiently. All she could think of was little Scottie, hanging by his neck. It was electrical ties in her imagination. That's how her waking nightmare, her morbid thoughts, crafted the scene of his death in her head.

'It's just that I got a private wire and—'

'Keep up if you want, but I've got to get down there.' She spun towards the stairwell.

Peter grabbed her arm. Roughly. A forceful grip.

'I'm sorry, ma'am, but I'm supposed to take you into custody—'

She whirled on him and saw how unsure of himself he looked.

'What did you say?'

'I'm just doing my duty, Sheriff, I swear.' Peter reached for his metal cuffs.

Juliette stared at him, disbelieving, as he snapped one link around her wrist and fumbled for the other.

'Peter, what's going on? I've got a friend I need to see to . . .'

He shook his head. 'The computer says you're a suspect, ma'am. I'm just doing what it tells me to do.'

And with that, the second link clicked around her other wrist and Juliette looked down at her predicament, dumbfounded, the image of her young friend hanging by his neck unable to be shaken loose from her mind.

26

She was allowed a visitor, but who would Juliette want to see her like this? No one. So she sat with her back against the bars, the bleak view outside brightening with the rising of an unseen sun, the floor around her bare of folders and ghosts. She was alone, stripped of a job she wasn't sure she had ever wanted, a pile of bodies in her wake, her simple and easily understood life having come unravelled.

'I'm sure this will pass,' a voice behind her said. Juliette leaned away from the steel rods and looked around to find Bernard standing behind her, his hands wrapped around the bars.

Juliette moved away from him and sat on the cot, turning her back to the grey view.

'You know I didn't do this,' she said. 'He was my friend.'

Bernard frowned. 'What do you think you're being held for? The boy committed suicide. He seems to have been distraught from recent tragedies. This is not unheard of when people move to a new section of the silo, away from friends and family, to take a job they're not entirely suited for—'

'Then why am I being held here?' Juliette asked. She realised suddenly that there may be no double cleaning after all. Off to the side, down the hallway, she could see Peter shuffling back and forth as if a physical barrier prevented him from coming any closer.

'Unauthorised entry on the thirty-fourth,' Bernard said. 'Threatening a member of the silo, tampering with IT affairs, removing IT property from secured quarters—'

'That's ratshit,' Juliette said. 'I was summoned by one of your workers. I had every right to be there!'

'We will look into that,' Bernard said. 'Well, Peter here will. I'm afraid he's had to remove your computer for evidence. My people down below are best qualified to see if—'

'*Your* people? Are you trying to be mayor or IT head? Because I looked into it, and the Pact clearly states you can't be both—'

'That will be put to a vote soon enough. The Pact has changed before. It's designed to change when events call for it.'

'And so you want me out of the way.' Juliette stepped closer to the bars so she could see Peter Billings, and have him see her. 'I suppose you were to have this job all along? Is that right?'

Peter slunk out of sight.

'Juliette. Jules.' Bernard shook his head and clicked his tongue at her. 'I don't want you out of the way. I wouldn't want that for any member of the silo. I want people to be in their *place*. Where they fit in. Scottie wasn't cut out for IT. I see that now. And I don't think you were meant for the up top.'

'So, what, I'm banished back to Mechanical? Is that what's going on? Over some ratshit charges?'

'Banished is such a horrible word. I'm sure you didn't mean that. And don't you want your old job back? Weren't you happier then? There's so much to learn up here that you've never shadowed for. And the people who thought you best fit for this job, who I'm sure hoped to ease you into it . . .'

He stopped right there, and it was somehow worse that he left the sentence hanging like that, forcing Jules to complete the image rather than just hear it. She pictured two mounds of freshly turned soil in the gardens, a few mourning rinds tossed on top of them.

'I'm going to let you gather your things, what isn't needed for evidence, and then allow you to see yourself back down. As long as you check in with my deputies on the way and report your progress, we'll drop these charges. Consider it an extension of my little . . . *forgiveness* holiday.'

Bernard smiled and straightened his glasses.

Juliette gritted her teeth. It occurred to her that she had never, in her entire life, punched someone in the face.

And it was only her fear of missing, of not doing it correctly and cracking her knuckles on one of the steel bars, that stopped her from putting an end to that streak.

It was just about a week since she had arrived at the up top, and Juliette was leaving with fewer belongings than she'd brought. A blue Mechanical overall had been provided, one much too big for her. Peter didn't even say goodbye – Juliette thought more from shame than anger or blame. He walked her through the cafeteria to the top of the stairs, and as she turned to shake his hand, she found him staring down at his toes, his thumbs caught in his overalls, her sheriff's badge pinned at an angle over his left breast.

Juliette began her long walk down through the length of the silo. It would be less physically taxing than her walk up had been, but more draining in other ways. What exactly had happened to the silo, and why? She couldn't help but feel in the middle of it all, to shoulder some of the blame. None of this would have happened had they left her in Mechanical, had they never come to see her in the first place. She would still be bitching about the alignment of the generator, not sleeping at night as she waited for the inevitable failure and a descent into chaos as they learned to survive on backup power for the decades it would take to rebuild the thing. Instead, she had been witness to a different type of failure: a throwing not of switches but of bodies. She felt the worst for poor Scottie, a boy with so much promise, so many talents, gone before his prime.

She had been sheriff for a short time, a star appearing on her breast for but a wink, and yet she felt an incredible urge to investigate Scottie's death. There was something not right about the boy killing himself. The signs were there, sure. He had been afraid to leave his office – but then, he'd also shadowed under Walker and had maybe picked up the habit of reclusiveness from the old man. Scottie had also been harbouring secrets too big for his young mind, had been fearful enough to wire her to come quickly – but she knew him like her own shadow, and knew he didn't have it in him. She suddenly wondered if Marnes had ever had it in him as well. If Jahns were here beside her, would the old mayor be screaming for Jules to investigate both their deaths? Telling her that none of this fitted?

'I can't,' Juliette whispered to the ghost, causing an upbound porter to turn his head as he passed.

She kept further thoughts to herself. As she descended towards her father's nursery, she paused at the landing, contemplating longer and harder about going in to see him than she had on her way up. Pride had prevented her the first time. And now shame set her feet into motion once again as she spiralled down away from him, chastising herself for thinking on the ghosts from her past that had long ago been banished from memory.

At the thirty-fourth, the entrance to IT, she again considered stopping. There would be clues in Scottie's office, maybe even some they hadn't managed to scrub away. She shook her head. The conspiracies were already forming in her mind. And as hard as it was to leave the scene of the crime behind, she knew she wouldn't be allowed anywhere near his office.

She continued down the staircase and thought, as she considered IT's location in the silo, that this couldn't be an accident either. She had another thirty-two floors to go before she checked in with the first deputy, who was located near the centre of the mids. The sheriff's office was thirty-three floors above her head. IT, then, was as far as it could get from any deputy station in the silo.

She shook her head at this paranoid thinking. It wasn't how diagnoses were made. Her father would have told her so.

After meeting with the first deputy around noon, and accepting a piece of bread and fruit, along with a reminder to eat, she made good time down through the mids, wondering as she passed the upper apartments which level Lukas lived on, or if he even knew of her arrest.

The weight of the past week seemed to pull her down the stairwell, gravity sucking at her boots, the pressures of being sheriff dissipating as she left that office far behind. Those pressures were slowly replaced with an eagerness to return to her friends, even in shame, as she got closer and closer to Mechanical.

She stopped to see Hank, the down-deep deputy, on level one-twenty. She had known him for a long time, was becoming surrounded with familiar faces, people who waved hello, their moods sombre as if they knew every detail of her time away. Hank tried to get her to stay and rest a while, but she only paused long enough to be polite, to refill her canteen, and then to shuffle the remaining twenty floors to the place she truly belonged.

Knox seemed thrilled to have her back. He wrapped her up in a crippling hug, lifting her feet off the ground and roughing up her face with his beard. He smelled of grease and sweat, a mix Juliette had never fully noticed in the down deep because she had never been free from it.

The walk to her old room was punctuated by slaps on her back, well wishes, questions about the up top, people calling her sheriff in jest, and the sort of rude frivolities she had grown up in and grown used to. Juliette felt more saddened by it all than anything. She had set out to do something and had failed. And yet her friends were just happy to have her back.

Shirly from second shift spotted her coming down the hallway and accompanied Juliette on the rest of the walk to her room. She updated Juliette on the status of the generator and the output from the new oil well, as if Juliette had simply been on vacation for a short while. Juliette thanked her at the door to her room, stepped inside, and kicked her way through all the folded notes slipped under the door. She lifted the strap of her daypack over her head and dropped it, then collapsed onto her bed, too exhausted and upset at herself to even cry.

She awoke in the middle of the night. Her small display terminal showed the time in green blocky numbers: 2.14 a.m.

Juliette sat at the edge of her old bed in overalls that weren't truly hers and took stock of her situation. Her life was not yet over, she decided. It just felt that way. Tomorrow, even if they didn't expect her to, she would be back at work in the pits, keeping the silo humming, doing what she did best. She needed to wake up to this reality, to set other ideas and responsibilities aside. Already, they felt so far away. She doubted she would even go to Scottie's funeral, not unless they sent his body down to be buried where it belonged.

She reached for the keyboard slotted into the wall rack. Everything was covered in a layer of grime, she saw. She had never noticed it before. The keys were filthy from the dirt she had brought back from each shift. The monitor's glass was limned with grease. She fought the urge to wipe the screen and smear the shiny coat of oil around, but she would have to clean her place a little deeper, she decided. She was viewing things with untainted and more critical eyes.

Rather than chase pointless sleep, she keyed the monitor awake to check the work logs for the next day, anything to get her mind off the past week. But before she could open her task manager, she saw that she had over a dozen wires in her inbox. She'd never seen so many. Usually people just slid recycled notes under each other's doors – but then, she had been a long way away when the news of her arrest had hit, and she hadn't been able to get to a computer since.

She logged onto her email account and pulled up the most recent wire. It was from Knox. Just a semicolon and a parenthesis – a half-chit smile.

Juliette couldn't help it, she smiled back. She could still smell Knox on her skin and realised, as far as the big brute was concerned, that all the troubles and problems percolating in whispers down the stairwell about her paled in comparison to her return. To him, the worst thing that had happened in the last week was probably the challenge of replacing her on first shift.

Jules went to the next message, one from the third-shift foreman welcoming her home – probably because of the extra time his crew was putting in to help cover her old shift.

There was more. A day's pay of a note from Shirly, wishing her well on her journey. These were all notes they had hoped she would receive up top, to make the trip down easier, hoping she wouldn't loathe herself or feel humiliated, or even a failure. Juliette felt tears well up at how considerate it all was. She had an image of her desk, Holston's desk, with nothing but unplugged wires snaking across its surface, her computer removed. There was no way she could've got these messages when they were meant to be read. She wiped her eyes and tried not to think of the wired notes as money wasted, but rather as extravagant tokens of her friendships in the down deep.

Reading each one, trying to hold it together, made the last message she came to doubly jarring. It was paragraphs long. Juliette assumed it was an official document, maybe a list of her offences, a formal ruling against her. She had seen such messages only from the mayor's office, usually on holidays, notes that went out to every silo member. But then she saw that it was from Scottie.

Juliette sat up straight and tried to clear her head. She started from the beginning, damning her blurred vision.

J--

    I lied. Couldn't delete this stuff. Found more. That tape I got you? Your joke was truth. And the program -- NOT for big screen. Pxl density not right. 32,768 x 8,192! Not sure what's that size. 8" x 2"? So many pxls if so.

    Putting more together. Don't trust porters, so wiring this. Screw cost, wire me back. Need transfr to Mech. Not safe here.

    --S

Juliette read it a second time, crying now. Here was the real voice of a ghost warning her of something, all of it too late. And it wasn't the voice of someone who was planning his own death – she was sure of that. She checked the timestamp of the wire; it was sent before she had even arrived back at her office the day before, before Scottie had died.

Before he had been *killed*, she corrected herself. They must have found him snooping, or maybe her visit had alerted them. She wondered what IT could see, if they could break into her wire account, even. They must not have yet, or the message wouldn't be there, waiting for her.

She leaped suddenly from her bed and grabbed one of the folded notes by the door. Digging a charcoal from her daypack, she sat back down on the bed. She copied the entire wire, every odd spelling, double-checking each number, and then deleted the message. She had chills up and down her arms by the time she finished, as if some unseen person was racing towards her, hoping to break into her computer before she dispensed with the evidence. She wondered if Scottie had been cautious enough to have deleted the note from his sent wires, and assumed, if he'd been thinking clearly, that he would.

She sat back on her bed, holding the copied note, thoughts about the work log for the next day gone. Instead, she studied the sinister mess revolving around her, spiralling through the heart of the silo. Things were bad, from top to bottom. A great set of gears had been thrown out of alignment. She could hear the noise from the past week, this thumping and clanging, this machine lumbering off its mounts and leaving bodies in its wake.

And Juliette was the only one who could hear it. She was the only one who knew. And she didn't know who she could trust to help set things right. But she did know this: it would require a diminishing of power to align things once again. And there would be no way to call what happened next a 'holiday'.

27

Juliette showed up at Walker's electronics workshop at five, worried she might find him asleep on his cot, but smelling instead the distinctive odour of vaporised solder wafting down the hallway. She knocked on the open door as she entered, and Walker looked up from one of his many green electronics boards, corkscrews of smoke rising from the tip of his soldering iron.

'Jules!' he shouted. He lifted the magnifying lens off his grey head and set it and the soldering iron down on the steel workbench. 'I heard you were back. I meant to send a note, but . . .' He waved around at the piles of parts with their work-order tags dangling from strings. 'Super busy,' he explained.

'Forget it,' she said. She gave Walker a hug, smelling the electrical fire scent on his skin that reminded her so much of him. And of Scottie.

'I'm going to feel guilty enough taking some of your time with this,' she said.

'Oh?' He stepped back and studied her, his bushy white brows and wrinkled skin furrowed with worry. 'You got something for me?' He looked her up and down for something broken, a habit formed from a lifetime of being brought small devices that needed repairing.

'I actually just wanted to pick your brain.' She sat down on one of his workbench stools, and Walker did the same.

'Go ahead,' he said. He wiped his brow with the back of his sleeve, and Juliette saw how old Walker had become. She remembered him without so much white in his hair, without the wrinkles and splotchy skin. She remembered him with his shadow.

'It has to do with Scottie,' she warned him.

Walker turned his head to the side and nodded. He tried to say something, tapped his fist against his chest a few times and cleared his throat. 'Damn shame,' was all he could manage. He peered down at the floor for a moment.

'It can wait,' Juliette told him. 'If you need time—'

'I *convinced* him to take that job,' Walker said, shaking his head. 'I remember when the offer came, being scared he'd turn it down. Because of me, you know? That he'd be too afraid of me bein' upset at him for leaving, that he might just stay for ever, so I urged him to take it.' He looked up at her, his eyes shining. 'I just wanted him to know he was free to choose. I didn't mean to push him away.'

'You didn't,' Juliette said. 'Nobody thinks that, and neither should you.'

'I just don't figure he was happy up there. That weren't his home.'

'Well, he was too smart for us. Don't forget that. We always said that.'

'He loved you,' Walker said, and wiped his eyes. 'Damn, how that boy looked up to you.'

Juliette felt her own tears welling up again. She reached into her pocket and brought out the wire she'd transcribed onto the back of the note. She had to remind herself why she was there, to hold it together.

'Just don't seem like him to take the easy way—' Walker muttered.

'No, it doesn't,' she said. 'Walker, I need to discuss some things with you that can't leave this room.'

He laughed. Mostly, it seemed, to keep from sobbing. 'Like I ever leave this room,' he said.

'Well, it can't be discussed with anyone else. No one. Okay?'

He bobbed his head.

'I don't think Scottie killed himself.'

Walker threw up his hands to cover his face. He bent forward and shook as he started to cry. Juliette got off her stool and went to him, put her arm around his trembling back.

'I knew it,' he sobbed into his palms. 'I knew it, I knew it.' He looked up at her, tears coursing through several days of white stubble. 'Who did this? They'll pay, won't they? Tell me who did it, Jules.'

'Whoever it was, I don't think they had far to travel,' she said.

'IT? Goddamn them.'

'Walker, I need your help sorting this out. Scottie sent me a wire not long before he . . . well, before I think he was killed.'

'Sent you a wire?'

'Yeah. Look, I met with him earlier that day. He asked me to come down to see him.'

'Down to IT?'

She nodded. 'I'd found something in the last sheriff's computer—'

'Holston.' He dipped his head. 'The last cleaner. Yeah, Knox brought me something from you. A program, looked like. I told him Scottie would know better than anyone, so we forwarded it along.'

'Well, you were right.'

Walker wiped his cheeks and bobbed his head. 'He was smarter than any of us.'

'I know. He told me this thing, that it was a program, one that made very detailed images. Like the images we see of the outside—'

She waited a beat to see how he would respond. It was taboo even to use the word in most settings. Walker was unmoved. As she had hoped, he was old enough to be beyond childhood fears – and probably lonely and sad enough not to have cared anyway.

'But this wire he sent, it says something about p-x-l's being too dense.' She showed him the copy she'd made. Walker grabbed his magnifiers and slipped the band over his forehead.

'Pixels,' he said, sniffing. 'He's talking about the little dots that make up an image. Each one is a pixel.' He took the note from her and read some more. 'He says it's not safe there.' Walker rubbed his chin and shook his head. 'Damn them.'

'Walker, what kind of screen would be eight inches by two inches?' Juliette looked around at all the boards, displays, and coils of loose wire strewn about his workshop. 'Do you have anything like that?'

'Eight by two? Maybe a readout, like on the front of a server or something. Be the right size to show a few lines of text, internal temps, clock cycles . . .' He shook his head. 'But you'd never make one with this kind of pixel density. Even if it were possible, it wouldn't make sense. Your eye couldn't make out one pixel from its neighbour if it were right at the end of your nose.'

He rubbed his stubble and studied the note some more. 'What's this nonsense about the tape and the joke? What's that mean?'

Juliette stood beside him and looked over the note. 'I've been wondering about that. He must mean the heat tape he scored for me a while back.'

'I think I remember something about that.'

'Well, do you remember the problems we had with it? The exhaust we wrapped it in almost caught fire. The stuff was complete crap. I think he sent a note asking if the tape had gotten here okay, and I sorta recall writing back that it did, and thanks, but the tape couldn't have self-destructed better if it'd been *engineered* to.'

'That was your joke?' Walker swivelled in his stool and rested his elbows on the workbench. He kept peering over the copied charcoal letters like they were the face of Scottie, his little shadow coming back one last time to tell him something important.

'And he says my joke was truth,' Juliette said. 'I've been up the last three hours thinking about this, dying to talk to someone.'

Walker looked back over his shoulder at her, his eyebrows raised.

'I'm not a sheriff, Walk. Never born to be one. Shouldn't have gone. But I know, as sure as everyone, that what I'm about to say should send me to cleaning . . .'

Walker immediately slid off his stool and walked away from her. Juliette damned herself for coming, for opening her mouth, for not just clocking into first shift and saying to hell with it all—

Walker shut the door to his workshop and locked it. He

looked at her and lifted a finger, went to his air compressor and pulled out a hose. Then he flipped the unit on so the motor would start to build up pressure, which just leaked out the open nozzle in a steady, noisy hiss. He returned to the bench, the clatter from the noisy compressor engine awful, and sat down. His wide eyes begged her to continue.

'There's a hill up there with a crook in it,' she told him, having to raise her voice a little. 'I don't know how long it's been since you've seen this hill, but there are two bodies nestled together in it, man and wife. If you look hard, you can see a dozen shapes like this all over the landscape, all the cleaners, all in various states of decay. Most are gone, of course. Rotted to dust over the long years.'

Walker shook his head at the image she was forming.

'How many years have they been improving these suits so the cleaners have a chance? Hundreds?'

He nodded.

'And yet nobody gets any further. And never once have they *not* had enough time to clean.'

Walker looked up and met her gaze. 'Your joke is truth,' he said. 'The heat tape. It's engineered to fail.'

Juliette pursed her lips. 'That's what I'm thinking. But not just the tape. Remember those seals from a few years back? The ones from IT that went into the water pumps, that were delivered to us by accident?'

'So we've been making fun of IT for being fools and dull-ards—'

'But *we're* the fools,' Juliette said. And it felt so damned good to say it to another human being. So good for these new ideas of hers to swim in the air. And she knew she was right about the cost of sending wires, that they didn't want people talking. Thinking was fine; they would bury you with your thoughts. But no collaboration, no groups coordinating together, no exchange of ideas.

'You think they have us down here to be near the oil?' she asked Walker. 'I don't think so. Not any more. I think they're keeping anyone with a lick of mechanical sense as far from them as possible. There're two supply chains, two sets of parts being made, all in complete secrecy. And who questions them? Who would risk being put to cleaning?'

'You think they killed Scottie?' he asked.

Juliette nodded. 'Walk, I think it's worse than that.' She leaned closer, the compressor rattling, the hiss of released air filling the room. 'I think they kill *everybody*.'

28

J uliette reported to first shift at six, the conversation with Walker playing over and over in her head. There was a sustained and embarrassing applause from the handful of techs present as she entered dispatch. Knox just glared at her from the corner, back to his gruff demeanour. He had already welcomed her home, and was damned if he'd do it again.

She said hello to the people she hadn't seen the night before, and looked over the job queue. The words on the board made sense, but she had a difficult time processing them. In the back of her mind, she thought about poor Scottie, confused and struggling while someone much larger than him – or several someones – choked him to death. She thought of his little body, probably riddled with evidence but soon to feed the roots of the dirt farms. She thought of a married couple lying together on a hill, never given a chance to make it any further, to see beyond the horizon.

She chose a job from the queue, one that would require little mental exertion on her part, and thought of poor Jahns and Marnes and how tragic their love – if she had been reading Marnes correctly – had been. The temptation to tell the entire room was crippling. She looked around at Megan and Ricks, at Jenkins and Marck, and thought about the small army of tight brotherhood she could form. The silo was rotten to the core; an evil man was acting mayor; a puppet stood where a good sheriff had been; and all the good men and women were gone.

It was comical to imagine: her rallying a band of mechanics to storm the upper levels and right a wrong. And then what? Was *this* the uprising they had learned about as children? Was this how it began? One silly woman with fire in her blood stirring the hearts of a legion of fools?

She kept her mouth shut and made her way to the pump room, riding the flow of morning mechanics, thinking more about what she should be doing above than on what needed repairing below. She descended one of the side stairwells, stopped by the tool room to check out a kit bag, and lugged the heavy satchel to one of the deep pits where pumps ran constantly to keep the deep silo from filling halfway up with water.

Caryl, a transfer from third shift, was already working near the pit basin patching rotten cement. She waved with her trowel, and Juliette dipped her chin and forced herself to smile.

The offending pump sat idle on one wall, the backup pump beside it struggling mightily and spraying water out of dry and cracked seals. Juliette looked into the basin to gauge the height of the water. A painted '9' was just visible above its murky surface. Juliette did some quick maths, knowing the diameter of the basin and it being almost nine feet full. The good news was they had at least a day before boots were getting wet. Worst case, they would replace the pump with a rebuilt one from spares and deal with Hendricks bitching at them for checking it out instead of fixing what they already had.

As she began stripping the failed pump down, pelted with spray from its smaller, leaking neighbour, Juliette considered her life with this new perspective provided by the morning's revelations. The silo was something she had always taken for granted. The priests said it had always been here, that it was lovingly created by a caring God, that everything they would ever need had been provided for. Juliette had a hard time with this story. A few years ago, she had been on the first team to drill past 10,000 feet and hit new oil reserves. She had a sense of the size and scope of the world below them. And then she had seen with her own eyes the view of the outside with its phantom-like sheets of smoke they called clouds rolling by at miraculous heights. She had even seen a star, which Lukas thought stood an inconceivable distance away. What god would make so much rock below and air above and just a measly silo between?

And then there was the rotting skyline and the images in the children's books, both of which seemed to hold clues. The priests, of course, would say that the skyline was evidence that man wasn't supposed to exceed his bounds. And the books with the faded colour pages? The fanciful imagination of authors, a class done away with for all the trouble they inspired.

But Juliette didn't see fanciful imagination in those books. She had spent a childhood in the nursery, reading each one over and over whenever they weren't checked out, and things in them and in the wondrous plays performed in the bazaar made more sense to her than this crumbling cylinder in which they lived.

She wiggled the last of the water hoses free and began separating the pump from its motor. The steel shavings suggested a chewed-up impeller, which meant pulling the shaft. As she worked on automatic, cruising through a job she'd performed numerous times before, she thought back on the myriad of animals that populated those books, most of which had never been seen by living eyes. The only fanciful part, she figured, was that they all talked and acted human. There were mice and chickens in several of the books that performed these stunts as well, and she knew their breeds were incapable of speech. All those other animals must exist somewhere, or used to. She felt this to the core, maybe because they didn't seem that fantastical. Each seemed to follow the same plan, just like all the silo's pumps. You could tell one was based on the other. A particular design worked, and whoever had made one had made them all.

The silo made less sense. It hadn't been created by a god – it was probably designed by IT. This was a new theory, but she felt more and more sure of it. They controlled all the important parts. Cleaning was the highest law and the deepest religion, and both of these were intertwined and housed within its secretive walls. And then there was the spacing from Mechanical and the spread of the deputy stations – more clues. Not to mention the clauses in the Pact, which practically granted them immunity. And now the discovery of a second supply chain, a series of parts engineered to fail, a reason behind the lack of progress in prolonging survival time on the outside. IT had built this place and IT was keeping them there.

Juliette nearly stripped a bolt, she was so agitated. She turned to look for Caryl, but the younger woman was already gone, her repair patch a darker shade of grey as it waited to dry and blend in with the rest. Looking up, Juliette scanned the ceiling of the pump room where conduits of wire and piping travelled through the walls and mingled overhead. A run of steam pipes stood clustered to the side to keep from melting any of the wires; a ribbon of heat tape hung off one of these pipes in a loose coil. It would have to be replaced soon, she thought. That tape might be ten or twenty years old. She considered the stolen tape that had caused so much of the mess she was in, and how it would've been lucky to survive twenty minutes up there.

And that's when Juliette realised what she must do. A project to pull the wool back from everyone's eyes, a favour to the next fool who slipped up or dared to hope aloud. And it would be so easy. She wouldn't have to build anything herself – they would do all the work for her. All it would take would be some convincing, and she was mighty good at that.

She smiled, a list of parts forming in her head as the broken impeller was removed from the faulty pump. All she would need to fix this problem was a replacement part or two. It was the perfect solution to getting everything in the silo working properly once more.

Juliette worked two full shifts, wearing her muscles to a numb ache before returning her tools and showering. She took a stiff brush to her nails over the bathroom sink, determined to keep them up-top clean. She headed towards the mess hall, looking forward to a tall plate of high-energy food rather than the weak rabbit stew from the cafeteria on level one, when she passed through Mechanical's entrance hall and saw Knox talking to Deputy Hank. The way they turned and stared, she knew they were talking about her. Juliette's stomach sank. Her first thought was of her father. And then Peter. Who else could they take away from her that she might care about? They wouldn't know to contact her about Lukas, whatever he was to her.

She made a swift turn and headed in their direction, even as the two of them moved to intercept her. The looks on their faces confirmed her every fear. Something awful had happened. Juliette barely noticed Hank reaching for his cuffs.

'I'm sorry, Jules,' he said, as they got close.

'What happened?' Juliette asked. 'Dad?'

Hank's brow wrinkled in confusion. Knox was shaking his head and chewing on his beard. He studied the deputy like he might eat the man.

'Knox, what's going on?'

'Jules, I'm sorry.' He shook his head. He seemed to want to say more but was powerless to do so. Juliette felt Hank reaching for her arm.

'You are under arrest for grave crimes against the silo.'

He recited the lines like they were from a sad poem. The steel clicked around her wrist.

'You will be judged and sentenced according to the Pact.'

Juliette looked up at Knox. 'What is this?' she asked. Was she really being arrested again?

'If you are found guilty, you will be given a chance at honour.'

'What do you want me to do?' Knox whispered, his vast muscles twitching beneath his overalls. He wrung his hands together, watching the second metal band clack around her other wrist, her two hands shackled together now. The large head of Mechanical seemed to be contemplating violence – or worse.

'Easy, Knox,' Juliette said. She shook her head at him. The thought of more people getting hurt because of her was too much to bear.

'Should humanity banish you from this world,' Hank continued to recite, his voice cracking, his eyes wet with shame.

'Let it go,' Juliette told Knox. She looked past him to where more workers were coming off second shift, stopping to see this spectacle of their prodigal daughter being put in cuffs.

'In that banishment, may you find your sins scrubbed, scrubbed away,' Hank concluded. He looked up at her, one hand gripping the chain between her wrists, tears streaking down his face.

'I'm sorry,' he said.

Juliette nodded to him. She set her teeth and nodded to Knox as well.

'It's all right,' she said. She kept bobbing her head. 'It's all right, Knox. Let it go.'

29

The climb up was to take three days. Longer than it should have, but there were protocols. A day trip up to Hank's office, a night in his cell, Deputy Marsh coming down the next morning from the mids to escort her up another fifty levels to his office.

She felt numb during this second day of climbing, the looks from passersby sliding off her like water on grease. It was difficult to concern herself with her own life – she was too busy tallying all the others lost, some of them because of her.

Marsh, like Hank, tried to make small talk, and all Juliette could think to say in return was that they were on the wrong side. That evil ran amok. Instead, she kept her mouth shut.

At the mids deputy station, she was shown to a familiar enough cell, just like the one in Hank's in the down deep. No wall screen, only a stack of primed breeze blocks. She collapsed onto the bunk before he even had the gate locked, and lay there for what felt like hours, waiting for night to come and pass to dawn, for Peter's new deputy to come and march her up the last leg of her journey.

She checked her wrist often, but Hank had confiscated her watch. He probably wouldn't even know how to wind it. The thing would eventually fall into disrepair and return to being a trinket, a useless thing worn upside down for its pretty band.

This saddened her more than it should have. She rubbed her bare wrist, dying to know the time, when Marsh came back and told her she had a visitor.

Juliette sat up on the cot and swung her legs around. Who would come up to the mids from Mechanical?

When Lukas appeared on the other side of the bars, the dam that held back all her emotions nearly broke. She felt her neck constrict, her jaws ache from fighting the sobs, the emptiness in her chest nearly puncture and burst. He grabbed the bars and leaned his head against them, his temples touching the smooth steel, a sad smile on his face.

'Hey,' he said.

Juliette barely recognised him. She was used to seeing him in the dark, had been in a hurry when they'd bumped into each other on the stairs. He was a striking man, his eyes older than his face, his light brown hair slicked back with sweat from what she assumed was a hurried walk down.

'You didn't need to come,' she said, speaking softly and slowly to keep from crying. What really saddened her was someone seeing her like this, someone she was beginning to realise she cared about. The indignity was too much.

'We're fighting this,' he said. 'Your friends are collecting signatures. Don't give up.'

She shook her head. 'It won't work,' she told him. 'Please don't get your hopes up.' She walked to the bars and wrapped her hands a few inches below his. 'You don't even know me.'

'I know this is ratshit—' He turned away, a tear streaking down his cheek. 'Another cleaning?' he croaked. 'Why?'

'It's what they want,' Juliette said. 'There's no stopping them.'

Lukas's hands slid down the bars and wrapped around hers. Juliette couldn't free them to wipe her cheeks. She tried to dip her head to use her shoulder.

'I was coming up to see you that day—' Lukas shook his head and took a deep breath. 'I was coming to ask you out—'

'Don't,' she said. 'Lukas. Don't do this.'

'I told my mom about you.'

'Oh, for God's sake, Lukas—'

'This can't happen,' he said. He shook his head. 'It can't. You can't go.'

When he looked back up, Juliette saw that there was more fear in his eyes than even she felt. She wiggled one hand free and peeled his other one off. She pushed them away. 'You need to let this go,' she said. 'I'm sorry. Just find someone. Don't end up like me. Don't wait—'

'I thought I had found someone,' he said plaintively.

Juliette turned to hide her face.

'Go,' she whispered.

She stood still, feeling his presence on the other side of those bars, this boy who knew about stars but nothing about her. And she waited, listening to him sob while she cried quietly to herself, until she finally heard his feet shuffle across the floor, his sad gait carrying him away.

That night, she spent another evening on a cold cot, another evening of not being told what she'd been arrested for, an evening to count the hurts she had unwittingly caused. The next day, there was a final climb up through a land of strangers, the whispers of a double cleaning chasing after her, Juliette falling into another stunned trance, one leg moving and then the other.

At the end of her climb, she was moved into a familiar cell, past Peter Billings and her old desk. Her escort collapsed into Deputy Marnes's squeaking chair, complaining of exhaustion.

Juliette could feel the shell that had formed around her during the long three days, that hard enamel of numbness and disbelief. People didn't talk softer; they just sounded that way. They didn't stand further from her; they just seemed more distant. She sat on the lone cot and listened to Peter Billings charge her with conspiracy. A data drive hung in a limp plastic bag like a pet fish that had gobbled all its water and now lay dead. Dug out of the incinerator, somehow. Its edges were blackened. A scroll was unspooled, only partly pulped. Details of her computer search were listed. She knew most of what they had found was Holston's data, not hers. She wasn't sure what the point would be of telling them this. They already had enough for several cleanings.

A judge stood beside Peter in his black overalls while her sins were listed, as if anyone were really there to decide her fate. Juliette knew the decision had already been made, and who had made it.

Scottie's name was mentioned, but she didn't catch the context. It could have been that the email on his account had been discovered. It could be that they were going to pin his death on her, just in case. Bones buried with bones, keeping the secrets held between them safe.

She tuned them out and instead watched over her shoulder as a small tornado formed on the flats and spun towards the hills. It eventually dissipated as it crashed into the gentle slope, dissolving like so many cleaners, thrown to the caustic breeze and left to waste away.

Bernard never showed himself. Too afraid or too smug, Jules would never know. She peered down at her hands, at the thin trace of grease deep under her nails, and knew that she was already dead. It didn't matter, somehow. There was a line of bodies behind and before her. She was just the shuffling present, the cog in the machine, spinning and gnashing its metal teeth until that one gear wore down, until the slivers of her self broke loose and did more damage, until she needed to be pulled, cast off, and replaced with another.

Pam brought her oatmeal and fried potatoes from the cafeteria, her favourite. She left it steaming outside the bars. Notes were ported up from Mechanical all day and passed through to her. She was glad none of her friends visited. Their silent voices were more than enough.

Juliette's eyes did the crying, the rest of her too numb to shake or sob. She read the sweet notes while tears dripped on her thighs. Knox's was a simple apology. She imagined he would rather have murdered and done something – even if he were cast out for the attempt – than the impotent display his note said he would regret all his life. Others sent spiritual messages, promises to see her on the other side, quotes from memorised books. Shirly maybe knew her best and gave her an update on the generator and the new centrifuge for the refinery. She told her all would remain well and largely because of her. This elicited the faintest of sobs from Juliette. She rubbed the charcoal letters with her fingers, transferring some of her friends' black thoughts to herself.

She was left at last with Walker's note, the only one she

couldn't figure. As the sun set over the harsh landscape, the wind dying down for the night and allowing the dust to settle, she read his words over and over, trying to deduce what he meant.

> Jules –
>> No fear. Now is for laughing. The truth is a joke and they're good in Supply.
>> – Walk

She wasn't sure how she fell asleep, only that she woke up and found notes like peeled chips of paint around her cot, more of them slipped between the bars overnight. Juliette turned her head and peered through the darkness, realising someone was there. A man stood behind the bars. When she stirred, he pulled away, a wedding band singing with the sound of steel on steel. She rose hurriedly from the cot and rushed to the bars on sleepy legs. She grabbed them with trembling hands and peered through the darkness as the figure melded with the black.

'Dad—?' she called out, reaching through the grate.

But he didn't turn. The tall figure quickened his pace, slipping into the void, a mirage now, as well as a distant childhood memory.

The following sunrise was something to behold. There was a rare break in the low dark clouds that allowed visible rays of golden smoke to slide sideways across the hills. Juliette lay in her cot, watching the dimness fade to light, her cheek resting on her hands, the smell of cold untouched oatmeal drifting from outside the bars. She thought of the men and women in IT working through the past three nights to construct a suit tailored for her, their blasted parts ported up from Supply. The suit would be timed to last her just long enough, to get her through the cleaning but no further.

In all the ordeal of her handcuffed climb, the days and nights of numb acceptance, the thought of the actual cleaning had never occurred to her until now, on the very morning of that duty. She felt, with absolute certainty, that she would not perform the act. She knew they all said this, every cleaner, and that they all experienced some magical, perhaps spiritual, transformation on the threshold of their deaths and performed nonetheless. But she had no one up top to clean for. She wasn't the first cleaner from Mechanical, but she was determined to be the first to refuse.

She said as much as Peter took her from her cell and led her to that yellow door. A tech from IT was waiting inside, making last-minute adjustments to her suit. Juliette listened to his instructions with a clinical detachment. She saw all the weaknesses in the design. She realised – if she hadn't been so busy working two shifts in Mechanical to keep the floods out, the oil in, the power humming – that she could make a better suit in her sleep. She studied the washers and seals, identical to the kind employed in pumps, but designed, she knew, to break down. The shiny coat of heat tape, applied in overlapping strips to form the skin of the suit, she knew to be purposefully inferior. She nearly pointed these things out to the tech as he promised her the latest and greatest. He zipped her up, tugged on her gloves, helped with her boots, and explained the numbered pockets.

Juliette repeated the mantra from Walker's note: *No fear. No fear. No fear.*

Now is for laughing. The truth is a joke. And they're in good Supply.

The tech checked her gloves and the Velcro seals over her zippers while Juliette puzzled over Walker's note. Why had he capitalised 'Supply'? Or was she even remembering it correctly? Now, she wasn't sure. A strip of tape went around one boot, then the other. Juliette laughed at the spectacle of it all. It was all so utterly pointless. They should bury her in the dirt farms, where her body might actually do some good.

The helmet came last, handled with obvious care. The tech had her hold it while he adjusted the metal ring collar around her neck. She looked down at her reflection in the visor, her eyes hollow and so much older than she remembered yet so much younger than she felt. Finally, the helmet went on, the room dimmer through the dark glass. The tech reminded her of the argon blast, of the fires that would follow. She would have to get out quickly or die a far worse death inside.

He left her to consider this. The yellow door behind her clanged shut, its wheel spun on the inside as if by a ghost.

Juliette wondered if she should simply stay and succumb to the flames, not give this spiritual awakening a chance to persuade her. What would they say in Mechanical when that tale spiralled its way through the silo? Some would be proud of her obstinacy, she knew. Some would be horrified at her having gone out that way, in a bone-charring inferno. A few might even think she'd not been brave enough to take the first step out the door, that she'd wasted the chance to see the outside with her own eyes.

Her suit crinkled as the argon was pumped into the room, creating enough pressure to temporarily hold the outside toxins at bay. She found herself shuffling towards the door, almost against her will. When it cracked, the plastic sheeting in the room flattened itself against every pipe, against the low-jutting bench, and she knew the end had come. The doors before her parted, the silo splitting like the skin of a pea, giving her a view of the outside through a haze of condensing steam.

One boot slid through that crack, followed by another. And Juliette moved out into the world, dead set on leaving it on her own terms, seeing it for the first time with her own eyes even through this limited portal, this roughly eight-inch-by-two-inch sheet of glass, she suddenly realised.

30

Bernard watched the cleaning from the cafeteria while his techs gathered their supplies in Peter's office. It was his habit to view these things alone – his techs rarely joined him. They lugged their equipment out of the office and headed straight for the stairwell. Bernard was ashamed sometimes of the superstitions, the fears, he fostered even in his own men.

First the dome of her helmet, and then the shiny spectre of Juliette Nichols staggered aboveground. She lumbered up the ramp, her movements stiff and unsure. Bernard checked the clock on the wall and reached for his cup of juice. He settled back to see if he could gauge another cleaner's reaction to what they were seeing: a world crisp, bright, and clean, studded with soaring life, grass wavering in a fresh breeze, a glimmering acropolis beckoning from over the hills.

He had watched nearly a dozen cleanings in his day, always enjoying that first pirouette as they took in their surroundings. He had seen men who had left families behind dance before the sensors, waving as if to beckon their loved ones out, trying to pantomime all the false goodness displayed on their visor screens, all to no avail, to no audience. He had seen people reaching madly for flying birds, mistaking them for insects much closer to their faces. One cleaner had even gone back down the ramp and presumably beaten on the door as if to signal something, before finally getting to cleaning. What were any of these various reactions but the proud reminder of a system that worked? That no matter the individual psychology, the sight of all their false hopes eventually drove them to do what they promised they wouldn't.

Perhaps that's why Mayor Jahns could never stomach to watch. She had no idea what they were seeing, feeling, responding to. She would come up with her weak stomach the next morning and take in a sunrise, mourn in her own way, the rest of the silo granting her some space. But Bernard cherished this transformation, this delusion he and his predecessors had honed to perfection. He smiled and took a sip of fresh fruit juice and observed this Juliette as she staggered around, coming to her misguided senses. There was the barest coat of grime on the sensor lenses, not even worth a hard scrub, but he knew from double cleanings in the past that she would do it anyway. No one had ever not.

He took another sip and turned to the sheriff's office to see if Peter had summoned the courage to come watch, but the door was closed all but a crack. He had high hopes for that boy. Sheriff today, and maybe one day mayor. Bernard might hold the post for a short while, maybe an election or two, but he knew he belonged in IT, that this was not the job for him. Or rather, that his other duties were far more difficult to replace.

He turned away from Peter's office and back to the view – and nearly dropped his paper cup of juice.

The silvery form of Juliette Nichols was already trudging up the hill. The grime on the sensors was still in place.

Bernard stood abruptly, knocking his chair over backwards. He staggered toward the wall screen, almost as if he could chase after her.

And then he watched, dumbfounded, as she strode up that dark crease and paused for a moment over the still form of two other cleaners. Bernard checked the clock again. Any moment now. Any moment. She would collapse and fumble for her helmet. She would roll in the dusty soil, kicking up a cloud, sliding down that slope until she came to a dead rest.

But the second hand ticked along, and so did Juliette. She left the two cleaners behind, her limbs still climbing with power, her steady gait guiding her far up to the crest of the hill where she stood, taking in a view of who-knew-what, before disappearing, impossibly, out of sight.

*

Bernard's hand was sticky with juice as he raced down the stairwell. He kept the crushed paper cup in his fist for three levels before catching up to his techs and hurling it at their backs. The ball of trash bounced off and went tumbling into space, destined to settle on some distant landing below. Bernard cursed the confused men and kept running, his feet dangerously close to tripping over themselves. A dozen floors down, he nearly collided with the first hopeful climbers ascending to see the second crisp sunrise in the past weeks.

He was sore and winded when he finally made it down to thirty-four, his spectacles sliding around on the sweaty bridge of his nose. He burst through the double doors and yelled for the gate to be opened. A frightened guard complied, scanning the reader with his own ID right before Bernard slammed through the stubby metal arm. He practically ran down the hallway, taking two turns before he got to the most heavily fortified door in the entire silo.

Swiping his card and punching in his security code, he hurried inside, past the thick wall of solid steel. It was hot in the room full of servers. The identical black cases rose from the tiled floor like monuments to what was possible, to the craft and engineering of human endeavour. Bernard walked among them, the sweat gathering in his eyebrows, light glittering in his vision, his upper lip wet with perspiration. He ran his hands along the faces of the machines, the flashing lights like happy eyes trying to dispel his anger, the electrical hum like whispers to their master, hoping to calm him.

Their soothing efforts were in vain. All Bernard felt was a surge of fear. He went over and over what could have gone wrong. It wasn't as if she would survive – she couldn't possibly survive – but his mandate, second only to preserving the data on these machines, was never to let anyone out of sight. It was the highest order. He understood why and trembled from the repercussions of the morning's failure.

He cursed the heat as he reached the server on the far wall. The vents overhead carried cool air from the down deep and deposited it into the server room. Large fans in the back whisked the heat away and pumped it through more ducts down the silo, keeping the cool and dingy nastiness of the triple-digit levels humanely warm. Bernard glared at the vents, remembering the power holiday, the week of rising temperatures that had threatened his servers, all for some generator, and all because of this woman he had just let out of his sight. The memory stoked the flames under his collar. He cursed the design flaw that left the control of those vents down in Mechanical with those grease monkeys, those uncivilised tinkerers. He thought of the ugly and loud machines down there, the smell of leaking exhaust and burning oil. He had only needed to see it once – to kill a man – but even that was too much.

Comparing those noisy engines with the sublime servers was enough to make him never want to leave IT. Here was where silicon chips released their tangy scent as they heated under the strain of crunching data. Here was where one could smell the rubber coating the wires, running in parallel, neatly bundled, labelled and coded, and streaming with gigabits of glorious data every second. Here was where he oversaw the refilling of their data drives with all that had been deleted from the last uprising. Here, a man could think, surrounded by machines quietly doing the same.

Somewhere down those vents, however, was the stench of the unclean. Bernard wiped the sweat from his head and rubbed it on the seat of his overalls. The thought of that woman, first *stealing* from him, then rewarded by Jahns with the highest office of law, and now daring to not clean, to wander off . . . It raised his temperature dangerously.

He reached the server at the end of the row and squeezed between it and the wall to the back. The key kept around his neck slid into the greased innards of the case locks. As he turned each one, he reminded himself that she couldn't have got far. And how much trouble could this really cause? More importantly, what had gone wrong? The timing should always be impeccable. It always had been.

The back of the server came free, revealing the mostly empty innards behind. Bernard slipped the key back into his overalls and set the panel of black steel aside, the metal damnably hot to the touch. There was a cloth case fastened inside the server's belly. Bernard unloosened the flap and reached inside, extracting the plastic headset. He pulled it down over his ears, adjusted the mic, and unspooled the cord.

He could keep this under control, he thought to himself. He was head of IT. He was mayor. Peter Billings was his man. People liked stasis, and he could maintain the illusion of it. They were afraid of change, and he could conceal it. With him in both offices, who would oppose him? Who was better qualified? He would explain this. Everything would be okay.

Still, he was mightily, uniquely afraid as he located the correct jack and plugged in the cord. There was an immediate beeping sound in the headphones, the connection automatically taking place.

He could still oversee IT from a distance, make sure this never happened again, be more on top of his reports. Everything was under control. He told himself this as his headphones clicked and the beeping stopped. He knew someone had picked up, even if they refused anything in the way of a greeting. He felt there was annoyance hanging in the silence.

Bernard dispensed with the pleasantries as well. He jumped right in to what he needed to say.

'Silo one? This is silo eighteen.' He licked the sweat off his lips and adjusted his mic. His palms suddenly felt cold and clammy, and he needed to pee.

'We, uh . . . we might have a, uh . . . slight problem over here—'

PART 4 – THE UNRAVELLING

31

The walk was long, and longer still for her young mind. Though Juliette took few of the steps with her own small feet, it felt as though she and her parents had travelled for weeks. To impatient youth, all things took for ever and any kind of waiting was torture.

She rode on her father's shoulders, clutched his chin, her legs wrapped choking around his neck. Riding so high, she had to stoop her head to avoid the undersides of the steps. Clangs from strangers' boots rang out on the treads above her, and sprinkles of rust-dust drifted into her eyes.

Juliette blinked and rubbed her face into her father's hair. As excited as she was, the rise and fall of his shoulders made it impossible to stay awake. When he complained of a sore back, she rode a few levels on her mother's hip, fingers interlocked around her neck, her young head lolling as she drifted off to sleep.

She enjoyed the sounds of the travelling, the footfalls and the rhythmic song of her mother and father chatting about adult things, their voices drifting back and forth as she faded in and out.

The journey became a haze of foggy recollections. She awoke to the squealing of pigs through an open door, was vaguely aware of a garden they toured, woke fully to the smell of something sweet and ate a meal – lunch or dinner, she wasn't sure. She hardly stirred that night as she slid from her father's arms into a dark bed. She awoke the next morning beside a cousin she didn't know in an apartment nearly identical to her own. It was a weekend. She could tell by the older kids playing loudly in the hallway instead of getting ready for school. After a cold breakfast, she returned to the stairs with her parents and the sensation that they'd been travelling all their lives instead of just one day. And then the naps returned with their gentle erasure of time.

After another day they arrived at the hundredth landing of the silo's unfathomable depths. She took the last steps herself, her mom and dad holding a hand each, telling her about the significance. She was now in a place called the 'down deep', they told her. The bottom third. They steadied her sleepy legs as she wobbled from the last tread of the ninety-ninth stairway to the landing of the hundredth. Her father pointed above the open and busy doors to a large painted number with an incredible third digit:

100

The two circles captivated Juliette. They were like wide-open eyes peering out at the world for the first time. She told her father that she could already count that high.

'I know you can,' he said. 'It's because you're so smart.'

She followed her mother into the bazaar while clutching one of her father's strong and rough hands with both of her own. There were people everywhere. It was loud, but in a good way. A happy noise filled the air as people lifted their voices to be heard – just like a classroom once the teacher was gone.

Juliette felt afraid of getting lost, and so she clung to her father. They waited while her mom bartered for lunch. It required stopping at what felt like a dozen stalls to get the handful of things she needed. Her dad talked a man into letting her lean through a fence to touch a rabbit. The fur was so soft, it was like it wasn't there. Juliette snapped her hand back in fear when the animal turned its head, but it just chewed something invisible and looked at her like it was bored.

The bazaar seemed to go on for ever. It wound around and out of sight, even when all the many-coloured adult legs were clear enough for her to see to the end. Off to the sides, narrower passages full of more stalls and tents twisted in a maze of colours and sounds, but Juliette wasn't allowed to go down any of these. She stuck with her parents until they arrived at the first set of square steps she'd ever seen in her young life.

'Easy now,' her mother told her, helping her up the steps.

'I can do it,' she said stubbornly, but took her mom's hand anyway.

'Two and one child,' her father said to someone at the top of the steps. She heard the clatter of chits going into a box that sounded full of them. As her father passed through the gate, she saw the man by the box was dressed in all colours and wearing a funny floppy hat that was much too big for him. She tried to get a better look as her mom guided her through the gates, a hand on her back and whispers in her ear to keep up with her father. The gentleman turned his head, bells jangling on his hat, and made a funny face at her, his tongue poking out to the side.

Juliette laughed, but still felt half afraid of the strange man as they found a spot to sit and eat. Her dad dug a thin bed sheet out of his pack and spread it across one of the wide benches. Juliette's mom made her take her shoes off before she stood on the sheet. She held her father's shoulder and looked down the slope of benches and seats towards the wide-open room below. Her father told her the open room was called a 'stage'. Everything in the down deep had different names.

'What're they doing?' she asked her father. Several men on the stage, dressed as colourfully as the gatesman, were throwing balls up into the air – an impossible number of them – keeping them all from hitting the ground.

Her father laughed. 'They're juggling. They're here to entertain us until the play starts.'

Juliette wasn't sure she wanted the play to start. This was it, the thing she wanted to see. The jugglers tossed balls and hoops between each other, and Juliette could feel her own arms windmilling as she watched. She tried counting the hoops, but they wouldn't stay in one place long enough.

'Eat your lunch,' her mother reminded her, passing her bites of a fruit sandwich.

Juliette was mesmerised. When the jugglers put the balls and hoops away and started chasing one another, falling down and acting silly, she laughed as loudly as the other kids. She looked constantly to her mom and dad to see if they were watching. She tugged on their sleeves, but they just nodded and continued to talk, eat, and drink. When another family sat close and a boy older than her laughed at the jugglers as well, Juliette felt suddenly like she had company. She began to squeal even louder. The jugglers were the brightest things she had ever seen. She could've watched them for ever.

But then the lights were dimmed and the play began, and it was boring by comparison. It started off well with a rousing sword fight, but then it was a lot of strange words and a man and woman looking at each other the way her parents did, talking in some funny language.

Juliette fell asleep. She dreamed of flying through the silo with one hundred colourful balls and hoops soaring all around her, always out of reach, the hoops round like the numbers at the end of the bazaar's level – and then she woke up to whistles and applause.

Her parents were standing and yelling while the people on the stage in the funny costumes took several bows. Juliette yawned and looked over at the boy on the bench beside her. He was sleeping with his mouth open, his head in his mom's lap, his shoulders shaking while she clapped and clapped.

They gathered up the sheet and her father carried her down to the stage where the sword-fighters and strange talkers were speaking to the audience and shaking hands. Juliette wanted to meet the jugglers. She wanted to learn how to make the hoops float in the air. But her parents waited instead until they could speak to one of the ladies, the one who had her hair braided and twisted into drooping curves.

'Juliette,' her father told her, lifting her onto the stage. 'I want you to meet . . . Juliette.' He gestured to the woman in the fluffy dress with the strange hair.

'Is that your real name?' the lady asked, kneeling down and reaching for Juliette's hand.

Juliette pulled it back like it was another rabbit about to bite her, but nodded.

'You were wonderful,' her mum told the lady. They shook hands and introduced themselves.

'Did you like the play?' the lady with the funny hair asked.

Juliette nodded. She could sense that she was supposed to and that this made it okay to lie.

'Her father and I came to this show years ago when we first started dating,' her mother said. She rubbed Juliette's hair. 'We were going to name our first child either Romeus or Juliette.'

'Well, be glad you had a girl, then,' the lady said, smiling.

Her parents laughed, and Juliette was beginning to be less afraid of this woman with the same name as her.

'Do you think we could get your autograph?' Her father let go of her shoulder and rummaged in his pack. 'I have a programme in here somewhere.'

'Why not a script for this young Juliette?' The lady smiled at her. 'Are you learning your letters?'

'I can count to a hundred,' Juliette said proudly.

The woman paused, then smiled. Juliette watched her as she stood and crossed the stage, her dress flowing in a way that overalls never could. The lady returned from behind a curtain with a tiny book of papers held fast with brass pins. She accepted a charcoal from Juliette's father and wrote her name large and curly across the cover.

The woman pressed the collection of papers into her small hands. 'I want you to have this, Juliette of the silo.'

Her mother protested. 'Oh, we couldn't. That's too much paper—'

'She's only five,' her father said.

'I have another,' the lady assured them. 'We make our own. I want her to have it.'

She reached out and touched Juliette's cheek, and this time Juliette didn't pull away. She was too busy flipping through the papers, looking at all the curly notes handwritten along the sides beside the printed words. One word, she noticed, was circled over and over among all the others. She couldn't make out many of them, but this one she could read. It was her name. It was at the beginning of so many sentences: Juliette.

This was her. She looked up at the lady, understanding at once why her parents had brought her there, why they had walked so far and for so long.

'Thank you,' she said, remembering her manners.

And then, after some consideration:

'I'm sorry I fell asleep.'

It was the morning of the worst cleaning of Lukas's life – and for once he considered going into work, to ignore the paid holiday, to pretend it was a day like any other. He sat at the foot of his bed as he worked up the courage to move, one of his many star charts in his lap. Lightly with his fingers, so as not to smear the marks away, he caressed the charcoal outline of one star in particular.

It wasn't a star like the others. Those were simple dots on a meticulous grid with details of date sighted, location, and intensity. This wasn't that kind of star – not one that lasted nearly so long. It was the five-pointed kind, the outline of a sheriff's badge. He remembered drawing the shape while she was talking to him one night, the steel on her chest glowing faintly as it caught the weak light from the stairwell. He remembered her voice being magical, the way she carried herself mesmerising, and her arrival into his boring routine had been as unexpected as the parting of clouds.

He also remembered how she had turned away from him in her cell two nights ago, had tried to save his feelings by pushing him away.

Lukas had no more tears. He had spent most of the night shedding them for this woman he hardly knew. And now he wondered what he would do with his day, with his life. The thought of her out there, doing anything for them – cleaning – made him sick. He wondered if that was why he'd had no appetite for two days. Some deep part of his gut must know he'd never keep anything down, even if he forced himself to eat.

He set the star chart aside and dropped his face into his palms. He rested there, so tired, trying to convince himself to just get up and go to work. If he went to work, at least he'd be distracted. He tried to remember where he'd left off in the server room last week. Was it the number eight tower that had gone down again? Sammi had suggested he swap out the control board, but Lukas had suspected a bad cable. That's what he'd been doing, he remembered now: toning out the Ethernet runs. It's what he should be doing right then, that very day. Anything but sitting around on a holiday, feeling like he could be physically ill over a woman he'd done little more than tell his mother about.

Lukas stood and shrugged on the same pair of overalls he'd worn the day before. He remained there a moment, staring at his bare feet, wondering why he'd got up. Where was he going? His mind was completely blank, his body numb. He wondered if he could stand there, unmoving, his stomach twisted in knots, for the rest of his life. Someone would eventually find him, wouldn't they? Dead and stiff, standing upright, a statue of a corpse.

He shook his head and these black thoughts loose and looked for his boots. He found them; it was an accomplishment. Lukas had done something by getting himself dressed.

He left his room and ambled towards the landing, weaving around kids squealing from another day off school, parents trying to corral them and get their boots and overalls on. The commotion was little more than background noise for Lukas. It was a hum, like the aches in his legs from the long climb down to see her and the even longer climb back up. He stepped out onto the apartment's landing and felt a habitual tug upward towards the cafeteria. All he could think about was all he had thought of for the past week: making it through another day so he could go up top for the chance to see her.

It suddenly occurred to Lukas that he still could. He wasn't one for sunrises – he much preferred the twilight and the stars – but if he wanted to see her, all he had to do was climb to the cafeteria and scan the landscape. There would be a new body there, a new suit with the shine still on it glimmering in whatever weak rays the sun dribbled through those blasted clouds.

He could see the image clearly in his head: her uncomfortable sprawl – legs twisted, arm pinned, helmet turned to the side, gazing back at the silo. Sadder still, he saw himself decades later, a lonely old man sitting in front of that grey wall screen and drawing not star charts but landscapes. The same landscapes over and over, looking up at a wasting might-have-been, sketching that same still pose while weeping tears that dripped and turned charcoal to mud.

He would be like Marnes, that poor man. And thinking of the deputy, who died with no one to bury him, it reminded Lukas of the last thing Juliette had told him. She had begged him to find someone, to not be like her, to never be alone.

He gripped landing fifty's cool steel railing and leaned over. Looking down, he could watch the stairwell drill its way deep into the earth. The landing for fifty-six was visible below, the several landings between jutting off in unseen angles. It was hard to gauge the distance but he figured it was more than enough. No need to walk down to eighty-two, which most jumpers preferred for its long clear path down to ninety-nine.

Suddenly, he saw himself in flight, tumbling down, arms and legs splayed. He reckoned he would just miss the landing. One of the railings would catch him and saw him near in half. Or maybe if he jumped out a little further, maybe if he aimed his head, he could make it quick.

He straightened, feeling a twinge of fear and a rush of adrenalin from picturing the fall, the end, so vividly. He glanced around and checked the morning traffic to see if anyone was watching him. He had seen other adults peer over railings before. He'd always assumed bad thoughts were going through their heads. Because he knew, growing up in the silo, that only children dropped physical things from the landings. By the time you got older, you knew to keep a grip on all that you could. Eventually, it was something else that slipped away, something else you lost that tumbled down through the heart of the silo, that made you ponder leaping after—

The landing shivered with the beat of a hurrying porter; the sound of bare feet slapping against steel treads came next and spiralled closer. Lukas slid away from the railing and tried to focus on what he was doing that day. Maybe he should just crawl back into bed and sleep, kill some hours with unconsciousness.

As he attempted to summon some sliver of motivation, the speeding porter flew past, and Lukas caught a glimpse of the boy's face twisted in consternation. Even as he sped out of sight – his pace swift and reckless – the image of his worry remained vividly lodged in Lukas's mind.

And Lukas knew. As the rapid patter of the boy's feet wound deeper into the earth, he knew something had happened that morning, something up top, something newsworthy about the cleaning.

A seed of hope. Some wishful kernel buried deep, where he was loath to acknowledge it lest it poison or choke him, began to sprout. Maybe the cleaning never happened. Was it possible her banishment had been reconsidered? The people of Mechanical had sent up a petition. Hundreds of daring signatures, risking their own necks to save hers. Had the mad gesture from the down deep worn the judges down? That tiny seed of hope sprang roots. It grew vine-like through Lukas's chest, filling him with an urgency to run up and see for himself. He left the railing, and the dream of leaping after his worries, and pushed his way through the morning crowd.

Whispers, he noticed, were already foaming in the porter's wake. He wasn't the only one who had noticed.

As he joined the upbound traffic, he realised the aches in his legs from the days before had vanished. He prepared to pass the slow-moving family in front of him – when he heard the loud squawk of a radio behind him.

Lukas turned to find Deputy Marsh a few treads back fumbling for the radio on his hip, a small cardboard box clutched to his chest, a sheen of sweat on his forehead. Lukas stopped and held the railing, waiting for the mids deputy to reach him.

'Marsh!'

The deputy finally got the volume down on his radio and

glanced up. He nodded to Lukas. The both of them squeezed against the railing as a worker and his shadow passed them, heading upward.

'What's the news?' Lukas asked. He knew the deputy well, and he knew he might spill it for free.

Marsh swiped his forehead and moved the box into the crook of his other arm. 'That Bernard is whoopin' my ass this mornin',' he complained. 'Done climbed *enough* this week!'

'No, what of the *cleaning*?' Lukas asked. 'A porter just hurried by like he'd seen a ghost.'

Deputy Marsh glanced up the steps. 'I was told to bring her things to thirty-four as quick as grease. Hank nearly killed himself bringing 'em partway up to me.' He started up the stairs as if he couldn't afford to stay. 'Look, I've gotta keep movin' if I wanna keep my job.'

Lukas held his arm, and traffic swelled below them as annoyed climbers squeezed past and against the occasional traveller heading down. 'Did the cleaning go through or not?' Lukas demanded to know.

Marsh sagged against the railing. Quiet chatter popped through his radio.

'No,' he whispered, and Lukas felt as though he could fly. He could fly straight up the space between the stairs and the concrete heart of the silo, could soar around the landings, could go fifty levels at a leap—

'She went out, but she didn't clean,' Marsh said, his voice low but laced with words sharp enough to pierce Lukas's dreams. 'She wandered over them hills—'

'Wait. What?'

Marsh nodded, and sweat dripped from the deputy's nose. 'Plumb out of sight,' he hissed, like a radio turned down low. 'Now I've got to get her things up to Bernar—'

'I'll do it,' Lukas said, reaching out his hands. 'I'm going to thirty-four anyway.'

Marsh shifted the box. The poor deputy seemed liable to collapse at any moment. Lukas begged him, just as he had two days earlier in order to see Juliette in her cell. 'Let me take them up for you,' he said. 'You know Bernard won't mind. He and I are good friends, just like you and I have always been—'

Deputy Marsh wiped his lip and nodded ever so slightly, thinking on this.

'Look, I'm going up anyway,' Lukas said. He found himself slowly taking the box from an exhausted Marsh, even though the waves of emotion surging through his own body made it difficult to focus. The traffic on the stairs had become background noise. The idea that Juliette may still be in the silo had slipped away, but the news that she hadn't cleaned, that she had made it over the hills – this filled him with something else. It touched the part of him that yearned to map the stars. It meant no one would ever have to watch her waste away.

'You'll be careful with that,' Marsh said. His eyes were on the box, now tucked into Lukas's arms.

'I'll guard it with my life,' Lukas told him. 'Trust me.'

Marsh nodded to let him know he did. And Lukas hurried up the stairs, ahead of those rising to celebrate the cleaning, the weight of Juliette's belongings rattling softly in a box tucked tightly against his chest.

33

Walker the electrician bent over a cluttered workbench and adjusted his magnifier. The great bulbous lens was attached to his head with a hoop that might've been uncomfortable had he not been wearing it for most of his sixty-two years. As he pushed the glass into position, the small black chip on the green electronics board came into crystal focus. He could see each of the silver metal legs bent out from its body like knees on a spider, the tiny feet seemingly trapped in silver puddles of frozen steel.

With the tip of his finest soldering iron, Walker prodded a spot of silver while he worked the suction bulb with his foot. The metal around the chip's tiny foot melted and was pulled through a straw, one little leg of sixteen free.

He was about to move to the other – he had stayed up all night pulling fried chips to distract his mind from other things – when he heard the recognisable patter of that new porter skittering down his hall.

Walker dropped the board and hot iron on the workbench and hurried to his door. He held the jamb and leaned out as the kid ran past.

'Porter!' he yelled, and the boy reluctantly stopped. 'What news, boy?'

The kid smiled, revealing the whites of youth. 'I've got *big* news,' he said. 'Cost you a chit, though.'

Walker grunted with disgust, but dug into his overalls. He waved the kid over.

'You're that Samson boy, right?'

The kid bobbed his head, his hair dancing around his youthful face.

'Shadowed under Gloria, didn't you?'

The kid nodded again as his eyes followed the silver chit drawn from Walker's rattling pockets.

'You know, Gloria used to take pity on an old man with no family and no life. Trusted me with news, she did.'

'Gloria's dead,' the boy said, lifting his palm.

'That she is,' Walker said with a sigh. He dropped the chit into the child's outstretched palm, then waved his aged and spotted own for the news. He was dying to know everything and would have gladly payed ten chits. 'The details, child. Don't skip a one.'

'No cleaning, Mr Walker!'

Walker's heart missed a beat. The boy turned his shoulder to run on.

'Stay, boy! What do you mean, no cleaning? She's been set free?'

The porter shook his head. His hair was long, wild, and seemingly built for flying up and down the staircase. 'Nossir. She *refused!*'

The child's eyes were electric, his grin huge with the possession of such knowledge. No one had ever refused to clean in his lifetime. In Walker's, neither. Maybe not ever. Walker felt a surge of pride in his Juliette.

The boy waited a moment. He seemed eager to run off.

'Anything else?' Walker asked.

Samson nodded and glanced at Walker's pockets.

Walker let out a long sigh of disgust for what had become of this generation. He dug into his pocket with one hand and waved impatiently with the other.

'She's *gone*, Mr Walker!'

He snatched the chit from Walker's palm.

'Gone? As in dead? Speak up, son!'

Samson's teeth flashed as the chit disappeared into his overalls. 'Nossir. Gone as in over the hill. No cleaning, Mr Walker, just strode right over and out of view. Gone to the city, and Mr Bernard witnessed the whole thing!'

The young porter slapped Walker on the arm, needing, obviously, to strike something with his enthusiasm. He swiped his hair off his face, smiled large, and turned to run along his route, his feet lighter and pockets heavier from the tale.

Walker was left stunned in the doorway. He gripped the jamb with an iron claw lest he tumble out into the world. He stood there swaying, looking down at the pile of dishes he'd slipped outside the night before. He glanced over his shoulder at the dishevelled cot that had been calling his name all night. Smoke still rose from the soldering iron. He turned away from the hall, which would soon be pattering and clinking with the sounds of first shift, and unplugged the iron before he started another fire.

He remained there a moment, thinking about Jules, thinking about this news. He wondered if she'd got his note in time, if it had lessened the awful fear he'd felt in his gut for her.

Walker returned to the doorway. The down deep was stirring. He felt a powerful tug to go out there, to cross that threshold, to be a part of the unprecedented. Shirly would probably be by soon with his breakfast and to take away his dishes. He could wait for her, maybe talk a bit. Perhaps this spell of insanity would pass. But the thought of waiting, of the minutes stacking up like work orders, of not knowing how far Juliette had got or what reaction the others might be having to her not cleaning, pressed him into motion.

Walker lifted his foot and reached out past his doorway, his boot hovering over untrammelled ground.

He took a deep breath, fell forward, and caught himself on it. And suddenly, he felt like an intrepid explorer himself. There he was, forty something years later, teetering down a familiar hallway, one hand brushing the steel walls, a corner coming up around which his eyes could remember nothing.

And Walker became one more old soul pushing into the great unknown, his brain dizzy with what he might find out there.

34

The heavy steel doors of the silo parted, and a great cloud of argon billowed out with an angry hiss. The cloud seemed to materialise from nowhere, the compressed gas blossoming into a whipped froth as it met the warmer, less dense air beyond.

Juliette Nichols stuck one boot through that narrow gap. The doors opened only partway to hold back the deadly toxins, to force the argon through with pent-up pressure, so she had to turn sideways to squeeze past, her bulky suit rubbing against the thick doors. All she could think of was the raging fire that would soon fill the airlock. Its flames seemed to lick at her back, forcing her to flee.

She pulled her other boot through – and she suddenly found herself outside.

Outside.

There was nothing above her helmeted head but clouds, sky, and the unseen stars.

She lumbered forward, emerging through the fog of hissing argon to find herself on an upward-sloping ramp, the corners by the walls caked high with wind-trapped dirt. It was easy to forget that the top floor of the silo was belowground. The view from her old office and the cafeteria created an illusion of standing on the surface of the earth, head up in the wild air, but that was because the sensors were located there.

Juliette looked down at the numbers on her chest and remembered what she was supposed to be doing. She trudged up the ramp, head down, focusing on her boots. She wasn't sure how she even moved, if it was the numbness one succumbed to in the face of execution – or if it was just automated self-preservation, simply a move away from the coming inferno in the airlock, her body delaying the inevitable because it couldn't think or plan beyond the next fistful of seconds.

As Juliette reached the top of the ramp, her head emerged into a lie, a grand and gorgeous untruth. Green grass covered the hills like newly laid carpet. The skies were intoxicatingly blue, the clouds bleached white like fancy linen, the air peppered with soaring things.

She spun in place and took in the spectacular fabrication. It was as if she'd been dropped into a book from her youth, a book where animals talked and children flew and grey was never found.

Even knowing it wasn't real, knowing that she was looking through an eight-by-two-inch fib, the temptation to *believe* was overwhelming. She wanted to. She wanted to forget what she knew of IT's devious program, to forget everything she and Walker had discussed, and to fall instead to the soft grasses that weren't there, to roll around in the life that wasn't, to strip off the ridiculous suit and go screaming happily across the lying landscape.

She looked down at her hands, clenched and unclenched them as much as the thick gloves would allow. This was her coffin. Her thoughts scattered as she fought to remember what was real and what was a false hope laid on top by IT and her visor. The sky was not real. The grass was not real. Her *death* was real. The ugly world she had always known was real. And then, for just a moment, she remembered that she was supposed to be doing something. She was supposed to be cleaning.

She turned and gazed at the sensor tower, seeing it for the first time. It was a sturdy block of steel and concrete with a rusted and pitted ladder running up one side. The bulge of sensor pods were stuck like warts on the faces of the tower. Juliette reached for her chest, grabbed one of the scrubbing pads, and tore it loose. The note from Walker continued to stream through her mind: *No fear.*

She took the coarse wool pad and rubbed it against the arm of her suit. The heat tape wrapping did not peel, did not flake away like the stuff she had once stolen from IT, the tape they had engineered to fail. This was the brand of heat tape Juliette was used to working with, Mechanical's design.

They're good in Supply, Walker's note had said. The good had referred to the *people* of Supply. After years of helping Juliette score spares when she needed them most, they had done something extraordinary for her. While she had spent three days climbing stairs and three lonely nights in three different holding cells on her way to banishment, they had replaced IT's materials with those from Mechanical. They had fulfilled their orders for parts in a most devious way, and it must've been at Walker's behest. IT had then – unwittingly and for once – built a suit designed to *last*, not to disintegrate.

Juliette smiled. Her death, however certain, was delayed. She took a long look at the sensors, relaxed her fingers, and dropped the wool pad into the fake grass. Turning for the nearest hill, she tried her best to ignore the false colours and the layers of life projected on top of what was truly there. Rather than give in to the euphoria, she concentrated on the way her boots clomped on the packed earth, noted the feel of the angry wind buffeting against her suit, listened for the faint hiss as grains of sand pelted her helmet from all sides. There was a terrifying world around her, one she could be dimly aware of if she concentrated hard enough, a world she knew but could no longer see.

She started up the steep slope and headed vaguely towards the gleaming metropolis over the horizon. There was little thought of making it there. All she wanted was to die beyond the hills where no one would have to watch her rot away, so that Lukas the star-hunter would not be afraid to come up at twilight for fear of seeing her still form.

And suddenly, it felt good to simply be walking, to have some purpose. She would take herself out of sight. It was a more solid goal than that false city, which she knew to be crumbling.

Partway up the hill, she came to a pair of large rocks. Juliette started to dodge around them before she realised where she was, that she had followed the most gentle path up the crook of two colliding slopes, and here lay the most horrible lie of them all.

Holston and Allison. Hidden from her by the magic of the visor. Covered by a mirage of stone.

There were no words. Nothing to see, nothing to say. She glanced down the hill and spotted other sporadic boulders resting in the grass, their position not random at all but where cleaners of old had collapsed.

She turned away, leaving these sad things behind. It was impossible to know how much time she had, how long in order to hide her body from those who might gloat – and the few who might mourn.

Climbing towards the crest of the hill, her legs still sore from ascending the silo, Juliette witnessed the first rips in IT's deceitful veil. New portions of the sky and the distant city came into view, parts that had been obscured by the hill from down below. There seemed to be a break in the program, a limit to its lies. While the upper levels of the distant monoliths appeared whole and gleamed in the false sunlight, below these sharp panes of glass and bright steel lay the rotted dinginess of an abandoned world. She could see straight through the bottom levels of many of the buildings, and with their heavy tops projected onto them, they seemed liable to topple at any moment.

To the side, the extra and unfamiliar buildings had no supports at all, no foundations. They hung in the air with dark sky beneath them. This same dark vista of grey clouds and lifeless hills stretched out across the low horizon, a hard line of painted blue where the visor's program met its end.

Juliette puzzled over the incompleteness of IT's deceit. Was it because they themselves had no idea what lay beyond the hills, and so couldn't guess what to modify? Or did they deem it not worth the effort, knowing nobody would ever make it this far? Whatever the reason, the jarring and illogical nature of the view left her dizzy. She concentrated instead on her feet, taking those last dozen steps up the painted green hill until she reached the crest.

At the top, she paused while heavy gusts of wind buffeted against her, causing her to lean into their turbulence. She scanned the horizon and saw that she stood on the divide between two worlds. Down the slope before her, on a landscape her eyes had never before seen, lay a bare world of dust and parched earth, of wind flurries and small tornadoes, of air that could kill. Here was new land, and yet it looked more familiar to her than anything she'd encountered thus far.

She turned and peered back along the path she had just climbed, at the tall grasses blowing in the gentle breeze, at occasional flowers dipping their heads at her, at the bright blue and brilliant white overhead. It was an evil concoction, inviting but false.

Juliette took one last admiring gaze at this illusion. She noted how the round depression in the centre of the hills seemed to mark the outline of her silo's flat roof, the rest of her habitable home nestled deep in the belly of the soil. The way the land rose up all around made it look as though a hungry god had spooned out a large bite of the earth. With a heavy heart, she realised that the world she had grown up in was now closed off to her, that her home and her people were safe behind bolted doors, and she must be resigned to her fate. She had been cast off. Her time was short. And so she turned her back on the alluring view and bright colours to face the dusty, the dead, and the real.

As she started down the hill, Juliette pulled cautiously on the air in her suit. She knew Walker had given her the gift of time, time no cleaner before her ever had, but how much? And for what? She had already reached her goal, had managed to haul herself out of the sensors' sight, so why was she was still walking, still staggering down this foreign hill? Was it inertia? The pull of gravity? The sight of the unknown?

She was barely down the slope, heading in the general direction of the crumbling city, when she stopped to survey the unfamiliar landscape before her. The elevation made it possible to choose a path for her final walk, this maiden walk, across the tall dunes of dry earth. And that's when she saw, gazing out towards the rusting city beyond, that the hollow in which her silo resided was no accident. The hills bore a clear pattern as they stretched into the distance. It was one circular bowl after another, the earth rising up between them as if to shield each spooned-out bite from the caustic wind.

Juliette descended into the next bowl, pondering this, watching her footing as she went. She kicked aside the larger rocks and controlled her breathing. She knew from working deep in the flooded basins, swimming beneath the muck that burly men cringed from as she unclogged the drains, that air could be conserved through calmness. She glanced up, wondering if she had enough in the suit to cross this bowl and make it up the next great hill.

And that's when she saw the slender tower rising from the centre of the bowl, its exposed metal glinting in the sparse sunlight. The landscape here was untouched by the program in her visor; reality passed through her helmet untarnished. And seeing this, the familiar sensor tower, she wondered if perhaps she'd got turned around, if she had surveyed the world one too many times from the crest of the hill, if she was in fact trudging back towards her silo, covering ground already crossed before.

The sight of a dead cleaner wasting away in the dirt seemed to confirm this. It was a bare outline, ribbons of an old suit, the husk of a helmet.

She stopped and touched the dome of the helmet with the toe of her boot, and the shell crumbled and caved in. Whatever flesh and bone had been inside had long ago drifted off on the winds.

Juliette looked down the hill for the sleeping couple, but the crook of those two dunes was nowhere in sight. She suddenly felt bewildered and lost. She wondered if the air had finally worked past the seals and heat tape, if her brain was succumbing to noxious fumes, but no. She was nearer the city, still walking towards that skyline, the tops of which were still rendered whole and gleaming, the sky above them blue and spotted with bright clouds.

It meant this tower below her . . . was not hers. And these dunes, these great mounds of dead earth, were not meant to block out the winds or hold back the air. They were meant to shield curious eyes. To block this sight, this view, of some *other*.

35

L ukas held the small box tightly against his chest as he hiked up to the landing on thirty-eight. Here was a mixed-use level of offices, shops, a plastics factory, and one of the small water treatment plants. He pushed through the doors and hurried down corridors quiet from the day's cleaning until he reached the main pump control room. His IT master key allowed him inside. The room housed a tall and familiar computer cabinet from his Tuesday maintenance schedule. Lukas left the overhead light off to keep the small window in the door darkened to passers-by. He slid behind the tall server rack and the wall, scooted to the ground, and fished his flashlight out of his overalls.

In the soft red glow of his night light, Lukas gently peeled the flaps of the box apart, revealing the contents inside.

The guilt was immediate. It punctured the anticipation, the thrill of discovery, of intimacy. It wasn't guilt from defying his boss or lying to Deputy Marsh, nor of delaying the delivery of items he had been told were important. It was the violation of her things. The reminder of her fate. Here were Juliette's remains. Not her body, which was lost and gone, but the remnants of the life she had lived.

He took a heavy breath, considered closing the flaps and forgetting the contents, and then thought of what would become of them anyway. His friends in IT would probably be the ones to paw through them. They would tear open the box and trade items like kids swapping candy. They would desecrate her.

He bent the flaps open further and decided to honour her instead.

He adjusted his light and saw a stack of silo vouchers on top, wrapped in a piece of wire. He pulled these out and flipped through them. They were vacation vouchers. Dozens of them. He lifted them to his nose and puzzled over the tangy scent of grease emanating from the box.

A few expired meal cards lay underneath these vouchers, the corner of an ID badge poking out. Lukas reached for the badge, coded silver from her job as sheriff. He searched for another ID among the various scattered cards, but it appeared it had not yet been replaced with whatever colour Mechanical used. There hadn't been that much time between her being fired for one offence and being put to death for another. He took a moment to study the picture on the badge. It looked recent, just as he remembered her. Her hair was tied back tight, leaving it flat on her head. He could see loose curls sticking out at either side of her neck and remembered the first night he had watched her work, how she had braided her long hair herself while she sat alone in a pool of light, peering at page after page in those folders of hers.

He ran his finger over the picture and laughed when he saw her expression. Her forehead was wrinkled, her eyes narrowed, as if trying to determine what the photographer was attempting or why in the heavens it was taking so long. He covered his mouth to prevent the laugh from becoming a sob.

The vouchers went back into the box, but the ID slid into the breast pocket of his overalls as if by Juliette's own stubborn accord. The next thing that caught his eye was a silver multi-tool, new-looking, a slightly different model from his own. He grabbed this and leaned forward to pull his own tool out of his back pocket. He compared the two, opening a few of the tools on hers and admiring the smooth motion and neat click as each attachment locked into place. Taking a moment to first clean his, wiping his prints off and removing a bit of melted rubber wire casing, he switched the tools over. He decided he would rather carry this reminder of her and have his own tool disappear into storage or be pawned off to a stranger who wouldn't appreciate—

Lukas froze at the sound of footsteps and laughter. He held

his breath and waited for someone to come in, for the overhead lights to burst on. The server clicked and whirred beside him. The noise in the hallway receded, the laughter fading.

He was pushing his luck, he knew, but there was more in the box to see. He rummaged inside again and found an ornate wooden box, a valuable antique. It was just slightly bigger than his palm, and he took a moment to figure out how to open it. The first thing he saw as the top slid away was a ring, a woman's wedding ring. It could've been solid gold, but it was difficult to tell. The red glow from his flashlight tended to wash out colours, causing everything to appear dull and lifeless.

He checked for an inscription, but found none. It was a curious artefact, this ring. He was certain Juliette hadn't been wearing it when he'd known her, and he wondered if it was a relative's, or a thing passed down from before the uprising. He placed it back in the wooden box and reached for the other item inside, a bracelet of some sort. No, not a bracelet. As he pulled it out, he saw that it was a watch, the face so tiny it melded with the design of the jewelled strap. Lukas studied the face, and after a moment he realised his eyes or the red flashlight were playing tricks on him. Or were they? He looked closely to be sure – and saw that one of the impossibly thin hands was ticking away the time. The thing worked.

Before he could contemplate the challenge of concealing such an item or the consequences of being discovered with it, Lukas slid the watch into his chest pocket. He looked at the ring sitting alone in the box, and after a moment's hesitation, palmed this and stashed it away as well. He fished through the cardboard box and gathered some of the loose chits at the bottom and placed these into the antique box before sealing it shut and returning it.

What was he doing? He could feel a trickle of sweat work its way from his scalp and run the length of his jawline. The heat from the rear of the busy computer seemed to intensify. He dipped his head and lifted his shoulder to dab the itchy run of sweat away. There was more in the box, and he couldn't help himself: he had to keep looking.

He found a small notepad and flipped through it. It contained one to-do list after another, all of the items neatly crossed out. He replaced this and reached for a folded piece of paper at the bottom of the box, then realised it was more than a piece. He pulled out a thick collection of papers held together with brass fasteners. Across the top, in handwriting similar to that in the notebook, was printed: Main Generator Control Room Operation Manual.

He flipped it open and found inscrutable diagrams and bulleted notes lining the margins. It looked like something she'd put together herself, either as a reminder from piecing the room's operation together over time, or perhaps a helpful guide for others. The paper was recycled without being pulped, he saw. She had just written on the back. He flipped the manual over and checked the lines and lines of printed text on the opposite side. There were notes in the margins and a name circled over and over: Juliette. Juliette. Juliette.

He flipped the manual over and surveyed the rear, only to find it was the original front. 'The Tragic Historye of Romeus and Juliette', it said. It was a play. One Lukas had heard of. In front of him, a fan kicked on in the heart of the server, blowing air over warm chips of silicon and wire. He wiped the sweat from his forehead and tucked the bound play back into the box. He neatly arranged the other items on top and folded the cardboard flaps together. Wiggling back to his feet, Lukas doused his light and shoved it back into his pocket where it nestled against Juliette's multi-tool. With the box secured under one arm, he patted his chest with his other hand and felt her watch, her ring and her ID there with its picture of her. All tight against his torso.

Lukas shook his head. He wondered what the hell he was thinking as he stole out the small and dark room, a tall panel of winking and blinking lights watching him go.

36

The bodies were everywhere. Covered in dust and dirt, suits worn down by the toxic eaters that lived in the winds, Juliette found herself stumbling over more and more of them. And then, they were constant, a mass of boulders jumbled together. A few were in suits similar to her own, but most wore rags that had been eaten away into streamers. When the wind blew past her boots and across the bodies, strips of clothing waved like kelp in the down deep's fish farms. Unable to pick her way around them all, she found herself stepping over the remains, working her way closer and closer to the sensor tower, the bodies easily in the hundreds, possibly the thousands.

These weren't people from her silo, she realised. However obvious, the sensation was startling. *Other* people. That they were dead did nothing to diminish the soul-shattering reality that people had lived so close and she had never known. Juliette had somehow crossed an uninhabitable void, had gone from one universe to another, was possibly the first ever to have done so, and here was a graveyard of foreign souls, of people just like her having lived and died in a world so similar and so near to her own.

She made her way through dead bodies thick as crumbling rock, the forms becoming indistinguishable from one another. They were piled high in places, and she had to choose her path carefully. As she neared the ramp leading down to this *other* silo, she found herself needing to step on a body or two in order to pass. It looked as though they'd been trying to get away and had scampered over one another, creating their own small hills in a mad attempt to reach the real ones. But then, when she reached the ramp leading down, she saw the crush of bodies at the steel airlock door and realised they had been trying to get *back in*.

Her own imminent death loomed large − a constant awareness, a new sense worn on her skin and felt keenly in every pore. She would soon join these bodies, and somehow she was not afraid. She had passed through that fear on the crest of the hill and was now in new lands, seeing new things, a terrible gift for which she had to be grateful. Curiosity drove her forward, or maybe it was the mentality of this frozen crowd, all in scrambling repose, bodies swimming over each other and reaching towards the doors below.

She swam among them. Waded, where she had to. She stepped through broken and hollow bodies, kicked aside bones and tattered remains, and fought her way to the partly cracked doors. There was a figure there frozen between its iron teeth, one arm in, one out, a scream trapped on a grey and withered face, two eye sockets empty and staring.

Juliette was one of them, one of these others. She was dead, or nearly so. But while they were frozen in motion, she was still pushing ahead. Shown the way. She tugged the body out of the gap, her breathing loud in her helmet, her exhalations misting on the screen before her nose. Half the body pulled free, the other half collapsed inside the door. A mist of powdered flesh drifted down in-between.

She wiggled one of her arms inside and tried to push through sideways. Her shoulder slipped through, then her leg, but her helmet caught. She turned her head and tried again, but the helmet still wedged tightly between the doors. There was a moment of panic as she could feel the steel jaws gripping her head, supporting the weight of her helmet, leaving her semi-dangling from its grasp. She swam her arm all the way through, trying to reach around the door for purchase, to pull herself the rest of the way, but her torso was stuck. One leg was in, the other out. There was nothing to push against or pull in order to go the rest of the way. She was trapped, an arm useless on the inside, waving frantically, her rapid breathing using up what remained of her air.

Juliette tried to fit her other arm through. She couldn't turn her waist, but she could bend her elbow and slide her fingers across her belly through the tight space between her stomach and the door. She curled her fingers around the edge of the steel and pulled. There was no leverage in those confines. It was just the strength in her fingers, in her grip. Juliette suddenly didn't want to die, not there. She curled her hand as if to make a fist, her fingers bent around the edge of those steel jaws, her knuckles singing out from the strain. Jerking her head against her helmet, trying to bang her face against the damned screen, twisting and shoving and yanking – she suddenly popped free.

She stumbled forward into the airlock, a boot catching briefly on the gap behind her, arms windmilling for balance as she kicked through a pile of charred bones and sent a cloud of black ash into the air. It was the remains of those who had been caught in the cleansing fire of the airlock. Juliette found herself in a burnt room eerily similar to the one she had recently left. Her exhausted and bewildered mind spun with outrageous delusions. Perhaps she was already dead, and these were the ghosts awaiting her. Maybe she had burned alive inside the airlock of her own silo, and these were her mad dreams, her escape from the pain, and now she would haunt this place for ever.

She stumbled through the scattered remains towards the inner door and pressed her head against the thick glass porthole. She looked for Peter Billings beyond, sitting at his desk. Or perhaps a glimpse of Holston wandering the hallways, a spectre searching for his ghostly wife.

But this was not the same airlock. She tried to calm herself. She wondered if her air was running low, if sucking on her own exhaust was like breathing the fumes of a hot motor, choking off her brain.

The door was sealed. It was real. The thousands were dead, but she wasn't. Not yet.

She tried to spin the large wheel that secured the door, but it was either frozen in place or locked from the inside. Juliette banged on the glass, hoping the silo sheriff would hear her, or maybe a cafeteria worker. It was dark inside, but the thought lingered that someone must be there. People lived *inside* silos. They didn't belong piled up around them.

There was no answer. No light flicked on. She leaned on the large wheel, remembered Marnes's instructions, how all the mechanisms worked, but those lessons felt like so long ago and she hadn't thought them important at the time. But she remembered something: after the argon bath and the fire, didn't the inner door unlock? Automatically? So the airlock could be scrubbed? This seemed like something she remembered Marnes saying. He had joked that it wasn't as if anyone could come back inside once the fire had run its course. Was she remembering this or making it up? Was it the wishful thinking of an oxygen-starved mind?

Either way, the wheel on the door wouldn't budge. Juliette pushed down with all her weight, but it definitely felt locked to her. She stepped back. The bench hanging from the wall where cleaners got suited up before their deaths looked inviting. She was tired from the walk, from the struggle to get inside. And why was she trying to get inside? She spun in place, indecisive. What was she doing?

She needed air. For some reason, she thought the silo might have some. She looked around at all the scattered bones of an uncountable number of bodies. How many dead? They were too jumbled to know. The skulls, she thought. She could count those and know. She shook this nonsense from her head. She was definitely losing her senses.

'The wheel on the door is a stuck nut,' some receding part of her said. 'It's a frozen bolt.'

And hadn't she made a reputation as a young shadow for working them free?

Juliette told herself that this could be done. Grease, heat, leverage. Those were the secrets to a piece of metal that wouldn't budge. She didn't have any of the three, but she looked around anyway. There was no squeezing back through the outer door, she knew she wouldn't make it a second time, not that kind of straining. So she had this room. The bench was secured to the wall along the back edge and hung from two chains. Juliette wiggled the chains, but didn't see how they could come free, or what good they would do her anyway.

In the corner, there was a pipe snaking up that led into a series of vents. It must be what delivered the argon, she thought. She wrapped her hands around the pipe, put her feet on the wall, and tugged.

The connection to the vent wiggled; the toxic air had corroded and weakened it. Juliette smiled, set her teeth, and yanked back ferociously.

The pipe came free of the vent and bent at its base. She felt a sudden thrill, like a wild rat standing over a large crumb. She grabbed the free end of the pipe and worked it back and forth, bending and wrenching the fastened end. Metal would snap if you could wiggle it even a little bit, if you did it long enough. She had felt the heat of weakened steel countless times while bending it over and over until it broke.

Sweat beaded on her brow and twinkled in the dim light allowed by her visor screen. It dripped down her nose, fogged the screen, and still she yanked and pushed, back and forth, growing frantic and desperate—

The pipe snapped, taking her by surprise. Just a faint pop bled through her helmet, and then the long piece of hollow metal was free. One end was crushed and twisted, the other whole and round. Juliette turned to the door, a tool now in hand. She slid the pipe through the wheel, leaving as much as she could hanging out the side, just long enough not to brush the wall. With both gloved hands wrapped around the pipe, she lifted herself to her waist, bending over the pipe, her helmet touching the door. She bounced her weight on the lever, knowing it was a jerking motion that freed a bolt, not a steady force. She wiggled her way towards the end of the pipe, watching it bend a little, worried it might snap in half long before the door budged.

When she got towards the end – maximum leverage – she threw her weight up and down with all her strength, and she cursed as the pipe snapped. There was a loud clang, barely muffled by her suit, and then she collapsed to the floor, landing painfully on her elbow.

The pipe was at an angle beneath her, digging into her ribs. Juliette tried to catch her breath. Her sweat dripped against the visor screen, blurring her view. She got up and saw that the pipe was unbroken. She wondered if it had slipped free, but it was still threaded through the spokes of the large wheel.

Disbelieving, excited, she slid the pipe out the other side. She wrapped her hands around the spokes and leaned into it.

And the wheel.

It budged.

37

Walker made it to the end of the hallway and found himself leaving the comforting confines of a tight corridor to enter the wider entrance hall to Mechanical. The room, he saw, was full of young shadows. They hung out in groups, whispering to themselves. Three boys crouched near one wall, throwing stones for chits. Walker could hear a dozen interwoven voices spilling out of the mess hall across the room. The casters had sent these young ears away while they discussed adult things. He took a deep breath and hurried through that damned open space, focusing on each step, moving one foot ahead of him at a time, each small patch of floor a thing to conquer.

After a short lifetime, he finally crashed into the wall on the other side and hugged the steel panels in relief. Behind him, the shadows laughed, but he was too frightened to care. Sliding across the riveted steel, he grabbed the edge of the mess-hall door and pulled himself inside. The relief was enormous. Even though the mess hall was several times the size of his workshop, it was at least full of crowding furniture and people he knew. With his back to the wall, his shoulder against the open door, he could almost pretend it was smaller. He slumped to the ground and rested, the men and women of Mechanical arguing among themselves, voices rising, agitated, competing.

'She'd be out of air by now, anyway,' Ricks was saying.

'You don't know that,' Shirly said. She was standing on a chair so she could be at least as tall as the others. She surveyed the room. 'We don't know what advances they've made.'

'That's because they won't tell us!'

'Maybe it's gotten better out there.'

The room quietened with this last. Waiting, perhaps, to see if the voice would dare speak again and break its anonymity. Walker studied the eyes of those facing his way. They were wide with a mixture of fear and excitement. A double cleaning had removed some taboos. Shadows had been sent away. The adults were feeling frisky and free to speak forbidden thoughts.

'What if it *has* gotten better?' someone else asked.

'Since two weeks ago? I'm telling you guys, it's the suits! They figured out the suits!' Marck, an oilman, looked around at the others, anger in his eyes. 'I'm sure of it,' he said. 'They've sorted the suits and now we have a chance!'

'A chance to what?' Knox growled. The grizzled head of Mechanical sat at one of the tables, digging into a breakfast bowl. 'A chance to send more of our people out to wander the hills until they run out of air?' He shook his head and took another bite, then jabbed at the lot of them with his spoon. 'What we need to be talking about,' he said, chewing, 'is this sham of an election, this rat-ass mayor, and us kept in the dark down here—!'

'They didn't figure out the suits,' Walker hissed, still breathless from his ordeal.

'*We're* the ones who keep this place humming,' Knox continued, wiping his beard. 'And what do we get? Busted fingers and ratshit pay. And now? Now they come and take our people and send them out for a view we don't care about!' He slammed the table with his mighty fist, sending his bowl hopping.

Walker cleared his throat. He remained crouched on the floor, his back against the wall. No one had seen him enter or heard him the first time. Now, while the room was scared quiet by Knox, he tried again.

'They did *not* figure out the suits,' he said, a little louder this time.

Shirly saw him from her perch. Her chin dropped, her mouth hanging open. She pointed, and a dozen other heads turned to follow.

They gaped at him. Walker was still trying to catch his breath and must've looked near death. Courtnee, one of the young plumbers who was always kind to him whenever she stopped by his workshop, left her seat and hurried to his side. She whispered his name in surprise and helped him to his feet, urging him to come to the table and take her chair.

Knox slid his bowl away from himself and slapped the table. 'Well, people are just wandering all over the damned place now, aren't they?'

Walker looked up sheepishly to see the old foreman chief smiling through his beard at him. There were two dozen other people staring at him, all at once. Walker half waved, then stared down at the table. It was suddenly too many people.

'All this shouting rouse you, old man? You setting off over the hills, too?'

Shirly jumped down from her chair. 'Oh, God, I'm so sorry. I forgot to take him his breakfast.' She hurried towards the kitchen to fetch him some food even as Walker tried to wave her off. He wasn't hungry.

'It isn't . . .' His voice cracked. He tried again. 'I came because I *heard*,' he whispered. 'Jules. Out of sight.' He made a gesture with his hand, arching it over some imaginary hill running across the table. 'But it wasn't them in IT that figured *nothing*,' he said. He made eye contact with Marck and tapped his own chest. 'I did it.'

A whispered conversation in the corner fell quiet. No one sipped their juice, no one moved. They were still half stunned to see Walker out of his workshop, much less among the crowd of them. Not one of them had been old enough to remember the last time he'd roamed about. They knew him as the crazy electrical man who lived in a cave and refused to cast shadows any more.

'What're you *sayin*'?' Knox asked.

Walker took a deep breath. He was about to speak when Shirly returned and placed a bowl of hot oats in front of him, the spoon standing off the rim the concoction was so thick. Just how he liked it. He pressed his hands against either side of the bowl, feeling the heat in his palms. He was suddenly very tired from lack of sleep.

'Walk?' Shirly asked. 'You okay?'

He nodded and waved her away, lifted his head and met Knox's gaze.

'Jules came to me the other day.' He bobbed his head, gaining confidence. He tried to ignore how many people were watching him speak, or the way the overhead lights twinkled in his watering eyes. 'She had a theory about these suits, about IT.' With one hand, he stirred his oats, steeling his resolve to say the unthinkable. But then, how old was he? Why did he care for taboos?

'You remember the heat tape?' He turned to Rachele, who worked first shift and knew Juliette well. She nodded. 'Jules sorted that it weren't no accident, the way the tape broke down.' He nodded to himself. 'She sorted it all, she did.'

He took a bite of his food, not hungry but enjoying the burn of the hot spoon on his tongue. The room was silent, waiting. The whispers and quiet play of the shadows outside could just barely be heard.

'I've built up favours and favours with Supply over the years,' he explained. 'Favours and favours. So I called them all in. Told them we'd be even.' He looked at this group of men and women from Mechanical, could hear more standing in the hallway who'd arrived late but could read from the frozen demeanours in the room to stay put. 'We've taken stuff out of IT's supply chain before. I know I have. All the best electronics and wire go to them that make the suits—'

'The ratshit bastards,' someone muttered, which got more than a few of them bobbing their heads.

'So I told Supply to return the favour. Soon as I heard they took her' – Walker paused and swiped at his eyes – 'soon as I heard, I wired in those favours, said to replace anything them bastards asked for with some of our own. Best of the best. And don't let 'em be the wiser.'

'You did *what*?' Knox asked.

Walker dipped his head over and over, feeling good to let out the truth. 'They've been making those suits to fail. Not 'cause it ain't bad out there, that's not what I figure. But they don't want your body wandering out of sight, no sir.' He stirred his oats. 'They want us all right here where they can see us.'

'So she's okay?' Shirly asked.

Walker frowned and slowly shook his head.

'I *told* you guys,' someone said. 'She'd have run out of air by now.'

'She was dead *anyway*,' someone else countered, and the argument began to build again. 'This just proves they're full of shit!'

Walker had to agree with that.

'Everybody, let's stay calm,' Knox roared. But he appeared the least calm of them all. More workers filed in now that the moment of silence appeared to be over. They gathered around the table, faces full of worry.

'This is it,' Walker said to himself, seeing what was happening, what he had started. He watched his friends and co-workers get all riled up, barking at the empty air for answers, their passions stirred. 'This is it,' he said again, and he could feel it brewing, ready to burst out. 'Thisisit, thisisit—'

Courtnee, still hovering over him, tending to him like he was an invalid, held his wrist with those delicate hands of hers.

'What is it?' she asked. She waved down the others so she could hear. She leaned close to Walker.

'Walk, tell me, what is it? What is this? What're you trying to say?'

'This is how it starts,' he whispered, the room quiet once more. He looked up at all the faces, scanned them, seeing in their fury, in all the exploded taboos, that he was right to worry.

'This is how the uprising begins . . .'

38

Lukas arrived at thirty-four breathless and clutching the small box, more exhausted from the laws he had broken than this habitual climb to work. He could still taste the metallic tang of adrenalin in his mouth from hiding behind the servers and rummaging through Juliette's things. He patted his chest, feeling the items there, and also his racing heart.

Once he was better composed, he reached for the doors to IT and nearly cracked a knuckle as they flew outward towards him. Sammi, a tech he knew, burst out in a hurry and stormed past. Lukas called his name, but the older tech was already gone, storming up the stairs and out of sight.

There was more commotion in the entrance hall: voices yelling over one another. Lukas entered warily, wondering what the fuss was about. He held open the door with his elbow and slid into the room, the box tight against his chest.

Most of the yelling, it seemed, was coming from Bernard. The head of IT stood outside the security gates and was barking at one tech after the other. Nearby, Sims, the head of IT security, similarly laid into three men in grey overalls. Lukas remained frozen by the door, intimidated by the angry duo.

When Bernard spotted him there, he snapped shut and waded through the trembling techs to greet him. Lukas opened his mouth to say something, but his boss was fixated less on him and more on what was in his hands.

'This is it?' Bernard asked, snatching the box from him.

'It—?'

'Everything that greaser owned fits in this little damn box?' Bernard tugged the flaps open. 'Is this everything?'

'Uh . . . that's what I was given,' Lukas stammered. 'Marsh said—'

'Yeah, the deputy wired about his cramps. I swear, the Pact should stipulate an age limit for their kind. Sims!' Bernard turned to his security chief. 'Conference room. Now.'

Lukas pointed towards the security gate and the server room beyond. 'I suppose I should get to—'

'Come with me,' Bernard said, wrapping his arm around Lukas's back and squeezing his shoulder. 'I want you in on this. There seems to be fewer and fewer ratshit techs I can trust around here.'

'Unless y-you want me on the servers. We had that thing with tower thirteen—'

'That can wait. This is more important.' Bernard ushered him towards the conference room, the hulking mass of Sims preceding them.

The security guard grabbed the door and held it open, frowning at Lukas as he went by. Lukas shivered as he crossed the threshold. He could feel the sweat running down his chest, could feel guilty heat in his armpits and around his neck. He had a sudden image of being thrown against the table, pinned down, contraband yanked from his pockets and waved in his face—

'Sit,' Bernard said. He put the box down on the table, and he and Sims began emptying its contents while Lukas lowered himself into a chair.

'Vacation chits,' Sims said, pulling out the stack of paper coupons. Lukas watched the way the man's arms rippled with muscle with even the slightest movement. Sims had been a tech once, until his body kept growing and made him too obviously suited for other, less cerebral, endeavours. He lifted the chits to his nose, took a sniff, and recoiled. 'Smells like sweaty greaser,' he said.

'Counterfeit?' Bernard asked.

Sims shook his head. Bernard was inspecting the small wooden box. He shook it and rapped it with his knuckles, listening to the rattle of chits inside. He searched the exterior for a hinge or clasp.

Lukas almost blurted out that the top slid, that it was so finely crafted you could barely see the joints and that it took a bit of effort. Bernard muttered something and set the box aside.

'What exactly are we looking for?' Lukas asked. He leaned forward and grabbed the box, pretended to be inspecting it for the first time.

'Anything. A fucking clue,' Bernard barked. He glared at Lukas. 'How did this greaser make it over the hill? Was it something she did? One of my techs? What?'

Lukas still couldn't figure out the anger. So what if she hadn't cleaned – it would've been a double anyway. Was Bernard furious because he didn't know *why* she'd survived so long? This made sense to Lukas. Whenever he fixed something by accident, it drove him nearly as nuts as having something break. He'd seen Bernard angry before, but this was something different. The man was livid. He was *manic*. It's just how Lukas would feel if he'd had such an unprecedented piece of success with no cause to pin it on.

Sims, meanwhile, found the notebook and began flipping through it. 'Hey, boss—'

Bernard snatched it from him and tore through the pages, reading. 'Someone'll have to go through all this,' he said. He pushed his glasses up his nose. 'There might be some sign of collusion in here—'

'Hey, look,' Lukas said, holding out the box. 'It opens.' He showed them the sliding lid.

'Lemme see that.' Bernard dropped the notebook to the table and snatched the wooden box away. He wrinkled his nose. 'Just chits,' he said disgustedly.

He dumped them on the table and was about to toss the box aside, but Sims grabbed it from him. 'That's an antique,' the large man said. 'You think it's a clue, or can I . . . ?'

'Yes, keep it, by all means.' Bernard waved his arms out towards the window with its view of the entrance hall. 'Because nothing of greater fucking importance is going on around here, is it, shit-for-brains?'

Sims shrugged non-committally and slid the wooden box into

his pocket. Lukas desperately wanted to be somewhere else, anywhere in the silo but there.

'Maybe she just got lucky,' Sims offered.

Bernard began dumping the rest of the box onto the table, shaking it to loosen the manual that Lukas knew was tightly wedged in the bottom. He paused from his efforts and squinted at Sims over the rims of his glasses.

'Lucky,' Bernard repeated.

Sims tilted his head.

'Get the fuck out of here,' Bernard told him.

Sims nodded. 'Yeah, you're right.'

'No, I mean get out!' Bernard pointed at the door. 'Getthefuckout!'

The head of security smiled like this was funny, but lumbered for the door. He slid out of the room and gently clicked the door shut behind him.

'I'm surrounded by morons,' Bernard said, once they were alone.

Lukas tried to imagine this was not meant as an insult directed at him.

'Present company excluded,' Bernard added, as if reading his mind.

'Thanks.'

'Hey, you at least can fix a goddamn server. What the hell do I pay these other ratshit techs to do?'

He pressed his glasses up the bridge of his nose again, and Lukas tried to remember if the IT head had always cursed this much. He didn't think so. Was it the strain of being interim mayor that was getting to him? Something had changed. It felt strange to even consider Bernard his friend any more. The man was so much more important now, so much busier. Perhaps he was cracking under the stress that came with the extra responsibility, the pain of being the one to send good people to cleaning—

'You know why I've never taken a shadow?' Bernard asked. He flipped through the manual, saw the play on the reverse side, and turned the bound sheets of paper around. He glanced up at Lukas, who lifted his palms and shrugged.

'It's because I shudder to think of anyone else ever running this place.'

Lukas assumed he meant IT, not the silo. Bernard hadn't been mayor very long.

Bernard set the play down and gazed out the window where muffled voices argued once more.

'But I'll have to, one of these days. I'm at that age where your friends, the people you grew up with, are dropping like flies, but you're still young enough to pretend it won't happen to you.'

His eyes fell to Lukas. The young tech felt uncomfortable being alone with Bernard. He'd never felt that before.

'Silos have burned to the ground before because of one man's hubris,' Bernard told him. 'All it takes is improper planning, thinking you'll be around for ever, but because one man disappears' – he snapped his fingers – 'and leaves a sucking void behind, that can be enough to bring it all down.'

Lukas was dying to ask his boss what the hell he was talking about.

'Today is that day, I think.' Bernard walked around the long conference table, leaving behind him the scattered remnants of Juliette's life. Lukas's gaze drifted over the items. The guilt of going through them himself vanished when he saw how they'd been treated by Bernard. He wished instead that he'd stashed away more of them.

'What I need is someone who already has access to the servers,' Bernard said. Lukas turned to the side and realised the short, full-bellied head of IT was standing right beside him. He moved his hand up to his chest pocket, making sure it didn't bulge open where Bernard could see.

'Sammi is a good tech. I trust him, but he's nearly as old as I am.'

'You aren't that old,' Lukas said, trying to be polite, to gather his wits. He wasn't sure what was going on.

'There's not many I consider a friend,' Bernard said.

'I appreciate that . . .'

'You're probably the closest thing—'

'I feel the same—'

'I knew your father. He was a good man.'

Lukas swallowed and nodded. He looked up at Bernard and realised the man was holding out his hand. Had been for a while. He extended his own to accept, still not sure what was being offered.

'I need a shadow, Lukas.' Bernard's hand felt small in Lukas's own. He watched as his arm was pumped up and down. 'I want you to be that man.'

39

J uliette forced her way through the inner airlock door and scrambled to get it closed. Darkness overwhelmed her as the heavy door squealed on its hinges and settled against its dry seals. She groped for the large locking wheel and leaned on the spokes, spinning it and sealing the door tight.

The air in her suit was growing stale; she could feel the dizziness overtaking her. Turning around, keeping one hand on the wall, she stumbled forward through the darkness. The puff of outside air that she'd allowed inside seemed to claw at her back like a horde of mad insects. Juliette staggered blindly down the hallway, trying to put distance between herself and the dead she'd left behind.

There were no lights on, no glow from the wall screens with their view of the outside world. She prayed the layout was the same, that she could find her way. She prayed the air in her suit would hold out a moment longer, prayed the air in the silo wouldn't be as foul and toxic as the wind outside. Or – and just as bad – that the air in the silo wouldn't be as devoid of oxygen as what little remained in her suit.

Her hand brushed the bars of a cell just where they should be, giving her hope that she could navigate the darkness. She wasn't sure what she hoped to find in the pitch black – she had no plan for salvation – she was simply stumbling away from the horrors outside. It hardly registered for her that she had been there, had gone *outside*, and was now in some place new.

As she fumbled through the office, sucking on the last breaths of air in her helmet, her feet knocked into something and Juliette went sprawling forward. She landed roughly on a soft mound, groped with her hand, and felt an arm. A body. Several bodies. Juliette crawled over them, the spongy flesh feeling more human and solid than the husks and bones outside – and more difficult to move across. She felt someone's chin. The weight of her body caused their neck to turn, and she nearly lost her balance. Her body recoiled at the sensation of what she was doing, the reflex to apologise, to pull her limbs away, but she forced herself forward over a pile of them, through the darkness, until her helmet slammed into the office door.

Without warning, the blow was hard enough that Juliette saw stars and feared blacking out. She reached up and fumbled for the handle. Her eyes might as well have been sealed shut, the utter darkness was so complete. Even the bowels of Mechanical had never seen such deep and perfect shadow.

She found the latch and pushed. The door was unlocked, but wouldn't budge. Juliette scrambled to her feet, her boots digging into lifeless bodies, and threw her shoulder against the door. She wanted out.

The door moved. A little. She could feel something slide on the other side and imagined more bodies piled up. She threw herself again and again into the door, grunts of effort and frustrated tiny screams echoing in her helmet. Her hair was loose, sweaty, and matting to her face. She couldn't see. Couldn't breathe. Was growing more faint as she poisoned her own internal atmosphere.

When the door slid open a crack, she tried to force her way through, one shoulder first, squeezing her helmet past, then pulling her other arm and leg after. She fell to the floor, scrambled around and shoved herself against the door, sealing it tight.

There was a dim light, almost impossible to notice at first. A barricade of tables and chairs were pressed in against her, scattered from her efforts to get through. Their hard edges and spindly legs seemed intent on ensnaring her.

Juliette heard herself wheezing for air and knew her time had run out. She imagined the poison all over her like grease. The toxic air that she'd let in was a cloud of vermin just waiting for her to crawl out of her shell so they could eat away at her.

She considered lying down and letting her air supply run out instead. She would be preserved in this chrysalis of a suit, a well-built suit, a gift from Walker and the people of Supply. Her body would lie for ever in this dim silo that shouldn't exist – but so much better than to rot on a lifeless hill and fly away, piece by piece, on a fickle breeze. It would be a good death. She panted, proud of herself for making it somewhere of her own choosing, for conquering these last few obstacles. Slumping against the door, she very nearly lay down and closed her eyes – but for the nagging of her curiosity.

Juliette held up her hands and studied them in the dim glow from the stairwell. The shiny gloves – wrapped in heat tape and melted to form a bright skin – made her look like a machine of sorts. She ran her hands over the dome of her helmet, realising she was like a walking toaster. When she had been a mere shadow in Mechanical, she'd had a bad habit of taking things apart, even those that already worked. What had Walker said of her? That she liked nothing more than peering inside of toasters.

Juliette sat up and tried to focus. She was losing sensation, and with it the will to live. She shook her head and pulled herself to her feet, sent a pile of chairs crashing to the floor. She was the toaster, she realised. Her curiosity wanted it open. This time, to see what was *outside*. To take one breath and know.

She swam through the tables and chairs, wanting more and more distance between herself and any bad air she had let in. The bodies she had crawled over in the sheriff's office had felt whole. Naturally dead. Trapped inside and starved or asphyxiated, perhaps. But not rotten. Still, and despite her lightheadedness and need to breathe, she wanted to somehow douse herself before cracking the helmet, wanted to dilute the toxins as she would with any other chemical spill back in Mechanical.

She escaped the barrier of tables and chairs and made her way across the open cafeteria floor. The emergency lights in the stairwell leaked a green glow to dimly show the way. She passed through the serving door and into the kitchen, and tried the taps on the large sink. The handles turned, but the spout didn't leak a drop, didn't knock with even a futile try from distant pumps.

She went to the dangling hose over the dish station and pulled that lever – and was similarly rewarded. There was no water.

Her next thought was the walk-ins, to maybe freeze the nastiness she could feel crawling all over her suit. She staggered around the cooking stations and pulled the large silver handle on the door, her breath wheezy in her helmet. The light in the back reaches of the kitchen was already so dim she could barely see. She couldn't feel any cold through her suit, but wasn't sure if she'd be able to. It was built to shield her, and built well. The overhead light didn't come on, so she assumed the freezer was dead. With the door open, she peered inside, looking for anything fluid, and saw what looked like vats of soup.

She was desperate enough to try anything. Juliette moved inside the walk-in, letting the door swing slowly shut behind her. She seized one of the large plastic containers, a bucket the size of the largest cooking pots, and tore the top off. The door clicked shut, returning her to solid darkness. Juliette knelt beneath the shelf and tipped the massive bucket over. She could feel the liquid soup splatter over her suit, crinkling it and splashing to the floor. Her knees slipped in the stuff. She felt for the next one and did the same, ran her fingers into the puddles and coated herself in it. There was no way of knowing if she was being crazy, if she was making things worse, or if any of it mattered. Her boot slipped, sending her flat onto her back, her helmet cracking against the floor.

Juliette lay there in a puddle of tepid soup, unable to see, her breath raspy and stale. Her time had run out. She was dizzy and could think of nothing else to try, didn't have the breath or energy, anyway. The helmet had to come off.

She fumbled for the latches, could barely feel them through her gloves. Her gloves were too thick. They were going to kill her.

She rolled to her belly and crawled through the soup, her hands and knees slipping. She reached the door, gasping, and fumbled for the handle, found it, threw the door open. There was a rack of knives gleaming behind the counter. She lurched to her feet and grabbed one, held the blade in her thick mitts, and slumped to the floor, exhausted and dizzy.

Turning the blade towards her own neck, Juliette groped for

the latch. She slid the point along her collar until it caught in the crack of the button. Steadying herself, her arm shaking, she moved the knife and pressed in, shoving it towards her body against all her most human instincts.

There was a faint click. Juliette gasped and groped along the rim with the blade for the other button until she found it. She repeated the manoeuvre.

Another click, and her helmet popped off.

Juliette's body took over for her, compelling her to take deep gulps of foul air. The stench was unbearable, but she couldn't stop gasping for more. Rotted food, biological decay, a tepid filth of stenches invaded her mouth, tongue, nose.

She turned to the side and wretched, but nothing came out. Her hands were still slippery with soup. Breathing was painful; she imagined a burning sensation on her skin, but it could've been her fevered state. She crawled away from the walk-in, towards the cafeteria, out of the fog of rotting soup, and took another gulp of air.

Air.

She took a lungful, the odour still overpowering, the soup coating her. But beyond the stench, something else was there. Something faint. Something *breathable* that began to force away the dizziness and the panic. It was *oxygen*. Life.

Juliette was still alive.

She laughed madly and stumbled towards the stairwell, drawn to the green glow of light, breathing deeply and too exhausted to appreciate this, the *impossible* life still in her.

40

Knox saw the uproar in Mechanical as just another emergency to overcome. Like the time the basement subwall had sprung a leak, or when the oil rig had hit that pocket of methane and they had to evacuate eight levels until the air handlers made it safe to return. Against the inevitable flow of commotion, what he needed to do was push for order. To assign tasks. He had to break a huge undertaking down to discrete bits and make sure they fell to the right hands. Only this time, he and his people wouldn't be setting out to repair something. There were things the good people of Mechanical meant to *break*.

'Supply is the key,' he told his foremen, pointing to the large-scale blueprint hanging on the wall. He traced the stairwell up the thirty flights to Supply's main manufacturing floor. 'Our greatest advantage is that IT doesn't know we're coming.' He turned to his shift leaders. 'Shirly, Marck, and Courtnee, you'll come with me. We'll load up with supplies and take your shadows with us. Walker, you can wire ahead to let 'em know we're coming. Be careful, though. Assume IT has ears. Say we have a load of your repairs to deliver.'

He turned to Jenkins, who had shadowed under Knox for six years before he grew his own beard and moved to third shift. The assumption everywhere was that Knox's job was his in waiting. 'Jenks, I want you to take over down here. There are no days off for a while. Keep the place running, but get ready for the worst. I want as much food stockpiled as possible. And water. Make sure the cistern is topped up. Divert from the hydroponics feed if you have to, but be discreet. Think of an excuse, like a leak or something, in case they notice. Meanwhile, have someone make the rounds and check every lock and hinge, just in case the fighting comes to us. And stockpile whatever weapons you can make up. Pipes, hammers, whatever.'

Some eyebrows were lifted at this, but Jenkins nodded at the list as if it all made sense and was doable. Knox turned to his foremen. 'What? You know where this is heading, right?'

'But what's the larger picture?' Courtnee asked, glancing at the tall blueprint of their buried home. 'Storm IT, and then what? Take over running this place?'

'We already run this place,' Knox growled. He slapped his hand across the floors of the mid-thirties. 'We just do it in the dark. Like these levels here are dark to us. But now I mean to shine a light in their rat hole and scare them out, see what else they're hiding.'

'You understand what they've been doing, right?' Marck turned to Courtnee. 'They've been sending people out to die. On purpose. Not because it *had* to happen, but because they wanted it to!'

Courtnee bit her lip and didn't say anything, just stared at the blueprint.

'We need to get going,' Knox said. 'Walker, get that wire out. Let's load up. And think of something pleasant to chat about while we're on the move. No grumbling about this where some porter can hear and make a chit or two ratting us out.'

They nodded. Knox slapped Jenkins on the back and dipped his chin at the younger man. 'I'll send word when we need everyone. Keep the bare bones you think you've gotta have down here and send the rest. Timing is everything, okay?'

'I know what to do,' Jenkins said. He wasn't trying to be uppity, just reassuring his elder.

'All right,' Knox said. 'Then let's get to it.'

They made it up ten flights with little complaint, but Knox could begin to feel the burn in his legs from the heavy load. He had a canvas sack stuffed full of welding smocks on his wide shoulders, plus a bundle of helmets. A rope had been strung through their chin straps, and they clattered down his wide back. Marck struggled with his load of pipe stock as they kept trying to slide against one another and slip out of his arms. The shadows brought up the rear, behind the women, with heavy sacks of blasting powder tied together so they hung around their necks. Professional porters with similarly full loads breezed past them in both directions, their glances signalling a mix of curiosity and competitive anger. When one porter – a woman Knox recognised from deliveries to the down deep – stopped and offered to help, he gruffly sent her on her way. She hurried up the steps, looking back over her shoulder before spiralling out of view, and Knox regretted taking his exhaustion out on her.

'Keep it up,' he told the others. Even with the small group, they were making a spectacle. And it was growing ever more tiresome to hold their tongues as news of Juliette's amazing disappearance gyred all around them. At almost every landing, a group of people, often younger people, stood around and gossiped about what it all meant. The taboo had moved from thought to whisper. Forbidden notions were birthed on tongues and swam through the air. Knox ignored the pain in his back and lumbered up and up, each step driving them closer to Supply, feeling more and more like they needed to get there in a hurry.

As they left the one-thirties, the grumblings were fully in the air. They were nearing the upper half of the down deep, where people who worked, shopped, and ate in the mids mingled with those who would rather they didn't. Deputy Hank was on the stairwell of one-twenty-eight, trying to mediate between two arguing crowds. Knox squeezed past, hoping the officer wouldn't turn and see his heavily loaded train and ask them what they were doing up this far. As he ascended past the ruckus, Knox glanced back to watch the shadows slink past, hugging the inner rail. Deputy Hank was still asking a woman to please calm down as the landing sank out of sight.

They passed the dirt farm on one-twenty-six, and Knox figured this to be a key asset. The thirties of IT were a long hike up, but if they had to fall back, they would need to hold at Supply. Between their manufacturing, the food on this level, and the machinery of Mechanical, they might be self-sufficient. He could think of a few weak links, but many more for IT. They could always shut off their power or stop treating their water – but he really hoped, as they approached Supply on weary legs, that it wouldn't come to any of that.

They were greeted on the landing of one-ten by frowns. McLain, the elder woman and head of Supply, stood with her arms crossed over her yellow overalls, her stance screaming unwelcome.

'Hello, Jove.' Knox fixed her with a wide smile.

'Don't *Jove* me,' McLain said. 'What's this nonsense you're after?'

Knox glanced up and down the stairwell, shrugged his heavy load higher up his shoulder. 'Mind if we step in and talk about it?'

'I don't want any trouble here,' she said, her eyes blazing beneath her lowered brow.

'Let's go inside,' Knox said. 'We haven't stopped once on the way up. Unless you want us collapsing out here.'

McLain seemed to consider this. Her arms loosened across her chest. She turned to three of her workers, who formed an imposing wall behind her, and nodded. While they pulled open the gleaming doors of Supply, she turned and grabbed Knox's arm. 'Don't get comfortable,' she told him.

Inside the front room of Supply, Knox found a small army of men and women in their yellow overalls, waiting. Most of them stood behind the low, long counter where the people of the silo normally waited for whatever parts they needed, whether newly fabricated or recently repaired. The parallel and deep aisles of shelves beyond ran into the gloomy distance, boxes and bins bulging off of them. The room was noticeably quiet. Usually, the mechanical thrumming and clanking sounds of fabrication could be heard worming their way through the space, or one might hear workers chatting unseen back in the stacks while they sorted newly fashioned bolts and nuts into hungry bins. Now it was just silence and distrustful glares.

Knox stood with his people, their sacks and loads slumping exhaustedly to the floor, sweat on their brows, while the men and women of Supply watched, unmoving. He had expected a more amicable welcome. Mechanical and Supply had a long history together. They jointly ran the small mine beneath the lowest levels of Mechanical that supplemented the silo's stockpile of ores.

But now, as McLain followed her boys back inside, she graced Knox with a look of scorn he hadn't seen since his mother passed away.

'What in the hell is the meaning of this?' she hissed at Knox.

He was taken aback by the language, especially in front of his people. He thought of himself and McLain as equals, but now he was being snapped at as if by one of Supply's dogs. Made to feel small and worthless.

McLain's gaze ranged down the exhausted line of mechanics and their shadows before turning back to him.

'Before we discuss how we're cleaning up this problem, I want to hear how you're handling your employees, whoever was responsible.' Her eyes bore through him. 'I *am* correct in assuming you had nothing to do with this, right? That you've come to apologise and shower me with bribes?'

Shirly started to say something, but Knox waved her off. There were a lot of people in the room just waiting for this to go undiplomatically.

'Yes, I do apologise,' Knox said, grinding his teeth together and bowing his head. 'And no, I just learned of this earlier today. After I found out about the cleaning, in fact.'

'So it was all your electrician,' McLain said, her thin arms crossed tightly over her chest. 'One man.'

'That's right. But—'

'I've meted out punishment to those involved here, let me tell you. And I suppose you'll have to do more than banish that old fart to his room.'

There was laughter behind the counter. Knox put a hand on Shirly's shoulder to keep her in place. He looked past McLain to the men and women arranged behind her.

'They came and took one of our workers,' he said. His chest may have been heavy, but his voice still boomed. 'You know how it happens. When they want a body for cleaning, they *take* it.' He thumped his chest. 'And I *let* them. I stood there because I trust this system. I *fear* it, just as any of you.'

'Well—' McLain began, but Knox cut her short, continuing in that voice that routinely gave calm commands over the racket of machines run amok.

'One of my people was taken, and it was the oldest of us, the wisest of us, who intervened on her behalf. It was the weakest and most scared who braved his neck. And whoever of you he turned to for help, and who gave it, I owe you my life.' Knox blinked away the blur and continued. 'You gave her more than a chance to walk over that hill, to die in peace and out of sight. You gave *me* the courage to open my eyes. To see this veil of lies we live behind—'

'That's quite enough,' McLain barked. 'Someone could be sent to cleaning for even *listening* to such nonsense, to such *drivel*.'

'It's not nonsense,' Marck cried down the line. 'Juliette is dead because of—'

'She's dead because she broke these very laws!' McLain snapped, her voice high and shrill. 'And now you march up here to break even more? On *my* level?'

'We aim to break heads!' Shirly said.

'Leave it!' Knox told them both. He saw the anger in McLain's eyes, but he also saw something else: the sporadic nods and raised brows among the rank and file behind her.

A porter entered the room with empty sacks in each hand and looked around at the tense silence. One of the large Supply workers by the door ushered him back onto the landing with apologies, telling him to return later. Knox composed his words carefully during the interruption.

'No person has ever been sent to cleaning for *listening*, however great the taboo.' He allowed that to sink in. He glared at McLain as she moved to interrupt, but she seemed to decide against it. 'So let me be sent to cleaning by any of you for what I'm about to say. I will welcome it if these facts do not move you to instead push forward with me and my men. For this is what Walker and a few of you brave souls have shown us this morning. We have cause for more hope than they dare give us. There's more at our disposal to broaden our horizons than they'll allow. We have been raised on a pack of lies, made to fear by the sight of our kinsmen rotting on the hills, but now one of us has crossed over that! They have seen new horizons! We have been given seals and washers and told that they should suffice, but what are they?'

He stared down the men and women behind the counter. McLain's arms seemed to loosen across her chest.

'Designed to fail, that's what! Fake. And who knows what other lies there are. What if we'd taken any cleaner back and done our best by them? Cleaned and disinfected them? Tried whatever we could? Would they survive? We can no longer trust IT to tell us they wouldn't!'

Knox saw chins rise and fall. He knew his own people were ready to storm the room if need be; they were as amped up and driven mad by all this as he was.

'We are not here to cause trouble,' he said, 'we are here to bring *order*! The uprising has already happened.' He turned to McLain. 'Don't you see? We've been *living* the uprising. Our parents were the children of it, and now we feed our own children to the same machine. This will *not* be the start of something new, but the end of something old. And if Supply is with us, we stand a chance. If not, then may our bodies haunt your view of the *outside*, which I now see as far less rotten than this blasted silo!'

Knox bellowed this last in open defiance of all taboo. He threw it out and savoured the taste of it, the admission that anything beyond those curved walls might be better than what was inside them. The whisper that had killed so many became a throaty roar shouted from his broad chest.

And it felt good.

McLain cringed. She took a step away, something like fear in her eyes. She turned her back on Knox and made to return to her people, and he knew he had failed. There had been a chance, however slim, in this silent and still crowd to inspire action, but the moment had slipped him by or he had scared it off.

And then McLain did something. Knox could see the tendons in her slender neck bulge. She lifted her chin to her people, her white hair in its tight knot high on her head, and she said, quietly, 'What say you, Supply?'

It was a question, not a command. Knox would later wonder if it had been asked in sadness; he would wonder if she had taken poor stock of her people, who had listened patiently during his madness. He would also wonder if she were just curious, or if she were challenging them to cast him and his mechanics out.

But now he wondered, tears streaming down his face, thoughts of Juliette swelling inside his heart, if he could even hear his handful of compatriots shouting, so drowned out were they by the angry war cries of the good men and women of Supply.

41

Lukas followed Bernard through the halls of IT, nervous techs scattering before them like night bugs startled by the light. Bernard didn't seem to notice the techs ducking into offices and peering through windows. Lukas hurried to keep up, his eyes darting side to side, feeling conspicuous with all these hidden others watching.

'Aren't I a little old to be shadowing for another job?' he asked. He was pretty sure he hadn't accepted the offer, not verbally anyway, but Bernard spoke as if the deal was done.

'Nonsense,' he said. 'And this won't be shadowing in the traditional sense.' He waved his hand in the air. 'You'll continue your duties as before. I just need someone who can step in, who knows what to do in case something happens to me. My will' – he stopped at the heavy door to the server room and turned to face Lukas – 'if it came to it, in an emergency, my will would explain everything to the next head, but' – he gazed over Lukas's shoulder and down the hall – 'Sims is my executor, which we'll have to change. I just don't see that ever going smoothly.'

Bernard rubbed his chin and lost himself in his thoughts. Lukas waited a moment, then stepped beside him and entered his code on the panel by the door, fished his ID out of his pocket – made sure it was *his* ID and not Juliette's – and swiped it through the reader. The door clicked open, snapping Bernard out of his thoughts.

'Yes, well, this will be much better. Not that I expect to go anywhere, mind you.' He adjusted his glasses and stepped through the heavy steel doorway. Lukas followed, pushing the monstrous enclosure shut behind them and waiting for the locks to engage.

'But if something did happen to you, I would oversee the cleanings?' Lukas couldn't imagine. He suspected there was more to learn about those suits than the servers. Sammi would be better at this, would actually *want* this job. Also – would he have to abandon his star charts?

'That's a small part of the job, but yes.' Bernard guided Lukas through the servers, past number thirteen with its blank face and still fans, all the way to the back of the room.

'These are the keys to the true heart of the silo,' Bernard said, fishing a jangling set out of his overalls. They were strung on a cord of leather that hung around his neck. Lukas had never noticed them before.

'There are other features to this cabinet that you'll learn about in time. For now, you simply need to know how to get downstairs.' He inserted the key into several locks on the back of the server, locks designed to look like recessed screws. What server was this? Twenty-eight? Lukas glanced around the room and tried to count its position, and realised he'd never been assigned to maintain this tower.

There was a gentle clang as the back came off. Bernard set it aside, and Lukas saw why he'd never worked on the machine. It was practically empty, just a shell, like it had been scrapped for parts over the long years.

'It's crucial that you lock this after coming back up.'

Lukas watched Bernard grab a handle in the bottom of the empty chassis. Bernard pulled it towards him, and there was a soft grinding noise nearby. 'When the grate's back in place, you simply press this down to secure it.'

Lukas was about to ask 'What grate?' when Bernard stepped aside and dug his fingers into the metal slats of the floor. With a grunt, he pulled the heavy surface of the flooring up and began sliding it over. Lukas jumped around to the other side and bent down to help.

'Wouldn't the stairs . . . ?' he started to ask.

'They don't access this part of thirty-five.' Bernard waved at a ladder leading down through the floor. 'You go first.'

Lukas's head spun from the day's sudden turn. As he bent to

grab the ladder he felt the contents of his breast pocket shift, and shot a hand up to hold the watch, ring, and ID steady. What had he been thinking? What was he thinking now? He lowered himself down the long ladder feeling like someone had initiated an automated routine in his brain, a rote program that had taken over his actions. From the bottom of the ladder, he watched as Bernard lowered himself down the first rungs before sliding the grate into place, sealing them both inside the dark dungeon beneath the already-fortressed server room.

'You are about to receive a great gift,' Bernard said in the darkness. 'Just as I was once granted the same.'

He flicked on a light, and Lukas saw that his boss was grinning maniacally, the anger from before gone. Here was a new man before him, a confident and eager man.

'All the silo and everyone in it hinges on what I'm about to show you,' Bernard said. He beckoned Lukas down the brightly lit but narrow corridor towards a wider room beyond. The servers felt very far above. Lukas felt closed off from every other soul in the silo; he was curious, but also afraid. He wasn't sure he wanted such responsibility and cursed himself for going along with this.

And yet, his feet moved. They carried him down that hidden passageway and into a room full of the strange and curious, a place that made the charting of stars seem insignificant, a den where the sense of the world's scale, of *size*, took on wholly new proportions.

42

J uliette left her soup-slathered helmet on the floor and moved towards the pale-green glow of light. It seemed brighter than before. She wondered how much of the darkness had been because of her helmet. As her senses returned, she remembered that it wasn't a piece of glass she'd been looking through, but some infernal screen that took the world as she saw it and overlaid it with half a lie. Maybe it had dimmed her view in the process.

She noticed the stench from her drenched suit followed her, the smell of rotten vegetables and mould – or possibly the toxic fumes from the outside world. Her throat burned a little as she crossed the cafeteria towards the stairwell. Her skin began to itch, and she couldn't tell if it was from fear, her imagination, or truly something in the air. She didn't dare risk finding out, so she held her breath and hurried as fast as her weary legs would take her, around the corner to where she knew the stairs would be.

This world is the same as my world, she thought to herself, stumbling down the first flight of stairs in the wan glow of emergency light strips. *God built more than one.*

Her heavy boots, still dripping with soup, felt unsteady on the metal treads. At the landing on two, she paused and took in a few big gulps of air, less painful gulps, and considered how best to remove the infernal and bulky outfit that made every movement awkward, that reeked of the fetid smell of rot and outside air. She looked down at her arms. The thing had required help to put on. There were double zippers in the back, layers of Velcro, miles of heat tape. She looked at the knife in her hand, suddenly grateful that she hadn't dropped it after using it to remove her helmet.

Gripping the knife with one clumsy glove, she carefully inserted the tip through the other sleeve, right above the top of her wrist. She forced the point through, pushing the blade over the top of her arm so it wouldn't jab her even if it pierced all the way. The fabric was difficult to cut, but a tear finally formed as she worked the handle in small circles. She slid the knife into this tiny rip, the dull side of the blade facing her skin, and slid it down her arm and towards her knuckles. When the tip of the blade ripped through the fabric between her fingers, she was able to free her hand from the long gash she'd made, the sleeve flopping from her elbow.

Juliette sat down on the grating, moved the knife to her newly freed hand, and worked on the other side. She freed it as well while soup dripped from her shoulders and down her arms. She next started a tear at her chest, having better control of the knife now without the thick gloves on. She ripped the metal foil exterior away, peeling herself like an orange. The solid collar for her helmet had to stay – it was attached to her charcoal fabric under-suit as well as the reinforced zippers up her back – but piece by piece she removed the shiny outer coat which was slathered with a nastiness she attributed partly to the soup and partly to her trek over the hills.

Next came her boots, which were cut free around the ankles until she was able to work them off, sawing a slit down the outside edge and popping one foot free, then the other.

Before she cleaned up the hanging tatters of fabric any further, or worried about the material still attached to the zipper at her back, she got up from the landing and hurried down the steps, putting more distance between herself and the air above, which seemed to scratch at her throat. She was another two flights down, swimming through the green glow of the stairwell, before she appreciated the fact that she was alive.

She was alive.

For however much longer, this was a brutal, beautiful, and brand-new fact for Juliette. She had spent three days climbing long stairs similar to these as she came to grips with her fate. Another day and night had been spent in a cell made for the future corpses who dotted the landscape. And then – *this*. An impossible trek through the wilderness of the forbidden, breaking in to the impenetrable and the unknown.

Surviving.

Whatever happened next, for this moment, Juliette flew down foreign steps in bare feet, the steel cool against her tingling skin, the air burning her throat less and less with each gulp of new air, the raw stench and memory of death receding further and further above her. Soon, it was just the patter of her joyous descent ringing out and drifting down a lonely and empty darkness like a muffled bell that rang not for the dead, but for the living.

She stopped on six and rested while she worked on what remained of her protective suit. With care, she sliced her black undersuit by her shoulders and collarbone, working the tear all the way around and clawing at her back as it ripped free, strips of heat tape still attached. Once the helmet collar was detached from the fabric – just the zipper hanging like a second spine along her back – she could finally remove it from her neck. She pulled it off and dropped it to the ground, then stripped off the rest of the black carbon fabric, peeling away the arms and legs and leaving all the material in a rough pile outside the double doors to level six.

Six should be an apartment level, she thought. She considered going inside and yelling out for help or looking for clothes and supplies in the many rooms, but her greater impulse was to descend. The up top felt poisoned and too close. It didn't matter if it was all in her imagination or from her miserable experiences living in the up top of her own silo – her body felt a revulsion for the place. Safe was the down deep. It had always felt this way.

One hopeful image did linger from the upper kitchen: the rows and rows of canned and jarred food for the lean harvests. Juliette figured there would be more in the lower mess halls as well. And the air in the silo seemed decent as she regained her breath; the sting in her lungs and on her tongue had faded. Either the vast silo held a lot of air that was now being consumed by no one, or there was still a source. All these thoughts gave her hope, these tallies of resources. So she left her spoiled and tattered clothing behind and, armed with only a large chef's knife, she stole down the curved stairs naked, her body becoming more and more alive with every step taken, her mind becoming more determined to keep the rest of her that way.

On thirteen, she stopped and checked inside the doors. There was always the chance that this silo was laid out completely differently, floor to floor, so it made little sense to plan ahead if she didn't know what to expect. There were only a handful of areas in the up top that she was intimately familiar with, and every bit of overlap so far had seemed a perfect copy. Thirteen, she would definitely know. There were certain things, learned so young and remembered so deep that they felt like little stones in the centre of her mind. These would be the parts of her that rotted last, the bits left over once the rest skittered off on the wind or was drunk deep by the roots. In her mind, as she pushed the door open a crack, she wasn't in a different silo, an abandoned husk of a silo, but in her past, pushing open a door on her youth.

It was dark inside, none of the security or emergency lights on. There was a different smell. The air was stagnant and had a tinge of decay.

Juliette shouted down the hallway: 'Hello?'

She listened to her voice echo back from the empty walls. The voice that returned sounded distant, weaker, higher than her own. She imagined herself at age nine, running through these very halls, crying out to her older self across the years. She tried to picture her mother chasing behind that girl, attempting to scoop her up and force her to be still, but the ghosts evaporated in the darkness. The last of the echoes faded, leaving her alone and naked in the doorway.

As her eyes adjusted, she could just barely make out a reception desk at the end of the hall. Light reflected off glass windows just where they should be. It was the exact same layout as her father's nursery in the mids, the place where she had been not just born, but raised. It was hard to believe that this was some place *different*. That *other* people had lived here, other children had been born, had played and had been raised just over a hill and down a dip, had given chase or challenged each other to Hop or whatever games they had invented, all of them unaware of the other. Maybe it was from standing in the doorway of a nursery, but she couldn't help but think of all the lives this place had contained. People growing up, falling in love, burying their dead.

All those people *outside*. People she had desecrated with her boots, scattering their bones and ashes as she kicked her way into the very place they had fled. Juliette wondered how long ago it had happened, how long since the silo had been abandoned. What *had* happened here? The stairwell was still lit, which meant the battery room still held juice. She needed paper to do the maths, to figure how recently or how long ago all this life had turned to death. There were practical reasons for wanting to know, beyond the mere itch of curiosity.

With one last look inside, one final shudder of regret for not stopping to see her father the last few times she'd passed his nursery, Juliette shut the door on the darkness and the ghosts and considered her predicament. She could very well be perfectly alone in a dying silo. The thrill of being alive at all was quickly draining away, replaced with the reality of her solitude and the tenuousness of her survival. Her stomach grumbled its agreement. She could somehow still smell the fetid soup on her, could taste the stomach acid from her retching. She needed water. She needed clothes. These primal urges were pushed to the forefront, drowning out the severity of her situation, the daunting tasks before her, leaving the regrets of the past behind.

If the layout was the same, the first hydroponic farm would be four floors below and the larger of the two upper dirt farms would lie just below that. Juliette shivered from an updraught of cold air. The stairwell was creating its own thermal cycle, and it would only be colder the further down she went. But she went anyway – lower was better. At the next level, she tried the door. It was too dark to see past the first interior hallway, but it seemed like offices or workrooms. She tried to remember what would be on the fourteenth in her own silo, but didn't know. Was it incredible not to know? The up top of her own home had somehow been strange to her. That made this silo something completely alien.

She held the door to fourteen open and stuck the blade of her knife between the slits of metal that formed every landing's grating. The handle was left sticking up to form a stop. She allowed the door to close on its sprung hinges until it rested on the handle, holding it open. This let in enough light for her to steal inside and grope around the first handful of rooms.

There were no overalls hanging on the backs of the doors, but one room was set up for conferences. The water in the pitchers had long evaporated, but the purple tablecloth looked warm enough. Warmer than being naked. Juliette moved the assortment of cups, plates, and pitchers and grabbed the cloth. She wrapped it around her shoulders, but it was going to slip off when she moved, so she tried knotting the corners in front of her. Giving up on this, she ran back to the landing, out into the welcomed light, and removed the fabric completely. Grabbing the knife – the door squealing eerily shut behind her – she pushed the blade through the centre of the tablecloth and cut a long gash. Her head went through this, the cloth falling past her feet in front and behind her. A few minutes with the blade and she'd cut away the excess, forming a belt out of a long strip and from another shock of fabric, enough to tie over her head and keep it warm.

It felt good to be making something, to be engineering her way through one particular problem. She had a tool, a weapon if need be, and clothes. The impossible list of tasks had been whittled down a few shavings. She descended further, her feet cold on the stairs, dreaming of boots, thirsty for water, very much aware of all that remained for her to do.

On fifteen, she was reminded of another necessity as her weary legs nearly gave way. Her knees buckled, she grabbed the railing, and she realised, as the adrenalin left her veins, that she was deathly tired. She paused on the landing, hands on her knees, and took a few deep breaths. How long had she been going? How much further could she push herself? She checked her reflection in the blade of the knife, saw how horrible she looked, and decided she needed rest before she went any further. Rest now, while it was still warm enough not to shiver to pieces.

It was tempting to explore that level for a bed, but she decided against it – there would be little comfort in the pitch black behind those doors. So she curled up on the steel grating of landing fifteen, tucked her arms under her head, and adjusted the tablecloth so every patch of bare skin was covered. And before she could go over the long list forming in her head, exhaustion took over. She drifted off to sleep with only a moment's panic that she shouldn't be so tired, that this might be the sort of nap one never woke up from, that she was destined to join the residents of this strange place, curled up and unmoving, frozen and lifeless, rotting and wasting away . . .

43

'Do you understand what you're proposing we do?'

Knox looked up at McLain, met her wrinkled and piercing eyes with as much confidence as he could muster. The tiny woman who controlled all the silo's spares and fabrication cast an oddly imposing figure. She didn't have Knox's barrel chest or thick beard, had wrists barely bigger than two of his fingers, but she possessed a wizened grey gaze and the weight of hard years that made him feel but a shadow in her presence.

'It's not an uprising,' he said, the forbidden words moving easily with the grease of habit and time. 'We're setting things to rights.'

McLain sniffed. 'I'm sure that's what my great-grandparents said.' She pushed back loose strands of silver hair and peered down at the blueprint spread out between them. It was as if she knew this was wrong, but had resigned herself to helping rather than hinder it. Maybe it was her age, Knox thought, peering at her pink scalp through hair so thin and white as to be like filaments of glass. Perhaps, with enough time in these walls, one could become resigned to things never getting better, or even changing all that much. Or maybe a person eventually lost hope that there was anything worth preserving at all.

He looked down at the blueprint and smoothed the sharp creases in the fine paper. He was suddenly aware of his hands, how thick and grease-limned his fingers appeared. He wondered if McLain saw him as a brute, storming up here with delusions of justice. She was old enough to consider him young, he realised. Young and hot-tempered, while he thought of himself as being old and wise.

One of the dozens of dogs that lived among Supply's stacks grunted discontentedly under the table as if all this war planning were spoiling its nap.

'I think it's safe to assume IT knows something is coming,' McLain said, running her small hands across the many floors between them and thirty-four.

'Why? You don't think we were discreet coming up?'

She smiled up at him. 'I'm sure you were, but it's safe to assume this because it would be dangerous to assume otherwise.'

He nodded and chewed on the part of his beard below his lower lip.

'How long will the rest of your mechanics take to get here?' McLain asked.

'They'll leave around ten, when the stairwell is dimmed, and be here by two, three at the latest. They'll be loaded down.'

'And you think a dozen of your men is sufficient to keep things running down below?'

'As long as nothing major breaks, yeah.' He scratched the back of his neck. 'Where d'ya think the porters will fall? Or the people from the mids?'

She shrugged. 'The mids see themselves as toppers mostly. I know, I spent my childhood up there. They go for the view and eat at the cafe as much as they can, justifying the climb. The toppers are another question. I think we have more hope among them.'

Knox wasn't sure he heard her correctly. 'Say again?'

She looked up at him, and Knox felt the dog nuzzling against his boots, looking for company or warmth.

'Think about it,' McLain said. 'Why are you so riled up? Because you lost a good friend? That happens all the time. No, it's because you were *lied* to. And the toppers will feel this ever more keenly, trust me. They live in sight of those who've been lied to. It's the mids, the people who aspire upward without knowing and who look down on us without compassion that will be the most reluctant.'

'So you think we have allies up top?'

'That we can't get to, yeah. And they would take some convincing. A fine speech like you poisoned my people with.'

She gifted him with a rare grin, and Knox felt himself beaming in return. And right then he knew, instantly, why her people were devoted to her. It was similar to the pull he had on others, but for different reasons. People feared him and wanted to feel safe. But they respected McLain and wanted to feel loved.

'The problem we're gonna have is that the mids are what separate us from IT.' She drew her hand across the blueprint. 'So we need to get through there quick but without starting a fight.'

'I thought we'd just storm up before dawn,' Knox grumbled. He leaned back and peered under the table at the dog, who was half sitting on one of his boots and looking up at him with its foolish tongue hanging out, tail wagging. All Knox saw in the animal was a machine that ate food and left shit behind. A furry ball of meat he wasn't allowed to eat. He nudged the filthy thing off his boot. 'Scram,' he said.

'Jackson, get over here.' McLain snapped her fingers.

'I don't know why you keep those things around, much less breed more of 'em.'

'You wouldn't,' McLain snapped back. 'They're good for the soul, for those of us who have them.'

He checked to see if she was serious and found her smiling a little more easily now.

'Well, after we set this place right, I'm gonna push for a lottery for them, too. Get their numbers under control.' He returned her sarcastic smile. Jackson whined until McLain reached down to pet him.

'If we were all as loyal as this to each other, there'd never need to *be* an uprising,' she said, peering up at him.

He dipped his head, unable to agree. There had been a few dogs in Mechanical over the years, enough for him to know that some people felt this way, even if he didn't. He always shook his head at those who spent hard-earned chits on food that would fatten an animal that would never repay the favour. When Jackson crossed under the table and rubbed against his knee, whining to be petted, Knox left his hands spread out on the blueprint, defiant.

'What we need for the trip up is a diversion,' McLain said. 'Something to thin the numbers in the mids. It'd be nice if we could get more of them to go up top, because we're going to make a racket moving this many people up the stairs.'

'We? Wait, you don't think you're coming—'

'If my people are, then of course I am.' She inclined her head. 'I've been climbing ladders in the stockroom for over fifty years. You think a few flights of stairs will give me grief?'

Knox wasn't sure *anything* could give her grief. Jackson's tail thumped the leg of the table as the mutt stood there, looking up at him with that dumb grin his breed habitually wore.

'What about welding doors shut on the way up?' Knox asked. 'Keep them in until this is all over.'

'And do what afterwards? Just apologise? What if this takes weeks?'

'Weeks?'

'You don't think it'll be that easy, do you? Just march up and take the reins?'

'I'm under no delusions about what comes next.' He pointed at her office door, which led out to the workshops full of clacking machinery. 'Our people are building the implements of war, and I aim to use them if it comes to that. I will gladly take a peaceful transfer, would be satisfied pushing Bernard and a few others out to clean, but I have never shied away from getting dirty, either.'

McLain nodded. 'Just so we're both clear—'

'Clear as glass,' he said.

He clapped his hands, an idea forming. Jackson ducked away from the sudden noise.

'I've got it,' he told her. 'A diversion.' He pointed to the lower floors of Mechanical on the blueprint. 'What if we have Jenkins cascade a power outage? We could start a few levels above this, or even better, with the farms and the mess halls. Blame it on the recent generator work—'

'And you think the mids'll clear out?' She narrowed her eyes.

'If they want a warm meal. Or they'll hunker down in the dark.'

'I think they'll be in the stairwell gossiping, wondering what all the fuss is about. Even more in our way.'

'Then we'll tell them we're going up to fix the problem!' Knox felt himself getting frustrated. The damn dog was sitting on his boot again.

'*Up* to fix a problem?' McLain laughed. 'When's the last time *that* made any sense?'

Knox pulled on his beard. He wasn't sure what was so complicated. There were a lot of them. They worked with tools all day. They were going to beat in tech heads, little men like Bernard who sat on their butts and clacked on keyboards like secretaries. They just needed to go up there and *do* it.

'You got any better ideas?' he asked.

'We need to keep in mind the *after*,' McLain said. 'After you've bludgeoned some people to death and the blood is dripping through the grates, what then? Do you want people living in fear of that happening again? Or of whatever you put them through to get there?'

'I only want to hurt those that lied,' he said. 'That's all any of us want. We've *all* lived in fear. Fear of the outside. Fear of cleaning. Afraid to even talk about a better world. And none of it was true. The system was rigged, and in a way to make us hang our heads and *take* it—'

Jackson barked up at him and began to whine, his tail swishing the floor like a dropped air hose with a stuck nozzle that had gone out of control.

'I think when we're done,' he said, 'and we start talking about using our know-how to explore a world we've only ever looked out at, I think that's gonna inspire some people. Hell, it gives me hope. Don't you feel anything?'

He reached down and rubbed Jackson's head, which stopped the animal from making so much noise. McLain looked at him for a while. She finally bobbed her head in agreement.

'We'll go with the power outage,' she said with finality. 'Tonight, before any who went to see the cleaning return disappointed. I'll lead up a squad with candles and flashlights, make it look like a goodwill mission headed by Supply. You'll follow a few hours later with the rest. We'll see how far the repair story gets us before we run into trouble. Hopefully, a good number will be staying in the up top, or back in their beds in the mids, too exhausted from climbing for a meal to care about the commotion.'

'There'll be less traffic those early hours,' Knox agreed, 'so maybe we won't run into too much trouble.'

'The goal will be to hit IT and contain it. Bernard is still playing mayor, so he probably won't be there. But either he'll come to us or we'll push up after him once the thirties are secure. I don't think he'll put up much of a fight, not once his floors are ours.'

'Agreed,' Knox said, and it felt good to have a plan. To have an ally. 'And hey, thanks for this.'

McLain smiled. 'You give a good speech for a greaser,' she said. 'And besides' – she nodded towards the dog – 'Jackson likes you, and he's hardly ever wrong. Not about men.'

Knox looked down and realised he was still scratching the mutt. He pulled his hand away and watched the animal pant, staring up at him. In the next room, someone laughed at a joke, the voices of his mechanics mixing with the members of Supply, all gently muffled by the wall and door. This laughter was joined by the sounds of steel rods bending into shape, flat pieces hammered sharp, machines for making rivets turned instead into making bullets. And Knox knew what McLain meant about loyalty. He saw it in that dumb dog's eyes, that it would do anything for him if only he would ask. And this weight bearing down on his chest, of the many who felt that way for him and for McLain – Knox decided that *this* was the heaviest burden of them all.

44

The dirt farm below filled the stairwell with the rich smell of fresh rot. Juliette was still waking up as she descended another level and began noticing the scent. She had no idea how long she'd slept – it had felt like days but could've been hours. She had woken with her face pressed to the grating, a pattern of red lines marking her cheek, and had got underway immediately. Her stomach was gnawing at her, the odour from the farm hurrying her along. By twenty-eight, the pungency hung in the air so thick it felt like she was swimming *through* the scents. It was the smell of death, she decided. Of funerals. Of loamy soil turned over, releasing all those tangy molecules into the air.

She stopped on thirty – the hydroponic farms – and tried the doors. It was dark inside. There was a sound down the hallway, the whir of a fan or a motor. It was a strange encounter, this small noise. For over a day, she had heard nothing but the sounds she made herself. The green glow of the emergency lights were no company; they were like the heat of a dying body, of batteries draining with the leak of photons. But this was something *moving*, some sound beyond her own breathing and footfalls, and it lurked deep in the dark corridors of the hydroponic farms.

Once again, she left her only tool and defence behind as a doorstop to allow in a trickle of light. She stole inside, the smell of vegetation not as strong as in the stairwell, and padded down the hallway with one hand on the wall. The offices and reception area were dark and lifeless, the air dry. There was no blinking light on the turnstile, and she had no card or chit to feed it. She placed her hands on the supports and vaulted over, this small act of defiance somehow powerful, as though she had come to accept the lawlessness of this dead place, the complete lack of civilisation, of rules.

The light spilling from the stairwell barely reached the first of the growing rooms. She waited while her eyes adjusted, thankful of this ability honed by the down deep of Mechanical and the dark interiors of broken machines. What she saw, barely, when she was finally able, did not inspire her. The hydroponic gardens had rotted away. Thick stalks, like ropes, hung here and there from a network of suspended pipes. It gave her an idea of how long ago these farms had succumbed, if not the silo. It hadn't been hundreds of years, and it hadn't been days. Even a window that wide felt like a treasure of information, the first clue towards an answer to this mysterious place.

She rapped one of the pipes with her knuckles and heard the solid thud of fullness.

No plants, but water! Her mouth seemed to dry out with just the prospect. Juliette leaned over the railing and into the growing room. She pressed her mouth to one of the holes in the top of a pipe where the stalk of a plant should be growing. She created a tight seal and sucked. The fluid that met her tongue was brackish and foul – but wet. And the taste was not of anything chemical or toxic, but stale organics. Dirt. It was only slightly more distasteful than the grease and oil she had practically been drenched in for two decades.

So she drank until she was full. And she realised, now that she had water, that if there were more crumbs to find, more clues, she might just live long enough to gather them.

Before she left, Juliette snapped a section of pipe off the end of a run, keeping the cap intact on one side. It was only a little over an inch in diameter and no more than two feet long, but it would work as a flask. She gently bent the broken pipe that remained down, allowing water to flow from the remaining loop. While she topped up her pipe, she splashed some water on her hands and arms, still fearful of contamination from the outside.

Once her pipe was full, Juliette stole back towards the lit doorway at the end of the hall. There were three hydroponic farms, all with closed loops that wound through long and twisting corridors. She tried to do a rough calculation in her head, but all she could come up with was enough to drink for a very long time. The aftertaste was awful, and she wouldn't be surprised if her stomach cramped from the contents, but if she could get a fire going, find enough fabric or leftover paper to burn, even that could be helped with a good boil.

Back in the stairwell, she returned to the rich odours she had left behind. She retrieved her knife and hurried down another thick slice of the silo, almost two times around the stairwell to the next landing, and checked the door.

The smell was definitely coming from the dirt farms. And Juliette could hear that whirring motor again, louder now. She stopped the door, propped her flask against the railing, and checked inside.

The smell of vegetation was overpowering. Ahead, in the dim green glow, she could see bushy arms reaching over the railings and into the pathway. She vaulted the security gate and explored the edge, one hand on the wall while her eyes adjusted again. There was definitely a pump running somewhere. She could also hear water dripping, either from a leak or a functioning tap. Juliette felt chills from the leaves brushing her arms. The smell of rot was distinguishable now: it was the odour of fruit and vegetables decaying in the soil and withering on the vine. She heard the buzz of flies, the sounds of life.

She reached into a thick stand of green and felt around until her hand hit something smooth. Juliette gave it a tug and held a plump tomato up to the light. Her timeline estimate suddenly shrank. How long could the dirt farms sustain themselves? Did tomatoes require seeding, or did they come back every year like the weeds? She couldn't remember. She took a bite, the tomato not yet fully ripe, and heard a noise behind her. Another pump clicking on?

She turned just in time to see the door to the stairwell slamming closed, plunging the dirt farm into absolute darkness.

Juliette froze. She waited for the sound of her knife rattling down through the staircase. She tried to imagine that it could've slipped and fallen on its own. With the light extinguished, her ears seemed to hijack the unused portion of her brain. Her breathing, even her pulse, seemed audible, the whirring of the pump louder now.

Tomato in hand, she crouched down and moved towards the other wall, arms stretched out to feel her way. She slid towards the exit, staying low to avoid the plants, trying to calm herself. There were no ghosts here, nothing to be spooked about. She repeated this to herself as she slowly crept forward.

And then an arm was on her, reaching over her shoulder. Juliette cried out and dropped the tomato. The arm pinned her, holding her in a crouch as she tried to stand. She slapped at this intruder, tried to pull away from it, the tablecloth bonnet yanked from her head – until finally she felt the hard steel of the turnstile, one of the waist bars jutting out in the hallway, and felt the fool.

'You 'bout gave me a heart attack,' she told the machine. She reached for its sides and lifted herself over. She would come back for more food once she had light. Leaving the turnstile and heading for the exit, one hand on the wall and another groping ahead of herself, Juliette wondered if she would start talking to objects now. Start going crazy. As the darkness absorbed her, she realised her mindset was changing by the minute. Resigned to her death the day before, now she was frightened of mere insanity.

It was an improvement.

Her hand finally bumped into the door, and Juliette pushed it open. She cursed the loss of the knife; it was certainly missing from the grating. She wondered how far it might have fallen, if she'd ever find it again or maybe a replacement. She turned to grab her flask—

And saw that it was missing as well.

Juliette felt her vision narrow, her heart quicken. She wondered if the closing of the door could have toppled her flask. She wondered how the knife had slipped through a gap in the grating narrower than its handle. And as the pounding in her temples receded, she heard something else.

Footsteps.

Ringing out on the stairwell below her.

Running.

45

The countertop in Supply rattled with the implements of war. Guns, freshly milled and wholly forbidden, were lined up like so many sticks of steel. Knox picked one up – could feel the heat in a barrel recently bored and rifled – and hinged the stock to expose the firing chamber. He reached into one of the buckets of shiny bullets, the casings chopped from thin tubes of pipe and packed with blasting powder, and slotted one into the brand-new gun. The operation of the machine seemed simple enough: point and pull the lever.

'Careful where you aim that,' one of the men of Supply said, leaning out of the way.

Knox raised the barrel towards the ceiling and tried to picture what one of these could do. He'd only ever seen a gun once, a smaller one on the hip of that old deputy, a gun he'd always figured was more for show. He stuffed a fistful of deadly rounds in his pocket, thinking how each one could end an individual life, and understanding why such things were forbidden. Killing a man should be harder than waving a length of pipe in their direction. It should take long enough for one's conscience to get in the way.

One of the Supply workers emerged from the stacks with a tub in his hands. The bend of his back and sag of his shoulders told Knox the thing was heavy. 'Just two dozen of these so far,' the man said, hoisting the bin to the counter.

Knox reached inside and pulled out one of the heavy cylinders. His mechanics and even some of the men and women in yellow eyed the bin nervously.

'Slam that end on something hard,' the man behind the

counter said, just as calmly as if he were doling out an electrical relay to a customer and giving some last-minute installation advice, 'like a wall, the floor, the butt of your gun – anything like that. And then get rid of it.'

'Are they safe to carry?' Shirly asked as Knox stuffed one into his hip pocket.

'Oh yeah, it takes some force.'

Several people reached in the tub and clattered around for one. Knox caught McLain's eyes as she took one for herself and slotted it into a pocket on her chest. The look on her face was one of cool defiance. She must see how disappointed he was in her coming, and he could tell at a glance that there would be no reasoning with her.

'All right,' she said, turning her grey-blue eyes towards the men and women gathered around the counter. 'Listen up. We've got to get back open for business, so if you're carrying a gun, grab some ammo. There are strips of canvas over there. Wrap these things up as best you can to keep them out of sight. My group is leaving in five minutes, got that? Those of you in the second wave can wait in the back, out of sight.'

Knox nodded. He glanced over at Marck and Shirly, both of whom would join him in the second wave; the slower climbers would go first and act casual. The stouter legs would follow and make a strong push, hopefully converging on thirty-four at the same time. Each group would be conspicuous enough – combined, they might as well sing their intentions while they marched.

'You okay, boss?' Shirly rested her rifle on her shoulder and frowned at him. He rubbed his beard and wondered how much of his stress and fear was shining through.

'Fine,' he grumbled. 'Yeah.'

Marck grabbed a bomb, stashed it away, and rested a hand on his wife's shoulder. Knox felt a pang of doubt. He wished the women didn't have to get involved – at least the wives. He continued to hope that the violence they were preparing for wouldn't be necessary, but it was getting harder and harder to pretend as eager hands took up arms. They were, all of them, now capable of taking lives, and he reckoned they were angry enough to do so.

McLain stepped through the opening in the counter and sized him up. 'This is it, then.' She reached out a hand.

Knox accepted it. He admired the strength in the woman. 'We'll see you on thirty-five and go up the last level together,' he said. 'Don't have all the fun without us.'

She smiled. 'We won't.'

'And good climbing.' He looked to the men and women gathering up behind her. 'All of you. Good luck and see you soon.'

There were stern nods and clenched jaws. The small army in yellow began to file for the door, but Knox held McLain back.

'Hey,' he said. 'No trouble until we catch up, okay?'

She slapped his shoulder and smiled.

'And when this does go down,' Knox said, 'I expect you at the very back, behind the—'

McLain stepped closer, a hand gripping Knox's sleeve. Her wrinkled face had suddenly hardened.

'And tell me, where will you be, Knox of Mechanical, when the bombs fly? When these men and women who look up to us are facing their gravest test, where will you be?'

Knox was taken aback by the sudden attack, this quiet hiss that landed with all the force of a shout.

'You know where I'll—' he started to answer.

'Damn straight,' McLain said, releasing his arm. 'And you'd better well know that I'll see you there.'

46

Juliette stood perfectly still and listened to the sound of footsteps retreating down the stairwell. She could feel the vibrations in the railing. Goose bumps rushed up her legs and down her arms. She wanted to call out, to yell for the person to stop, but the sudden rush of adrenalin made her chest feel cold and empty. It was like a chill wind had forced itself deep into her lungs, crowding out her voice. People were alive and in the silo with her. And they were running away.

She pushed away from the railing and dashed across the landing, hit the curved steps at a dead run and took them as fast as her legs could take her. A flight down, as the adrenalin subsided, she found the lungs to yell 'Stop!', but the sound of her bare feet on the metal stairs seemed to drown out her voice. She could no longer hear the person running, dared not stop and listen for fear they would get too far ahead, but as she passed the doorway on thirty-one, she worried that they might slip inside some level and get away. And if there were only a handful of them hiding in the vast silo, she may never find them. Not if they didn't want to be found.

Somehow, this was more terrifying than anything else: that she might live the rest of her days foraging and surviving in a dilapidated silo, talking to inanimate objects, while a group of people did the same and stayed out of sight. It so stressed her that it took a while to consider the opposite: that this might instead be a group who *would* seek her out, and not have the best intentions.

They wouldn't have the best intentions, but they would have her knife.

She stopped on thirty-two to listen, hands clamped to the railing. Holding her breath to keep quiet was almost impossible: her lungs were crying out for deep gulps of air. But she remained still, the pulse in her palms beating against the cool railing, the distinct sound of footsteps still below her and louder now. She was catching up! She took off again, emboldened, taking the steps three at a time, her body sideways as she danced down the stairs as she had in youth, one hand on the curving railing, the other held out in front of her for balance, the balls of her feet just barely touching a tread before she was flying down to the next, concentrating lest she slip. A spill could be deadly at such speeds. Images of casts on arms and legs and stories of the unfortunate elderly with broken hips came to mind. Still, she pushed her limits, positively flying. Thirty-three went by in a blaze. Half a spiral later, over her footfalls, she heard a door slam. She stopped and looked up. She leaned over the railing and peered down. The footfalls were gone, leaving just the sound of her panting for air.

Juliette hurried down another rotation of the steps and checked the door on thirty-four. It wouldn't open. It wasn't locked, though. The handle clicked down and the door moved, but caught on something. Juliette tugged as hard as she could – but to no avail. She yanked again and heard something crack. With a foot braced on the other door, she tried a third time, yanking sharply, snapping her head back, pulling her arms towards her chest and kicking with her foot—

Something snapped. The door flew open, and she lost her grip on the handle. There was an explosion of light from inside, a bright burst of illumination spilling out the door before it slammed shut again.

Juliette scrambled across the landing and grabbed the handle again. She pulled the door open and struggled to her feet. One broken half of a broomstick lay inside the hallway; the other half hung from the handle of the neighbouring door. Both stood out in the blinding light all around her. The overhead lamps inside the room were fully lit, the bright rectangles in the ceiling marching down the hall and out of sight. Juliette listened for footsteps, but heard little more than the buzzing of the bulbs. The turnstile ahead of her winked its red eye over and over, like it knew secrets but wouldn't tell.

She got up and approached the machine, looked to the right where a glass wall peeked into a conference room, the lights full on in there as well. She hopped over the stile, the motion a habit already, and called out another hello. Her voice echoed back, but it sounded different in the lit air, if that were possible. There was life in here, electricity, other ears to hear her voice, which made the echoes somehow fainter.

She passed offices, peeking in each one to look for signs of life. The place was a mess. Drawers dumped on the floor, metal filing cabinets tipped over, precious paper everywhere. One of the desks faced her, and Juliette could see that the computer was on, the screen full of green text. It felt as though she'd entered a dreamworld. In two days – assuming she'd slept that long – her brain had gradually acclimatised to the pale-green glow of the emergency lights, had grown used to a life in the wilderness, a life without power. She still had the taste of brackish water on her tongue, and now she strolled through a dishevelled but other-wise normal workplace. She imagined the next shift (did offices like these have shifts?) returning, laughing, from the stairwell, shuffling papers and righting furniture and getting back to work.

The thought of work had her wondering what they did here. She had never seen such a layout. She almost forgot her flight down the stairs as she poked about, as curious about the rooms and power as the footsteps that had brought her there. Around a bend she came to a wide metal door that, unlike the others, wouldn't open. Juliette heaved on it and felt it barely budge. She pressed her shoulder against the metal door and pushed it, a few inches at a time, until she could squeeze through. She had to step over a tall metal filing cabinet that had been yanked down in front of the heavy door in an attempt to hold it closed.

The room was massive, at least as big as the generator room and far larger than the cafeteria. It was full of tall pieces of furni-ture bigger than filing cabinets but with no drawers. Instead, their fronts were covered with blinking lights, red, green, and amber.

Juliette shuffled through paper that had spilled from the filing cabinet. And she realised, as she did so, that she couldn't be alone in the room. Someone had pulled the cabinet across the door, and they had to have done this from *inside*.

'Hello?'

She passed through the rows of tall machines, for that's what she figured they were. They hummed with electricity, and now and then seemed to whir or clack like their innards were busy. She wondered if this were some sort of exotic power plant – providing the lighting perhaps? Or did these have stacks of batteries inside? Seeing all the cords and cables at the backs of the units had her leaning towards batteries. No wonder the lights were blaring. This was like twenty of Mechanical's battery rooms combined.

'Is anyone here?' she called out. 'I mean you no harm.'

She worked her way through the room, listening for any movement, until she came across one of the machines with its door hinged open. Peering inside, she saw not batteries but boards like the kind Walker was forever soldering. In fact, the guts of this machine looked eerily similar to the inside of the dispatch room's computer – Juliette stepped back, realizing what these were. 'The servers,' she whispered. She was in this silo's IT. Level thirty-four. Of course.

There was a scraping sound near the far wall, the sound of metal sliding on metal. Juliette ran in that direction, darting between the tall units, wondering who the hell this was running from her, and where they planned to hide.

She rounded the last row of servers to see a portion of the floor moving, a section of metal grate sliding to cover a hole. Juliette dived for the floor, her tablecloth garb wrapping around her legs, her hands seizing the edge of the cover before it could close. Right in front of her, she saw the knuckles and fingers of a man's hands gripping the edge of the grate. There was a startled scream, a grunt of effort. Juliette tried to yank back on the grate, but had no leverage. One of the hands disappeared. A knife took its place, snicking against the grate, hunting for her fingers.

Juliette swung her feet beneath her and sat up for leverage.

She yanked on the grate and felt the knife bite into her finger as she did so.

She screamed. The man below her screamed. He emerged and held the knife between them, his hand shaking, the blade catching and reflecting the overhead lights. Juliette tossed the metal hatch away and clutched her hand, which was dripping blood.

'Easy!' she said, scooting out of reach.

The man ducked his head down, then poked it back up. He looked past Juliette as if others were coming up behind her. She fought the urge to check – but decided to trust the silence just in case he was trying to fool her.

'Who are you?' she asked. She wrapped part of her garment around her hand to bandage it. She noticed the man, his beard thick and unkempt, was wearing grey overalls. They could've been made in her silo, with just slight differences. He stared at her, his dark hair wild and hanging shaggy over his face. He grunted, coughed into his hand, seemed prepared to duck down under the floor and disappear.

'Stay,' Juliette said. 'I mean you no harm.'

The man looked at her wounded hand and at the knife. Juliette glanced down to see a thin trace of blood snaking towards her elbow. The wound ached, but she'd had worse in her time as a Mechanic.

'S-s-sorry,' the man muttered. He licked his mouth and swallowed. The knife was trembling uncontrollably.

'My name's Jules,' she said, realising this man was much more frightened of her than the other way around. 'What's yours?'

He glanced at the knife blade held sideways between them, almost as if checking a mirror. He shook his head.

'No name,' he whispered, his voice a dry rasp. 'No need.'

'Are you alone?' she asked.

He shrugged. 'Solo,' he said. 'Years.' He looked up at her. 'Where did' – he licked his lips again, cleared his throat; his eyes watered and glinted in the light – 'you come from? What level?'

'You've been by yourself for *years*?' Juliette said in wonder. She couldn't imagine. 'I didn't come from any level,' she told him.

'I came from another silo.' She enunciated this last softly and slowly, worried what this news might do to such a seemingly fragile man.

But Solo nodded as if this made sense. It was not the reaction Juliette had expected.

'The outside . . .' Solo looked again at the knife. He reached out of the hole and set it on the grating, slid it away from both of them. 'Is it safe?'

Juliette shook her head. 'No,' she said. 'I had a suit. It wasn't a far walk. But still, I shouldn't be alive.'

Solo bobbed his head. He looked up at her, wet tracks running from the corners of his eyes and disappearing into his beard. 'None of us should,' he said. 'Not a one.'

47

'What is this place?' Lukas asked Bernard. The two of them stood before a large chart hanging on the wall like a tapestry. The diagrams were precise, the lettering ornate. It showed a grid of circles evenly spaced with lines between them and intricacies inside each. Several of the circles were crossed out with thick red marks of ink. It was just the sort of majestic diagramming he hoped to achieve one day with his star charts.

'This is our Legacy,' Bernard said simply.

Lukas had often heard him speak similarly of the mainframes upstairs.

'Are these supposed to be the servers?' he asked, daring to rub his hands across a piece of paper the size of a small bed sheet. 'They're laid out like the servers.'

Bernard stepped beside him and rubbed his chin. 'Hmm. Interesting. So they are. I never noticed that before.'

'What are they?' Lukas looked closer and saw each was numbered. There was also a jumble of squares and rectangles in one corner with parallel lines spaced between them, keeping the blocky shapes separate and apart. These figures contained no detail within them, but the word 'Atlanta' was written in large letters beneath.

'We'll get to that. Come, let me show you something.'

At the end of the room was a door. Bernard led him through this, turning on more lights as he went.

'Who else comes down here?' Lukas asked, following along. Bernard glanced back over his shoulder. 'No one.'

Lukas didn't like that answer. He glanced back over his own

shoulder, feeling like he was descending into something people didn't return from.

'I know this must seem sudden,' Bernard said. He waited for Lukas to join him, threw his small arm around Lukas's shoulder. 'But things changed this morning. The world is changing. And she rarely does it pleasantly.'

'Is this about . . . the cleaning?' He'd nearly said 'Juliette'. The picture of her felt hot against his breastbone.

Bernard's face grew stern. 'There was no cleaning,' he said abruptly. 'And now all hell will break loose, and people will die. And the silos, you see, were designed from the ground down to prevent this.'

'Designed,' Lukas repeated. His heart beat once, twice. His brain whirred through its circuits and finally computed that Bernard had said something that had made no sense.

'I'm sorry,' he said. 'Did you say *silos*?'

'You'll want to familiarise yourself with this.' Bernard gestured towards a small desk which had a fragile-looking wooden chair tucked up against it. There was a book on the desk unlike any Lukas had ever seen, or even heard of. It was nearly as thick as it was wide. Bernard patted the cover, then inspected his palm for dust. 'I'll give you the spare key, which you are never to remove from your neck. Come down when you can and read. Our history is in here, as well as every action you are to take in any emergency.'

Lukas approached the book, a lifetime's worth of paper, and hinged open the cover. The contents were machine printed, the ink pitch-black. He flipped through a dozen pages of listed contents until he found the first page of the main text. Oddly, he recognised the opening lines immediately.

'It's the Pact,' he said, looking up at Bernard. 'I already know quite a bit of—'

'This is the Pact,' Bernard told him, pinching the first half-inch of the thick book. 'The rest is the Order.'

He stepped back.

Lukas hesitated, digesting this, then reached forward and flopped the tome open near its middle.

In the Event of an Earthquake:

- For casement cracking and outside leak, *see* AIRLOCK BREACH (p. 2,180)
- For collapse of one or more levels, *see* SUPPORT COLUMNS *under* SABOTAGE (p. 751)
- For fire outbreak, *see* . . .

'Sabotage?' Lukas flipped a few pages and read something about air handling and asphyxiation. 'Who came up with all this stuff?'

'People who experienced many bad things.'

'Like . . . ?' He wasn't sure if he was allowed to say this, but it felt like taboos were allowed to be broken down there. 'Like the people before the uprising?'

'The people before *those* people,' Bernard said. 'The one people.'

Lukas closed the book. He shook his head, wondering if this was all a gag, some kind of initiation. The priests usually made more sense than this. The children's books, too.

'I'm not *really* supposed to learn all this, am I?'

Bernard laughed. His countenance had fully transformed from earlier. 'You just need to know what's in there so you can access it when you need to.'

'What does it say about this morning?' He turned to Bernard, and it dawned on him suddenly that no one knew of his fascination, his enchantment, with Juliette. The tears had evaporated from his cheeks; the guilt of possessing her forbidden things had overpowered his shame for falling so hard for someone he hardly knew. And now this secret had wandered out of sight. It could be betrayed only by the flush he felt on his cheeks as Bernard studied him and pondered his question.

'Page seventy-two,' Bernard said, the humour draining from his face and replaced with the frustration from earlier.

Lukas turned back to the book. This was a test. A shadowing rite. It had been a long time since he'd performed under a caster's glare. He began flipping through the pages and saw at once that the section he was looking for came right after the Pact, was at the very beginning of the Order.

He found the page. At the very top, in bold print, it said:

In the Event of a Failed Cleaning:

And below this rested terrible words strung into awful meaning. Lukas read the instructions several times, just to make sure. He glanced over at Bernard, who nodded sadly, before Lukas turned back to the print.

In the Event of a Failed Cleaning:
*   **Prepare for War.**

48

Juliette followed Solo through the hole in the server-room floor. There was a long ladder there and a passageway that led to thirty-five, a part of thirty-five she suspected was not accessible from the stairwell. Solo confirmed this as they ducked through the narrow passageway and followed a twisting and brightly lit corridor. A blockage seemed to have come unstuck from the man's throat, releasing a lone-stricken torrent. He talked about the servers above them, saying things that made little sense to Juliette, until the passageway opened into a cluttered room.

'My home,' Solo said, spreading his hands. There was a mattress on the floor in one corner, a tangled mess of sheets and pillows trailing from it. A makeshift kitchen had been arranged across two shelving units: jugs of water, canned food, empty jars and boxes. The place was a wreck and smelled foul, but Juliette figured Solo couldn't see or smell any of that. There was a wall of shelves on the other side of the room stocked with metal canisters the size of large ratchet sets, some of them partially open.

'You live here alone?' Juliette asked. 'Is there no one else?' She couldn't help but hear the thin hope in her voice.

Solo shook his head.

'What about further down?' Juliette inspected her wound. The bleeding had almost stopped.

'I don't think so,' he said. 'Sometimes I do. I'll find a tomato missing, but I figure it's the rats.' He stared at the corner of the room. 'Can't catch them all,' he said. 'More and more of them—'

'Sometimes you think there's more of you, though? More survivors?' She wished he would focus.

'Yeah.' He rubbed his beard, looked around the room like there was something he should be doing for her, something you offered guests. 'I find things moved sometimes. Find things left out. The grow lights left on. Then I remember *I* did them.'

He laughed to himself. It was the first natural thing she'd seen him do, and Jules figured he'd been doing a lot of it over the years. You laughed either to keep yourself sane or because you'd given up on staying that way. Either way, you laughed.

'Thought the knife in the door was something I did. Then I found the pipe. Wondered if it was left behind by a really, really big rat.'

Juliette smiled. 'I'm no rat,' she said. She adjusted her table-cloth, patted her head and wondered what had happened to her other scrap of cloth.

Solo seemed to consider this.

'So how many years has it been?' she asked.

'Thirty-four,' he said, no pause.

'Thirty-four *years*? Since you've been *alone*?'

He nodded, and the floor seemed to fall away from her. Her head spun with the concept of that much time with no other person around.

'How *old* are you?' she asked. He didn't seem all that much older than her.

'Fifty,' he said. 'Next month, I'm pretty sure.' He smiled. 'This is fun, talking.' He pointed around the room. 'I talk to things sometimes, and whistle.' He looked straight at her. 'I'm a good whistler.'

Juliette realised she probably had only just been *born* when whatever happened here took place. 'How exactly have you *survived* all these years?' she asked.

'I dunno. Didn't set out to survive for years. Tried to last hours. They stack up. I eat. I sleep. And I . . .' He looked away, went to one of the shelves and sorted through some cans, many of them empty. He found one with the lid hinged open, no label, and held it out towards her. 'Bean?' he asked.

Her impulse was to decline, but the eager look on his poor face made it impossible. 'Sure,' she said, and she realised how hungry she was. She could still taste the brackish water from earlier, the tang of stomach acid, the unripe tomato. He stepped closer, and she dug into the wet juice in the can and came out with a raw green bean. She popped it into her mouth and chewed.

'And I poop,' he said bashfully while she was swallowing. 'Not pretty.' He shook his head and fished for a bean. 'I'm by myself, so I just go in apartment bathrooms until I can't stand the smell.'

'In *apartments*?' Juliette asked.

Solo looked for a place to set down the beans. He finally did, on the floor, among a small pile of other garbage and bachelor debris.

'Nothing flushes. No water. I'm by myself.' He looked embarrassed.

'Since you were sixteen,' Juliette said, having done the maths. 'What happened here thirty-four years ago?'

He lifted his arms. 'What always happens. People go crazy. It only needs to happen once.' He smiled. 'We get no credit for being sane, do we? I get no credit. Even from me. From myself. I hold it together and hold it together and I make it another day, another year, and there's no reward. Nothing great about me being normal. About not being crazy.' He frowned. 'Then you have one bad day, and you worry for yourself, you know? It only takes one.'

He suddenly sat down on the floor, crossed his legs, and twisted the fabric of his overalls where they bunched up at his knees. 'Our silo had one bad day. Was all it took.' He looked up at Juliette. 'No credit for all the years before that. Nope. You wanna sit?'

He gestured at the floor. Again, she couldn't say no. She sat down, away from the reeking bed, and rested her back against the wall. There was so much to digest.

'How did you survive?' she asked. 'That bad day, I mean. And since.'

She immediately regretted asking. It wasn't important to know. But she felt some need, maybe to glimpse what awaited her, maybe because she feared that surviving in this place could be worse than dying on the outside.

'Staying scared,' he said. 'My dad's caster was the head of IT.

Of this place.' He nodded. 'My dad was a big shadow. Knew about these rooms, one of maybe two or three who did. In just the first few minutes of fighting, he showed me this place, gave me his keys. He made a diversion, and suddenly I became the only one who knew about this place.' He looked down at his lap a moment, then back up. Juliette realised why he seemed so much younger. It wasn't just the fear, the shyness, that made him seem that way – it was in his eyes. He was locked in the perpetual terror of his teenage ordeal. His body was simply growing old around the frozen husk of a frightened little boy.

He licked his lips. 'None of them made it, did they? The ones who got out?' Solo searched her face for answers. She could feel the dire hope leaking out of his pores.

'No,' she said sadly, remembering what it felt like to wade through them, to crawl over them. It felt like weeks ago rather than days.

'So you saw them out there? Dead?'

She nodded.

He dipped his chin. 'The view didn't stay on for long. I only snuck up once in the early days. There was still a lot of fighting going on. As time went by, I snuck out more often and further. I found a lot of the mess they made. But I haven't found a body in' – he thought carefully – 'maybe twenty years?'

'So there were others in here for a while?'

He pointed towards the ceiling. 'Sometimes they would come in here. With the servers. And fight. They fought everywhere. Got worse as it went along, you know? Fight over food, fight over women, fight over fighting.' He twisted at the waist and pointed back through another door. 'These rooms are like a silo in a silo. Made to last ten years. But it lasts longer if you're solo.' He smiled.

'What do you mean? A silo in a silo?'

He nodded. 'Of course,' he said. 'Sorry. I'm used to talking with someone who knows everything I know.' He winked at her, and Juliette realised he meant himself. 'You don't know what a silo is.'

'Of course I do,' she said. 'I was born and raised in a place just like this. Only, I guess you could say that we're still having good days and not giving ourselves credit for them.'

Solo smiled. 'Then what's a silo?' he asked, that teenage defiance bubbling to the surface.

'It's . . .' Juliette searched for the words. 'It's our home. A building like those over the hill, but underground. The silo is the part of the world you can live in. The *inside*,' she said, realising it was harder to define than she thought.

Solo laughed.

'That's what the word means to *you*. But we use words all the time without really understanding them.' He pointed towards the shelf with all the metal canisters. 'All the real knowing is in those. Everything that ever happened.' He shot her a look. 'You've heard the term "raging bull"? Or someone being "bull-headed"?'

She nodded. 'Of course.'

'But what's a bull?' he asked.

'Someone who's careless. Or mean, like a bully.'

Solo laughed. 'So much we don't know,' he said. He studied his fingernails. 'A silo isn't the world. It's nothing. The term, this word, comes from a long time ago, back when crops grew in the outside further than you could see' – he waved his hand over the floor like it was some vast terrain – 'back when there were more people than you could count, back when everyone had lots of kids.' He glanced up at her. His hands came together and kneaded one another, almost as if embarrassed to bring up the making of kids around a woman.

'They grew so much food,' he continued, 'that even for all these people they couldn't eat it all, not at once. So they stored it away in case times got bad. They took more seeds of grain than you could count and they would pour them into these great silos that stood aboveground—'

'Aboveground,' Juliette said. 'Silos.' She felt as though he must be making this up, some delusion he'd concocted over the lonely decades.

'I can show you pictures,' he said petulantly, as if upset by her doubt. He got up and hurried to the shelf with the metal canisters. He read the small white labels on the bottom, running his fingers across them.

'Ah!' He grabbed one – it looked heavy – and brought it to

her. The clasp on the side released the lid, revealing a thick object inside.

'Let me,' he said, even though she hadn't moved a muscle to help. He tilted the box and let the heavy object fall onto his palm, where it balanced expertly. It was the size of a children's book, but ten or twenty times as thick. Still, it was a book. She could see the edges of miraculously fine-cut paper.

'I'll find it,' he said. He flipped pages in large chunks, each flap a fortune in pressed paper clapping solidly against more fortunes. Then he whittled his search down more finely, a pinch at a time, before moving to a single page at a time.

'Here.' He pointed.

Juliette moved closer and looked. It was like a drawing, but so exact as to almost seem real. It was like looking at the view of the outside from the cafeteria, or the picture of someone's face on an ID, but in colour. She wondered if this book had batteries in it.

'It's so real,' she whispered, rubbing it with her fingers.

'It *is* real,' he said. 'It's a picture. A photograph.'

Juliette marvelled at the colours, the green field and blue sky reminding her of the lies she had seen in her visor's false images. She wondered if this was false as well. It looked nothing like the rough and smeared photos she'd ever seen.

'These buildings' – he pointed to what looked like large white cans sitting on the ground – 'these are silos. They hold seed for the bad times. For until the times get good again.'

He looked up at her. They were just a few feet apart, Juliette and him. She could see the wrinkles around his eyes, could see how much the beard concealed his age.

'I'm not sure what you're trying to say,' she told him.

He pointed at her. Pointed at his own chest. 'We are the seeds,' he said. 'This is a silo. They put us here for the bad times.'

'Who? Who put us here? And what bad times?'

He shrugged. 'But it won't work.' He shook his head, then sat back on the floor and peered at the pictures in the massive book. 'You can't leave seeds this long,' he said. 'Not in the dark like this. Nope.'

He glanced up from the book and bit his lip, water welling up in his eyes. 'Seeds don't go crazy,' he told her. 'They don't. They have bad days and lots of good ones, but it doesn't matter. You leave them and leave them, however many you bury, and they do what seeds do when they're left alone too long . . .'

He stopped. Closed the book and held it to his chest. Juliette watched as he rocked back and forth, ever so slightly.

'What do seeds do when they're left too long?' she asked him. He frowned.

'We rot,' he said. 'All of us. We go bad down here, and we rot so deep that we won't grow any more.' He blinked and looked up at her. 'We'll never grow again.'

49

The waiting beyond the stacks of Supply was the worst. Those who could, napped. Most engaged in nervous banter. Knox kept checking the time on the wall, picturing all the pieces moving throughout the silo. Now that his people were armed, all he could hope for was a smooth and bloodless transfer of power. He hoped they could get their answers, find out what had been going on in IT – those secretive bastards – and maybe vindicate Jules. But he knew bad things could happen.

He saw it on Marck's face, the way he kept looking at Shirly. The worry there was evident in the man's frown, the tilt of his eyebrows, the wrinkles above the bridge of his nose. Knox's shift leader wasn't hiding the concern for his wife as well as he probably thought he was.

Knox pulled out his multi-tool and checked the blade. He flashed his teeth in the reflection to see if anything from his last meal was stuck there. As he was putting it away, one of Supply's shadows emerged from behind the stacks to let them know they had visitors.

'What colour visitors?' Shirly asked, as the group gathered their guns and lurched to their feet.

The young girl pointed at Knox. 'Blue. Same as you.'

Knox rubbed the girl's head as he slipped between the shelving units. This was a good sign. The rest of his people from Mechanical were running ahead of schedule. He made his way to the counter while Marck gathered the others, waking a few, the extra rifles clattering as they were gathered up.

As Knox rounded the counter, he saw Pieter enter through

the front door, the two Supply workers guarding the landing having allowed him past.

Pieter smiled as he and Knox clasped hands. Members of Pieter's refinery crew filed in behind, their customary black overalls replaced with the more discreet blue.

'How goes it?' Knox asked.

'The stairs sing with traffic,' Pieter said. His chest swelled as he took in and held a deep breath, then blew it out. Knox imagined the pace they'd maintained to shave off so much time.

'Everyone's underway?' He and Pieter slid to the side while their two groups merged, members of Supply introducing themselves or embracing those they already knew.

'They are.' He nodded. 'I'd give the last of them another half-hour. Though I fear the whispers on porters' lips travel even faster than we do.' He looked towards the ceiling. 'I'd wager they echo above our heads even now.'

'Suspicions?' Knox asked.

'Oh, aye. We had a run-in by the lower market. People wanted to know the fuss. Georgie gave them lip, and I thought it'd come to blows.'

'God, and not in the mids yet.'

'Aye. Can't help but think a smaller incursion would've had a greater chance of success.'

Knox frowned, but he understood Pieter thinking so. The man was used to doing a great deal with only a handful of strong backs. But it was too late for them to argue over plans already in action. 'Well, the blackouts have likely begun,' Knox said. 'There's nothing to it but for us to chase them up.'

Pieter nodded gravely. He looked around the room at the men and women arming themselves and repacking their gear for another quick climb. 'And I suppose we mean to bludgeon our way up.'

'Our plan is to be heard,' Knox said. 'Which means making some noise.'

Pieter patted his boss on the arm. 'Well then, we are already winning.'

He left to pick out a gun and top up his canteen. Knox joined

Marck and Shirly by the door. Those without guns had armed themselves with fearsome shanks of flattened iron, the edges bright silver from the shrill work of the grinder. It was amazing to Knox that they all knew, instinctively, how to build implements of pain. It was something even shadows knew how to do at a young age, knowledge somehow dredged up from the brutal depths of their imagination, this ability to deal harm to one another.

'Are the others running behind?' Marck asked Knox.

'Not too bad,' Knox said. 'More that these guys made good time. The rest'll catch up. You guys ready?'

Shirly nodded. 'Let's get moving,' she said.

'All right, then. Onward and upward, as they say.' Knox scanned the room and watched his mechanics meld with members of Supply. More than a few faces were turned his way, waiting for some sign, maybe another speech. But Knox didn't have another one in him. All he had was the fear that he was leading good people to their slaughter, that the taboos were falling in some runaway cascade, and it was all happening much too quickly. Once guns were made, who would unmake them? Barrels rested on shoulders and bristled like pincushions above the crowd. There were things, like spoken ideas, that were almost impossible to take back. And he reckoned his people were about to make many more of them.

'On me,' he growled, and the chatter began to die down. Packs rustled into place, pockets jangling with danger. 'On me,' he said again to the quieting room, and his soldiers began to form up in columns. Knox turned to the door, thinking this was certainly all *on him*. He made sure his rifle was covered, tucked it under his arm, and squeezed Shirly's shoulder as she pulled the door open for him.

Outside, two workers from Supply stood by the railing. They had been turning the sparse traffic away with a made-up power outage. With the doors open, bright light and the noise of Supply's machinery leaked out into the stairwell, and Knox saw what Pieter meant by whispers travelling swifter than feet. He adjusted his pack of supplies – the tools, candles, and flashlights that made it seem as if he were marching to aid rather than war. Beneath this beguiling layer were secreted more bullets and an extra bomb, bandages and pain salve for just in case. His rifle was wrapped in a strip of cloth and remained tucked under his arm. Knowing what it was, he found the concealment ridiculous. Looking at the others marching with him, some in welding smocks, some holding construction helmets, he saw their intentions were all too obvious.

They left the landing and the light spilling from Supply behind and began their climb. Several of his people from Mechanical had changed into yellow overalls, the better to blend in the mids. They moved noisily up the dimmed night-time glow of the stairwell, the shiver of traffic from below giving Knox hope that the rest of his people would be catching up soon. He felt sorry for their weary legs but reminded himself that they were travelling light.

He tried his damnedest to picture the coming morning as positively as he could. Perhaps the clash would conclude before any more of his people arrived. Maybe they would end up being nothing more than a wave of supporters coming to join in the celebrations. Knox and McLain would have already entered the forbidden levels of IT, would have yanked the cover off the inscrutable machinery inside, exposing those evil whirring cogs once and for all.

They made good progress while Knox dreamed of a smooth overthrow. They passed one landing where a group of women were hanging laundry over the metal railing to dry. The women spotted Knox and his people in their blue overalls and complained of the power outages. Several of his workers stopped to hand out supplies and to spread lies. It wasn't until after they had left and had wound their way up to the next level that Knox saw the cloth had come unwrapped from Marck's barrel. He pointed this out and it was fixed before the next landing.

The climb turned into a silent, gruelling ordeal. Knox let others take the lead while he slid back and checked on the status of his people. Even those in Supply, he considered his responsibility. Their lives were hanging in the balance of decisions he'd made. It was just as Walker had said, that crazy fool. This was it. An uprising, just like the fables of their youth. And Knox suddenly felt a dire kinship with those old ghosts, those ancestors of myth and lore. Men and women had done this before – maybe for different reasons, with a less noble anger caught in their throats, but somewhen, on some level, there had been a march like this. Similar boots on the same treads. Maybe some of the same boots, just with new soles. All with the jangle of mean machines in hands not afraid to use them.

It startled Knox, this sudden link to a mysterious past. And it wasn't that terribly long ago, was it? Less than two hundred years? He imagined, if someone lived as long as Jahns had, or McLain for that matter, that three long lives could span that distance. Three handshakes to go from that uprising to this one. And what of the years between? That long peace sandwiched between two wars?

Knox lifted his boots from one step to another, thinking over these things. Had he become the bad people he'd learned about in youth? Or had he been lied to? It hurt his head to consider, but here he was, leading a revolution. And yet it felt so right. So *necessary*. What if that former clash had felt the same? Had felt the same in the breasts of the men and women who'd waged it?

50

'I t would take ten lifetimes to read all these.'

Juliette looked up from the pile of scattered tins and stacks of thick books. There was more to marvel at in their text-heavy pages than in any of the children's books of her youth.

Solo turned from the stove where he was heating soup and boiling water. He waved a dripping metal spoon at the scattered mess she'd made. 'I don't think they were meant to be read,' he told her. 'At least, not like I've been reading them, front to back.' He touched his tongue to the spoon, then stuck it back in the pot and stirred. 'Everything's out of order. It's more like a backup to the backup.'

'I don't know what that means,' Juliette admitted. She looked down at her lap where pictures of animals called 'butterflies' filled the pages. Their wings were comically bright. She wondered if they were the size of her hands or the size of people. She had yet to find any sense of scale for the beasts.

'The servers,' Solo said. 'What did you think I meant? The backup.'

He sounded flustered. Juliette watched him busy about the stove, his movements jerky and manic, and realised *she* was the one cloistered away and ignorant, not him. He had all these books, decades of reading history, the company of ancestors she could only imagine. What did she have as her experience? A life in a dark hole with thousands of fellow, ignorant savages?

She tried to remember this as she watched him dig a finger in his ear and then inspect his fingernail.

'The backup of what exactly?' she finally asked, almost afraid of the cryptic answer to come.

Solo found two bowls. He began wiping one out with the fabric in the belly of his overalls. 'The backup of *everything*,' he said. 'All that we know. All that ever was.' He set the bowls down and adjusted a knob on the stove. 'Follow me,' he said, waving his arm. 'I'll show you.'

Juliette closed the book and slotted it into its tin. She rose and followed Solo out of the room and into the next one.

'Don't mind the mess,' he said, gesturing at a small hill of trash and debris piled up against one wall. It looked like a thousand empty cans of food, and smelled like ten thousand. Juliette wrinkled her nose and fought the reflex to gag. Solo seemed unaffected. He stood beside a small wooden desk and flipped through diagrams hanging from the wall on enormous sheets of paper.

'Where's the one I want?' he wondered aloud.

'What are these?' Juliette asked, entranced. She saw one that looked like a schematic of the silo, but unlike any they'd had in Mechanical.

Solo turned. He had several sheets flopped over one shoulder, his body practically disappearing between the layers of them. 'Maps,' he said. 'I want to show you how much is out there. You'll shit yourself.'

He shook his head and muttered something to himself. 'Sorry, didn't mean to say that.'

Juliette told him it was fine. She held the back of her hand to her nose, the stench of rotting food intolerable.

'Here it is. Hold this end.' Solo held out the corner of a half-dozen sheets of paper. He took the other side and they lifted them away from the wall. Juliette felt like pointing out the grommets at the bottom of the maps and how there were probably sticks or hooks around here somewhere for propping them up, but held her tongue. Opening her mouth just made the smell of the rotting cans worse.

'This is us,' Solo said. He pointed to a spot on the paper. Dark, squiggly lines were everywhere. It didn't look like a map or schematic of anything Juliette had ever seen. It looked like children had drawn it. Hardly a straight line existed anywhere.

'What's this supposed to show?' she asked.

'Borders. Land!' Solo ran his hands over one uninterrupted shape that took up nearly a third of the drawing. 'This is all water,' he told her.

'Where?' Juliette's arm was getting tired of holding up her end of the sheet. The smell and the riddles were getting to her. She felt a long way from home. The thrill of survival was in danger of being replaced with the depression of a long and miserable existence looming for years and years before her.

'Out there! Covering the land.' Solo pointed vaguely at the walls. He narrowed his eyes at Juliette's confusion. 'The silo, *this silo*, would be as big around as a single hair on your head.' He patted the map. 'Right here. All of them. Maybe all of us left. No bigger than my thumb.' He placed a finger in a knot of lines. Juliette thought he seemed so sincere. She leaned closer to see better, but he pushed her back.

'Let those go,' he said. He slapped at her hand holding the corners of paper, and smoothed the maps against the wall. 'This is us.' He indicated one of the circles on the top sheet. Juliette eyeballed the columns and rows, figured there were four dozen or so of them. 'Silo seventeen.' He slid his hand up. 'Number twelve. This is eight. And silo one up here.'

'No.'

Juliette shook her head and reached for the desk, her legs weak.

'Yes. Silo one. You're probably from sixteen or eighteen. Do you remember how far you walked?'

She grabbed the small chair and pulled it out. Sat down heavily.

'How many hills did you cross?'

Juliette didn't answer. She was thinking about the *other* map and comparing the scales. What if Solo was right? What if there were fifty or so silos and all of them could be covered by a thumb? What if Lukas had been right about how far away the stars were? She needed something to crawl inside, something to cover her. She needed some sleep.

'I once heard from silo one,' Solo said. 'A long time ago. Not sure how well any of these others are doing—'

'Wait.' Juliette sat up straight. 'What do you mean, you *heard* from them?'

Solo didn't turn from the map. He ran his hands from one circle to another, a childlike expression on his face. 'They called. Checking in.' He looked away from the map and her, towards the far corner of the room. 'We didn't talk for long. I didn't know all the procedures. They weren't happy.'

'Okay, but how did you do this? Can we call someone now? Was it a radio? Did it have a little antennae, a small black pointy thing—' Juliette stood and crossed to him, grabbed his shoulder and turned him around. How much did this man know that could help her but that she couldn't get out of him? 'Solo, how did you talk to them?'

'Through the wire,' he said. He cupped his hands and covered his ears with them. 'You just talk in it.'

'You need to show me,' she said.

Solo shrugged. He flipped up a few of the maps again, found the one he wanted and pressed the others against the wall. It was the schematic of the silo she had seen earlier, a side-on view of it divided into thirds, each third side by side. She helped him hold the other sheets out of the way.

'Here are the wires. They run every which way.' He traced thick branches of lines that ran from the exterior walls and off the edges of the paper. They were labelled with minuscule print. Juliette leaned closer to read; she recognised many of the engineering marks.

'These are for power,' she said, pointing at the lines with the jagged symbols above them.

'Yup.' Solo nodded. 'We don't get our own power any more. Borrow it from others, I think. All automatic.'

'You get it from others?' Juliette felt her frustration rise. How many crucial things did this man know that he considered trifling? 'Anything else you want to add?' she asked him. 'Do you have a flying suit that can whisk me back to my silo? Or are there secret passages beneath all the floors so we can just stroll there as easy as we like?'

Solo laughed and looked at her like she was crazy. 'No,' he

said. 'Then it would be *one* seed, not many. One bad day would ruin us all. Besides, the diggers are dead. They buried them.' He pointed at a nook, a rectangular room jutting off from the edge of Mechanical. Juliette peered closer. She recognised every floor of the down deep at a glance, but this room wasn't supposed to exist.

'What do you mean, *the diggers?*'

'The machines that removed the dirt. You know, that made this place.' He ran his hand down the length of the silo. 'Too heavy to move, I guess, so they poured the walls right over them.'

'Do they work?' Juliette asked. An idea formed. She thought of the mines, of how she'd helped excavate rock by hand. She thought of the sort of machine that could dig out an entire silo, wondered if it could be used to dig *between* them.

Solo clicked his tongue. 'No way. Nothing down there does. All toast. Besides' – he chopped his hand partway up the down deep – 'there's flooding up to . . .' He turned to Juliette. 'Wait. Are you wanting *out*? To *go* somewhere?' He shook his head in disbelief.

'I want to go *home*,' Juliette said.

His eyes widened. 'Why would you go *back*? They sent you away, didn't they? You'll stay here. We don't want to leave.' He scratched his beard and shook his head side to side.

'Someone has to know about all of this,' Juliette told him. 'All these other people out there. All that space beyond. The people in my silo need to know.'

'People in your silo already *do*,' he said.

He studied her quizzically, and it dawned on Juliette that he was right. She pictured where they currently stood in this silo. They were in the heart of IT, deep inside the fortress room of the mythical servers, below the servers in a hidden passage, hidden probably even from the people who had access to the innermost kernels of the silo's mysteries.

Someone in her own silo *did* know. He had helped keep these secrets for generations. Had decided, alone and without input from anyone, what they should and should not know. It was the same man who had sent Juliette to her death, a man who had killed who knew how many more . . .

'Tell me about these wires,' Juliette said. 'How did you talk to the other silo? Give me every detail.'

'Why?' Solo asked, seemingly shrinking before her. His eyes were wet with fear.

'Because,' she said. 'I have someone I very much wish to call.'

51

The waiting was interminable. It was the long silence of itchy scalps and trickling sweat, the discomfort of weight on elbows, of backs bent, of bellies flat against an unforgiving conference table. Lukas peered down the length of his fearsome rifle and through the conference room's shattered glass window. Little fragment jewels remained in the side of the jamb like transparent teeth. Lukas could still hear, ringing in his ears, the incredible bang from Sims's gun that had taken out the glass. He could still smell the acrid scent of gunpowder in the air, the looks of worry on the faces of the other techs. The destruction had seemed so unnecessary. All this preparation, the toting of massive black guns out of storage, the interruption of his talk with Bernard, news of people coming from the down deep, it all made little sense.

He checked the *slide* on the side of the rifle and tried to remember the five minutes of instruction he'd been given hours earlier. There was a *round* in the *chamber*. The *gun* was *cocked*. More *bullets* waited patiently in the *clip*.

And the boys in security gave *him* a hard time for his tech jargon. Lukas's vocabulary had exploded with new terms. He thought about the rooms beneath the servers, the pages and pages of the Order, the rows of books he'd only got a glimpse of. His mind sagged under the weight of it all.

He spent another minute practising his *sighting*, looking down the *barrel* and lining up the small cross in the tiny circle. He aimed at the cluster of conference chairs that had been rolled into an obstructing jumble by the door. For all he knew, they would be waiting like this for days and nothing would ever happen. It had been a while since any porter had brought an update on what was going on below.

For practice, he gently slid his finger into the guard and against the *trigger*. He tried to get comfortable with the idea of pulling that lever, of fighting the upward kick Sims had told them to expect.

Bobbie Milner – a shadow no more than sixteen – made a joke beside him, and Sims told them both to shut the fuck up. Lukas didn't protest at being included in the admonishment. He glanced over at the security gate where a bristle of black barrels poked through the stanchions and over the metal duty desk. Peter Billings, the new silo sheriff, was over there fiddling with his small gun. Bernard stood behind the sheriff, doling out instructions to his men. Bobbie Milner shifted his weight beside Lukas and grunted, trying to get more comfortable.

Waiting. More waiting. They were all waiting.

Of course, had Lukas known what was coming, he wouldn't have minded.

He would've begged to wait there for ever.

Knox led his group through the sixties with just a few stops for water, a pause to secure their packs and tighten their laces. They passed several curious porters with overnight deliveries who prodded for details about where they were heading, about the blackouts. Each porter left unhappy. And hopefully, empty-headed.

Pieter had been right: the stairwell was singing. It vibrated with the march of too many feet. Those who lived above were generally moving upward, away from the blackouts and towards the promise of power, of warm food and hot showers. Meanwhile, Knox and his people mobilised behind them to squelch a different *kind* of power.

At fifty-six, they had their first spot of trouble. A group of farmers stood outside the hydroponic farm lowering a cluster of power cables over the railing, presumably towards the small group they had seen the last landing down. When the farmers spotted the blue overalls of Mechanical, one of them called out, 'Hey, we keep you fed, why can't you keep the juice on?'

'Talk to IT,' Marck replied from the front of the queue. 'They're the ones blowing fuses. We're doing what we can.'

'Well, do it faster,' the farmer said. 'I thought we just had a ratdamned power holiday to prevent this nonsense.'

'We'll have it by lunchtime,' Shirly told them.

Knox and the others caught up with the head of the group, creating a jam by the landing.

'The faster we get up there the faster you'll get your juice,' Knox explained. He tried to hold his concealed gun casually, like it was any other tool.

'Well, how about giving us a hand with this tap then? They've had power on fifty-seven for most of the morning. We'd like enough to get our pumps cranking.' He indicated the trunk of wires coiling over the railing.

Knox considered this. What the man was asking for was technically illegal. Challenging him about it would mean delays, but telling him to go ahead might look suspicious. He could sense McLain's group several levels up, waiting on them. Pace and timing were everything.

'I can spare two of my men to help out. Just as a favour. As long as it doesn't get back to me that Mechanical had shit to do with this.'

'Like I care,' the farmer said. 'I just want water moving.'

'Shirly, you and Courtnee give them a hand. Catch up when you can.'

Shirly's mouth dropped open. She begged with her eyes for him to reconsider.

'Get going,' he told her.

Marck came to her side. He lifted his wife's pack and handed her his multi-tool. She begrudgingly accepted it, glowered at Knox a moment longer, then turned to go, not saying a word to him or her husband.

The farmer let go of the cables and took a step towards Knox. 'Hey, I thought you said you'd lend me two of—'

Knox levelled a glare harsh enough to make the man pause.

'Do you want the best I got?' he asked. 'Because you've got it.'

The farmer lifted his palms and backed away. Courtnee and Shirly could already be heard stomping their way below to co-ordinate with the men on the lower landing.

'Let's go,' Knox said, hitching up his pack.

The men and women of Mechanical and Supply lurched forward once more. They left behind the group of farmers on landing fifty-six, who watched the long column wind its way upward.

Whispers rose as the power cables were lowered. Powerful forces were merging over these people's heads, bad intentions coming together and heading for something truly awful.

And anyone with eyes and ears could tell: some kind of reckoning was coming.

There was no warning for Lukas, no countdown. Hours of quiet anticipation, of insufferable nothingness, simply erupted into violence. Even though he had been told to expect the worst, Lukas felt like the waiting so long for something to happen just made it a fiercer surprise when it finally did.

The double doors of landing thirty-four blew open. Solid steel peeled back like curls of paper. The sharp ring made Lukas jump, his hand slip off the stock of his rifle. Gunfire erupted beside him, Bobbie Milner shooting at nothing and screaming in fear. Maybe excitement. Sims was yelling impossibly over the roar. When it died down, something flew through the smoke, a canister, bouncing towards the security gate.

There was a terrible pause – and then another explosion like a blow to the ears. Lukas nearly dropped his gun. The smoke by the security gate couldn't quite fog the carnage. Pieces of people Lukas had known came to a sick rest in the entrance hall of IT. The people responsible began to surge through before he could take stock, before he could become fearful of another explosion occurring right in front of him.

The rifle beside him barked again, and this time Sims didn't yell. This time, several other barrels joined in. The people trying to push through the chairs tumbled into them instead, their bodies shaking as if pulled by invisible strings, arcs of red like hurled paint flying from their bodies.

More came. A large man with a throaty roar. Everything moved so slowly. Lukas could see the man's mouth part, a yell in the centre of a burly beard, a chest as wide as two men. He held a rifle at his waist. He fired at the ruined security station. Lukas watched Peter Billings spin to the floor, clutching his shoulder. Bits of glass shivered from the window frame in front of Lukas as barrel after barrel erupted across the conference table, the shattered window seeming insignificant now. A prudent move.

The hail of bullets hit the man unseen. The conference room was an ambush, a side-on attack. The large man shook as some of the wild fire got lucky. His beard sagged open. His rifle was cracked in half, a shiny bullet between his fingers. He tried to reload.

The guns of IT loosed their own bullets too fast to count. Levers were held, and springs and gunpowder did the rest. The giant man fumbled with his rifle, but never got it reloaded. He tumbled into the chairs, sending them crashing across the floor. Another figure appeared through the door, a tiny woman. Lukas watched her down the length of his barrel, saw her turn and look right at him, the smoke from the explosion drifting towards her, white hair flowing about her shoulders as if the smoke were a part of her.

He could see her eyes. He had yet to shoot his gun, had watched, jaw slack, as the fighting took place.

The woman bent her arm back and made to throw something his way.

Lukas pulled the trigger. His rifle flashed and lurched. In the time it took, the long and terrible time it took for the bullet to cross the room, he realised it was just an old woman. Holding something.

A bomb.

Her torso spun and her chest blossomed red. The object fell. There was another awful wait, more attackers appearing, screaming in anger, until an explosion blew the chairs and the people among them apart.

Lukas wept while a second surge made a futile attempt. He wept until his clip was empty, wept as he fumbled for the clasp, shoved a spare into the butt, the salt bitter on his lips as he drew back that bolt and let loose with another menacing hail of metal – so much stouter and quicker than the flesh it met.

52

Bernard came to at the sound of shouting, his eyes burning from the smoke, his ears ringing with a long-ago blast.

Peter Billings was shaking his shoulders, yelling at him, a look of fright in his wide eyes and soot-stained brow. Blood stained his overalls in a wide rust-coloured pool.

'Hrm?'

'Sir! Can you hear me?'

Bernard pushed Peter's hands away and tried to sit up. He groped about his body, looking for anything bleeding or broken. His head throbbed. His hand came away from his nose wet with blood.

'What happened?' he groaned.

Peter crouched by his side. Bernard saw Lukas standing just behind the sheriff, rifle on his shoulder, peering towards the stairwell. There was shouting in the distance, and then the patter of gunfire.

'We've got three men dead,' Peter said. 'A few wounded. Sims led a half dozen into the stairwell. They got it a lot worse than us. A *lot* worse.'

Bernard nodded. He checked his ears, was surprised they weren't bleeding as well. He dotted his sleeve with blood from his nose and patted Peter on the arm. He nodded over his shoulder. 'Get Lukas,' he said.

Peter frowned but nodded. He spoke with Lukas, and the young man knelt by Bernard.

'Are you okay?' Lukas asked.

Bernard nodded. 'Stupid,' he said. 'Didn't know they'd have guns. Should've guessed about the bombs.'

'Take it easy.'

He shook his head. 'Shouldn't have had you here. Dumb. Could have been us both—'

'Well, it was *neither* of us, sir. We've got 'em running down the stairwell. I think it's over.'

Bernard patted his arm. 'Get me to the server,' he said. 'We'll need to report this.'

Lukas nodded. He knew which server Bernard meant. He helped Bernard to his feet, an arm around his back, Peter Billings frowning as the two of them staggered down the smoky hallway together.

'Not good,' Bernard told Lukas, once they were away from the others.

'But we won, right?'

'Not yet. The damage won't be contained here. Not today. You'll have to stay below a while.' Bernard grimaced and tried to walk alone. 'Can't risk something happening to us both.'

Lukas seemed unhappy about this. He entered his code into the great door, pulled out his ID, wiped someone else's blood off it and his hand, then swiped it through the reader.

'I understand,' he finally said.

Bernard knew he'd picked the right man. He left Lukas to close the heavy door while he made his way to the rearmost server. He staggered once and fell against number eight, catching himself and resting a moment until the wooziness went away. Lukas caught up and was pulling his copy of the master key out of his overalls before Bernard got to the back of the room.

Bernard rested against the wall while Lukas opened the server. He was still too shaken up to notice the flashing code on the server's front panel. His ears were too full of a false ringing to notice the real one.

'What's that mean?' Lukas asked. 'That noise?'

Bernard looked at him quizzically.

'Fire alarm?' Lukas pointed up at the ceiling. Bernard finally heard it as well. He stumbled towards the back of the server as Lukas opened the last lock, pushed the young man out of the way.

What were the chances? Did they already know? Bernard's life had become unhinged in two short days. He reached inside the cloth pouch, grabbed the headset, and pulled it over his tender ears. He pushed the jack into the slot labelled '1' and was surprised to hear a beep. The line was *ringing*. He was making a call.

He pulled the jack out hurriedly, cancelling the call, and saw that the light above '1' wasn't blinking; the light above '17' was.

Bernard felt the room spin. A dead silo was calling him. A survivor? After all these years? With access to the servers? His hand trembled as he guided the jack into the slot. Lukas was asking something behind him, but Bernard couldn't hear anything through the headphones.

'Hello?' he croaked. 'Hello? Is anyone there?'

'Hello,' a voice said.

Bernard adjusted his headphones. He waved for Lukas to shut the fuck up. His ears were still ringing, his nose bleeding into his mouth.

'Who is this?' he asked. 'Can you hear me?'

'I hear you,' the voice said. 'Is this who I think it is?'

'Who the fuck is this?' Bernard sputtered. 'How do you have access to—'

'You sent me out,' the voice said. 'You sent me to die.'

Bernard slumped down, his legs numb. The cord on the headphones uncoiled and nearly pulled the cups from his head. He clutched the headphones and fought to place this voice. Lukas was holding him by the armpits, keeping him from collapsing onto his back.

'Are you there?' the voice asked. 'Do you know who this is?'

'No,' he said. But he knew. It was impossible, but he knew.

'You sent me to die, you fuck.'

'You knew the rules!' Bernard cried, yelling at a ghost. 'You *knew*!'

'Shut up and listen, Bernard. Just shut the fuck up and listen to me very carefully.'

Bernard waited. He could taste the copper of his own blood in his mouth.

'I'm coming for you. I'm coming home, and I'm coming to *clean*.'

PART 5 – THE STRANDED

53

• Silo 18 •

Marck stumbled down the great stairway, his hand sliding against the cool railing, a rifle tucked under his arm, his boots slipping in blood. He could barely hear the screams all around him: the wails from the wounded as they were half dragged down the steps, the horrified cries from the curious crowds on every landing who witnessed their passage, or the shouts of promised violence from the men chasing him and the rest of his mechanics from level to level.

The ringing in his ears drowned out most of the noise. It was the blast, the god-awful blast. Not the one that had peeled open the doors of IT – he had been ready for that one, had hunkered down with the rest. And it wasn't the second bomb, the one Knox had lobbed deep into the heart of their enemy's den. It was the *last* one, the one he didn't see coming, the one that spilled from the hands of that small white-haired woman from Supply.

McLain's bomb. It had gone off right in front of him, had taken his hearing as it took her *life*.

And Knox, that stout and unmovable head of Mechanical – his boss, his good friend – gone.

Marck hurried down the steps, wounded and afraid. He was a long way from the safety of the down deep – and he desperately wanted to find his wife. He concentrated on this rather than the past, tried not to think of the explosion that had taken his friends, had wrecked their plans, had engulfed any chance at justice.

Muffled shots rang out from above, followed by the piercing

zing of bullets striking steel – only steel, thank God. Marck stayed away from the outer railing, away from the aim of the shooters who hounded them from the landings above with their smoothly firing rifles. The good people of Mechanical and Supply had been running and fighting for over a dozen levels; Marck silently begged the men above to stop, to give them a chance to rest, but the boots and the bullets kept coming.

Half a level later, he caught up to three members of Supply, the one in the middle wounded and being carried, his arms draped over shoulders, blood dotting the backs of their yellow overalls. He yelled at them to keep moving, couldn't hear his own voice, could just feel it in his chest. Some of the blood he was slipping in was his own.

With his injured arm tight against his chest, his rifle cradled in the crook of his elbow, Marck kept his other hand on the railing to keep from tumbling headfirst down the steep stairwell. There were no allies behind him, none still alive. After the last shootout, he had sent the others ahead, had barely got away himself. And yet they kept coming, tireless. Marck would pause now and then, fumble with the unreliable ammunition, chamber a shot, and fire wildly up the stairwell. Just to *do* something. To slow them down.

He stopped to take a breath, leaned out over the railing, and swung his rifle towards the sky. The next round was a dud. The bullets buzzing back at him *weren't*. Huddling against the stairwell's central post, he took the time to reload. His rifle wasn't like theirs. One shot at a time and difficult to aim. They had modern things he'd never heard of, shots coming as fast as a frightened pulse. He moved towards the railing and checked the landing below, could see curious faces through a cracked doorway, fingers curled around the edge of the steel jamb. This was it. Landing fifty-six. The last place he'd seen his wife.

'Shirly!'

Calling her name, he staggered down a quarter turn until he was level with the landing. He kept close to the interior, out of sight from his pursuers, and searched the shadowed faces.

'My wife!' he yelled across the landing, a hand cupped to his cheeks, forgetting that the incredible ringing was only in *his* ears, not theirs. 'Where is she?'

A mouth moved in the dark crowd. The voice was a dull and distant drone. Someone else pointed down. The faces cringed; the cracked door twitched shut as another ricochet screamed out; the stairway shook with all the frightened boots below and the chasing ones above. Marck eyed the illicit power cables draped over the railing and remembered the farmers attempting to steal electricity from the level below. He hurried down the stairs, following the thick cords, desperate to find Shirly.

One level down, positive that his wife would be inside, Marck braved the open space of the landing and rushed across. He threw himself against the doors. Shots rang out. Marck grabbed the handle and tugged, shouting her name to ears as deaf as his own. The door budged, was being held fast with the sinewy restraint of unseen arms. He slapped the glass window, leaving a pink palm print, and yelled for them to open up, to let him in. Eager bullets rattled by his feet – one of them left a scar down the face of the door. Crouching and covering his head, he scurried back to the stairwell. Marck forced himself to move downward. If Shirly was behind those doors she might be better off. She could strip herself of incriminating gear, blend in until things settled down. If she were below – he needed to hurry after her. Either way, *down* was the only direction.

At the next landing, he caught up with the same three members of Supply he'd passed earlier. The wounded man was sitting on the decking, eyes wide. The other two were tending to him, blood on their sides from supporting his weight. One of the Supply workers was a woman Marck vaguely recognised from the march up. There was a cold fire in her eyes as Marck paused to see if they needed help.

'I can carry him,' he shouted, kneeling by the wounded man.

The woman said something. Marck shook his head and pointed to his ears.

She repeated herself, lips moving in exaggeration, but Marck wasn't able to piece it together. She gave up and shoved at his arm, pushing him away. The wounded man clutched his stomach, a red stain ballooning out from his abdomen all the way to his crotch. His hands clasped something protruding there, a small wheel spinning on the end of a steel post. The leg of a chair.

The woman pulled a bomb from her satchel, one of those pipes that promised so much violence. It was solemnly passed to the wounded man, who accepted it, his knuckles white, his hands trembling.

The two members of Supply pulled Marck away – away from the man with the large piece of office furniture sprouting from his oozing stomach. The shouts sounded distant, but he knew they were nearby. They were practically in his ear. He found himself yanked backwards, transfixed by the vacant stare on the face of this doomed and wounded man. His eyes locked on to Marck's. The man held the bomb away from himself, fingers curled around that terrible cylinder of steel, a grim clench of teeth jutting along his jawline.

Marck glanced up the stairwell where the boots were finally gaining on them, coming into view, black and bloodless, this tireless and superior enemy. They came down the dripping trail Marck and the others had left behind, coming for them with their ammo that never failed.

He stumbled down the stairwell backwards, half dragged by the others, one hand on the railing, eyes drifting to the swinging door opening behind the man they'd left behind.

A young face appeared there, a curious boy, rushing out to see. A tangle of adult hands scrambled to pull him back.

Marck was hauled down the stairs, too far down the curving stairs to see what happened next. But his ears, as deadened as they were, caught the popping and zinging of gunfire, and then a blast, a roaring explosion that shook the great stairwell, that knocked him and the others down, slamming him against the railing. His rifle clattered towards the edge – Marck lunged for it. He grabbed it before it could escape and go tumbling into space.

Shaking his head, stunned, he pushed himself up to his hands and knees and managed to rise slowly to his feet. Senseless, he staggered forward down the shuddering steps, the treads beneath his feet ringing and vibrating as the silo around them all continued its spiral into dark madness.

54

• Silo 18 •

The first moment of true rest came hours later at Supply, on the upper edge of the down deep. There was talk of holding there, of setting up some kind of barrier, but it wasn't clear how the entire stairway could be blocked to include the open space between the railing and the concrete cylinder beyond. This was the gap where the singing bullets lived, a place where jumpers were known to meet their ends, and where their enemy could surely find some way to scamper down.

Marck's hearing had improved during the last leg of his run. Enough to grow weary of the rhythmic clomp of his own boots, the sound of his pained grunts, the noise of his exhausted pants for air. He heard someone say that the last explosion had wrecked the stairway, had impeded the chase. But for how long? What was the damage? No one knew.

Tensions ran high on the landing; the news of McLain's death had unsettled the people of Supply. The wounded in yellow overalls were taken inside, but it was suggested – and not gently – that Mechanical's injured would be better off receiving treatment further below. Where they belonged.

Marck waded through these arguments, the voices still somewhat muffled and distant. He asked everyone about Shirly, several in yellow shrugging as if they didn't know her. One guy said she'd already gone down with some of the other wounded. He said it a second time, louder, before Marck was sure he'd heard him.

It was good news, and he figured as much. He was about to leave when his wife emerged without warning from the anxious crowd, startling him.

Her eyes widened as she recognised him. And then her gaze fell to his wounded arm.

'Oh, God!'

She threw her arms around him, pressed her face against his neck. Marck hugged her with one arm, his rifle between them, the barrel cold against his quivering cheek.

'Are you okay?' he asked.

She latched to his neck, her forehead finding his shoulder, and said something he couldn't hear but could feel against his skin. She made room to inspect his arm.

'I can't hear,' he told her.

'I'm fine,' she said, louder. She shook her head, her eyes wide and wet. 'I wasn't there. I wasn't there for any of it. Is it true about Knox? What happened? How bad was it?'

She focused on his wound, and her hands felt good on his arm – strong and confident. The crowd was thinning as members of Mechanical retreated further down the stairwell. Several in Supply yellow treated Marck to cold stares, eyeing his wound as if worried it would soon be *their* problem.

'Knox is dead,' he told her. 'McLain, too. A few others. I was right there when the blast went off.'

He looked down at his arm, which she had exposed by tearing away his ripped and stained undershirt.

'Were you shot?' she asked.

He shook his head. 'I don't know. It happened so *fast*.' He looked over his shoulder. 'Where's everyone going? Why aren't we holing up here?'

Shirly set her teeth and jerked her head at the door, which was two deep with yellow overalls. 'Don't think we're wanted,' she said, her voice raised so he could hear. 'I've got to clean this wound. I think some of the bomb is in you.'

'I'm fine,' he insisted. 'I've just been looking for you. I've been worried sick.'

He saw that his wife was crying, unbroken tear tracks standing out amid the beads of sweat.

'I thought you were gone,' she said. He had to read her lips to make it out. 'I thought they had . . . that you were . . .'

She bit her lip and stared at him with uncharacteristic fear. Marck had never seen his wife fazed, not by a sprung casement leak, not by a cave-in deep in the mine that trapped several of their close friends, not even when Juliette was sent to cleaning. But heaps of dread were locked up in her expression now. And that scared him in a way the bombs and bullets couldn't.

'Let's hurry after the others,' he said, taking her hand. He could feel the exposed nerves on the landing, the gazes begging them to be off.

When shouts rang down from above once more and the members of Supply retreated to the safety of their doorway, Marck knew this brief moment of respite was over. But it was okay. He'd found his wife. She was unharmed. There was little anyone could do to him now.

When they reached one-thirty-nine together, Marck knew they'd made it. His legs had somehow held out. The blood loss hadn't stopped him. With his wife helping him along, they passed the last landing before Mechanical, and all he could think about was holding the line against those bastards who were taking shots at them from above. Inside Mechanical, they would have power, safety in numbers, the advantage of home turf. More importantly, they would be able to bandage wounds and get some rest. That's what he sorely needed: rest.

He nearly tripped and fell down the last few steps, his legs not used to an end to the descent, a flat piece of ground rather than one more tread to sink to. As his knees buckled, and Shirly caught him, he finally noticed the jam of people at the security station leading into Mechanical.

The crew that had stayed behind while the rest marched up to fight had been busy. Steel plates had been welded solid across the wide security entrance. The diamond-studded sheeting stood from floor to ceiling, wall to wall. Sparks hissed along one edge as someone worked to complete the job from the inside. The sudden flurry of refugees and wounded amassed in a crowd desperate to get in. Mechanics shoved and jostled against the barrier. They screamed and beat on the steel plates, mad with fear.

'What the hell?' Marck cried. He followed Shirly as she pressed into the back of the crowd. At the front, someone was crawling on the floor, wiggling on their belly through the tightest of gaps, a rectangle left open below the security turnstile wide enough to slide through, easy enough to defend.

'Easy! Wait your turn,' someone ahead of them shouted.

Yellow overalls were mixed in with the others. Some were mechanics who had donned disguises – some seemed to be from Supply, helping the wounded, mixed up in the wrong crowd or not trusting their own level for safety.

As Marck attempted to usher Shirly towards the front, a shot rang out, the thwack and clatter of a hot ball of lead striking nearby. He changed direction and pulled her back towards the stairs. The crush around the impossibly small entrance grew frantic. There was a lot of yelling back and forth through the hole, people on this side shouting that they were being shot at, those on the other side yelling 'One at a time!'

Several were on their bellies, scrambling for the tiny hole. One got his arms inside and was pulled through, sliding across the steel grating and disappearing into the dark space. Two others tried to be next, jostling for position. They were all exposed to the open stairwell above. Another shot rang out, and someone fell, clutching a shoulder and screaming 'I'm hit!' The throng dispersed. Several ran back to the stairs where the overhang of the treads protected them from the gunfire. The rest were in chaos, all trying to fit through a space expressly designed to allow no more than one at a time.

Shirly screamed and squeezed Marck's arm as another person was shot nearby. A mechanic fell to the ground and doubled over in pain. Shirly yelled at her husband, asking him what they should do.

Marck dropped his rucksack, kissed her cheek, and ran with his rifle back up the stairs. He tried to take them two at a time, but his legs were too sore. Another shot rang out, the ricochet of a miss. His body felt incredibly heavy, slow like in a bad dream. He approached the landing of one-thirty-nine with his gun level, but the shooters were further up, peppering the crowd from higher above.

He checked that he had a fresh round in the home-built gun, cocked it, and edged out onto the landing. Several men in the grey of Security were leaning out over the railing above, barrels trained down towards the ground floor of Mechanical. One of the men tapped his neighbour and pointed towards Marck. Marck watched all this down the length of his own barrel.

He fired a shot, and a black rifle tumbled towards him from above, the arms of its wielder slumping over the railing before sagging down and disappearing.

Gunfire erupted, but he was already diving back towards the stairs. The shouting grew furious both above and below him. Marck went to the other side of the stairs, away from where he'd last been seen, and peered down. The crowd was thinning by the security barrier. More and more people were being pulled through. He could see Shirly looking up, shielding her eyes against the stairway lights above.

Boots rang out behind him. Marck reloaded, turned, and aimed at the highest step he could see along the upward spiral. He waited for whatever was heading down towards him.

When the first boot appeared, he steadied himself, allowed more of the man to sink before his barrel, and then he pulled the trigger.

Another black rifle clattered against the steps and bounced through the railing; another man sagged to his knees.

Marck turned and ran. He lost his grip on his own gun, felt it bang against his shins as it skittered away from him, and he didn't stop to retrieve it. He slid down the steps, lost his footing, landed on his bottom and bounced back up. He tried taking the steps two at a time, was running as if in a dream, not fast enough, legs like rusted steel—

There was a bang, a muffled roar behind him, and somehow, someone had caught up, had punched him in the back, had hit him.

Marck sprawled forward and bounced down the steps, his chin striking the steel treads. Blood poured into his mouth. He tried to crawl, got his feet beneath him, and stumbled forward.

Another roar, another punch to the back, the feeling that he'd been bitten and kicked at the same time.

This is what it feels like to be shot, he thought numbly. He spilled down the last few steps, lost sensation in his legs, crashed to the grating.

The bottom floor was nearly empty. One person stood beside the tiny hole. Another was half in and half out, boots kicking.

Marck saw that it was Shirly, on her belly, looking back at him. They were both lying on the floor. So comfortable on the floor. The steel was cool against his cheek. There were no more steps to run down, no bullets to load, nothing to shoot.

Shirly was screaming, not as happy as he was to be lying there.

One of her arms extended back out of that small black rectangle, reached for him past the rough cuts in the steel plates. Her body slid forward, pulled by some force beyond, pushed by this nice person in yellow still standing by the strange wall of steel where the entrance to his home used to be.

'Go,' Marck told her, wishing she wouldn't scream. Blood flecked the floor before him, marking his words. 'I love you—'

And as if by command, her feet slid into the darkness, her screams swallowed by that rectangular, shadowy maw.

And the person in yellow turned. The nice man's eyes grew wide, his mouth fell open, and then his body jerked from the violence of gunfire.

It was the last thing Marck saw, this man's deathly dance.

And he only distantly felt, but for a tremble of time, the end of him that came next.

55

Three Weeks Later

• Silo 18 •

Walker remained in his cot and listened to the sounds of distant violence. Shouts echoed down his hallway, emanating from the entrance to Mechanical. The familiar patter of gunfire came next, the *pop pop pop* of the good guys followed by the *ratatatat* of the bad.

There was an incredible bang, the roar of blasting powder against steel, and the back-and-forth crackle ended for a moment. More shouting. Boots clomping down his hallway, past his door. The boots were the constant beat to the music of this new world. He could hear this music from his cot, even with the blankets drawn over his head, even with his pillow on top, even as he begged, out loud, over and over, for it to please stop.

The boots in the hallway carried with them more shouting. Walker curled up into a tight ball, knees against his chest, wondering what time it was, dreading that it was morning, time to get up.

A brief respite of silence formed, that quiet of tending to the wounded, their groans too faint to penetrate his sealed door.

Walker tried to fall asleep before the music was turned back up. But, as always, the quiet was worse. During the quiet, he grew anxious as he waited for the next patter of gunfire to erupt. His impatience for sleep often frightened that very sleep away. And he would grow terrified that the resistance was finally over, that the bad guys had won and were coming for him—

Someone banged on his door – a small and angry fist unmistakable to his expert ears. Four harsh knocks, and then she was gone.

Shirly. She would have left his breakfast rations in the usual place and taken away last night's picked-over and mostly uneaten dinner. Walker grunted and rolled his old bones over to the other side. Boots clomped. Always rushing, always anxious, forever warring. And his once quiet hallway, so far from the machines and pumps that really needed tending to, was now a busy thoroughfare. It was the entrance hall that mattered now, the funnel into which all the hate was poured. Screw the silo, the people above and the machines below, just fight over this worthless patch of ground, pile the bodies on either side until one gives, do it because it was yesterday's cause, and because nobody wanted to remember back any further than yesterday.

But Walker did. He remembered—

The door to his workshop burst open. Through a gap in his filthy cocoon, Walker could see Jenkins, a boy in his twenties but with a beard that made him appear older, a boy who had inherited this mess the moment Knox died. The lad stormed through the maze of workbenches and scattered parts, aiming straight for Walker's cot.

'I'm *up*,' Walker groaned, hoping Jenkins would go away.

'No you're not.' Jenkins reached the cot and prodded Walker in the ribs with the barrel of his gun. 'C'mon, old man, up!'

Walker tensed away from him. He wiggled an arm loose to wave the boy away.

Jenkins peered down gravely, a frown buried in his beard, his young eyes wrinkled with worry. 'We need that radio fixed, Walk. We're getting battered out there. And if I can't listen in, I don't think I can defend this place.'

Walker tried to push himself upright. Jenkins grabbed the strap of his overalls and gave him some rough assistance.

'I was up all night on it,' Walker told him. He rubbed his face. His breath was awful.

'Is it fixed? We need that radio, Walk. You do know Hank risked his life to get that thing to us, right?'

'Well, he should've risked a bit more and sent a *manual*,' Walker complained. He pressed his hands to his knees, and with much complaint from his joints, he stood and staggered towards the workbench, his blankets spilling to the floor in a heap. His legs were still half asleep, his hands tingling with the weak sensation of not being able to form a proper fist.

'I got the battery sorted,' he told Jenkins. 'Turns out that wasn't the problem.' Walker glanced towards his open door and saw Harper, a refinery worker turned soldier, standing in the hallway. Harper had become Jenks's number two when Pieter was killed. Now he was peering down at Walker's breakfast, practically salivating into it.

'Help yourself,' Walker called out. He waved dismissively at the steaming bowl.

Harper glanced up, eyes wide, but that was as long as he hesitated. He leaned his rifle against the wall and sat down in the workshop doorway, shovelling food into his mouth.

Jenkins grunted disapprovingly but didn't say anything.

'So, see here?' Walker showed him the arrangement on the workbench where various pieces of the small radio unit had been separated and were now wired together so everything was accessible. 'I've got constant power.' He patted the transformer he had built to bypass the battery. 'And the speakers work.' He keyed the transmit button, and there was a pop and hiss of static from his bench speakers. 'But nothing comes through. They aren't *saying* anything.' He turned to Jenkins. 'I've had it on all night, and I'm not a deep sleeper.'

Jenkins studied him.

'I would've heard,' he insisted. 'They aren't talking.'

Jenkins rubbed his face, made a fist. He kept his eyes closed, his forehead resting in one palm, a weariness in his voice. 'You think maybe something *broke* when you tore it apart?'

'Disassembled,' Walker said with a sigh. 'I didn't *tear it apart*.'

Jenkins gazed up at the ceiling and relaxed his fist. 'So you think they aren't using them any more, is that it? Do you reckon they know we have one? I swear, I think this damn priest they sent is a spy. Shit's been fallin' apart since we let him in here to give last rites.'

'I don't *know* what they're doing,' Walker admitted. 'I think they're still using the radios, they've just excluded this one somehow. Look, I made another antenna, a stronger one.'

He showed him the wires snaking up from the workbench and spiralling around the steel beam rafters overhead.

Jenkins followed his finger, then snapped his head towards the door. There was more shouting down the hallway. Harper stopped eating for a moment and listened. But only for a moment. He dug his spoon back into the cornmush.

'I just need to know when I'll be able to listen in again.' Jenkins tapped the workbench with his finger, then picked his rifle up. 'We've been shooting blind for almost a week now. I need results, not lessons on all this' – he waved a hand at Walker's work – 'all this *wizardry*.'

Walker plopped down on his favourite stool and peered at the myriad circuits that had once been jammed into the radio's cramped innards. 'It's not wizardry,' he said. 'It's electrics.' He pointed at two of the boards, connected by wires he had lengthened and re-soldered so he could analyse all the bits more closely. 'I know what most of these do, but you've gotta remember that nothing about these devices are known, not outside of IT, anyway. I'm havin' to theorise while I tinker.'

Jenkins rubbed the bridge of his nose. 'Just let me know when you've got something. All your other work orders can wait. This is the only thing that matters. Got that?'

Walker nodded. Jenkins turned and barked at Harper to get the hell off the floor.

They left Walker on his stool, their boots picking up the beat of the music again.

Alone, he stared down at the machine strung out across his workbench, its little green lights on its mysterious boards lit up and taunting him. His hand drifted to his magnifiers as if by their own accord, as if by decades of habit, when all Walker really wanted was to crawl back into his cot, to wrap his cocoon around himself, to disappear.

He needed help, he thought. He looked around at all that required doing and, as ever, his thoughts turned to Scottie, his little shadow, gone to work in IT where they hadn't been able to protect him. There had been a slice of time, sliding away from him now and fading into the slippery past, when Walker had been a happy man. When his life should've ended to keep him from enduring any of the suffering beyond. But he had made it through that brief bliss and now could hardly recall it. He couldn't imagine what it felt like to rise with anticipation in the morning, to fall asleep with contentment at the end of the day.

It was only fear and dread any more. And also regret.

He had started all this, all the noise and violence. Walker was convinced of that. Every life lost was on his wrinkled hands. Every tear shed was by his actions. Nobody said it, but he could feel them thinking it. One little message to Supply, one favour for Juliette, just a chance at dignity, an opportunity to test her wild and horrible theory, to bury herself out of sight – and now look at the cascade of events, the eruption of anger, the senseless violence.

It wasn't worth it, he decided. This was how the maths always added up: not worth it. Nothing seemed worth it any more.

He bent over his workbench and set his old hands to tinkering. This was what he did, what he had always done. There was no escaping it now, no stopping those fingers with their papery skin, those palms with their deep lines that seemed to never end, not when they should. He followed those lines down to his bony wrists where weak little veins ran like buried wire with blue insulation.

One snip, and off he would go to see Scottie, to see Juliette. It was tempting.

Especially since, Walker figured, wherever they were, whether the priests were on to something or simply ratshit mad, both of his old friends were in far better places than him . . .

A tiny strand of copper wire stood at right angles to the rest. It was like a silo landing shooting off the great stairway, a bit of flat amid the twisted spiral. As Juliette wrapped the pads of her fingers around the wire and worked the splice into place, this jutting barb sank into her finger, stinging her like some angry insect.

Juliette cursed and shook her hand. She very nearly dropped the other end of the wire, which would've sent it tumbling several levels down.

She wiped the welling spot of blood onto her grey overalls, then finished the splice and secured the wires to the railing to keep the strain off. She still didn't see how they had come loose, but everything in this cursed and dilapidated silo seemed to be coming apart. Her senses were the least of it.

She leaned far out over the railing and placed her hand on the hotchpotch of pipes and tubing fastened to the concrete wall of the stairwell. She tried to discern, with hands chilled by the cool air of the deep, any vibration from water gurgling through the pipe.

'Anything?' she called down to Solo. There seemed to be the slightest tremor in the plastic tubing, but it could've been her pulse.

'I think so!'

Solo's thin voice echoed from far below.

Juliette frowned and peered down the dimly lit shaft, down that gap between steel step and thick concrete. She would have to go see for herself.

Leaving her small tool bag on the steps – no danger of anyone coming along to trip over it – she took the treads two at a time and spiralled her way deeper into the silo. The electrical wiring and the long snake of pipes spun into view with each rotation, drips of purple adhesive marking every laborious joint she'd cut and fastened by hand.

Other wiring ran alongside hers, electrical cables snaking from IT far above to power the grow lights of the lower farms. Juliette wondered who had rigged this stuff up. It hadn't been Solo: this wiring had been strung during the early days of silo seventeen's downfall. Solo had simply become the lucky beneficiary of someone else's hard and desperate work. Grow lights now obeyed their timers, the greenery obeyed the urge to blossom, and beyond the stale stench of oil and gas, of floods and unmoving air, the ripe tinge of plants growing out of control could be nosed from several landings away.

Juliette stopped at the landing of one-thirty-six, the last dry landing before the flood. Solo had tried to warn her, had tried to tell her even as she lusted over the image of the massive diggers on the wall-sized schematic. Hell, she should've known about the flood without being told. Groundwater was forever seeping into her own silo, a hazard of living below the water table. Without power to the pumps, the water would naturally make its way in and rise.

Out on the landing, she leaned on the steel railing and caught her breath. A dozen steps below, Solo stood on the single dry tread their efforts had exposed. Nearly three weeks of wiring and plumbing, of scrapping a good section of the lower hydroponics farm, of finding a pump and routing the overflow to the water treatment facility tanks, and they had uncovered a single step.

Solo turned and smiled up at her. 'It's working, right?' He scratched his head, his wild hair jutting at all angles, his beard flecked with a grey that his youthful jubilance denied. The hopeful question hung in the air, a cloud visible from the cold of the down deep.

'It's not working *enough*,' Juliette told him, annoyed with the progress. She peered over the railing, past the jutting toes of borrowed boots to the colourful slick of water below. The mirrored surface of oil and gas stood perfectly still. Beneath this coat of slime, the emergency lights of the stairwell glowed eerily green, lending the depths a haunting look that matched the rest of the empty silo.

In that silence, Juliette heard a faint gurgle in the pipe beside her. She even thought she could hear the distant buzz of the submerged pump a dozen or so feet below the oil and gas. She tried to *will* the water up that tube, up twenty levels and hundreds of joints to the vast and empty treatment tanks above.

Solo coughed into his fist. 'What if we install another—'

Juliette raised her hand to quieten him. She was doing the maths.

The volume of the eight levels of Mechanical was difficult to calculate – so many corridors and rooms that may or may not be flooded – but she could guess the height of the cylindrical shaft from Solo's feet to the security station. The lone pump had moved the level of the flood a little less than a foot in two weeks. Eighty or ninety feet to go. With another pump, say a year to get to the entrance of Mechanical. Depending on how watertight the intervening levels were, it could be much more. Mechanical itself could take three or four times as long to clear.

'What about another pump?' Solo insisted.

Juliette felt nauseous. Even with three more of the small pumps from the hydroponic farms, and with three more runs of pipe and wiring to go with them, she was looking at a year, possibly two, before the silo was perfectly dry. She wasn't sure if she had a year. Just a few weeks of being in that abandoned place, alone with a half-sane man, and she was already starting to hear whispers, to forget where she was leaving things, finding lights on she swore she'd turned off. Either she was going crazy, or Solo found humour in making her feel that way. Two years of this life, of her home so close but so impossibly far away . . .

She leaned over the railing, feeling like she really might be sick. As she gazed down at the water and through her reflection cast in that film of oil, she suddenly considered risks even crazier than two years of near-solitude.

'Two years,' she told Solo. It felt like voicing a death sentence. 'Two years. That's how long this'll take if we add three more pumps. Six months at least on the stairwell, but the rest will go slower.'

'Two years!' Solo sung. 'Two years, two years!' He tapped his boot twice against the water on the step below, sending her reflection into sickening waves of distortion. He spun in place, peering up at her. 'That's no time!'

Juliette fought to control her frustration. Two years would feel like for ever. And what would they find down there, anyway? What condition would the main generator be in? Or the diggers? A machine submerged under fresh water might be preserved as long as air didn't get to it, but as soon as any of it was exposed by the pumps, the corrosion would begin. It was the nastiness of oxygen working on wet metal that spelled doom for anything useful down there. Machines and tools would need to be dried immediately and then oiled. And with only two of them—

Juliette watched, horrified, as Solo bent down, waved away the film of grease at his feet, and scooped up two palms of the brackish filth below. He slurped noisily and happily.

Okay, with only *one* of them working diligently at salvaging the machines, it wouldn't be enough.

Maybe she'd be able to salvage the backup generator. It would require less work and still provide plenty of power.

'What to do for two years?' Solo asked, wiping his beard with the back of his hand and looking up at her.

Juliette shook her head. 'We're not waiting two years,' she told him. The last three *weeks* in silo seventeen had been too much. This, she didn't say.

'Okay,' he said, shrugging. He clomped up the stairwell in his too-big boots. His grey overalls were also baggy, as if he were still a young boy trying to wear clothing tailored for his father. He joined Juliette on the landing, smiled at her through his glistening beard. 'You look like you have more projects,' he said happily.

She nodded silently. Anything the two of them worked on, whether it was fixing the sloppy wiring of the long-ago dead, or improving the farms, or repairing a light fixture's ballast, Solo referred to as a 'project'. And he professed to *love* projects. She decided it was something from his youth, some sort of survival mechanism he'd concocted over the years that allowed him to tackle whatever needed doing with a smile instead of horror or loneliness.

'Oh, we've got quite a project ahead of us,' Juliette told him, already dreading the job. She started making a mental list of all the tools and spares they'd need to scrounge on their way back up.

Solo laughed and clapped his hands. 'Good,' he said. 'Back to the workshop!' He twirled his finger over his head, pointing up at the long climb ahead of them.

'Not yet,' she said. 'First, some lunch at the farms. Then we need to stop by Supply for some more things. And *then* I need some time alone in the server room.' Juliette turned away from the railing and that deep shaft of silver-green water below. 'Before we get started in the workshop,' she said, 'I'd like to make a call—'

'A call!' Solo pouted. 'Not a call. You spend all your time on that stupid thing.'

Juliette ignored him and hit the stairs. She began the long slog up to IT, her fifth in three weeks. And she knew Solo was right: she *was* spending too much time making calls, too much time with those headphones pulled down over her ears, listening to them beep. She knew it was crazy, that she was going slowly mad in that place, but sitting at the back of that empty server with her microphone close to her lips and the world made quiet by the cups over her ears – just having that wire linking her from a dead world to one that harboured life – it was the closest she could get in silo seventeen to making herself feel sane.

• Silo 18 •

'. . . *was the year the Civil War consumed the thirty-three states. More American lives were lost in this conflict than in all the subsequent ones combined, for any death was a death among kin. For four years, the land was ravaged, smoke clearing over battlefields of ruin to reveal brother heaped upon brother. More than half a million lives were lost. Some estimates range to almost twice that. Disease, hunger, and heartbreak ruled the life of man . . .*'

The pages of the book flashed crimson just as Lukas was getting to the descriptions of the battlefields. He stopped reading and glanced up at the overhead lights. Their steady white had been replaced with a throbbing red, which meant someone was in the server room above him. He retrieved the loose silver thread curled up on the knee of his overalls and laid it carefully into the spine of the book. Closing the old tome, he returned it to its tin case with care, then slid it into the gap on the bookshelf, completing the vast wall of silvery spines. Padding silently across the room, he bent down in front of the computer and shook the mouse to wake the screen.

A window popped up with live views of the servers, only distorted from such wide angles. It was another secret in a room overflowing with them, this ability to see distant places. Lukas searched through the cameras, wondering if it was Sammi or another tech coming to make a repair. His grumbling stomach, meanwhile, hoped it was someone bringing him lunch.

In camera four, he finally spotted his visitor: a short figure in grey overalls sporting a moustache and glasses. He was slightly stooped, a tray in his hands dancing with silverware, a sloshing glass of water, and a covered plate, all of it partly supported by his protruding belly. Bernard glanced up at the camera as he walked by, his eyes piercing Lukas from a level away, a tight smile curling below his moustache.

Lukas left the computer and hurried down the hallway to get the hatch for him, his bare feet slapping softly on the cool steel grating. He scrambled up the ladder with practised ease and slid the worn red locking handle to the side. Just as he lifted the grate, Bernard's shadow threw the ladderway into darkness. The tray came to a clattering rest as Lukas shifted the section of flooring out of the way.

'I'm spoiling you today,' Bernard said. He sniffed and uncovered the plate. A fog of trapped steam billowed out of the metal hood, two stacks of pork ribs revealing themselves underneath.

'Wow.' Lukas felt his stomach rumble at the sight of the meat. He lifted himself out of the hatch and sat on the floor, his feet dangling down by the ladder. He pulled the tray into his lap and picked up the silverware. 'I thought we had the silo on strict rations, at least until the resistance was over.'

He cut a piece of tender meat free and popped it in his mouth. 'Not that I'm complaining, mind you.' He chewed and savoured the rush of proteins, reminded himself to be thankful for the animal's sacrifice.

'The rations haven't been lifted,' Bernard said. 'We had a pocket of resistance flare up in the bazaar, and this poor pig found himself in the crossfire. I wasn't about to let him go to waste. Most of the meat, of course, went to the wives and husbands of those we've lost.'

'Mmm?' Lukas swallowed. 'How many?'

'Five, plus the three from that first attack.'

Lukas shook his head.

'It's not bad, considering.' Bernard brushed his moustache with his hand and watched Lukas eat. Lukas gestured with his fork while he chewed, offering him some, but Bernard waved him away. The older man leaned back on the empty server that housed the uplink and the locking handle for the ladderway. Lukas tried not to react.

'So how long will I need to stay in here?' He tried to sound calm, like any answer would do. 'It's been three weeks, right?' He cut off another bite, ignoring the vegetables. 'You think a few more days?'

Bernard rubbed his cheeks and ran his fingers up through his thinning hair. 'I hope so, but I don't know. I've left it up to Sims, who's convinced the threat isn't over. Mechanical have themselves barricaded pretty good down there. They've threatened to cut the power, but I don't think they will. I think they finally understand that they don't control the juice up here on our levels. They probably tried to cut it before they stormed in, and then were surprised to see us all lit up.'

'You don't think they'll cut the power to the farms, do you?' He was thinking of the rations, his fear of the silo being starved.

Bernard frowned. 'Eventually. Maybe. If they get desperate enough. But that'll just erode whatever support those greasers have up here. Don't worry, they'll get hungry enough and give in. It's all going by the book.'

Lukas nodded and took a sip of water. The pork was the best he thought he'd ever had.

'Speaking of the book,' Bernard asked, 'are you catching up with your studies?'

'Yeah,' Lukas lied. He nodded. In truth, he had hardly touched the book of Order. The more interesting details were found elsewhere.

'Good. When this annoyance is over, we'll schedule you some extra shifts in the server room. You can spend that time shadowing. Once we reschedule the election, and I don't think anyone else will run, especially not after all this, I'll be up top a lot more. IT will be *yours* to run.'

Lukas set down the glass and picked up the cloth napkin. He wiped his mouth and thought about this. 'Well, I hope you're not talking weeks from now. I feel like I've got years of—'

A buzzing noise cut him off. Lukas froze, the napkin falling out of his hand and flopping to the tray.

Bernard started away from the server as if it had physically shocked him or its black metallic skin had grown suddenly warm.

'Goddammit!' he said, banging the server with his fist. He fumbled inside his overalls for his master key.

Lukas forced himself to take a bite of food, to act normal. Bernard had grown more and more agitated by the constant ringing of the server. It made him irrational. It was like living with his father again, back before the tub-gin finally bore him a hole beneath the potatoes.

'I fucking swear,' Bernard grumbled, working the series of locks in sequence. He glanced over at Lukas, who slowly chewed a piece of meat, unable suddenly even to taste it.

'I've got a project for you,' he said, wiggling the last lock free, which Lukas knew could stick a bit. 'I want you to add a panel on the back here, just a simple LED array. Figure out some code so we can see who's calling us. I wanna know if it's important or if we can safely ignore it.'

He yanked the back panel off the server and set it noisily against the front of server forty, behind him. Lukas took another sip of water while Bernard peered into the machine's dark and cavernous interior, studying the blinking lights above the little communication jacks. The black guts of the server tower and its frantic buzzing drowned out Bernard's whispered curses.

He pulled his head out, which was bright red with anger, and turned to Lukas, who set his cup on his tray. 'In fact, what I want right here is *two* lights.' Bernard pointed to the side of the tower. 'A red light if it's silo seventeen calling. Green if it's *anyone else*. You got that?'

Lukas nodded. He looked down at his tray and started cutting a potato in half, thinking suddenly of his father again. Bernard turned and grabbed the server's rear panel.

'I can pop that back on.' Lukas mumbled this around a hot mouthful of potato; he breathed out steam to keep his tongue from burning, swallowed, and chased it with water.

Bernard left the panel where it was. He turned and glared angrily into the pit of the machine, which continued to buzz and buzz, the overhead lights winking in alarm. 'Good idea,' he said. 'Maybe you can knock this project out first thing.'

Finally, the server quit its frantic calls, and the room fell silent save for the clinking of Lukas's fork on his plate. This was like the moments of rye-stench quiet from his youth. Soon – just like his father passing out on the kitchen floor or in the bathroom – Bernard would leave.

As if on cue, his caster and boss stood, the head of IT again throwing Lukas into darkness as he blocked the overhead lights.

'Enjoy your dinner,' he said. 'I'll have Peter come by later for the dishes.'

Lukas jabbed a row of beans with his fork. 'Seriously? I thought this was lunch.' He popped them into his mouth.

'It's after eight,' Bernard said. He adjusted his overalls. 'Oh, and I spoke with your mother today.'

Lukas set his fork down. 'Yeah?'

'I reminded her that you were doing important work for the silo, but she really wants to see you. I've talked with Sims about allowing her in here—'

'Into the server room?'

'Just inside. So she can see that you're okay. I'd set it up elsewhere, but Sims thinks it's a bad idea. He's not so sure how strong the allegiance is among the techs. He's still trying to ferret out any source of leaks—'

Lukas scoffed. 'Sims is paranoid. None of our techs are gonna side with those greasers. They're not going to betray the silo, much less you.' He picked up a bone and gnawed at the remaining meat.

'Still, he has me convinced to keep you as safe as possible. I'll let you know if I can set something up so you can see her.'

Bernard leaned forward and squeezed Lukas's shoulder. 'Thanks for being patient. I'm glad to have someone under me who understands how important this job is.'

'Oh, I understand completely,' Lukas said. 'Anything for the silo.'

'Good.' Another squeeze of his hand, and Bernard stood. 'Keep reading the Order. Especially the sections on insurrections and uprisings. I want you to learn from this one just in case, God forbid, it ever happens on *your* watch.'

'I will,' Lukas said. He set down the clean bone and wiped his fingers on the napkin. Bernard turned to go.

'Oh—' Bernard stopped and turned back to him. 'I know you don't need me to remind you, but under no circumstances are you to answer this server.' He jabbed his finger at the front of the machine. 'I haven't cleared you with the other IT heads yet, so your position could be in . . . well, *grave* danger if you were to speak with *any* of them before the induction.'

'Are you kidding?' Lukas shook his head. 'Like I want to talk with anyone who makes *you* nervous. No frickin' thanks.'

Bernard smiled and wiped at his forehead. 'You're a good man, Lukas. I'm glad I've got you.'

'And I'm glad to serve,' Lukas said. He reached for another rib and smiled up at his caster while Bernard beamed down at him. Finally, the older man turned to go, his boots ringing across the steel grates and fading towards that massive door that held Lukas prisoner among the machines and all their secrets.

Lukas ate and listened as Bernard's new code was keyed into the lock, a cadence of familiar but unknown beeps – a code Lukas no longer possessed.

For your own good, Bernard had told him. He chewed a piece of fat as the heavy door clanged shut, the red lights below his feet and down the ladderway blinking off.

Lukas dropped the bone onto his plate. He pushed the potatoes aside, fighting the urge to gag at the sight of them, thinking of where his father's bones lay. Setting the tray on the grating, he pulled his feet out of the ladderway and moved to the back of the open and quiet server.

The headphones slid easily out of their pouch. He pulled them down over his ears, his palms brushing the three-week growth of beard on his face. Grabbing the cord, he slotted it into the jack labelled '17'.

There was a series of beeps as the call was placed. He imagined the buzzing on the other side, the flashing lights.

Lukas waited, unable to breathe.

'Hello?'

The voice sang in his earphones. Lukas smiled.

'Hey,' he said.

He sat down, leaned back against server forty, and got more comfortable.

'How's everything going over there?'

Walker waved his arms over his head as he attempted
to explain his new theory for how the radio probably
worked. 'So the sound, these transmissions, they're
like ripples in the air, you see?' He chased the invisible voices with
his fingers. Above him, the third large antenna he'd built in two
days hung suspended from the rafters. 'These ripples run up and
down the wire, up and down' – he gesticulated to show the length
of antenna – 'which is why longer is better. It snags more of them
out of the air.'

*But if these ripples are everywhere, then why aren't we catching
any?*

Walker bobbed his head and wagged his finger in appreciation. It was a good question. A damn good question. 'We'll catch
them this time,' he said. 'We're getting close.' He adjusted the
new amplifier he'd built, one much more powerful than the tiny
thing in Hank's old hip radio. 'Listen,' he said.

A crackling hiss filled the room, like someone twisting fistfuls
of plastic sheeting.

I don't hear it.

'That's because you aren't being quiet. *Listen.*'

There. It was faint, but a crunch of transmitted noise emerged
from the hiss.

I heard it!

Walker nodded with pride. Less from the thing he was
building and more for his bright understudy. He glanced at the
door, made sure it was still closed. He only spoke with Scottie
when it was closed.

'What I don't get is why I can't make it clearer.' He scratched his chin. 'Unless it's because we're too deep in the earth.'

We've always been this deep, Scottie pointed out. *That sheriff we met years ago, he was always talking on his radio just fine.*

Walker scratched the stubble on his cheek. His little shadow, as usual, had a good point.

'Well, there *is* this one little circuit board I can't figure out. I think it's supposed to clean up the signal. Everything seems to pass through it.' Walker spun around on his stool to face the workbench, which had become dominated by all the green boards and colourful tangles of wires needed for this most singular project. He lowered his magnifier and peered at the board in question. He imagined Scottie leaning in for a closer inspection.

What's this sticker? Scottie pointed to the tiny dot of a white sticker with the number '18' printed on it. Walker was the one who had taught Scottie that it's always okay to admit when you didn't know something. If you couldn't do this, you would never truly know *anything*.

'I'm not sure,' he admitted. 'But you see how this little board slotted into the radio with ribbon cables?'

Scottie nodded.

'It's like it was meant to be swapped out. Like maybe it burns up easy. I'm thinking this is the part that's holding us up, like a blown fuse.'

Can we bypass it?

'Bypass it?' Walker wasn't sure what he meant.

Go around it. In case it's burned out. Short it.

'We might blow something else. I mean, it wouldn't be *in* here if it weren't truly needed.' Walker thought for a minute. He wanted to add that the same could be said of Scottie, of the boy's calming voice. But then, he never was good at telling his shadow how he felt. Only what he knew.

Well, that's what I would try—

There was a knock at the door followed by the squeal of hinges left purposefully loud. Scottie melted into the shadows beneath the workbench, his voice trailing off in the hiss of static from the speakers.

'Walk, what the hell's going on here?'

He swivelled around on his stool, the lovely voice and harsh words soldered together as only Shirly could. She came into his workshop with a covered tray, a thin-lipped frown of disappointment on her face.

Walker lowered the volume on the static. 'I'm trying to fix the—'

'No, what's this nonsense I hear about you not eating?' She set the tray in front of him and pulled off the cover, releasing the steam from a plate of corn. 'Did you eat your breakfast this morning, or did you give it to someone else?'

'That's too much,' he said, looking down at three or four rations of food.

'Not when you've been giving yours away it isn't.' She slapped a fork into his hand. 'Eat. You're about to fall out of your overalls.'

Walker stared at the corn. He stirred the food with his fork, but his stomach was cramped beyond hunger. He felt like he'd gone without for so long, he'd never be hungry again. The cramp would just tighten and tighten into a little fist and then he'd be just fine for ever—

'Eat, dammit.'

He blew on a bite of the stuff, had no desire to consume it, but put some in his mouth to make Shirly happy.

'And I don't want to hear that any of my men are hanging around your door sweet-talking you, okay? You are *not* to give them your rations. Got that? Take another bite.'

Walker swallowed. He had to admit, the burn of the food felt good going down. He gathered up another small bite. 'I'll be sick if I eat all this,' he said.

'And I'll murder you if you don't.'

He glanced over at her, expecting to see her smiling. But Shirly didn't smile any more. Nobody did.

'What the hell is that *noise?*' She turned and surveyed the workshop, hunting for the source of it.

Walker set down his fork and adjusted the volume. The knob was soldered onto a series of resistors; the knob itself was called a potentiometer. He had a sudden impulse to explain all of this, anything to keep from eating. He could explain how he had figured out the amplifier, how the potentiometer was really just an adjustable resistor, how each little twist of the dial could hone the volume to whatever he— Walker stopped. He picked up his fork and stirred his corn. He could hear Scottie whispering from the shadows.

'That's better,' Shirly said, referring to the reduced hiss. 'That's a worse sound than the old generator used to make. Hell, if you *can* turn that down, why ever have it up so loud?'

Walker took a bite. While he chewed, he set down his fork and grabbed his soldering iron from its stand. He rummaged in a small parts bin for another scrap potentiometer.

'Hold these,' he told Shirly around his food. He showed her the wires hanging off the potentiometer, and lined them up with the sharp silver prods from his multimeter.

'If it means you'll keep eating.' She pinched the wires and the prods together between her fingers and thumbs.

Walker scooped up another bite, forgetting to blow on it. The corn burned his tongue. He swallowed without chewing, the fire melting its way through his chest. Shirly told him to slow down, to take it easy. He ignored her and twisted the knob of the potentiometer. The needle on his multimeter danced, letting him know the part was good.

'Why don't you take a break from this stuff and eat while I'm here to watch?' Shirly slid a stool away from the workbench and plopped down on it.

'Because it's too hot,' he said, waving his hand at his mouth. He grabbed a spool of solder and touched it to the tip of the hot soldering iron, coating it with bright silver. 'I need you to hold the black wire to this.' He lightly touched the iron to the tiny leg of a resistor on the board labelled '18'. Shirly leaned over the bench and squinted at the one he was indicating.

'And then you'll finish your dinner?'

'Swear.'

She narrowed her eyes at him as if to say that she took this promise seriously, then did as he had shown her.

Her hands weren't as steady as Scottie's, but he lowered his magnifier and made quick work of the connection. He showed her where the red wire went and tacked that one on as well. Even if none of this worked, he could always remove it and tinker with something else.

'Now don't let it get cold,' Shirly told him. 'I know you won't eat it if it cools, and I'm not going back to the mess hall to warm it up for you.'

Walker stared at the little board with the numbered sticker on it. He grudgingly picked up the fork and scooped a sizable bite.

'How're things out there?' he asked, blowing on the corn.

'Things are shit,' Shirly said. 'Jenkins and Harper are arguing over whether or not they should kill the power to the entire silo. But then some of the guys who were there, you know, when Knox and . . .'

She looked away, left the sentence unfinished.

Walker nodded and chewed his food.

'Some of them say the power in IT was up to the max that morning, even though we had it shut down from here.'

'Maybe it was rerouted,' Walker said. 'Or battery backups. They have those, you know.' He took another bite, but was dying to spin the potentiometer. He was pretty sure the static had changed when he'd made the second connection.

'I keep telling them it'll do us more harm than good to screw with the silo like that. It'll just turn the rest of them against us.'

'Yeah. Hey, can you adjust this? You know, while I eat?'

He turned the volume up on the static, needing two hands to work the loose knob as it dangled from its bright wires. Shirly seemed to shrink from the noise crackling out of his home-built speakers. She reached for the volume knob as if to turn it down.

'No, I want you to spin the one we just installed.'

'What the hell, Walk? Just eat your damn food already.'

He took another bite. And for all her cussing and protests, Shirly began adjusting the knob.

'Slowly,' he said, his mouth full of food.

And sure enough, the static from the speakers modulated. It was as if the crunching plastic had begun to move and bounce around the room.

'What am I even doing?'

'Helping an old man—'

'—yeah, I might need you up here on this one—'

Walker dropped his fork and held out his hand for her to stop. She had gone past it though, into the static once more. Shirly seemed to intuit this. She bit her lip and wiggled the knob the other way until the voices returned.

'Sounds good. It's quiet down here anyway. You need me to bring my kit?'

'You did it,' Shirly whispered to Walker, as if these people could hear her if she spoke too loudly. 'You fixed—'

Walker held up his hand. The chatter continued.

'Negative. You can leave the kit. Deputy Roberts is already here with hers. She's sweeping for clues as I speak—'

'What I'm doing is working while he does nothing!' a faint voice called out in the background.

Walker turned to Shirly while laughter rolled through the radio, more than one person enjoying the joke. It had been a long time since he'd heard anyone laugh. But *he* wasn't laughing. Walker felt his brows furrow in confusion.

'What's wrong?' Shirly asked. 'We did it! We fixed it!' She got off her stool and turned as if to run and tell Jenkins.

'Wait!' Walker wiped his beard with his palm and jabbed his fork towards the strewn collection of radio parts. Shirly stood a pace away, looking back at him, smiling.

'Deputy *Roberts*?' Walker asked. 'Who in all the levels is *that*?'

• Silo 17 •

Juliette flicked the lights on in the Suit Lab as she hauled in her latest load from Supply. Unlike Solo, she didn't take the constant source of power for granted. Not knowing where it came from made her nervous that it wouldn't last. So while he had the habit, the compulsion even, of turning every light on to full and leaving it there, she tried to conserve the mysterious energy as much as possible.

She dropped her recent scavenges on her cot, thinking of Walker as she did so. Is this how he ended up living among his work? Was it the obsession, the drive, the need to keep hammering away at a series of never-ending problems until he couldn't sleep more than a few paces from them?

The more she understood the old man, the further away from him she felt, the lonelier. She sat down and rubbed her legs, her thighs and calves tight from the most recent hike up. She may've been gaining her porter legs these last weeks, but they were still sore all the time, the ache in them a constant new sensation. Squeezing the muscles transformed that ache into pain, which she somehow preferred. The sharp and definable sensations were better than the dull and nameless kind. She liked feelings she could understand.

Juliette kicked her boots off – strange to think of these scavenged things as *hers* – and stood up. That was enough rest. It was as much rest as she could allow herself to have. She carried her canvas sacks to one of the fancy workbenches, everything in the Suit Lab nicer than what she'd had in Mechanical. Even the parts engineered to fail were constructed with a level of chemical and engineering sophistication she could only begin to appreciate now that she understood their evil intent. She had amassed piles of washers and seals, the good from Supply and the leftover bad from the Lab, to see how the system worked. They sat along the back of her main workbench, a reminder of the diabolical murderousness with which she'd been sent away.

She dumped the parts from Supply and thought about how strange it was to have access to, to *live* in this forbidden heart of some *other* silo. It was stranger still to appreciate these workbenches, these immaculate tools, all arranged for the purpose of sending people like her to their death.

Looking around at the walls, at the dozen or so cleaning suits hanging from racks in various states of repair, it was like living and working in a room full of ghostly apparitions. If one of those suits jumped down and started moving about on its own, it wouldn't surprise her. The arms and legs on each one were puffy as if full, the mirrored visors easily concealing curious faces. It was like having company, these hanging forms. They watched her impassively while she sorted her finds into two piles: one of items she needed for her next big project, the other of useful titbits she had snagged with no specific idea of what she might use them for.

A valuable rechargeable battery went in this second group, some blood still on it that she hadn't been able to wipe off. Images flashed through her mind of some of the scenes she'd found while scrounging for materials, like the two men who had committed suicide in the head office of Supply, their hands interlocked, opposite wrists slit, a rust-coloured stain all around them. This was one of the worst scenes, a memory she couldn't shake. There was more evidence of violence scattered about the silo. The entire place was haunted and marred. She completely understood why Solo limited his rounds to the gardens. She also empathised with his habit of blocking off the server room every night with the filing cabinet, even though he had been alone for years. Juliette didn't blame him. She slid the deadbolts on the Suit Lab every night before she went to sleep. She didn't really believe in ghosts, but that conviction was being sorely tested by the constant feeling of being watched by − if not actual people − the silo itself.

She began her work on the air compressor and, as always, it

felt good to be doing something with her hands. *Fixing* something. Staying distracted. The first few nights, after surviving the horrible ordeal of being sent to clean, of fighting her way inside this carcass of a silo, she had searched long and hard for some place that she could actually sleep. It was never going to be below the server room, not with the stench of Solo's debris piles pervading the place. She tried the apartment for IT's head, but thoughts of Bernard made it impossible even to sit still. The couches in the various offices weren't long enough. The pad she'd tried to put together on the warm server-room floor was nice, but the clicking and whirring of all those tall cabinets nearly drove her insane.

The Suit Lab, strangely enough, with the spectres and ghouls hanging about, was the only spot where she'd won a decent night of sleep. It was probably the tools everywhere, the welders and wrenches, the walls of drawers full of every socket and driver imaginable. If she was going to fix anything, even herself, it was there in that room. The only other place she'd felt at home in silo seventeen was in the two jail cells she sometimes slept in on trips up and down. There, and sitting behind that empty server, talking to Lukas.

She thought about him as she crossed the room to grab the right size tap from one of the expansive metal tool chests. She pocketed this and pulled down one of the complete cleaning suits, admiring the heft of the outfit, remembering how bulky it had felt when she'd worn one just like it. She lifted it onto a workbench and pulled off the helmet's locking collar, took this to the drill press and carefully bored a starter hole. With the collar in a vice, she began working the tap into the hole, creating new threads for the air hose. She was wrestling with this and thinking about her last conversation with Lukas when the smell of fresh bread entered the lab, followed by Solo.

'Hello!' he called from the doorway. Juliette looked up and jerked her chin for him to enter. Turning the tap required effort, the metal handle digging into her palms, sweat forming on her brow.

'I baked more bread.'

'Smells great,' she grunted.

Ever since she'd taught Solo how to bake flatbread, she couldn't get him to stop. The large tins of flour that had been holding up his canned-goods shelves were being removed one at a time while he experimented with recipes. She reminded herself to teach him more things to cook, to put this industriousness of his to good use by having him mix it up a little.

'And I sliced cucumbers,' he said, proud as if it were a feast beyond compare. In so many ways, Solo was stuck with the mind of a teenager – culinary habits included.

'I'll have some in a bit,' she told him. With effort, she finally got the tap all the way through the pilot hole, creating a threaded connection as neat as if it had come from Supply. The tap backed out easily, just like a fitted bolt would.

Solo placed the plate of bread and vegetables on the workbench and grabbed a stool. 'Wotcha working on? Another pump?' He peered at the large wheeled air compressor with the hoses trailing off it.

'No. That was going to take too long. I'm working on a way to breathe underwater.'

Solo laughed. He started munching on a piece of bread until he realised she wasn't joking.

'You're serious.'

'I am. The pumps we *really* need are in the sump basins at the very bottom of the silo. I just need to get some of this electricity from IT *down* to them. We'll have the place dry in weeks or months instead of years.'

'Breathe underwater,' he said. He looked at her like *she* was the one losing her mind.

'It's no different from how I got here from my silo.' She wrapped the male end of the air hose coupler with silicone tape, then began threading it into the collar.

'These suits are airtight, which makes them watertight. All I need is a constant supply of air to breathe, and I can work down there as long as I like. Long enough to get the pumps going, anyway.'

'You think they'll still work?'

'They should.' She grabbed a wrench and tightened the coupler as hard as she dared. 'They're designed to be submerged, and they're simple. They just need power, which we've got plenty of up here.'

'What will *I* do?' Solo wiped his hands, sprinkling bread-crumbs on her workbench. He reached for another piece of bread.

'You'll be watching the compressor. I'll show you how to crank it, how to top it up with fuel. I'm going to install one of the portable deputy radios in the helmet here so we can talk back and forth. There'll be a whole mess of hose and electrical wire to play out.' She smiled up at him. 'Don't worry, I'll keep you busy.'

'I'm not worried,' Solo said. He puffed out his chest and crunched on a cucumber, his eyes drifting to the compressor.

And Juliette saw – just like a teenager with little practice but great need – that Solo had not yet mastered the art of lying convincingly.

'. . . *boys from the other side of the camp. These results were closely observed by the experimenters, who were posing as camp counsellors. When the violence got out of hand, the experiment was halted before it could run its full course. What began at Robber Cave as two sets of boys, all with nearly identical backgrounds and values, had turned into what became known in the field of psychology as an in-grouping and out-grouping scenario. Small perceived differences, the way one wore a hat, the inflections in speech, turned into unforgivable transgressions. When stones started flying, and the raids on each other's camps turned bloody, there was no recourse for the experimenters but to put an end to* . . .'

Lukas couldn't read any more. He closed the book and leaned back against the tall shelves. He smelled something foul, brought the spine of the old book to his nose and sniffed. It was *him*, he finally decided. When was the last time he'd showered? His routine was all out of whack. There were no screaming kids to wake him in the morning, no evenings hunting for stars, no dimmed stairwell to guide him back to his bed so he could repeat it all the following day. Instead, it was fitful periods of tossing and turning in the hidden bunk room of level thirty-five. A dozen bunks, but him all alone. It was flashing red lights to signal that he had company, conversations with Bernard and Peter Billings when they brought him food, long talks with Juliette whenever she called and he was free to answer. Between it all, the books. Books of history out of order, of billions of people, of even more stars. Stories of violence, of the madness of crowds, of the staggering timeline of life, of orbited suns that would one day burn out, of weapons that could end it all, of diseases that nearly had.

How long could he go on like this? Reading and sleeping and eating? The weeks already felt like months. There was no keeping track of the days, no way to remember how long he'd worn this pair of overalls, if it was time to change out of them and into the pair in the dryer. Sometimes he felt like he changed and washed his clothes three times a day. It could easily have been twice a week. It smelled like longer.

He leaned his head back against the tins of books and closed his eyes. The things he was reading couldn't all be true. It made no sense, a world so crowded and strange. When he considered the scale of it all, the idea of this life burrowed beneath the earth, sending people to clean, getting worked up over who stole what from whom – he sometimes felt a sort of mental vertigo, this frightening terror of standing over some abyss, seeing a dark truth far below, but unable to make it out before his senses returned and reality snatched him back from the edge.

He wasn't sure how long he'd been sitting like that, dreaming of a different time and place, before he realised the throbbing red lights had returned.

Lukas returned the book to its tin and struggled to his feet. The computer screen showed Peter Billings at the server door, as deep as he was allowed into the room. A tray with Lukas's dinner sat on top of the work-log filing cabinet inside the door.

He turned away from the computer, hurried down the corridor, and scrambled up the ladder. After removing the grate, he carefully dropped it back into place and picked a circuitous path through the tall humming servers.

'Ah, here's our little protégé.' Peter smiled, but his eyes narrowed at the sight of Lukas.

Lukas dipped his chin. 'Sheriff,' he said. He always had this sense that Peter was silently mocking him, looking down on him, even though they were about the same age. Whenever Peter showed up with Bernard, especially the day Bernard had explained the need to keep Lukas safe, there had seemed some sort of competitive tension between the two more junior men – a tension Lukas was aware of, even if he didn't share it. In private, Bernard had committed Lukas to secrecy and told him that he was grooming Peter for the eventual job of mayor, that he and Lukas would one day work hand in hand. Lukas tried to remember this as he slid the tray off the cabinet. Peter watched him, his brow lowered in thought.

Lukas turned to go.

'Why don't you sit and eat here?' Peter asked, not budging from where he leaned against the thick server-room door.

Lukas froze.

'I see you sitting here with Bernard while you eat, but you're always in a hurry to scurry off when I come by.' Peter leaned out and peered into the stacks of servers. 'What is it you do in here all day, anyway?'

Lukas felt trapped. In truth, he wasn't even all that hungry, had thought about saving it for later, but eating his food to completion was usually the fastest way out of these conversations. He shrugged and sat down on the floor, leaned against the work-log cabinet, and stretched his legs out in front of him. Uncovering the tray revealed a bowl of unidentifiable soup, two slices of tomato, and a piece of cornbread.

'I work on the servers mostly, just like before.' He started with a bite of the bread, something bland. 'Only difference is I don't have to walk home at the end of the day.' He smiled at Peter while he chewed the dry bread.

'That's right, you live down in the mids, don't you?' Peter crossed his arms and seemed to get even more comfortable against the thick door. Lukas leaned to the side and gazed past him and down the hallway. Voices could be heard around the corner. He had a sudden impulse to get up and run, just for the sake of running. 'Barely,' he answered. 'My apartment's practically in the up top.'

'All the mids are,' Peter laughed, 'to those who live there.'

Lukas worked on the cornbread to keep his mouth occupied. He eyed the soup warily while he chewed.

'Did Bernard tell you about the big assault we've got planned? I was thinking of going down to take part.'

Lukas shook his head. He dipped his spoon into the soup.

'You know that wall Mechanical built, how those idiots boxed themselves in? Well, Sims and his boys are gonna blast it to smithereens. They've had all the time in the world to work on it from our side, so this little rebellion nonsense should be over in a few days, max.'

While he slurped the hot soup, all Lukas could think about was the men and women of Mechanical trapped behind that wall of steel, and how he knew precisely what they were going through.

'Does that mean I'll be out of here soon?' He pressed the edge of his spoon into an under-ripe tomato rather than use the knife and fork. 'There can't be any threat out there for me, can there? Nobody even knows who I am.'

'That's up to Bernard. He's been acting strange lately. A lot of stress, I suppose.' Peter slid down the door and rested on his heels. It was nice for Lukas not to have to crane his neck to look up at him.

'He did say something about bringing your mother up for a visit. I took that to mean you might be in here at least a week longer.'

'Great.' Lukas pushed his food around some more. When the distant server started buzzing, his body practically jerked as if tugged by some string. The overhead lights winked faintly, meaningful to those in the know.

'What's that?' Peter peered into the server room, rising on his toes a little.

'That means I need to get back to work.' Lukas handed him the tray. 'Thanks for bringing this.' He turned to go.

'Hey, the mayor said to make sure you ate everything—'

Lukas waved over his shoulder. He disappeared around the first tall server and began to jog towards the back of the room, wiping his mouth with his hand, knowing Peter couldn't follow.

'Lukas—!'

But he was gone. He hurried towards the far wall, digging his keys out of his collar as he went.

While he worked on the locks, he saw the overhead lights stop their flashing. Peter had closed the door. He removed the back panel and dug the headphones out of their pouch, plugged them in.

'Hello?' He adjusted his microphone, made sure it wasn't too close.

'Hey.' Her voice filled him up in a way mere food couldn't. 'Did I make you run?'

Lukas took a deep breath. He was getting out of shape living in such confinement, not walking to and from work every day. 'No,' he lied. 'But maybe you should go easy with the calling. At least during the day. You-know-who is in here all the time. Yesterday, when you let it ring so long, we were sitting *right beside* the server while it buzzed and buzzed. It really pissed him off.'

'You think I care if he gets angry?' Juliette laughed. 'And I *want* him to answer. I'd love to talk to him some more. Besides, what would you suggest? I want to talk to you, I need to talk to *someone*. And you're always right there. It's not like you can call me and expect me to be here waiting. Hell, I'm all over the damn place over here. You know how many times I've been from the thirties to Supply in the last week? Guess.'

'I don't want to guess.' Lukas rubbed his eyelids.

'Probably a half dozen times. And you know, if he's in there all the time, you could just do me a favour and kill him for me. Save me all this trouble—'

'*Kill* him?' Lukas waved his arm. 'What, just *bludgeon* him to death?'

'Do you really want some pointers? Because I've dreamt up a number of—'

'No, I don't want pointers. And I don't want to *kill* anybody! I never *did*.' Lukas dug his index finger into his temple and rubbed in tiny forceful circles. These headaches were forever popping up. They had been ever since—

'Forget it,' Juliette said, the disgust in her voice zipping through the wires at the speed of light.

'Look—' Lukas readjusted his mic. He hated these conversations. He preferred it when they just talked about nothing. 'I'm sorry, it's just that . . . things are crazy over here. I don't know who's doing what. I'm in this box with all this information, I've got this radio that just blares out people fighting all the time, and yet I seem to know ratshit compared to everyone else.'

'But you know you can trust me, right? That I'm one of the good guys? I didn't do anything wrong to be sent away, Lukas. I need you to know that.'

He listened as Juliette took in a deep breath and let it out with a sigh. He imagined her sitting over there, alone in that silo with a crazy man, the mic pressed close to her lips, her chest heaving with exasperation, her mind full of all these expectations of him.

'Lukas, you do know that I'm on the right side here, don't you? And that you're working for an insane man?'

'Everything's crazy,' he said. 'Everyone is. I do know this: we were sitting here in IT, hoping nothing bad would happen, and the worst things we could think of came to *us*.'

Juliette released another deep breath, and Lukas thought about what he had told her of the uprising, the things he had omitted.

'I know what you say my people did, but do you understand why they came? Do you? Something needed to be done, Luke. It *still* needs doing.'

Lukas shrugged, forgetting she couldn't see him. As often as they chatted, he still wasn't used to conversing with someone like this.

'You're in a position to help,' she told him.

'I didn't *ask* to be here.' He felt himself growing frustrated. Why did their conversations have to drift off to bad places? Why couldn't they go back to talking about the best meals they'd ever had, their favourite books as kids, the likes and annoyances they had in common?

'None of us asked to be where we are,' she reminded him coolly.

This gave Lukas pause, thinking of where she was, what she'd been through to get there.

'What we control,' Juliette said, 'is our actions once fate puts us there.'

'I probably need to get off.' Lukas took a shallow breath. He didn't want to think of actions and fate. He didn't want to have this conversation. 'Pete'll be bringing me my dinner soon,' he lied.

There was silence. He could hear her breathing. It was almost like listening to someone think.

'Okay,' she said. 'I understand. I need to go test this suit anyway. And hey, I might be gone a while if this thing works. So if you don't hear from me for a day or so . . .'

'Just be careful,' Lukas said.

'I will. And remember what I said. What we do going forward defines who we are. You aren't one of them. You don't belong there. Please don't forget this.'

Lukas mumbled his agreement, and Juliette said goodbye, her voice still in his ears as he reached in and unplugged the jack.

Rather than slot the headphones into their pouch, he slumped back against the server behind him, wringing the ear pads in his hands, thinking about what he had done, about who he was.

He felt like curling up into a ball and crying, just closing his eyes and making the world go away. But he knew if he closed them, if he allowed himself to sink into darkness, all he would see there was *her*. That small woman with the white hair, her body jumping from the impacts of the bullets, *Lukas's* bullets. He would feel his finger on the trigger, his cheeks wet with salt, the stench of spent powder, the table ringing with the clink of empty brass and the jubilant and victorious cries of the men and women he had aligned himself with.

'— Said Thursday that I'd get it to you in two days.'

'Well, dammit, it's been two days, Carl. You do realise the cleaning's tomorrow morning, right?'

'And you realise that today is still today, don't you?'

'Don't be a smartass. Get me that file and get it up here, pronto. I swear, if this shit falls through because you were—'

'I'll bring it. C'mon, man. I'm busting your balls. Relax.'

'Relax. Screw you, I'll relax tomorrow. I'm getting off the line. Now don't dick around.'

'I'm coming right now . . .'

Shirly held the sides of her head, her fingers tangled in her hair, elbows digging into Walker's workbench. 'What in the depths is going on?' she asked him. 'Walk, what is this? Who *are* these people?'

Walker peered through his magnifiers. He dipped the single bristle plucked from the cleaning brush into the white paint on the wet lid of primer. With utmost care, his other hand steadying his wrist, he dragged the bristle across the outside of the potentiometer directly opposite the fixed mark he'd painted on the knob itself. Satisfied, he counted the ticks he'd made so far, each one marking the position of another strong signal.

'Eleven,' he said. He turned to Shirly, who had been saying something, he wasn't sure what. 'And I don't think we've found ours yet.'

'*Ours?* Walk, this is freaking me out. Where are these voices *coming* from?'

He shrugged. 'The city? Over the hills? How should I know?'

He started spinning the knob slowly, listening for more chatter. 'Eleven besides us. What if there's more? There has to be more, right? What're the chances we've found them all already?'

'That last one was talking about a cleaning. Do you think they meant? Like . . . ?'

Walker nodded, sending his magnifiers out of whack. He readjusted them, then went back to tuning the dial.

'So they're in silos. Like us.'

He pointed to the tiny green board she'd helped him wire the potentiometer to. 'It must be what this circuit does, modulates the wave frequency, maybe.' Shirly was freaking out over the voices; he was more fascinated by these other mysteries. There was a crackle of static; he paused in turning the knob, scrubbed back and forth across it, but found nothing. He moved on.

'You mean the little board with the number *eighteen* on it?'

Walker looked at her dumbly. His fingers stopped their searching. He nodded.

'So there's at least *that* many,' she said, putting it together quicker than he had. 'I've got to find Jenkins. We've got to tell him about this.' Shirly left her stool and headed for the door. Walker bobbed his head. The implications made him dizzy, the bench and walls seeming to slide sideways. The idea of *people* beyond these walls—

A violent roar rattled his teeth and shook the thought loose. His feet slipped out from underneath him as the ground trembled, decades of dust raining down from the tangle of pipes and wires crisscrossing overhead.

Walker rolled to his side, coughing, breathing the musky mildew drifting in the air. His ears were ringing from the blast. He patted his head, groped for his magnifiers, when he saw the frame lying on the steel decking before him, the lens broken into gravel-sized shards.

'Oh, no. I need . . .' He tried to get his hands underneath him, felt a twinge in his hip, a powerful ache where bone had smacked steel. He couldn't think. He waved his hand, begging Scottie to come out of the shadows and help him.

A heavy boot crunched on what remained of his magnifiers.

Strong, young hands gripped his overalls, pulling him to his feet. There was shouting everywhere. The pop and rattle of gunfire.

'Walk! You okay?'

Jenkins held him by his overalls. Walker was pretty sure he would collapse if the boy let go.

'My magni—'

'Sir! We've gotta go! They're inside!'

Walker turned towards the door, saw Harper helping Shirly to her feet. Her eyes were wide, stunned, a film of grey dust on her shoulders and in her dark hair. She was looking towards Walker, appearing as dazed as he felt.

'Get your things,' Jenkins said. 'We're falling back.' He scanned the room, his eyes drifting to the workbench.

'I fixed it,' Walker said, coughing into his fist. 'It works.'

'A little too late, I think.'

Jenkins let go of his overalls, and Walker had to catch himself on his stool not to go tumbling back to the ground. The gunfire outside drew nearer. Boots thundered by, more shouting, another loud blast that could be felt through the floor. Jenkins and Harper were at the doorway shouting orders and waving their arms at the people running past. Shirly joined Walker at his workbench. Her eyes were on the radio.

'We need this,' she said, breathing hard.

Walker looked down at the glittering jewels on the floor. Two months' wages for those magnifiers—

'Walk! What do I grab? Help me.'

He turned to find Shirly gathering up the radio parts, the wires between the boards folded up, tangled. There was a single loud pop from one of the good guns right outside his door, causing him to cower, his mind to wander.

'Walk!'

'The antenna,' he whispered, pointing to where the dust was still drifting from the rafters. Shirly nodded and jumped up on his workbench. Walker looked around the room, a room he had promised himself he would never leave again, a promise he really had meant to keep this time. What to grab? Stupid mementos. Junk. Dirty clothes. A pile of schematics. He grabbed his parts bin and dumped it on the floor. The radio components were swept in, the transformer unplugged from its outlet and added. Shirly was yanking down the antenna, the wires and metal rods bundled against her chest. He snatched his soldering iron, a few tools; Harper yelled that it was now or never.

Shirly grabbed Walker by the arm and pulled him along, towards the door.

And Walker realised it wasn't going to be *never*.

62

• Silo 17 •

The panic she felt from donning the suit was unexpected. Juliette had anticipated some degree of fear from slipping into the water, but it was the simple act of putting on the cleaning suit that filled her with a hollow dread, that gave her a cold and empty ache in the pit of her stomach. She fought to control her breathing while Solo zipped up the back and pressed the layers of Velcro into place.

'Where's my knife?' she asked him, patting the pockets on the front and searching among her tools.

'It's over here,' he said. He bent down and fished it out of her gear bag, out from under a towel and change of clothes. He passed her the knife handle first, and Juliette slotted it into the thick pocket she'd added on the suit's belly. It was easier to breathe, just having it within reach. This tool from the upper café was like a security blanket of sorts. She found herself checking for it the way she used to check her wrist for that old watch.

'Let's wait with the helmet,' she told Solo as he lifted the clear dome from the landing. 'Grab that rope first.' She pointed with her puffy mitts. The thick material and the two layers of undersuit were making her warm. She hoped that boded well for not freezing to death in the deep water.

Solo lifted the coils of spliced rope, a large adjustable wrench the length of his forearm knotted at the end.

'Which side?' he asked.

She pointed to where the gracefully curving steps plunged into the green-lit water. 'Lower it over steady. And hold it out so it doesn't get caught on the steps below.'

He nodded. Juliette checked her tools while he dropped the wrench into the water, the weight of the hunk of metal tugging the rope straight down to the very bottom of the great stairwell. In one pocket, she had a range of drivers. Each one was tied to the pocket with a few feet of string. She had a spanner in another pocket, cutters behind pocket number four. Looking down at herself, more memories flooded back from her walk outside. She could hear the sound of fine grit pelting her helmet, could sense her air supply running thin, could feel the clomp of her heavy boots on the packed earth . . .

She gripped the railing ahead of her and tried to think of something else. Anything else. Wire for power and hose for air. Concentrate. She would need a lot of both. She took a deep breath and checked the tall coils of tubing and electrical wire laid out on the deck. She had flaked them in figure eights so they would be impossible to tangle. Good. The compressor was ready; all Solo had to do was make sure everything fed down to her, didn't get caught up—

'It's on the bottom,' Solo said. She watched him knot the line to the stairway railing. He was in good spirits today. Lucid and energetic. This would be a good time to get it over with. Shifting the flood to the treatment plant would've been an inelegant, temporary solution. It was time to get those big pumps down below churning through that water properly, pumping it through the concrete walls and back into the earth beyond.

Juliette shuffled to the edge of the landing and looked down at the silvery surface of the foul water. Was this plan of hers crazy? Shouldn't she be afraid? Or was it the years of waiting and doing this safely that was more terrifying to her? The prospect of going mad, inch by inch, seemed the greater risk. This would be just like going outside, she reminded herself, which she had already done and had survived. Except . . . this was safer. She was taking an unlimited supply of air, and there was nothing toxic down there, nothing to eat away at her.

She gazed at her reflection in the still water, the bulky suit making her look enormous. If Lukas were standing there with her, if he could see what she was about to do, would he try to talk her out of it? She thought he might. How well did they really know each other? They had had what, two, three encounters in person?

But then there were the dozens of talks since. Could she know him from just his voice? From stories about his childhood? From his intoxicating laughter when everything else in her day made her want to cry? Was this why wires and emails were expensive, to prevent this kind of life, this kind of relationship? How could she be standing there, thinking of a man she hardly knew rather than the insanity of the task before her?

Maybe Lukas had become her lifeline, some slender thread of hope connecting her to home. Or was he more like a tiny spot of light seen occasionally through the murk, a beacon guiding her return?

'Helmet?' Solo stood beside her, watching her, the clear plastic dome in his hands, a single flashlight strapped to its top.

Juliette reached for it. She made sure the flashlight was securely fastened and tried to clear her head of pointless ruminations.

'Hook up my air first,' she said. 'And turn on the radio.'

He nodded. She held the dome while he clicked the air hose into the adapter she'd threaded through the collar. There was a hiss and spit of residual air from the line as it locked into place. His hand brushed the back of her neck as he reached in to flick on the radio. Juliette dipped her chin, squeezing the handmade switch sewn into her undersuit. 'Hello, hello,' she said. There was a strange squeal from the unit on Solo's hip as her voice blared out of it.

'Little loud,' he said, adjusting his volume.

She lifted the dome into place. It had been stripped of its screen and all the plastic linings. Once she'd scraped the paint off the exterior, she was left with an almost completely transparent half-sphere of tough plastic. It felt good to know, clicking it into the collar, that whatever she saw out of it was really there.

'You good?'

Solo's voice was deadened by the airtight connection between the helmet and the suit. She lifted her glove and gave him a thumbs-up. She pointed to the compressor.

He nodded, knelt down by the unit, and scratched his beard. She watched him flick the portable unit's main power, push the priming bulb five times, then yank the starting cord. The little unit spat out a breath of smoke and whirred to life. Even with its rubber tyres, it danced and rattled the landing, sending vibrations up through her boots. Juliette could hear the awful acoustics through her helmet, could imagine the violent racket echoing up through the abandoned silo.

Solo held the choke an extra second, just like she'd shown him, and then pushed it all the way in. While the machine pattered and chugged, he looked up at her, smiling through his beard, looking like one of the dogs in Supply staring up at its faithful owner.

She pointed to the red can of extra fuel and gave him another thumbs-up. He returned the gesture. Juliette shuffled towards the steps, her gloved hand on the railing for balance. Solo squeezed past and went to the railing and the knotted rope. He held out a hand to steady her while she lumbered down the slippery treads in the suit's clunky boots.

Her hope was that it would be easier to move once she was in the water, but she had no way of knowing, just an intuitive feel for the physics of it all, the way she could gauge a machine's intent simply by poring over it. She took the last dry steps, and then her boots broke the oily surface of the water and found the step below. She waded down two more, anticipating the frigid cold to seep through, but it never came. The suit and her undergarments kept her toasty. Almost too warm, in fact – she could see a humid mist forming on the inside of her helmet. She dipped her chin into the radio switch and told Solo to open her valve to let the air in.

He fumbled at her collar and twisted the lever to allow the flow of air. It hissed by her ear, quite noisily, and she could feel the suit puff out around her. The overflow valve she'd screwed into the other side of the collar squealed as it opened and let out the excess pressure, preventing her suit – and her head, she suspected – from bursting.

'Weights,' she said, clicking the radio.

He ran back to the landing and returned with the round exercise weights. Kneeling on the last dry step, he strapped these below her knees with heavy Velcro, then looked up to see what was next.

Juliette struggled to lift one foot, then the other, making sure that the weights were secure.

'Wire,' she said, getting the hang of working the radio.

This was the most important part: the power from IT would run the lifeless pumps below. Twenty-four volts of juice. She had installed a switch on the landing so Solo could test it while she was down there. She didn't want to travel with the wires live.

Solo unspooled a dozen feet of the two-connector wire and tied a loop around her wrist. His knots were good, both with the rope and the wire. Her confidence in the endeavour was growing by the minute, her discomfort in the suit lessening.

Solo smiled down through her clear plastic dome from two steps above, yellow teeth flashing in his scraggly beard. Juliette returned the smile. She stood still while he fumbled with the flashlight strapped to her helmet, clicking it on. The battery was freshly charged and would last a full day, much longer than she possibly needed.

'Okay,' she said. 'Help me over.'

Releasing the radio contact with her chin, she turned and leaned against the railing, worked her belly up onto it, then eased her head over. It was an incredible sensation, throwing herself over that rail. It felt suicidal. This was the great stairwell; this was her silo; she was four levels up from Mechanical; all that space below her, that long plummet only madmen dived into, and she was going just as willingly.

Solo helped with her weighted feet. He splashed down onto the first wet step to assist her. Juliette threw her leg over the railing as he lifted. Suddenly, she was straddling that narrow bar of slippery steel, wondering if the water would truly hold her, if it would catch and slow her fall. And there was a moment of raw panic, the taste of metal in her mouth, the sinking of her stomach and the dire need to urinate, all while Solo heaved her other foot over the railing, her gloved hands clawing madly for the rope he'd tied, her boots splashing noisily and violently into the silvery skin of the flooded waters.

'Shit!'

She blew her breath out into the helmet, gasping from the shock of splashing in so quickly, her hands and knees wrapping around the twisting rope, her body moving inside the puffy suit like a layer of too-large skin had become detached.

'You okay?' Solo shouted, his hands cupped around his beard.

She nodded, her helmet unmoving. She could feel the tug of the weights on her shins, trying to drag her down. There were a dozen things she wanted to say to Solo, reminders and tips, words of luck, but her mind was racing too fast to think of using the radio. Instead, she loosened her grip with her gloves and knees, felt the rope slide against her body with a distant squeak, and she began her long plummet down.

63

• Silo 18 •

Lukas sat at the little desk constructed from an embarrassment of wood and stared down at a book stuffed with a fortune in crisp paper. The chair beneath him was probably worth more than he'd make in a lifetime, and he was *sitting* on it. If he moved, the joints of the dainty thing twisted and squeaked, like it could come apart at any moment.

He kept his boots firmly planted on either side, his weight on his toes, just in case.

Lukas flipped a page, pretending to read. It wasn't that he didn't want to be reading, he just didn't want to be reading *this*. Entire shelves of more interesting works seemed to mock him from within their tin boxes. They sang out to be perused, for him to put away the Order with its rigid writing, bulleted lists, and internal labyrinth of page references that led in more circles than the great stairwell itself.

Each entry in the Order pointed to another page, every page another entry. Lukas flipped through a few and wondered if Bernard was keeping tabs on him. The head of IT sat on the other side of the small study, just one room of many in the well-stocked hideaway beneath the servers. While Lukas pretended to shadow for his new job, Bernard alternated between fiddling with the small computer on the other desk and going over to the radio mounted on the wall to give instructions to the security forces in the down deep.

Lukas pinched a thick chunk of the Order and flopped it to the side. He skipped past all the recipes for averting silo disasters and checked out some of the more academic reference material towards the back. This stuff was even *more* frightening: chapters on group persuasion, on mind control, on the effects of fear during upbringing; graphs and tables dealing with population growth . . .

He couldn't take it. He adjusted his chair and watched Bernard for a while as the head of IT and acting mayor scrolled through screen after screen of text, his head notching back and forth as he scanned the words there.

After a moment, Lukas dared to break the silence. 'Hey, Bernard?'

'Hm?'

'Hey, why isn't there anything in here about how all this came to be?'

Bernard's office chair squealed as he swivelled it around to face Lukas. 'I'm sorry, what?'

'The people who made all this, the people who wrote these books. Why isn't there anything in the Order about them? Like how they built all this stuff in the first place.'

'Why would there be?' Bernard half turned back to his computer.

'So we would *know*. I dunno, like all the stuff in the other books—'

'I don't want you reading those other books. Not yet.' Bernard pointed to the wooden desk. 'Learn the Order first. If you can't keep the silo together, the Legacy books are pulp. They're as good as processed wood if no one's around to read them.'

'Nobody *can* read them but the two of us if they stay locked up down here—'

'No one *alive*. Not today. But one day, there'll be plenty of people who'll read them. But only if you study.' Bernard nodded towards the thick and dreadful book before turning back to his keyboard and reaching for his mouse.

Lukas sat there a while, staring at Bernard's back, the knotted cord of his master keys sticking out of the top of his undershirt.

'I figure they must've known it was coming,' Lukas said, unable to stop himself from going on about it. He had always wondered about these things, had suppressed them, had found his thrills in piecing together the distant stars that were so far away as to be immune to the hillside taboos. And now he lived in this vacuum, this hollow of the silo no one knew about where forbidden topics were allowed and he had access to a man who seemed to know the precious truth.

'You aren't studying,' Bernard said. His head remained bent over his keyboard, but he seemed to know that Lukas was watching him.

'But they had to've seen it coming, right?' Lukas lifted his chair and turned it around a little more. 'I mean, to have built all these silos before it got so bad out there . . .'

Bernard turned his head to the side, his jaw clenching and unclenching. His hand fell away from the mouse and came up to smooth his moustache. 'These are the things you want to know? How it happened?'

'Yes.' Lukas nodded. He leaned forward, elbows on his knees. 'I want to know.'

'Do you think it matters? What happened out there?' Bernard turned and looked up at the schematics on the wall, then at Lukas. 'Why would it matter?'

'Because it *happened*. And it only happened one way, and it kills me not to know. I mean, they saw it coming, right? It would take years to build all—'

'Decades,' Bernard said.

'And then move all this stuff in, all the people—'

'That took much less time.'

'So you know?'

Bernard nodded. 'The information is stored here, but not in any of the books. And you're wrong. It *doesn't* matter. That's the past, and the past is not the same thing as our Legacy. You'll need to learn the difference.'

Lukas thought about the difference. For some reason, a conversation with Juliette sprang to mind, something she was forever telling him—

'I think I know,' he said.

'Oh?' Bernard pushed his glasses up his nose and stared at him. 'Tell me what you *think* you know.'

'All our hope, the accomplishments of those before us, what the world *can* be like, that's our Legacy.'

Bernard's lips broke into a smile. He waved his hand for Lukas to continue.

'And the bad things that can't be stopped, the mistakes that got us here, that's the past.'

'And what does this difference mean? What do *you* think it means?'

'It means we can't change what's already happened, but we can have an impact on what happens next.'

Bernard clapped his small hands together. 'Very good.'

'And this' – Lukas turned and rested one hand on the thick book; he continued, unbidden – 'the Order. *This* is a road map for how to get through all the bad that's piled up between our past and the future's hope. *This* is the stuff we can prevent, that we can fix.'

Bernard raised his eyebrows at Lukas's last statement, as if it were a new way of looking at an old truth. Finally, he smiled, his moustache curling up, his glasses rising on the wrinkled bridge of his nose.

'I think you're almost ready,' he said. 'Soon.' Bernard turned back to his computer, his hand falling to his mouse. 'Very soon.'

The descent to Mechanical was oddly tranquil, almost mesmerising. Juliette slid through the green flood, pushing herself away from the curved railing each time the staircase spiralled around beneath her feet. The only sounds anywhere were the hiss of air entering her helmet and the excess gurgling out the other side. A never-ending stream of bubbles rolled up her visor like beads of solder, drifting up in defiance of gravity.

Juliette watched these silver spheres chase one another and play like children through the metal stairs. They broke up where they touched the railing, leaving just minuscule dots of gas stuck to the surface, rolling and colliding. Others marched in wavy lines inside the stairway. They gathered in crowds beneath the hollow steps, bubbles becoming pockets of air that wobbled and caught the light radiating from the top of her helmet.

It was easy to forget where she was, what she was doing. The familiar had become distorted and strange. Everything seemed magnified by the plastic dome of her visor, and it was easy to imagine that she wasn't sinking at all, but that the great stairway was rising, pushing up through the deep earth and heading towards the clouds. Even the sensation of the rope sliding through her gloved hands and across her padded belly felt more like something tugged inexorably from above rather than a line she was descending.

It wasn't until she arched her back and looked straight up that Juliette remembered how much water was stacking up above her. The green glow of the emergency lights faded to an eerie black in the space of a landing or two. The light from her flashlight barely dented it. Juliette inhaled sharply and reminded herself that she had all the air in the silo. She tried to ignore the sensation of so much liquid piled up on her shoulders, of being buried alive. If she had to, if she panicked, she could just cut the weights free. One flick with the chef's knife and she would bob right back to the surface. She told herself this as she continued to sink. Letting go of the rope with one hand, she patted for the knife, making sure it was still there.

'SLOWER!' her radio barked.

Juliette grabbed the rope with both hands and squeezed until she came to a stop. She reminded herself that Solo was up there, watching the air hose and electrical wires as they spooled off their neat coils. She imagined him tangled up in the lines, hopping around on one foot. Bubbles raced out of her overflow valve and jiggled through the lime-green water back towards the surface. She leaned her head back and watched them swirl around the taut rope, wondering what was taking him so long. In the undersides of the helical steps, the air pockets danced mercury silver, wavering in the turbulence of her passing—

'OKAY.' The radio speaker behind her neck crackled. 'GOOD HERE.'

Juliette cringed from the volume of Solo's voice and wished she'd checked that before closing up her helmet. There was no fixing it now.

With ears ringing and the silence and majesty of the tranquil descent broken, she slid down another level, keeping her pace steady and slow as she studied the slack in the wire and the air hose for any sign of their pulling taut. As she passed close to the landing of one-thirty-nine, she saw that one of the doors was missing; the other door had been wrenched violently from its hinges. The entire level must be flooded, which meant more water for the pumps to move. Just before the landing rose out of sight, she saw dark forms down the corridor, shadows floating in the water. The flashlight on her helmet barely illuminated a pale and bloated face before she drifted past, leaving the long dead to rise out of sight.

It hadn't occurred to Juliette that she might come across more bodies. Not the drowned of course – the flood would've risen too slowly to take anyone by surprise – but any violence that occurred in the down deep would now be preserved in its icy depths. The chill of the water around her seemed to finally penetrate the layers of her suit. Or perhaps it was just her imagination.

Her boots thumped to the lowermost floor of the stairwell while she was still looking up, keeping an eye on the slack in the lines. Her knees were jarred by the startling end to her descent. It had taken her far less time than a dry hike would have. With a grip on the rope for balance, Juliette let go with her other hand and waved it through the thick atmosphere of green groundwater. She dipped her chin against the radio switch. 'I'm down,' she transmitted to Solo.

She took a few lumbering and tentative steps, waving her arms and half swimming towards the entrance to Mechanical. The light from the stairwell barely penetrated past the security gates. Beyond, the oily depths of a home both foreign and familiar awaited her.

'I HEAR YOU,' Solo answered after some delay.

Juliette felt her muscles tense up as his voice rattled around inside her helmet. Not being able to adjust the volume was going to drive her mad.

After a dozen halting steps, she eventually got the hang of the awkward wading motion and learned to drag her weighted boots across the steel decking. With the suit inflated and her arms and legs brushing around on the inside, it was like guiding a bubble by throwing oneself against its skin. She paused once to look back at her air hose, making sure it wasn't getting caught on the stairs, and she gave the rope she had descended one last glance. Even from this distance it appeared as an impossibly slender thread, a thread hanging in that submerged straw of a stairwell. It wavered slightly in the wake she was causing, almost as if saying goodbye.

Juliette tried not to read anything into it; she turned back to the entrance to Mechanical. *You don't have to do this*, she reminded herself. She could hook up two, maybe three more small pumps plus a few additional runs of hydroponic piping. The work might take a few months, the water level would recede for years, but eventually these levels would be dry and she could investigate those buried diggers Solo had told her about. It could be done with minimal risk – other than to her sanity.

And if her only reason for getting back home was vengeance, if that was her only motivation, she might have chosen to wait, to take that safe route. She could feel the temptation even then to yank the weights off her boots and float up through the stairwell, to fly past the levels like she used to dream she could, arms out, buoyant and free . . .

But Lukas had kept her apprised of the horrible mess her friends were in, the mess her leaving had caused. There was a radio mounted to his wall below the servers that leaked violence day and night. Solo's underground apartment was equipped with an identical radio, but it could communicate only with silo seventeen's portables. Juliette had given up fiddling with it.

A part of her was glad she couldn't hear. She didn't want to have to listen to the fighting – she just wanted to get home and make it stop. This had become a desperate compulsion: returning to her silo. It was maddening to think that she was only a short walk away, but those doors were only ever opened to kill people. And what good would her return do, anyway? Would her surviving a cleaning and revealing the truth be enough to expose Bernard and all of IT?

As it happened, she had other, less sane plans. It was a fantasy, maybe, but it gave her hope. She dreamed of fixing up one of the diggers that had built this place, a machine buried and hidden at the long end of its vertical toil, and driving it through the earth itself to eighteen's down deep. She dreamed of breaking that blockade, of leading her people back to these dry corridors and getting this dead place *working* again. She dreamed of operating a silo without all the lies and deceptions.

Juliette waded through the heavy water towards the security gate, dreaming these childish dreams, discovering that they somehow steeled her resolve. She approached the security turnstile and saw that the lifeless and unguarded gate would pose the first true obstacle of her descent. Getting over it wouldn't be easy. Turning her back to the machine, she placed her hands on either side and pushed, squirming and kicking her heavy heels against the low wall, until she was just barely sitting on the control box.

Her legs were too heavy to lift . . . not high enough to swing over, anyway. The weights had ended up being more than she'd needed to counter the suit's buoyancy. She wiggled backwards until her butt was more secure and tried to turn sideways. With a thick glove under her knee, she strained and leaned back until her boot was on the edge of the wall. She rested a moment, breathing hard and filling her helmet with muffled laughter. It felt ridiculous, all this effort to do something so outrageously simple, so benign. With one boot already up, the other was easier to lift. She felt the muscles in her abdomen and thighs, muscles sore from weeks of a porter's hustle, finally help her lift her own damn foot up.

She shook her head in relief, sweat trickling down the back of her neck, already dreading repeating the manoeuvre on the return trip. Dropping to the other side was easy: the weights did all the work. She took a moment to make sure the wires knotted around her wrist and the air hose attached to her collar weren't getting tangled, and then started down the main corridor, the flashlight on top of her helmet her only illumination.

'YOU OKAY?' Solo asked, his voice startling her again.

'I'm fine,' she said. She held her chin down against her chest, leaving the contact open. 'I'll check in if I need you. The volume is a little high down here. Scares the hell out of me.'

She released the contact and turned to see how her lifeline was doing. All along the ceiling, her overflow bubbles danced in the glow of her flashlight like tiny jewels—

'OKAY. GOTCHA.'

With her boots hardly leaving the floor, pushing forward on them one at a time, she slowly made her way across the main intersection and past the mess hall. To her left, if she made her way down the hallway and took two turns, she could reach Walker's workshop. Had it always been a workshop? She had no idea. In this place, it might be a storeroom. Or an apartment.

Her small apartment would be in the opposite direction. She turned to peer down that hallway, her cone of light brushing away the darkness to reveal a body pressed up against the ceiling, tangled in the runs of pipe and conduit. She looked away. It was easy to imagine that being George or Scottie or someone else she had cared about and lost. It was easy to imagine it being herself.

She shuffled towards the access stairs, her body wavering in the thick but crystal-clear water, the weight of her boots and the buoyancy of her torso keeping her upright even though she felt on the verge of toppling. She paused at the top of the square steps leading down.

'I'm about to descend,' she said, chin down. 'Make sure you keep everything feeding. And please don't respond unless there's a problem. My ears are still ringing from the last time.'

Juliette lifted her chin from the contact switch and took the first few steps, waiting for Solo to blare something in her ear, but it never came. She kept a firm grip on the wire and hose, dragging it around the sharp corners of the square stairwell as she descended into the darkness. The black water all around was disturbed only by her rising bubbles and the feeble cone of her sweeping, flash-lit gaze.

Six floors down, the hose and wire became difficult to pull, too much friction from the steps. She stopped and gathered more and more of it around herself, letting the slack coil drift in the weightlessness of the water. Several of her careful splices in both the wire and tubing slid through her gloves. She paused and checked the taped and glued joints of the latter to see how they were holding up. Minuscule bubbles were trailing out of one joint, leaving a perforated and wavy line of tiny dots in the dark water. It was hardly anything.

Once she had enough slack at the bottom of the stairs to reach the sump basin, she turned and marched purposefully towards her work. The hardest part was over. The air was flowing in, cool and fresh and hissing by her ear. The excess streamed out through the other valve, the bubbles shooting up in a curtain whenever she turned her head. She had enough wire and hose to reach her goal, and all of her tools intact. It felt like she could finally relax now that she knew she wouldn't be going any deeper. All she had to do was hook up the power lines, two easy connections, and make her way out.

Being so close, she dared to think of getting free, of rescuing this silo's Mechanical spaces, resuscitating one of its generators and then one of its hidden and buried diggers. They were making progress. She was on her way to rescuing her friends. It all seemed perfectly attainable, practically in her grasp, after weeks of frustrating setbacks.

Juliette found the sump room just where it was supposed to be. She slid her boots to the edge of the pit in the centre. Leaning forward, her flashlight shone down on the numbers signifying how deep the waters had risen. They seemed comical under so many hundreds of feet of water. Comical and sad. This silo had failed its people.

But then Juliette corrected herself: these *people* had failed their *silo*.

'Solo, I'm at the pump. Gonna hook up the power.'

She peered down at the bottom of the pit to make sure the pump's pick-up was clear of debris. The water down there was amazingly clear. All the oil and grime she'd worked hip-deep in at the bottom of her own basin had been made diffuse, spread out into who knew how many gallons of groundwater seepage. The result was crystal-clear stuff she could probably drink.

She shivered, suddenly aware that the chill of the deep water was making its way through her layers and wicking away her body heat. Halfway there, she told herself. She moved towards the massive pump mounted on the wall. Pipes as thick as her waist bent to the ground and snaked over the edge of the pit. The outflow ran up the wall in a similarly sized pipe and joined the jumble of mechanical runs above. As she stood by the large pump and worked the knotted wires off her wrist, she remembered the last job she'd ever performed as a mechanic. She had pulled the shaft on an identical pump and had discovered a worn and broken impeller. As she selected a Phillips driver from her pocket and began loosening the positive power terminal, she took the time to pray that *this* pump had not been in a similar condition when the power had blown. She didn't want to have to come down and service it again. Not until she could do it while keeping her boots dry.

The positive power line came free more easily than she had hoped. Juliette twisted the new one into place. The sound of her own breathing rattled in the confines of her helmet and provided her only company. As she was tightening the terminal around the new wire, she realised she could hear her breathing because the air was no longer hissing by her cheek.

Juliette froze. She tapped the plastic dome by her ear and saw that the overflow bubbles were still leaking out, but slower now. The pressure was still inside her suit; there just wasn't any more air being forced inside.

She dipped her chin against the switch, could feel the sweat form around her collar and drip down the side of her jaw. Her feet were somehow freezing while from the neck up she was beginning to sweat.

'Solo? This is Juliette. Can you hear me? What's going on up there?'

She waited, turned to aim her flashlight down the air hose, and looked for any sign of a kink. She still had air, the air in her suit. Why wasn't he responding?

'Hello? Solo? Please say something.'

The flashlight on her helmet needed to be adjusted, but she could feel the ticking of some silent clock in her head. How much air would she have starting *right then*? It had probably taken her an hour to get down there. Solo would fix the compressor before her air ran out. She had plenty of time. Maybe he was pouring in more fuel. Plenty of time, she told herself as the driver slipped off the negative terminal. The damn thing was stuck.

This, she didn't have time for, not for anything to be corroded. The positive wire was already spliced and locked tight. She tried to adjust the flashlight strapped to her helmet; it was aimed too high: good for walking, horrible for working. She was able to twist it a little and aim it at the large pump.

The ground wire could be connected to any part of the main housing, right? She tried to remember. The entire case was the ground, wasn't it? Or was it? Why couldn't she remember? Why was it suddenly difficult to think?

She straightened the end of the black wire and tried to give the loose copper strands a twist with her heavily padded fingers. She jabbed this bundle of raw copper into a cowling vent on the back, a piece of conducting metal that appeared connected to the rest of the pump. She twisted the wire around a small bolt, knotted the slack so it would hold, and tried to convince herself that this would work, that it would be enough to run the damn thing. Walker would know. Where the hell was he when she needed him?

The radio by her neck squawked – a burst and pop of static – what sounded like part of her name in a faraway distance – a dead hiss – and then nothing.

Juliette wavered in the dark, cold water. Her ears were ringing from the outburst. She dipped her chin to tell Solo to hold the radio away from his mouth, when she noticed through the glass window of her helmet's visor that there were no more bubbles spilling from the overflow valve and rising in that gentle curtain across her vision. The pressure in her suit was gone.

A different sort of pressure quickly took its place.

• Silo 18 •

Walker found himself shoved down the square stairs, past a crew of mechanics working to weld another set of steel plates across the narrow passage. He had most of the home-built radio in the spare parts tub, which he desperately clutched with two hands. He watched the electrical components rattle together as he jostled through the crowd of mechanics fleeing from the attack above. In front of him, Shirly carried the rest of the radio gear against her chest, the antenna wires trailing behind her. Walker skipped and danced on his old legs so he wouldn't get tangled up.

'Go! Go! Go!' someone yelled. Everyone was pushing and shoving. The rattle of gunfire seemed to grow louder behind him, while a golden shower of fizzling sparks rained through the air and peppered Walker's face. He squinted and stormed through the glowing hail as a team of miners in striped overalls fought their way up from the next landing with another large sheet of steel.

'This way!' Shirly yelled, tugging him along. At the next level, she pulled him aside. His poor legs struggled to keep up. A duffle bag was dropped; a young man with a gun spun and hurried back for it.

'The generator room,' Shirly told him, pointing.

There was already a stream of people moving through the double doors. Jenkins was there, managing the traffic. Some of those with rifles took up position near an oil pump, the counter-weighted head sitting perfectly still like it had already succumbed to the looming battle.

'What is that?' Jenkins asked as they approached the door. He jerked his chin at the bundle of wires in Shirly's arms. 'Is that . . . ?'

'The radio, sir.' She nodded.

'Fat lot of good it does us now.' Jenkins waved two other people inside. Shirly and Walker pressed themselves out of the way.

'Sir—'

'Get him inside,' Jenkins barked, referring to Walker. 'I don't need him getting in the way.'

'But sir, I think you're gonna want to hear—'

'C'mon, go!' Jenkins yelled to the stragglers bringing up the rear. He twirled his arm at the elbow for them to hurry. Only the mechanics who had traded their wrenches for guns remained. They formed up like they were used to this game, arms propped on railings, long steel barrels trained in the same direction.

'In or out,' Jenkins told Shirly, starting to close the door.

'Go,' she told Walker, letting out a deep breath. 'Let's get inside.'

Walker numbly obeyed, thinking all the while of the parts and tools he should have grabbed, things a few levels overhead now that were lost to him, maybe for good.

'Hey, get those people out of the control room!'

Shirly ran across the generator room as soon as they were inside, wires trailing behind her, bits of rigid aluminium antenna bouncing across the floor. 'Out!'

A mixed group of mechanics and a few people wearing the yellow of Supply sheepishly filed out of the small control room. They joined the others around a railing cordoning off the mighty machine that dominated the cavernous facility and gave the generator room its name. At least the noise was tolerable. Shirly imagined all these people being stuck down there in the days when the roar of the rattling shaft and loose engine mounts could deafen a person.

'All of you, out of my control room.' She waved the last few out. Shirly knew why Jenkins had sealed off this floor. The only power they had left was the literal kind. She waved the last man out of the small room studded with sensitive knobs, dials, and readouts and immediately checked the fuel levels.

Both tanks were topped up, so at least they had planned *that* properly. They would have a few weeks of power, if nothing else. She looked over all the other knobs and dials, the jumble of cords still held tightly against her chest.

'Where should I . . . ?'

Walker held his box out. The only flat surfaces in the room were covered with switches and the sorts of things one didn't want to bump. He seemed to understand that.

'On the floor, I guess.' She set her load down and moved to shut the door. The people she'd hurried outside gazed longingly through the window at the few tall stools in the climate-controlled space. Shirly ignored them.

'Do we have everything? Is it all here?'

Walker pulled pieces of the radio out of the box, tsking his tongue at the twisted wires and jumbled components. 'Do we have power?' he asked, holding up the plug of a transformer.

Shirly laughed. 'Walk, you do know where you are now, right? Of course we have power.' She took the cord and plugged it into one of the feeds on the main panel. 'Do we have everything? Can we get it up and running again? Walk, we need to let Jenkins hear what we heard.'

'I know.' He bobbed his head and sorted the gear, twisting some loose wires together as he went. 'We need to string that out.' He jerked his head at the tangled antenna in her arms.

Shirly looked up. There were no rafters.

'Hang it from the railing out there,' he told her. 'Straight line, make sure that end reaches back in here.'

She moved towards the door, trailing the loops out behind her.

'Oh, and don't let the metal bits touch the railing!' Walker called after her.

Shirly recruited a few mechanics from her work shift to help out. Once they saw what needed doing, they took over, coordinating as a team to undo the knots while she went back to Walker.

'It'll just be a minute,' she told him, shutting the door behind her, the wire fitting easily between it and the padded jamb.

'I think we're good,' he said. He looked up at her, his eyes sagging, his hair a mess, sweat glistening in his white beard. 'Shit,' he said. He slapped his forehead. 'We don't have speakers.'

Shirly felt her heart drop to hear Walker swear, thinking they'd forgotten something crucial. 'Wait here,' she told him, running back out and to the earmuff station. She picked one of the sets with a dangling cord, the kind used to talk between the control room and anyone working on the primary or secondary generators. She jogged past the curious and frightened-looking crowd to the control room. It occurred to her that she should be more afraid, like they were, that a real war was grinding closer to them. But all she could think about were the voices that war had interrupted. Her curiosity was much stronger than her fear. It was how she'd always been.

'How about these?'

She shut the door behind herself and showed him the headphones.

'Perfect,' he said, his eyes wide with surprise. Before she could complain, he snipped the jack off with his multi-tool and began stripping wires. 'Good thing it's quiet in here,' he said, laughing.

Shirly laughed as well, and it made her wonder what the hell was going on. What were they going to do, sit in there and fiddle with wires while the deputies and the security people from IT came and dragged them away?

Walker got the ear cones wired in, and a faint hiss of static leaked out of them. Shirly hurried over to join him; she sat down and held his wrist to steady his hand. The headphones trembled in them.

'You might have to . . .' He showed her the knob with the white marks he'd painted on.

Shirly nodded and realised they'd forgotten to grab the paint. She held the dial and studied the various ticks. 'Which one?' she asked.

'No.' He stopped her as she began dialling back towards one of the voices they'd found. 'The other way. I need to see how many—' He coughed into his fist. 'We need to see how many there are.'

She nodded and turned the knob gradually towards the black unpainted portion. The two of them held their breath, the hum of the main generator barely audible through the thick door and double-paned glass.

Shirly studied Walker while she spun the dial. She wondered what would become of him when they were rounded up. Would they all be put to cleaning? Or could he and a few of the others claim to be bystanders? It made her sad, thinking about the consequences of their anger, their thirst for revenge. Her husband was gone, ripped from her, and for what? People were dying, and for what? She thought how things could've gone so differently, how they'd had all these dreams, unrealistic perhaps, of a real change in power, an easy fix to impossible and intractable problems. Back then she'd been unfairly treated, but at least she'd been safe. There had been injustice, but she'd been in love. Did that make it okay? Which sacrifice made more sense?

'A little faster,' Walker said, growing impatient with the silence. They'd heard a few hits of crackling static, but no one talking. Shirly very slightly increased the rate she spun the knob.

'You think the antenna—' she started to ask.

Walker raised his hand. The little speakers in his lap had popped. He jerked his thumb to the side, telling her to go back. Shirly did. She tried to remember how far she had gone since the sound, using a lot of the same skills she'd learned in that very room to adjust the previously noisy generator—

'Solo? This is Juliette. Can you hear me? What's going on up there?'

Shirly dropped the knob. She watched it swing on its soldered wire and crash to the floor.

Her hands felt numb. Her fingertips tingled. She turned, gaped at Walker's lap where the ghostly voice had risen, and found him looking dumbly down at his own hands.

Neither of them moved. The voice, the name, they were unmistakable.

Tears of confused joy winked past Walker's beard and fell into his lap.

Juliette grabbed the limp air hose with both hands and squeezed. Her reward was a few weak bubbles rolling up her visor – the pressure inside the tube was gone.

She whispered a curse, tilted her chin against the radio, and called Solo's name. Something had happened to the compressor. He must be working on it, maybe topping up the fuel. She had told him not to turn it off for that. He wouldn't know what to do, wouldn't be able to restart it. She hadn't thought this through clearly at all; she was an impossible distance from breathable air, from any hope of survival.

She took a tentative breath. She had what was trapped in the suit and the air that remained in the hose. How much of the air in the hose could she suck with just the power of her lungs? She didn't think it would be much.

She took one last look at the large sump pump, her hasty wiring job, the loose trail of wires streaming through the water that she'd hoped to have time to secure against vibration and accidental tugs. None of it likely mattered any more, not for her. She kicked away from the pump and waved her arms through the water, wading through the viscous fluid that seemed to both impede her while giving her nothing to push or pull against.

The weights were holding her back. Juliette bent to release them, and found she couldn't. The buoyancy of her arms, the stiffness of the suit . . . she groped for the Velcro straps, but watched her fingers through the magnified view of helmet and water as they waved inches from the blasted things.

She took a deep breath, sweat dripping from her nose and

splattering the inside of her dome. She tried again and came close, her fingertips nearly brushing the black straps, both hands outstretched, grunting and throwing her shoulders into the simple act of reaching her damned shins . . .

But she couldn't. She gave up and shuffled a few more steps down the hallway, following the wire and hose, both visible in the faint cone of white light emanating from above her head. She tried not to bump against the wire, thinking of what one accidental pull might do, how tenuous the connection was that she'd made to the pump's ground. Even as she struggled for a deep breath, her mind was ever playing the mechanic. She cursed herself for not taking longer to prepare.

Her knife! She remembered her knife and stopped dragging her feet. It slid out of its home-made sheath sewn across her belly and gleamed in the glow from her flashlight.

Juliette bent down and used the extra reach of the blade; she slid the point of the knife between her suit and one of the straps. The water was dark and thick all around her. With the limited amount of light from her helmet, and being at the bottom of Mechanical under all that heap of flood, she felt more remote and alone, more afraid, than she had in all her life.

She gripped the knife, terrified of what dropping it could mean, and bobbed up and down, using her stomach muscles. It was like doing sit-ups while standing. She attacked the strap with a laboured sawing motion, cursed in her helmet from the effort, the strain, the pain in her abdomen from lurching forward, from throwing her head down . . . when finally the exercise weight popped free. Her calf felt suddenly naked and light as the round hunk of iron clanged mutely to the plate-steel flooring.

Juliette tilted to the side, held down by one leg, the other trying to rise up. She worked the knife carefully beneath the second strap, fearful of cutting her suit and seeing a stream of precious bubbles leak out. With desperate force, she shoved and pulled the blade against the black webbing just like before. Nylon threads popped in her magnified vision; sweat spattered her helmet; the knife burst through the fabric; the weight was free.

Juliette screamed as her boots flew up behind her, rising above her head. She twisted her torso and waved her arms as much as she could, but her helmet slammed into the runs of pipes at the top of the hallway.

There was a bang – and the water all around her went black. She fumbled for her flashlight, to turn it back on, but it wasn't there. Something bumped her arm in the darkness. She fumbled for the object with one hand, knife in the other, felt it spill through her gloved fingers, and then it was gone. While she struggled to put the knife away, her only source of light tumbled invisible to the ground below.

Juliette heard nothing but her rapid breathing. She was going to die like this, pinned to the ceiling, another bloated body in these corridors. It was as if she were destined to perish in one of those suits, one way or another. She kicked against the pipes and tried to wiggle free. Which way had she been going? Where was she facing? The pitch black was absolute. She couldn't even see her own arms in front of her. It was worse than being blind, to *know* her eyes were working but somehow taking nothing in. It heightened her panic, even as the air in her suit seemed to grow more and more stale.

The air.

She reached for her collar and found the hose, could just barely feel it through her gloves. Juliette began to gather it in, hand over hand, like pulling a mining bucket up a deep shaft.

It felt like miles of it went through her hands. The slack gathered around her like knotted noodles, bumping and sliding against her. Juliette's breathing began to sound more and more desperate. She was panicking. How much of her shallow breaths were coming from the adrenalin, the fear? How much because she was using up all her precious air? She had a sudden terror that the hose she was pulling had been cut, that it had been sawn through on the stairwell, that the free end would at any moment slip through her fingers, that her next frantic reach for more of the lifeline would result in a fistful of inky water and nothing else . . .

But then she grabbed a length of hose with tension, with *life*. A stiff line that held no air, but led the way out.

Juliette cried out in her helmet and reached forward to grab another handhold. She pulled herself, her helmet bumping against a pipe and bouncing her away from the ceiling. She kept reaching, lunging one hand forward in the black to where the line should be, finding it, grasping, yanking, hauling herself through the midnight soup of the drowned and the dead, wondering how far she'd get before she joined them and breathed her very last.

67

• Silo 18 •

Lukas sat with his mother on the thick jamb of the open server-room door. He looked down at her hands, both of them wrapped around one of his. She let go with one of them and picked a piece of lint off his shoulder, then cast the offending knot of string away from her precious son.

'And you say there'll be a promotion in this?' she asked, smoothing the shoulder of his undershirt.

Lukas nodded. 'A pretty big one, yeah.' He looked past her to where Bernard and Sheriff Billings were standing in the hallway, talking in low voices. Bernard had his hands tucked inside the stretched belly of his overalls. Billings looked down and inspected his gun.

'Well, that's great, sweetheart. It makes it easier to bear you being away.'

'It won't be for much longer, I don't think.'

'Will you be able to vote? I can't believe my boy is doing such important things!'

Lukas turned to her. 'Vote? I thought the election was put off.'

She shook her head. Her face seemed more wrinkled than it had a month ago, her hair whiter. Lukas wondered if that were possible in so brief a time.

'It's back on,' she said. 'This nasty business with those rebels is supposed to be just about over.'

Lukas glanced towards Bernard and the sheriff. 'I'm sure they'll figure out a way to let me vote,' he told his mother.

'Well, that's nice. I like to think I raised you proper.' She cleared her throat into her fist, then returned it to the back of his hand. 'And they're feeding you? With the rationing, I mean.'

'More than I can eat.'

Her eyes widened. 'So I suppose there'll be some sort of a raise . . . ?'

He shrugged. 'I'm not sure. I'd think so. And look, you'll be taken care of—'

'Me?' She pressed her hand to her chest, her voice high. 'Don't you worry about me.'

'You know I do. Hey, look, Ma – I think our time's up.' He nodded down the hallway. Bernard and Peter were heading towards them. 'Looks like I've got to get back to work.'

'Oh. Well, of course.' She smoothed the front of her red overalls and allowed Lukas to help her to her feet. She puckered her lips, and he presented his cheek.

'My little boy,' she said, kissing him noisily and squeezing his arm. She stepped back and gazed up at him with pride. 'You take good care of yourself.'

'I will, Ma.'

'Make sure you get plenty of exercise.'

'Ma, I will.'

Bernard stopped by their side, smiling at the exchange. Lukas's mother turned and looked the silo's acting mayor up and down. She reached out and patted Bernard on his chest. 'Thank you,' she said, her voice cracking.

'It's been great to meet you, Mrs Kyle.' Bernard took her hand and gestured towards Peter. 'The sheriff here will see you out.'

'Of course.' She turned one last time and waved at Lukas. He felt a little embarrassed but waved back.

'Sweet lady,' Bernard said, watching them go. 'She reminds me of my own mother.' He turned to Lukas. 'You ready?'

Lukas felt like voicing his reluctance, his hesitation. He felt like saying, *I suppose*, but he straightened his back instead, rubbed his damp palms together and dipped his chin. 'Absolutely,' he managed, feigning a confidence he didn't feel.

'Great. Let's go make this official.' He squeezed Lukas's

shoulder before heading into the server room. Lukas walked around the edge of the thick door and leaned into it, slowly sealing himself in as the fat hinges groaned shut. The electric locks engaged automatically, thumping into the jamb. The security panel beeped, its happy green light flicking over to the menacing red eye of a sentry.

Lukas took a deep breath and picked his way through the servers. He tried not to go the same way as Bernard, tried never to go the same way twice. He chose a longer route just to break the monotony, to have one less routine in that prison.

Bernard had the back of the server open by the time he arrived. He held the familiar headphones out to Lukas.

Lukas accepted them and put them on backwards, the microphone snaking around the rear of his neck.

'Like this?'

Bernard laughed at him and twirled his finger. 'Other way around,' he said, lifting his voice so Lukas could hear through the muffs.

Lukas fumbled with the headphones, tangling his arm in the cord. Bernard waited patiently.

'Are you ready?' Bernard asked, once they were in place. He held the loose jack in one hand. Lukas nodded. He watched Bernard turn and aim the plug at the banks of receptacles. He pictured Bernard's hand swinging down and to the right, slamming the plug home into number seventeen, then turning and confronting Lukas about his favourite pastime, his secret crush . . .

But his boss's small hand never wavered; it clicked into place, Lukas knowing exactly how that felt, how the receptacle hugged the plug tightly, seemed to welcome it in, the pads of one's fingers getting a jolt from the flicking of that spring-loaded plastic retainer—

The light above the jack started blinking. A familiar buzzing throbbed in Lukas's ears. He waited for her voice, for Juliette to answer.

A click.

'Name.'

A thrill of fear ran up Lukas's back, bumps erupting across

his arms. The voice, deep and hollow, impatient and aloof, came and went like the glimpse of a star. Lukas licked his lips.

'Lukas Kyle,' he said, trying not to stammer.

There was a pause. He imagined someone, somewhere, writing this down or flipping through files or doing something awful with the information. The temperature behind the server soared. Bernard was smiling at him, oblivious to the silence on his end.

'You shadowed in IT.'

It felt like a statement, but Lukas nodded and answered. 'Yessir.'

He wiped his palm across his forehead and then the seat of his overalls. He desperately wanted to sit down, to lean back against server number forty, to relax. But Bernard was smiling at him, his moustache lifting, his eyes wide behind his glasses.

'What is your primary duty to the silo?'

Bernard had prepped him on likely questions.

'To maintain the Order.'

Silence. No feedback, no sense if he was right or wrong.

'What do you protect above all?'

The voice was flat and yet powerfully serious. Dire and somehow calm. Lukas felt his mouth go dry.

'Life and Legacy,' he recited. But it felt wrong, this rote façade of knowledge. He wanted to go into detail, to let this voice, like a strong and sober father, understand that he *knew* why this was important. He wasn't dumb. He had more to say than memorised facts—

'What does it take to protect these things we hold so dear?'

He paused.

'It takes sacrifice,' Lukas whispered. He thought of Juliette – and the calm demeanour he was projecting for Bernard nearly crumbled. There were some things he wasn't sure about, things he *didn't* understand. This was one of them. It felt like a lie, his answer. He wasn't sure the sacrifice was worth it, the danger so great that they had to let people, *good* people, go to their—

'How much time have you had in the Suit Labs?'

The voice had changed, relaxed somewhat. Lukas wondered if the ceremony was over. Was that *it*? Had he passed? He blew out his held breath, hoping the microphone didn't pick it up, and tried to relax.

'Not much, sir. Bernar— Uh, my boss, he's wanting me to schedule time in the labs after, you know . . .'

He looked to Bernard, who was pinching one side of his glasses and watching him.

'Yes. I do know. How is that problem in your lower levels going?'

'Um, well, I'm only kept apprised of the overall progress, and it sounds good.' He cleared his throat and thought of all the sounds of gunfire and violence he'd heard through the radio in the room below. 'That is, it sounds like progress is being made, that it won't be much longer.'

A long pause. Lukas forced himself to breathe deeply, to smile at Bernard.

'Would you have done anything differently, Lukas? From the beginning?'

Lukas felt his body sway, his knees go a little numb. He was back on that conference table, black steel pressed against his cheek, a line from his eye extending through a small cross, through a tiny hole, pointing like a laser at a small woman with white hair and a bomb in her hand. Bullets were flying down that line. His bullets.

'Nossir,' he finally said. 'It was all by the Order, sir. Everything's under control.'

He waited. Somewhere, he felt, his measure was being taken.

'You are next in line for the control and operation of silo eighteen,' the voice intoned.

'Thank you, sir.'

Lukas reached for the headphones, was preparing to take them off and hand them to Bernard in case he needed to say something, to hear that it was official.

'Do you know the worst part of my job?' the hollow voice asked.

Lukas dropped his hands. 'What's that, sir?'

'Standing here, looking at a silo on this map, and drawing a red cross through it. Can you imagine what that feels like?'

Lukas shook his head. 'I can't, sir.'

'It feels like a parent losing thousands of children, all at once.' A pause.

'You will have to be cruel to your children so as not to lose them.'

Lukas thought of his father. 'Yessir.'

'Welcome to Operation Fifty of the World Order, Lukas Kyle. Now, if you have a question or two, I have the time to answer, but briefly.'

Lukas wanted to say that he had no questions; he wanted to get off the line; he wanted to call and speak with Juliette, to feel a puff of sanity breathed into this crazy and suffocating room. But he remembered what Bernard had taught him about admitting ignorance, how this was the key to knowledge.

'Just one, sir. And I've been told it isn't important, and I understand why that's true, but I believe it will make my job here easier if I know.'

He paused for a response, but the voice seemed to be waiting for him to get to the question.

Lukas cleared his throat. 'Is there . . . ?' He pinched the mic and moved it closer to his lips, glanced at Bernard. 'How did this all begin?'

He wasn't sure – it could have been a fan on the server whirring to life – but he thought he heard the man with the deep voice sigh.

'How badly do you wish to know?'

Lukas feared answering this question honestly. 'It isn't crucial,' he said, 'but I would appreciate a sense of what we're accomplishing, what we survived. It feels like it gives me – gives us a purpose, you know?'

'The reason *is* the purpose,' the man said cryptically. 'Before I tell you, I'd like to hear what you think.'

Lukas swallowed. 'What I think?'

'Everyone has ideas. Are you suggesting you don't?'

A hint of humour could be heard in that hollow voice.

'I think it was something we saw coming,' Lukas said. He watched Bernard, who frowned and looked away.

'That's one possibility.'

Bernard removed his glasses and began wiping them on the sleeve of his undershirt, his gaze falling to his feet.

'Consider this . . .' The deep voice paused. 'What if I told you that there were only fifty silos in all the world, and that here we are in this infinitely small corner of it?'

Lukas thought about this. It felt like another test.

'I would say that we were the only ones . . .' He almost said that they were the only ones with the resources, but he'd seen enough in the Legacy to know this wasn't true. Many parts of the world had buildings rising above their hills. Many more could have been prepared. 'I'd say we were the only ones who *knew*,' Lukas suggested.

'Very good. And why might that be?'

He hated this. He didn't want to puzzle it out, he just wanted to be told.

And then, like a cable splicing together, like electricity zipping through connections for the very first time, the truth hit him.

'It's because . . .' He tried to make sense of this answer in his head, tried to imagine that such an idea could possibly verge on truth. 'It's not because we knew,' Lukas said, sucking in a gasp of air. 'It's because we *did it*.'

'Yes,' the voice said. 'And now you know.'

He said something else, just barely audible, like it was being said to someone else. 'Our time is up, Lukas Kyle. Congratulations on your assignment.'

The headphones were sticky against his head, his face clammy with sweat.

'Thank you,' he managed.

'Oh, and Lukas?'

'Yessir?'

'Going forward, I suggest you concentrate on what's beneath your feet. No more of this business with the stars, okay, son? We know where most of them are.'

68

• Silo 18 •

'Hello? Solo? Please say something.'

There was no mistaking that voice, even through the small speakers in the dismantled headset. It echoed bodiless in the control room, the same control room that had housed that very voice for so many years. The location was what nailed it for Shirly; she stared at the tiny speakers spliced into the magical radio, knowing it couldn't be anyone else.

Neither she nor Walker dared breathe. They waited what felt like for ever before she finally broke the silence.

'That was Juliette,' she whispered. 'How can we . . . ? Is her voice *trapped* down here? In the air? How long ago would that have been?'

Shirly didn't understand how any of the science worked; it was all beyond her pay grade. Walker continued to stare at the headset, unmoving, not saying a word, tears shining in his beard.

'Are these . . . these *ripples* we're grabbing with the antenna, are they just bouncing around down here?'

She wondered if the same was true of *all* the voices they'd heard. Maybe they were simply picking up conversations from the *past*. Was that possible? Like some kind of electrical echo? Somehow, this seemed far less shocking than the alternative.

Walker turned to her, a strange expression on his face. His mouth hung partway open, but there was a curl at the edges of his lips, a curl that began to rise.

'It doesn't work like that,' he said. The curl transformed into a smile. 'This is *now*. This is *happening*.' He grabbed Shirly's arm.

'You heard it too, didn't you? I'm not crazy. That really was her, wasn't it? She's alive. She made it.'

'No . . .' Shirly shook her head. 'Walk, what're you saying? That Juliette's *alive*? Made it where?'

'You heard.' He pointed at the radio. 'Before. The conversations. The cleaning. There's more of them *out there*. More of *us*. She's *with* them, Shirly. This is *happeningrightnow*.'

'Alive.'

Shirly stared at the radio, processing this. Her friend was still *somewhere*. Still breathing. It had been so solid in her head, this vision of Juliette's body just over the hills, lying in silent repose, the wind flecking away at her. And now she was picturing her moving, breathing, talking into a radio somewhere.

'Can we talk to her?' she asked.

She knew it was a dumb question. But Walker seemed to startle, his old limbs jumping.

'Oh, God. God, yes.' He set the mish-mash of components down on the floor, his hands trembling, but with what Shirly now read as excitement. The fear in *both* of them was gone, drained from the room, the rest of the world beyond that small space fading to meaninglessness.

Walker dug into the parts bin. He dumped some tools out and pawed into the bottom of the container.

'No,' he said. He turned and scanned the parts on the ground. 'No, no, no.'

'What is it?' Shirly slid away from the string of components so he could better see. 'What're we missing? There's a microphone right there.' She pointed to the partially disassembled headphones.

'The transmitter. It's a little board. I think it's on my workbench.'

'I swiped everything into the bin.' Her voice was high and tense. She moved towards the plastic bucket.

'My *other* workbench. It wasn't needed. All Jenks wanted was to *listen in*.' He waved at the radio. 'I did what he wanted. How could I have known I'd need to transmit—'

'You couldn't,' Shirly said. She rested her hand on his arm. She could tell he was heading towards a bad place. She had seen him go there often enough, knew he had short cuts he could take to get there in no time. 'Is there anything in here we can use? Think, Walk. Concentrate.'

He shook his head, wagged his finger at the headphones. 'This mic is dumb. It just passes the sound through. Little membranes vibrating . . .' He turned and looked at her. 'Wait — there *is* something.'

'Down here? Where?'

'The mining storehouse would have them. Transmitters.' He pretended to hold a box and twist a switch. 'For the blasting caps. I repaired one just a month ago. It would work.'

Shirly rose to her feet. 'I'll go get it,' she said. 'You stay here.'

'But the stairwell . . .'

'I'll be safe. I'm going *down*, not up.'

He bobbed his head.

'Don't change anything with that.' She pointed to the radio. 'No looking for more voices. Just hers. Leave it there.'

'Of course.'

Shirly bent down and squeezed his shoulder. 'I'll be right back.'

Outside, she found dozens of faces turning her way, frightened and questioning looks in their wide eyes, their slack mouths. She felt like shouting over the hum of the generator that Juliette was alive, that they weren't alone, that other people lived and breathed in the forbidden outside. She wanted to, but she didn't have the time. She hurried to the rail and found Courtnee.

'Hey—'

'Everything okay in there?' Courtnee asked.

'Yeah, fine. Do me a favour, will you? Keep an eye on Walker for me.'

Courtnee nodded. 'Where are you . . . ?'

But Shirly was already gone, running to the main door. She squeezed through a group huddled in the entranceway. Jenkins was outside with Harper. They stopped talking as she hurried past.

'Hey!' Jenkins seized her arm. 'Where the hell're *you* going?'

'Mine storeroom.' She twisted her arm out of his grasp. 'I won't be long—'

'You won't be *going*. We're about to blow that stairwell. These idiots are falling right into our hands.'

'You're *what*?'

'The stairwell,' Harper repeated. 'It's rigged to blow. Once they get down there and start working their way through . . .' He put his hands together in a ball, then expanded the sphere in a mock explosion.

'You don't understand.' She faced Jenkins. 'It's for the radio.'

He frowned. 'Walk had his chance.'

'We're picking up a *lot* of chatter,' she told him. 'He needs this one piece. I'll be right back, swear.'

Jenkins looked at Harper. 'How long before we do this?'

'Five minutes, sir.' His chin moved back and forth, almost imperceptibly.

'You've got four,' he said to Shirly. 'But make sure—'

She didn't hear the rest. Her boots were already pounding the steel, carrying her towards the stairwell. She flew past the oil rig with its sad and lowered head, past the row of confused and twitching men, their guns all pointing the way.

She hit the top of the steps and slid around the corner. Someone half a flight up yelled in alarm. Shirly caught a glimpse of two miners with sticks of TNT before she skipped down the flight of stairs.

At the next level, she turned and headed for the mineshaft. The hallways were silent, just her panting and the clop, clop, clop of her boots.

Juliette. Alive.

A person sent to *cleaning*, alive.

She turned down the next hallway and ran past the apartments for the deep workers, the miners and the oil men, men who now bore guns instead of boring holes in the earth, who wielded weapons rather than tools.

And this new knowledge, this impossible bit of news, this secret, it made the fighting seem surreal. Petty. How could anyone fight if there were places to go beyond these walls? If her friend was still out there? Shouldn't they be going as well?

She made it to the storeroom. Probably been two minutes.

Her heart was racing. Surely Jenkins wouldn't do anything to that stairway until she got back. She moved down the shelves, peering in the bins and drawers. She knew what the thing looked like. There should be several of them floating about. Where were they?

She checked the lockers, threw the dingy overalls hanging inside them to the ground, tossed work helmets out of the way. She didn't see anything. How much time did she have?

She tried the small foreman's office next, throwing the door open and storming to the desk. Nothing in the drawers. Nothing on the shelves mounted on the wall. One of the big drawers on the bottom was stuck. Locked.

Shirly stepped back and kicked the front of the metal drawer with her boot. She slammed the steel toe into it once, twice. The lip curled down, away from the drawer above. She reached in, yanked the flimsy lock off its lip, and the warped drawer opened with a groan.

Explosives. Sticks of dynamite. There were a few small relays that she knew went into the sticks to ignite them. Beneath these, she found three of the transmitters Walker was looking for.

Shirly grabbed two of them, a few relays, and put them all in her pocket. She took two sticks of the dynamite too – just because they were there and might be useful – and ran out of the office, through the storeroom, back towards the stairs.

She had used up too much time. Her chest felt cool and empty, raspy, as she laboured to breathe. She ran as fast as she could, concentrating on throwing her boots forward, lunging for more floor, gobbling it up.

Turning at the end of the hall, she again thought about how ridiculous this fighting was. It was hard to remember why it had begun. Knox was gone, so was McLain. Would their people be fighting if these great leaders were still around? Would they have done something different long ago? Something more sane?

She cursed the folly of it all as she reached the stairs. Surely it had been five minutes. She waited for a blast to ring out above her, to deafen her with its concussive ferocity. Leaping up two treads at a time, she made the turn at the top and saw that the miners were gone. Anxious eyes peered at her over home-made barrels.

'Go!' someone yelled, waving their arms to the side, hurrying her along.

Shirly focused on Jenkins, who crouched down with his own rifle, Harper by his side. She nearly tripped over the wires leading away from the stairwell as she ran towards the two men.

'Now!' Jenkins yelled.

Someone threw a switch.

The ground lurched and buckled beneath Shirly's feet, sending her sprawling. She landed hard on the steel floor, her chin grazing the diamond plating, the dynamite nearly flying from her hands.

Her ears were still ringing as she got to her knees. Men were moving behind the railing, guns popping into the bank of smoke leaking from a new maw of twisted and jagged steel. The screams of the distant wounded could be heard on the other side. While men fought, Shirly patted her pockets, fished inside for the transmitters.

Once again, the noise of war seemed to fade, to become insignificant, as she hurried through the door to the generator room, back to Walker, her lip bleeding, her mind on more important things.

69

• Silo 17 •

Juliette pulled herself through the cold, dark waters, bumping blindly against the ceiling, a wall, no way to tell which. She gathered the limp air hose with blind and desperate lunges, no idea how fast she was going – until she crashed into the stairs. Her nose crunched against the inside of her helmet, and the darkness was momentarily shouldered aside by a flash of light. She floated, dazed, the air hose drifting from her hands.

Juliette groped for the precious line as her senses gradually returned. She hit something with her glove, grabbed it, and was about to pull herself along when she realised it was the smaller power line. She let go and swept her arms in the blind murk, her boots bumping against something. It was impossible to know top from bottom. She began to feel turned around, dizzy, disoriented.

A rigid surface pressed against her; she decided she must be floating *up*, away from the hose.

She kicked off what she assumed was the ceiling and swam in the direction that she hoped was down. Her arms tangled in something – she felt it across her padded chest – she found it with her hands, expecting the power cord, but was rewarded with the spongy nothingness of the empty air tube. It no longer offered her air, but it did lead the way out.

Pulling in one direction gathered slack, so she tried the other way. The hose went taut. She pulled herself into the stairs again, bounced away with a grunt, and kept gathering line. The hose led up and around the corner – and she found herself pulling, reaching out an arm to fend off the blind assaults from walls, ceiling, steps – bumping and floating up six flights, a battle for every inch, a struggle that seemed to take for ever.

By the time she reached the top, she was out of breath and panting. And then she realised she wasn't out of breath, she was out of *air*. She had burned through whatever remained in the suit. Hundreds of feet of exhausted hose lay invisible behind her, sucked dry.

She tried the radio again as she pulled herself through the corridor, her suit rising slowly towards the ceiling, not nearly as buoyant as before.

'Solo! Can you hear me?'

The thought of how much water still lay above her, all those levels of it pressing down, hundreds of feet of solid flood – it was suffocating. What did she have left in the suit? Minutes? How long would it take to swim or float to the top of the stairwell? Much, much longer. There were probably oxygen bottles down one of those pitch-black hallways, but how would she find them? This wasn't her home. She didn't have time to look. All she had was a mad drive to reach the stairwell, to race to the surface.

She pulled and kicked her way around the last corner and into the main hallway, her muscles screaming from being used in new ways, from fighting the stiff and bulky suit, the viscous atmosphere, when she realised the inky water had lightened to something nearer charcoal instead of pitch black. There was a *green tint* to her blindness.

Juliette scissored her legs and gathered in the tubing, bumping along the ceiling, sensing the security station and stairwell ahead. She had travelled corridors like these thousands of times, twice in utter darkness when main breakers had failed. She remembered staggering through hallways just like this, telling co-workers it would be okay, just to stay still, she'd handle it.

Now she tried to do the same for herself, to lie and say it would all be okay, to just keep moving, don't panic.

The dizziness began to set in as she reached the security gate. The water ahead glowed lime green and looked so inviting, an end to the blind scrambling, no more of her helmet bumping into what she couldn't see.

Her arm briefly tangled with the power cord; she shook it free and hauled herself towards that tall column of water ahead, that flooded straw, that sunken stairway.

Before she got there, she had her first spasm, like a hiccup, a violent and automatic gasp for air. She lost her grip on the line and felt her chest nearly burst from the effort of breathing. The temptation to shed her helmet and take a deep inhalation of water overpowered her. Something in her mind insisted she could breathe the stuff. Just give her a chance, it said. One lungful of the water. Anything other than the toxins she had exhaled into her suit, a suit designed to keep such things *out*.

Her throat spasmed again, and she started coughing in her helmet as she pulled her way into the stairwell. The rope was there, held down by the wrench. She swam for it, knowing it was too late. As she yanked down, she felt the slack coming – the loose end of the rope spiralling in sinking knots towards her.

She drifted slowly towards the surface, very little of the built-up pressure inside her suit, no quick ride to the top. Another throat spasm, and the helmet had to come off. She was getting dizzy, would soon pass out.

Juliette fumbled for the clasps on her metal collar. The sense of déjà vu was overpowering. Only this time, she wasn't thinking clearly. She remembered the soup, the fetid smell, crawling out of the dark walk-in. She remembered the knife.

Patting her chest, she felt the handle sticking out from its sheath. Some of the other tools had wiggled out of their pockets; they dangled from lines meant to keep them from getting lost, lines that now just made them a nuisance, turned them into more weights holding her down.

She rose gently up the stairwell, her body shivering from the cold and convulsing from the absence of breathable air. Forgetting all reason, all sense of where she was, she became singularly aware of the noxious fog hanging all around her head, trapped by that dome, killing her. She aimed the blade into the first latch in her collar and pressed hard.

There was a click and a fine spray of cold water against her neck. A feeble bubble lurched out of her suit and tumbled up her visor. Groping for the other latch, she shoved the knife into it, and the helmet popped off, water flooding over her face, filling her suit, shocking her with the numbing cold and dragging her, sinking, back down to where she'd come from.

The freezing cold jolted Juliette to her senses. She blinked against the sting of the green water and saw the knife in her hands, the dome of her helmet spinning through the murk like a bubble heading in the wrong direction. She was slowly sinking after it, no air in her lungs, hundreds of feet of water pressing down on her.

She jabbed the knife into the wrong pocket on her chest, saw the drivers and spanners hanging by their cords from her struggle through the blackness, and kicked towards the hose that still led through four levels of water to the surface.

Bubbles of air leaked out of her collar and across her neck, up through her hair. Juliette seized the hose and stopped her plummet, pulled upward, her throat screaming for an intake of air, of water, of anything. The urge to swallow was overpowering. She started to pull herself up, when she saw, in the undersides of the steps, a shimmering flash of hope.

Trapped bubbles. Maybe from her descent. They moved like liquid solder in the hollow undersides of the spiral staircase.

Juliette made a noise in her throat, a raw cry of desperation, of effort. She pawed through the water, fighting the sinking of the suit, and grasped the railing of the submerged stairway. Pulling herself up and kicking off of the railing, she made it to the nearest shimmer of bubbles, grabbed the edge of the stairs, and pushed her mouth right up to the metal underside of the step.

She inhaled a desperate gasp of air and sucked in a lot of water in the process. She ducked her head below the surface and coughed into the water, which brought the burn of fluids invading her nose. She nearly sucked in a lungful of water, felt her heart racing and ready to burst out of her chest, stuck her face back up against the wet rusty underside of the step and, her lips pursed and trembling, managed to take in a gentle sip of air.

The tiny flashes of light in her vision subsided. She lowered her head and blew out, away from the step, watching the bubbles of her exhalation rise, and then pressed her face close for another taste.

Air.

She blinked away underwater tears of effort, of frustration, of relief. Peering up the twisted maze of metal steps, many of them moving like flexible mirrors where the trapped air was stirred by her mad gyrations, she saw a pathway like no other. She kicked off and took a few steps at a time, pulling herself hand over hand in the gaps between, drinking tiny bubbles of air out of the inches-deep hollow beneath each tread, praising the tight welds where the diamond plate steps had been joined many hundreds of years ago. The steps had been boxed in for strength, to handle the traffic of a million impacts of boots, and now they held the gaseous overflow from her descent. Her lips brushed each one, tasting metal and rust, kissing her salvation.

The green emergency lights all around her remained steady, so Juliette never noticed the landings drifting past. She just concentrated on taking five steps with each breath, six steps, a long stretch with hardly any air, another mouthful of water where the bubble was too thin to breathe, a lifetime of rising against the tug of her flooded suit and dangling tools, no thought for stopping and cutting things free, just kick and pull, hand over hand, up the undersides of the steps, a deep and steady pull of air, suck this shallow step dry, don't exhale into the steps above, easy now. Five more steps. It was a game, like Hop, five squares in a leap, don't cheat, mind the chalk, she was good at this, getting better.

And then a foul burn on her lips, the taste of water growing toxic, her head coming up into the underside of a step and breaking through a film of gas-stench and slimy oil.

Juliette blew out her last breath and coughed, wiping at her face, her head still trapped below the next step. She wheezed and laughed and pushed herself away, banging her head on the sharp steel edge of the stairs. She was free. She briefly bobbed below the surface as she swam around the railing, her eyes burning from the oil and gas floating on top. Splashing loudly, crying for Solo, she made it over the railing. With her padded and shivering knees, she finally found the steps.

She'd survived. Clinging to the dry treads above her, neck bent, gasping and wheezing, her legs numb, she tried to cry out that she'd made it, but it escaped as a whimper. She was cold. She was freezing. Her arms shivered as she pulled herself up the quiet steps, no rattle from the compressor, no arms reaching to assist her.

'Solo . . . ?'

She crawled the half-dozen treads to the landing and rolled onto her back. Some of her tools were caught on steps below, tugging at her where they were tied to her pockets. Water drained out of her suit and splashed down her neck, pooled by her head, ran into her ears. She turned her head – she needed to get the freezing suit off – and found Solo.

He was lying on his side, eyes shut, blood running down his face, some of it already caked dry.

'Solo?'

Her hand was a shivering blur as she reached out and shook him. What had he done to himself?

'Hey. Wakethefuckup.'

Her teeth were chattering. She grabbed his shoulder and gave him a violent shake. 'Solo! I need help!'

One of his eyes parted a little. He blinked a few times, then bent double and coughed, blood flecking the landing by his face.

'Help,' she said. She fumbled for the zipper at her back, not realising it was Solo who needed *her*.

Solo coughed into his hand, then rolled over and settled once again on his back. The blood on his head was still flowing from somewhere, fresh tracks trickling across what had dried some time before.

'Solo?'

He groaned. Juliette pulled herself closer, could barely feel her body. He whispered something, his voice a rasp on the edge of silence.

'Hey—' She brought her face close to his, could feel her lips swollen and numb, could still taste the gasoline.

'Not my name . . .'

He coughed a mist of red. One arm lifted from the landing a few inches as if to cover his mouth, but it never had a chance of getting there.

'Not my name,' he said again. His head lolled side to side, and Juliette finally realised that he was badly injured. Her mind began to clear enough to see what state he was in.

'Hold still,' she groaned. 'Solo, I need you to be still.'

She tried to push herself up, to will herself the strength to move. Solo blinked and looked at her, his eyes glassy, blood tinting the grey in his beard crimson.

'Not Solo,' he said, his voice straining. 'My name's Jimmy—'

More coughing, his eyes rolling up into the back of his head.

'—and I don't think—'

His eyelids sagged shut, and then squinted in pain.

'—don't think I was—'

'Stay with me,' Juliette said, hot tears cutting down her frozen face.

'—don't think I ever *was* alone,' he whispered, the lines on his face relaxing, his head sagging to the cold steel landing.

70

• Silo 18 •

The pot on the stove bubbled noisily, steam rising off the surface, tiny drops of water leaping to their freedom over the edge. Lukas shook a pinch of tea leaves out of the resealable tin and into the tiny strainer. His hands were shaking as he lowered the little basket into his mug. As he lifted the pot, some water spilled directly on the burner; the drops made spitting sounds and gave off a burnt odour. He watched Bernard out of the corner of his eye as he tilted the boiling water through the leaves.

'I just don't understand,' he said, holding the mug with both hands, allowing the heat to penetrate his palms. 'How could anybody—? How could you *do* something like this on *purpose*?' He shook his head and peered into his mug, where a few intrepid shreds of leaf had already got free and swam outside the basket. He looked up at Bernard. 'And you knew about this? How—? How could you *know* about this?'

Bernard frowned. He rubbed his moustache with one hand, the other resting in the belly of his overalls. 'I wish I *didn't* know it,' he told Lukas. 'And now you see why some facts, some pieces of knowledge, have to be snuffed out as soon as they form. Curiosity would blow across such embers and burn this silo to the ground.' He looked down at his boots. 'I pieced it together much as you did, just knowing what we have to know to do this job. This is why I chose you, Lukas. You and a few others have some idea what's stored on these servers. You're already prepped for learning more. Can you imagine if you told any of this to someone who wears red or green to work every day?'

Lukas shook his head.

'It's happened before, you know. Silo ten went down like that. I sat back there' – he pointed towards the small study with the books, the computer, the hissing radio – 'and I listened to it happen. I listened to a colleague's shadow broadcast his insanity to anyone who would listen.'

Lukas studied his steeping tea. A handful of leaves swam about on hot currents of darkening water; the rest remained in the grip of the imprisoning basket. 'That's why the radio controls are locked up,' he said.

'And it's why *you* are locked up.'

Lukas nodded. He'd already suspected as much.

'How long were you kept in here?' He glanced up at Bernard, and an image flashed in his mind, one of Sheriff Billings inspecting his gun while his mother had visited him. Had they been listening in? Would he have been shot, his mother too, if he'd said anything?

'I spent just over two months down here until my caster knew I was ready, that I had accepted and understood everything I'd learned.' He crossed his arms over his belly. 'I really wish you hadn't asked the question, hadn't put it together so soon. It's much better to find out when you're older.'

Lukas pursed his lips and nodded. It was strange to talk like this with someone his senior, someone who knew so much more, was so much wiser. He imagined this was the sort of conversation a man had with his father – only not about the planned and carried-out destruction of the entire world.

Lukas bent his head and breathed in the smell of the steeping leaves. The mint was like a direct line through the trembling stress, a strike to the calm pleasure centre in the deep regions of his brain. He inhaled and held his breath, finally let it out. Bernard crossed to the small stove in the corner of the storeroom and started making his own mug.

'How did they do it?' Lukas asked. 'To kill so many. Do you know how they did it?'

Bernard shrugged. He tapped the tin with one finger, shaking out a precise amount of tea into another basket. 'They might still be doing it for all I know. Nobody talks about how long it's supposed to go on. There's fear that small pockets of survivors might be holed up elsewhere around the globe. Operation Fifty is completely pointless if anyone else survives. The population has to be homogenous—'

'The man I spoke to, he said we were *it*. Just the fifty silos—'

'Forty-seven,' Bernard said. 'And we *are* it, as far as we know. It's difficult to imagine anyone else being so well prepared. But there's always a chance. It's only been a few hundred years.'

'A few *hundred*?' Lukas leaned back against the counter. He lifted his tea, but the mint was losing its power to reach him. 'So hundreds of years ago, we decided—'

'*They.*' Bernard filled his mug with the still-steaming water. 'They decided. Don't include yourself. Certainly don't include me.'

'Okay, *they* decided to destroy the world. Wipe everything out. Why?'

Bernard set his mug down on the stove to let it steep. He pulled off his glasses, wiped the steam off them, then pointed them towards the study, towards the wall with the massive shelves of books. 'Because of the worst parts of our Legacy, that's why. At least, that's what I *think* they would say if they were still alive.' He lowered his voice and muttered, 'Which they aren't, thank God.'

Lukas shuddered. He still didn't believe anyone would make that decision, no matter what the conditions were like. He thought of the billions of people who supposedly lived beneath the stars all those hundreds of years ago. Nobody could kill so many. How could anyone take that much life for granted?

'And now we *work* for them,' Lukas spat. He crossed to the sink and pulled the basket out of his mug, set it on the stainless steel to drain. He took a cautious sip, slurping lest it burn him. 'You tell me not to include us, but we're a part of this now.'

'No.' Bernard walked away from the stove and stood in front of the small map of the world hanging above the dinette. 'We weren't any part of what those crazy fucks did. If I had those guys, the men who did this, if I had them in a room with me, I'd kill every last goddamned one of them.' Bernard smacked the map with his palm. 'I'd kill them with my bare hands.'

Lukas didn't say anything. He didn't move.

'They didn't give us a *chance*. That's not what this is.' He gestured at the room around him. 'These are prisons. Cages, not homes. Not meant to protect us, but meant to force us, by pain of death, to bring about *their* vision.'

'Their vision for *what*?'

'For a world where we're too much the same, where we're too tightly invested in each other to waste our time fighting, to waste our resources guarding those *same* limited resources.' He lifted his mug and took a noisy sip. 'That's my theory, at least. From decades of reading. The people who did this, they were in charge of a powerful country that was beginning to crumble. They could see the end, *their* end, and it scared them suicidal. As the time began to run out – over decades, keep in mind – they figured they had *one* chance to preserve themselves, to preserve what they saw as their way of life. And so, before they lost the only opportunity they might ever have, they put a plan into motion.'

'Without anybody knowing? How?'

Bernard took another sip. He smacked his lips and wiped his moustache. 'Who knows? Maybe nobody could believe it anyway. Maybe the reward for secrecy was inclusion. They built other things in factories bigger than you can imagine that nobody knew about. They built bombs in factories like these that I suspect played a part in all this. All without anyone knowing. And there are stories in the Legacy about men from a long time ago in a land with great kings, like mayors but with many more people to rule. When these men died, elaborate chambers were built below the earth and filled with treasure. It required the work of hundreds of men. Do you know how they kept the locations of these chambers a secret?'

Lukas lifted his shoulders. 'They paid the workers a ton of chits?'

Bernard laughed. He pinched a stray tea leaf off his tongue. 'They didn't have chits. And no, they made perfectly sure these men would keep quiet. They killed them.'

'Their own men?' Lukas glanced towards the room with the books, wondering which tin this story was in.

'It is not beyond us to kill to keep secrets.' Bernard's face hardened as he said this. 'It'll be a part of your job one day, when you take over.'

Lukas felt a sharp pain in his gut as the truth of this hit. He caught the first glimmer of what he'd truly signed on for. It made shooting people with rifles seem an honest affair.

'We are not the people who made this world, Lukas, but it's up to us to survive it. You need to understand that.'

'We can't control where we are right now,' he mumbled, 'just what we do going forward.'

'Wise words.' Bernard took another sip of tea.

'Yeah. I'm just beginning to appreciate them.'

Bernard set his cup in the sink and tucked a hand in the round belly of his overalls. He stared at Lukas a moment, then looked again to the small map of the world.

'Evil men did this, but they're gone. Forget them. Just know this: they locked up their brood as a fucked-up form of their own survival. They put us in this game, a game where breaking the rules means we all die, every single one of us. But *living* by those rules, obeying them, means we all suffer.'

He adjusted his glasses and walked over to Lukas, patted him on the shoulder as he went past. 'I'm proud of you, son. You're absorbing this much better than I ever did. Now get some rest. Make some room in your head and heart. Tomorrow, more studies.' He headed towards the study, the corridor, the distant ladder.

Lukas nodded and remained silent. He waited until Bernard was gone, the muted clang of distant metal telling him that the grate was back in place, before walking through to the study to gaze up at the big schematic, the one with the silos crossed out. He peered at the roof of silo one, wondering just who in hell was in charge of all this and whether they too could rationalise their actions as having been foisted upon them, as not really being culpable but just going along with something they'd inherited, a crooked game with ratshit rules and almost everyone kept ignorant and locked up.

Who the fuck were these people? Could *he* see himself being *one* of them? How did Bernard not see that *he* was one of them?

71

• Silo 18 •

The door to the generator room slammed shut behind her, dulling the patter of gunfire to a distant hammering. Shirly ran towards the control room on sore legs, ignoring her friends and co-workers asking her what was going on outside. They cowered along the walls and behind the railing from the loud blast and the sporadic gunfire. Just before she reached the control room, she noticed some workers from second shift on top of the main generator toying with the rumbling machine's massive exhaust system.

'I got it,' Shirly wheezed, slamming the control-room door shut behind her. Courtnee and Walker looked up from the floor. The wide eyes and slack jaw on Courtnee's face told Shirly she'd missed something.

'What?' she asked. She handed the two transmitters to Walker. 'Did you hear? Walk, does she know?'

'How is this possible?' Courtnee asked. 'How did she survive? And what happened to your face?'

Shirly touched her lip, her sore chin. Her fingers came away wet with blood. She used the sleeve of her undershirt to dab at her mouth.

'If this works,' Walker grumbled, fiddling with one of the transmitters, 'we can ask Jules herself.'

Shirly turned and peered through the control room's observation window. She lowered her sleeve away from her face. 'What's Karl and them doing with the exhaust feed?' she asked.

'They've got some plan to reroute it,' Courtnee said. She got up from the floor while Walker started soldering something, the smell reminding her of his workshop. He grumbled about his eyesight while Courtnee joined her by the glass.

'Reroute it where?'

'IT. That's what Heline said, anyway. The cooling feed for their server room runs through the ceiling here before shooting up the Mechanical shaft. Someone spotted the proximity on a schematic, thought of a way to fight back from here.'

'So, we choke them out with our fumes?' Shirly felt uneasy about the plan. She wondered what Knox would say if he were still alive, still in charge. Surely all the men and women riding desks up there weren't the problem. 'Walk, how long before we can talk? Before we can try and contact her?'

'Almost there. Blasted magnifiers . . .'

Courtnee rested her hand on Shirly's arm. 'Are you okay? How're you holding up?'

'Me?' Shirly laughed and shook her head. She checked the bloodstains on her sleeve, felt the sweat trickling down her chest. 'I'm walking around in shock. I have no idea what the hell's going on any more. My ears are still ringing from whatever they did to the stairwell. I think I've screwed up my ankle. And I'm starving. Oh, and did I mention my friend isn't as dead as I thought she was?'

She took a deep breath.

Courtnee continued to stare at her worryingly. Shirly knew none of this was what her friend was asking her about.

'And yeah, I miss Marck,' she said quietly.

Courtnee put her arm around her friend and pulled her close. 'I'm sorry,' she said. 'I didn't mean to—'

Shirly waved her off. The two of them stood quietly and watched through the window as a small crew from second shift worked on the generator, trying to reroute the outpouring of noxious fumes from the apartment-sized machine to the floors of the thirties high above.

'You know what, though? There are times when I'm *glad* he's not here. Times when I know I won't be around much longer either, not once they get to us, and I'm glad he's not here to stress about it, to worry about what they'll do to us. To me. And I'm glad I haven't had to watch him do all this fighting, living on rations, this sort of craziness.' She dipped her chin at the crew outside. She knew Marck would either be up there leading that terrible work or outside with a gun pressed to his cheek.

'Hello. Testing. Hello, hello.'

The two women turned around to see Walker clicking the red detonate switch, the microphone from the headset held beneath his chin, furrows of concentration across his brow.

'Juliette?' he asked. 'Can you hear me? Hello?'

Shirly moved to Walker's side, squatted down, rested a hand on his shoulder. The three of them stared at the headphones, waiting for a reply.

'Hello?' A quiet voice leaked out of the tiny speakers.

Shirly clapped a hand to her chest, her breath stolen from the miracle of a reply. It was a fraction of a second later, after this surge of desperate hope, that she realised this wasn't Juliette. The voice was different.

'That's not her,' Courtnee whispered, dejected. Walker waved his hand to silence her. The red switch clicked noisily as he prepared to transmit.

'Hello. My name is Walker. We received a transmission from a friend. Is there anyone else there?'

'Ask them where they are,' Courtnee hissed.

'Where exactly are you?' Walker added, before releasing the switch.

The tiny speakers popped.

'We are nowhere. You'll never find us. Stay away.'

There was a pause, a hiss of static.

'And your friend is dead. We killed him.'

72

• Silo 17 •

The water inside the suit was freezing, the air cold, the combination lethal. Juliette's teeth chattered noisily while she worked the knife. She slid the blade into the soggy skin of the suit, the feeling of having already been here, having done all this before, unmistakable.

The gloves came off first, the suit destroyed, water pouring out of every cut. Juliette rubbed her hands together, could barely feel them. She hacked away at the material over her chest, her eyes falling to Solo, who had gone deathly still. His large wrench was missing, she saw. Their supply bag was gone as well. The compressor was on its side, the hose kinked beneath it, fuel leaking from the loose filling cap.

Juliette was freezing. She could hardly breathe. Once the chest of the suit was cut open, she wiggled her knees and feet through the hole, spun the material around in front of herself, then tried to pry the Velcro apart.

Her fingers were too senseless even to do this. She ran the knife down the joint instead, sawing the Velcro apart until she could find the zipper.

Finally, squeezing her fingers until they were white, she pulled the small tab free of the collar and threw the suit away from herself. The thing weighed double with all the water in it. She was left in two layers of black undersuit, still soaking wet and shivering, a knife in her trembling hand, the body of a good man lying beside her, a man who had survived everything this nasty world could throw at him except for her arrival.

Juliette moved to Solo's side and reached for his neck. Her

hands were icy; she couldn't feel a pulse, wasn't sure if she would be *able* to. She could barely feel his neck with her frozen fingers.

She struggled to her feet, nearly collapsed, hugged the landing's railing. She teetered towards the compressor, knowing she needed to warm up. She felt the powerful urge to go to sleep but knew she'd never wake up if she did.

The fuel can was still full. She tried to work the cap, but her hands were useless. They were numb and vibrating from the cold. Her breath fogged in front of her, a chilly reminder of the heat she was losing, what little heat she had left.

She grabbed the knife. Holding it in both hands, she pressed the tip into the cap. The flat handle was easier to grasp than the plastic cap; she spun the knife and cracked the lid on the jug of fuel. Once the cap was loose, she pulled the blade out and did the rest with her palms, the knife resting in her lap.

She tilted the can over the compressor, soaking the large rubber wheels, the carriage, the entire motor. She would never want to use it again anyway, never rely on it or anything else for her air. She put the can down, still half full, and slid it away from the compressor with her foot. Fuel dripped through the metal grating and made musical impacts in the water below, drips that echoed off the concrete walls of the stairwell and added to the flood's toxic and colourful slick.

Wielding the knife with the blade down, the dull side away from her, she smacked it against the metal fins of the heat exchanger. She yanked her arm back with each strike, expecting the whoosh of an immediate flame. But there was no spark. She hit it harder, hating to abuse her precious tool, her only defence. Solo's stillness nearby was a reminder that she might need it if she were able to survive the deadly cold—

The knife struck with a snick, there was a pop, heat travelling up her arm, a wash of it against her face.

Juliette dropped the knife and waved her hand, but it wasn't on fire. The compressor *was*. Part of the grating, too.

As it began to die down, she grabbed the can and sloshed some more fuel out of it, large balls of orange flame rewarding her, leaping up in the air with a whoosh. The wheels crackled as they burned. Juliette collapsed close to the fire, felt the heat from the dancing flame as it burned all across the metal machine. She began to strip, her eyes returning now and then to Solo, promising herself that she wouldn't leave his body there, that she would come back for him.

Feeling returned to her extremities – at first gradually, but then with a tingling pain. Naked, she curled into a ball next to the small and feeble fire and rubbed her hands together, breathing her warm and visible breath into her palms. Twice she had to feed the hungry and stingy fire. Only the wheels burned reliably, but they kept her from needing another spark. The glorious heat travelled somewhat through the landing's grated decking, warming her bare skin where it touched the metal.

Her teeth chattered violently. Juliette eyed the stairs, this new fear coursing through her that boots could rumble down at any moment, that she was trapped between these other survivors and the freezing water. She retrieved her knife, held it in front of her with both hands, tried to will herself not to shiver so violently.

Glimpses of her face in the blade caused her to worry more. She looked as pale as a ghost. Lips purple, eyes ringed dark and seeming hollow. She nearly laughed at the sight of her lips vibrating, the clacking blur of her teeth. She scooted closer to the fire. The orange light danced on the blade, the unburnt fuel dripping and forming silvery splashes of colour below.

As the last of the gas burned and the flames dwindled, Juliette decided to move. She was still shaking, but it was cold in the depths of the shaft so far from the electricity of IT. She patted the black underlinings she'd stripped off. One of them had been left balled up and was still soaked. The other she had at least dropped flat; if she'd been thinking clearly she would've hung it up. It was damp, but better to wear it and heat it up herself than allow the cold air to wick her body temperature away. She worked her legs in, struggled to get her arms through the sleeves, zipped up the front.

On bare, numb, and unsteady feet, she returned to Solo. She could feel his neck this time. He felt warm. She couldn't remember how long a body stayed that way. And then she felt a weak and slow thrumming in his neck. A beat.

'Solo!' She shook his shoulders. 'Hey . . .' What name had he whispered? She remembered: 'Jimmy!'

His head lolled from side to side while she shook his shoulder. She checked his scalp beneath all that crazy hair, saw lots of blood. Most of it was dry. She looked around again for her bag – they had brought food, water, and dry clothes for when she got back up – but the satchel was gone. She grabbed her other undersuit instead. She wasn't sure about the quality of the water in the fabric, but it had to be better than nothing. Wrenching the material in a tight ball, she dripped what she could against his lips. She squeezed more on his head, brushed his hair back to inspect the wound, probed the nasty cut with her fingers. As soon as the water hit the open gash, it was like pushing a button. Solo lurched to the side, away from her hand and the drip from the undersuit. His teeth flashed yellow in his beard as he screamed in pain, his hands rising from the landing and hovering there, arms tensed, still senseless.

'Solo. Hey, it's okay.'

She held him as he came to, his eyes rolling around, lids blinking.

'It's okay,' she said. 'You're gonna be okay.'

She used the balled-up undersuit to dab at his wound. Solo grunted and held her wrist but didn't pull away.

'Stings,' he said. He blinked and looked around. 'Where am I?'

'The down deep,' she reminded him, happy to hear him talking. She felt like crying with relief. 'I think you were attacked . . .'

He tried to sit up, hissing between his teeth, a powerful grip pinching her wrist.

'Easy,' she said, trying to hold him down. 'You've got a nasty cut on your head. A lot of swelling.'

His body relaxed.

'Where are they?' he asked.

'I don't know,' Juliette said. 'What do you remember? How many were there?'

He closed his eyes. She continued to dab at his wound.

'Just one. I think.' He opened his eyes wide as if shocked by the memory of the attack. 'He was *my* age.'

'We need to get up top,' she told him. 'We need to get where it's warm, get you cleaned up, get me dry. Do you think you can move?'

'I'm not crazy,' Solo said.

'I know you're not.'

'The things that moved, the lights, it wasn't me. I'm not crazy.'

'No,' Juliette agreed. She remembered all the times she had thought the same thing of herself, always in the down deep of this place, usually while rummaging around Supply. 'You aren't crazy,' she said, comforting him. 'You aren't crazy at all.'

• Silo 18 •

Lukas couldn't force himself to study, not what he was supposed to be studying. The Order sat flopped open on the wooden desk, the little lamp on its thousand-jointed-neck bent over and warming it in a pool of light. He stood before the wall schematics instead, staring at the arrangement of silos, which were spaced out like the servers in the room above him, and listened to the radio crackle with the sounds of distant warring.

The final push was being made. Sims's team had lost a few men in an awful explosion, something about a stairwell – but not the great stairwell – and now they were in a fight they hoped would be the last. The little speakers by the radio crackled with static as the men coordinated themselves, as Bernard shouted orders from his office one level up, always with the crackle of gunfire erupting behind the voices.

Lukas knew he shouldn't listen, and yet he couldn't stop. Juliette would call him anytime now and ask him for an update. She would want to know what had happened, how the end had come, and the only thing worse than telling her would be admitting he didn't know, that he couldn't bear to listen.

He reached out and touched the round roof of silo seventeen. It was as though he were a god surveying the structures from up high. He pictured his hand piercing the dark clouds above Juliette and spanning a roof built for thousands. He rubbed his fingers over the red X drawn across the silo, those two slashes that admitted to such a great loss. The marks felt waxy beneath his fingers like they'd been drawn with crayon or something similar. He tried to imagine getting the news one day that an entire people were gone, wiped out. He would have to dig in Bernard's desk – *his* desk – and find the red stick, cross out another chance at their Legacy, another pod of buried hope.

Lukas looked up at the overhead lights, steady and constant, unblinking. Why hadn't she called?

His fingernail caught on one of the red marks and flaked a piece of it away. The wax stuck under his fingernail, the paper beneath still stained blood red. There was no taking it back, no cleaning it off, no making it whole again—

Gunfire erupted from the radio. Lukas went to the shelf where the little unit was mounted and listened to orders being barked, men being killed. His forehead went clammy with sweat. He knew how that felt, to pull that trigger, to end a life. He was conscious of an emptiness in his chest and a weakness in his knees. Lukas steadied himself with the shelf, palms slick, and looked at the transmitter hanging there inside its locked cage. How he longed to call those men and tell them not to do it, to stop all the insanity, the violence, the pointless killing. There could be a red X on them all. *This* was what they should fear, not each other.

He touched the metal cage that kept the radio controls locked away from him, feeling the truth of this and the silliness of broadcasting it to everyone else. It was naive. It wouldn't change anything. The short-term rage to be sated at the end of a barrel was too easy to act on. Staving off extinction required something else, something with more vision, something impossibly patient.

His hand drifted across the metal grating. He peered inside at one of the dials, the arrow pointing to the number '18'. There were fifty numbers in a dizzying circle, one for each silo. Lukas gave the cage a futile tug, wishing he could listen to something else. What was going on in all those other distant lands? Harmless things, probably. Jokes and chatter. Gossip. He could imagine the thrill of breaking in on one of those conversations and introducing himself to people who weren't in the know. 'I am Lukas from silo eighteen,' he might say. And they would want to know why silos had numbers. And Lukas would tell them to be good to each other, that there were only so many of them left, and that all the books and all the stars in the universe were pointless with no one to read them, no one to peer through the parting clouds for them.

He left the radio alone, left it to its war, and walked past the desk and its eager pool of light spilling across that dreary book. He checked the tins for something that might hold his attention. He felt restless, pacing like a pig in its pen. He should go for another jog among the servers, but that would mean showering, and somehow showering had begun to feel like an insufferable chore.

Crouching down at the far end of the shelves, he sorted through the loose, un-tinned stacks of paper there. Here was where the handwritten notes and the additions to the Legacy had amassed over the years. Notes to future silo leaders, instructions, manuals, mementos. He pulled out the generator control-room manual, the one Juliette had written. He had watched Bernard shelve the papers weeks ago, saying it might come in handy if the problems in the down deep went from bad to worse.

And the radio was blasting the worse.

Lukas went to his desk and bent the neck of the lamp so he could read the handwriting inside. There were days that he dreaded her calling, dreaded getting caught or Bernard answering or her asking him to do things he couldn't, things he would never do again. And now, with the lights steady overhead and nothing buzzing, all he wanted was a call. His chest ached for it. Some part of him knew that what she was doing was dangerous, that something bad could've happened. She was living beneath a red X, after all, a mark that meant death for anyone below it.

The pages of the manual were full of notes she'd made with sharp lead. He rubbed one of them, feeling the grooves with his fingers. The actual content was inscrutable. Settings for dials in every conceivable order, valve positions, electrical diagrams. Riffling through the pages, he saw the manual as a project not unlike his star charts, created by a mind not unlike his own. This awareness made the distance between them worse. Why couldn't they go back? Back to before the cleaning, before the string of burials. She would get off work every night and come sit with him while he gazed into the darkness, thinking and watching, chatting and waiting.

He turned the manual around and read some of the printed words from the play, which were nearly as indecipherable. In the margins sat notes from a different hand – Lukas assumed Juliette's mother, or maybe one of the actors. There were diagrams on some pages, little arrows showing movement. An actor's notes, he decided. Directions on a stage. The play must've been a souvenir to Juliette, this woman he had feelings for whose name was in the title.

He scanned the lines, looking for something poetic to capture his dark mood. As the text flowed by, his eyes caught a brief flash of familiar scrawl, not the actor's. He flipped back, looking for it a page at a time until he found it.

It was Juliette's hand, no mistaking. He moved the play into the light so he could read the faded marks:

George:
    There you lay, so serene. The wrinkles in your
brow and by your eyes, nowhere seen. A touch when
others look away, look for a clue, but only I know what
happened to you. Wait for me. Wait for me. Wait
there, my dear. Let these gentle pleas find your ear, and
bury them there, so this stolen kiss can grow on the
quiet love that no other shall know.

Lukas felt a cold rod pierce his chest. He felt his longing replaced by a flash of temper. Who was this George? A childhood fling? Juliette was never in a sanctioned relationship; he had checked the official records the day after they'd met. Access to the servers afforded certain guilty powers. A crush, perhaps? Some man in Mechanical who was already in love with another girl? To Lukas, this would be even worse. A man she longed for in a way she never would feel for him. Was that why she'd taken a job so far from home? To get away from the sight of this George she couldn't have, these feelings she'd hidden in the margins of a play about forbidden love?

He turned and plopped down in front of Bernard's computer. Shaking the mouse, he logged into the upstairs servers remotely, his cheeks feeling flush with this sick feeling, this new feeling, knowing it was called jealousy but unfamiliar with the heady rush that came with it. He navigated to the personnel files and searched the down deep for 'George'. There were four hits. He copied the ID numbers of each and put them in a text file, then fed them to the ID department. While the pictures of each popped up, he skimmed their records, feeling a little guilty for the abuse of power, a little worried about this discovery, and a lot less agonisingly bored having found something to do.

Only one of the Georges worked in Mechanical. Older guy. As the radio crackled behind him, Lukas wondered what would become of this man if he was still down there. There was a chance that he was no longer alive, that the records were a few weeks out of date, the blockade a barrier to the truth.

A couple of the hits were too young. One wasn't even a year old yet. The other was shadowing a porter. It left one man, thirty-two years old. He worked in the bazaar, occupation listed as 'other', married with two kids. Lukas studied the blurry image of him from the ID office. Moustache. Receding hair. A sideways smirk. His eyes were too far apart, Lukas decided, his brows too dark and much too bushy.

Lukas held up the manual and read the poem again.

The man was dead, he decided. *Bury these pleas.*

He did another search, this time a global one that included the closed records. Hundreds of hits throughout the silo popped up, names from all the way back to the uprising. This did not dissuade Lukas. He knew Juliette was thirty-four, and so he gave her an eighteen-year window, figured if she were younger than sixteen when she'd had this crush, he wouldn't stress, he would let go of the envious and shameful burn inside him.

From the list of Georges, there were only three deaths in the down deep for the eighteen-year period. One was in his fifties, the other in his sixties. Both died of natural causes. Lukas thought to cross-reference them with Juliette, see if there had been any work relations, if they shared a family tree perhaps.

And then he saw the third file. *This* was his George. *Her* George. Lukas knew it. Doing the maths, Lukas saw he would be thirty-eight if he were still alive. He had died just over three years earlier, had worked in Mechanical, had *never married*.

He ran the ID search, and the picture confirmed his fears. He was a handsome man, a square jaw, a wide nose, dark eyes. He was smiling at the camera, calm, relaxed. It was hard to hate the man. Difficult, especially, since he was dead.

Lukas checked the cause and saw that it was investigated and then listed as an industrial accident. *Investigated*. He remembered hearing something about Jules when the up top got its new sheriff. Her qualifications had been a source of debate and tension, a wind of whispers. Especially around IT. But there had been chatter that she'd helped out on a case a long time ago, that this was why she'd been chosen.

This was the case. Was she in love with him before he died? Or did she fall for the memory of the man after? He decided it had to be the former. Lukas searched the desk for a charcoal, found one, and jotted down the man's ID and case number. Here was something to occupy his time, some way of getting to know her better. It would distract him, at least, until she finally got around to calling him back. He relaxed, pulled the keyboard into his lap, and started digging.

Juliette shivered from the cold as she helped Solo to his feet. He wobbled and steadied himself, both hands on the railing.

'Do you think you can walk?' she asked. She kept an eye on the empty stairs spiralling down towards them, wary of whoever else was out there, whoever had attacked him and nearly got her killed.

'I think so,' he said. He dabbed at his forehead with his palm, studied the smear of blood he came away with. 'Don't know how far.'

She guided him towards the stairs, the smell of melted rubber and gasoline stinging her nose. The black undersuit was still damp against her skin; her breath billowed out before her; and whenever she stopped talking, her teeth chattered uncontrollably. She bent to retrieve her knife while Solo clutched the curved outer railing. Looking up, she considered the task before them. A straight run to IT seemed impossible. Her lungs were exhausted from the swim, her muscles cramped from the shivering and cold. And Solo looked even worse. His mouth was slack, his eyes drifting to and fro. He seemed barely cognisant of where he was.

'Can you make it to the deputy station?' she asked. Juliette had spent nights there on supply runs. The holding cell made for an oddly comfortable place to sleep. The keys were still in the box – maybe they could rest easy if they locked themselves inside and kept the key with them.

'That's how many levels?' Solo asked.

He didn't know the down deep of his own silo as well as Jules. He rarely risked venturing so far.

'A dozen or so. Can you make it?'

He lifted his boot to the first step, leaned into it. 'I can try.'

They set off with only a knife between them, which Juliette was lucky to have at all. How it had survived her dark pull through Mechanical was a mystery. She held it tightly, the handle cold, her hand colder. The simple cooking utensil had become her security totem, had replaced her watch as a necessary thing she must always have with her. As they made their way up the stairs, its handle clinked against the inner railing each time she reached over to steady herself. She kept her other arm around Solo, who struggled up each step with grunts and groans.

'How many of them do you think there are?' she asked, watching his footing and then glancing nervously up the stairway.

Solo grunted. 'Shouldn't be any.' He wobbled a little, but Juliette steadied him. 'All dead. Everyone.'

They stopped to rest at the next landing. '*You* made it,' she pointed out. 'All these years, and you survived.'

He frowned, wiped his beard with the back of his hand. He was breathing hard. 'But I'm Solo,' he said. He shook his head sadly. 'They were all gone. All of them.'

Juliette peered up the shaft, up the gap between the stairs and the concrete. The dim green straw of the stairwell rose into a tight darkness. She pinned her teeth together to keep them from chattering while she listened for a sound, for any sign of life. Solo staggered ahead for the next flight of stairs. Juliette hurried beside him.

'How well did you see him? What do you remember?'

'I remember – I remember thinking he was just like me.'

Juliette thought she heard him sob, but maybe it was the exertion from tackling more of the steps. She looked back at the door they were passing, the interior dark, no power being leached from IT. Were they passing Solo's assailant? Were they leaving some living ghost behind?

She powerfully hoped so. They had so much further to go, even to the deputy station, much less to any place she might call home.

They trudged in silence for a level and a half, Juliette shivering and Solo grunting and wincing. She rubbed her arms now and then, could feel the sweat from the climb and from helping to steady him. It was nearly enough to warm her but for the damp undersuit, and she was so hungry by the time they cleared three levels that she thought her body was simply going to give out. It needed fuel, something to burn and keep itself warm.

'One more level and I'm going to need to stop,' she told Solo. He grumbled his agreement. It felt good to have the reward of a rest as their goal – the steps were an easier climb when they were countable, finite. At the landing of one-thirty-two, Solo used the railing to lower himself to the ground, hand over hand like the bars of a ladder. When his bottom hit the decking, he laid out supine and folded his hands over his face.

Juliette hoped it was nothing more than a concussion. She'd seen her fair share of them working around men who were too tough to wear helmets – but not so tough when a tool or a steel beam caught them on the head. There was nothing for Solo but to rest.

The problem with resting was that it made her colder. Juliette stomped her feet to keep the blood circulating. The slight sweat she'd worked up from the hike was working against her. She could feel a draught cycling through the stairwell, cold air from below passing over the chilled waters like a natural air-conditioning unit. Her shoulders shook, the knife vibrating in her hand until her reflection became a silvery blur. Moving was difficult; staying in one place would kill her. And she still didn't know where this attacker was, could only hope he was below them.

'We should get going,' she told Solo. She looked to the doors beyond him, the windows dark. What would she do if someone burst out at that very moment and attacked them? What kind of fight could she hope to put up?

Solo lifted his arm and waved it at her. 'Go,' he said. 'I'll stay.'

'No, you're coming with me.' She rubbed her hands together, blew on them, summoned the strength to continue. She went to Solo and tried to grab his hand, but he withdrew it.

'More rest,' he said. 'I'll catch up.'

'I'll be damned if I'm—' Her teeth clacked uncontrollably.

She shivered and turned the involuntary spasm into an excuse to shake her arms, waggling them and forcing the blood to her extremities. '—damned if I'm leaving you alone,' she finished.

'So thirsty,' he told her.

Despite having seen quite enough water for a lifetime, Juliette was thirsty as well. She glanced up. 'One more level and we're at the lower farms. C'mon. That'll be far enough for today. Food and water, find me something dry. C'mon, Solo, up. I don't care if it takes us a week to get home, we aren't giving up right here.'

She grabbed his wrist. This time he didn't pull away.

The next flight took for ever to climb. Solo stopped several times to lean on the railing and gaze senselessly at the next step. There was fresh blood trickling down his neck. Juliette stomped her frozen feet some more and cursed to herself. This was all stupid. She'd been so damned stupid.

A few steps from the next landing, she left Solo behind and went to check the doors to the farms. The jury-rigged power cables descending from IT and snaking their way inside were a legacy from decades ago, a time when the survivors, like Solo, were cobbling together what they could to stave off their demise. Juliette peeked inside and saw that the grow lights were off.

'Solo? I'm gonna go hit the timers. You rest here.'

He didn't answer. Juliette held the door open and tried to slot her knife into the metal grating by her feet, leaving the handle to prop it open. Her arm shook so violently, it took her considerable effort just to aim it into a gap. Her undersuit, she noticed, smelled like burning rubber, like the smoke from the fire.

'Here,' Solo said. He held the door open and slumped down against it, pinning it to the railing.

Juliette clutched the knife against her chest. 'Thanks.'

He nodded and waved his hand. His eyes drooped shut. 'Water,' he said, licking his lips.

She patted his shoulder. 'I'll be right back.'

The farm's entrance hall gobbled up the emergency lights from the stairway, the dim green quickly fading to pitch black. A circulating pump whirred in the distance, the same noise that had greeted her in the upper farms so many weeks ago. But now she knew what the sound was, knew there would be water available. Water and food, perhaps a change of clothes. She just needed to get the lights on so she could see. She cursed herself for not bringing a spare flashlight, for the loss of her pack and their gear.

The darkness accepted her as she climbed over the security gate. She knew her way. These farms had been nourishing her and Solo for weeks while they worked on the pathetic hydroponics pump and all that plumbing. Juliette thought of the new pump she'd wired; the mechanic in her was curious about the connection, wondered whether the thing would work, if she should've thrown the switch on the landing before they left. It was a crazy thought, but even if she didn't live to see it, some part of her wanted that silo dry, that flood removed. Her ordeal in its depths already seemed oddly distant, like something she had seen in a dream but hadn't really gone through, and yet she wanted it to have *mattered* for something. She wanted Solo's wounds to have mattered for something.

Her undersuit swished noisily while she walked, her legs rubbing together, her damp feet squeaking as she lifted them from the floor. She kept one hand on the wall, her knife comforting her in the other. Already, she could feel the residual warmth in the air from the last burn of the grow lights. She was thankful to be out of that frigid stairwell. In fact, she felt *better*. Her eyes began to adjust to the darkness. She would get some food, some water, find them a safe place to sleep. Tomorrow, they would aim for the mids deputy station. They could arm themselves, gather their strength. Solo would be stronger by then. She would need him to be.

At the end of the hall, Juliette groped for the doorway to the control room. Her hand habitually went to the switch inside, but it was already up. It hadn't worked in over three decades.

She fumbled blindly through the room, arms out in front of her, expecting to hit the wall long before she did. The tip of the knife scraped one of the control boxes. Juliette reached up to find the wire hanging from the ceiling, tacked up by someone long ago. She traced the wire to the timer it had been rigged to, felt for the programmable knob and slowly turned it until it clicked.

A series of loud pops from the relays outside rattled down the growing halls. A dim glow appeared. It would take a few minutes for them to warm all the way up.

Juliette left the control room and headed down one of the overgrown walkways railed off between the long plots of dirt. The nearest plots were picked clean. She pushed through the greenery, plants from either side of the hall shaking hands in the middle, and made her way to the circulation pump.

Water for Solo, warmth for herself. She repeated this mantra, begging the lights to heat up faster. The air around her remained dim and hazy like the view of an outside morning beneath the heavy clouds.

She made her way through the pea plants, long neglected. Popping a few pods off their vines, she gave her stomach something to do besides ache. The pump whirred louder as it worked to push water through the drip pipes. Juliette chewed a pea, swallowed, slipped through the railing and made her way to the small clearing around the pump.

The soil beneath the pump was dark and packed flat from weeks of her and Solo drinking there and refilling their containers. A few cups were scattered on the ground. Juliette knelt beside the pump and chose a tall glass. The lights above her were slowly brightening. She already imagined she could feel their warmth.

With a bit of effort, she managed to loosen the drain plug at the bottom of the pump a few turns. The water was under pressure and jetted out in a fine spray. She held the cup tightly against the pump to minimise the spillage. The cup gurgled as it was filled.

She drank out of one cup while filling another, some loose dirt crunching between her teeth.

Once both were full, she screwed them into the wet dirt so they wouldn't tip over, and then twisted the plug until the spray stopped. Juliette tucked the knife under her arm and grabbed the two cups. She went to the railing, passed everything through, then threw her leg over the lowermost bar and scrambled out.

Now she needed warmth. She left the cups where they were

and grabbed the knife. There were offices around the corner, a dining room. She remembered her first outfit in silo seventeen: a tablecloth with a slit in the middle. She laughed to herself as she turned the corner, feeling like she was regressing, like her weeks of working to make things better were taking her back to where she'd started.

The long hallway between the two grow stations was dark. A handful of wires hung from the pipes overhead, drooping between the spots where they'd been hastily attached. They marched in these upside-down leaps towards the hum and glow of the growing plots in the distance.

Juliette checked the offices and found nothing for warmth. No overalls, no curtains. She moved towards the dining hall, was turning to enter, when she thought she heard something beyond the next plot of plants. A click. A crackle. More relays for the lights? Stuck, perhaps?

She peered down the hall and into the grow station beyond. The lights were brighter there, warming up. Maybe they had come on sooner. She crept down the hallway towards them, drawn like a shivering fly to a flame, her arms bursting with goosebumps at the thought of drying out, of getting truly warm.

At the edge of the station, she heard something else. A squeal, maybe metal on metal, possibly another circulation pump trying to kick over. She and Solo hadn't checked the other pumps on this level. There was more than two people could eat or drink in the first patches.

Juliette froze and turned around to look behind herself.

Where would she set up camp if she were trying to survive in this place? In IT, for the power? Or here, for the food and water? She imagined another man like Solo squeezing through the cracks in the violence, lying low and surviving the long years. Maybe he'd heard the air compressor earlier, had come down to investigate, got scared, hit Solo over the head and ran. Maybe he grabbed their gear bag just because it was there, or maybe it had been knocked under the railing by accident and had sunk to the pits of Mechanical.

She held the knife out in front of herself and slid down the hallway between the burgeoning plants. The wall of green before her parted with a rustle as she pushed through. Things were more overgrown here. Unwelcoming. Not picked over. This filled her with a mix of emotions. She was probably wrong, was probably hearing things again, just as she had for weeks, but part of her *wanted* to be right. She wanted to find this man who was like Solo. She wanted to make contact. Better that than living in fear of someone lurking in every shadow, behind every corner.

But what if there was more than one of them? Could a group of people have survived this long? How many could there be and go undetected? The silo was a massive place, but she and Solo had spent *weeks* in the down deep, had been in and out of these farms several times. Two people, an oldish couple, no more. Solo had said the man was his age. He would have to be.

These calculations and more ran through her mind, convincing her that she had nothing to be afraid of. She was shivering, but her adrenalin was pumping. She was armed. The leaves of wild and unkempt plants brushed against her face; Juliette pushed through this dense outer barrier and knew she'd found something on the other side.

The farms here were different. Groomed. Tamed. Recently guided by the hand of man. Juliette felt a wash of fear and relief, those two opposites twisting together like staircase and rail. She didn't want to be alone, didn't want this silo to be so desolate and empty, but she didn't want to be attacked. The first part of her felt an urge to call out, to tell whoever was in there that she meant no harm. The second part tightened its grip on the knife, clenched chattering teeth together, and begged her to turn and run.

At the end of the groomed grow station, the hallway took a dark turn. She peered around the corner into more unexplored territory. A long patch of darkness stretched towards the other side of the silo, a distant glow of light emanating from what was probably yet another crop station sucking juice from IT.

Someone was here. She knew it. She could feel the same eyes she'd felt for weeks, could sense the whispers on her skin, but this time she wasn't imagining it; she didn't have to fight the awareness or think she was going crazy. With her knife at the ready and the welcomed thought that she was between this someone and the defenceless Solo, she moved slowly but bravely into the dark hall, passing open offices and tasting rooms to either side, one hand on the wall to guide and steady herself—

Juliette stopped. Something wasn't right. Had she heard something? A person crying? She backed up to the previous door, could barely see it in front of herself, and realised it was closed. The only one she could see along the hall that was closed.

She stepped away from the door and knelt down. There had been a noise inside. She was sure of it. Almost like a faint wail. Looking up, she saw in the wan light that some of the overhead wires diverted perpendicularly from the rest and snaked through the wall above the door.

Juliette moved closer. She crouched down and put her ear to the door. Nothing. She reached up and tried the knob, felt that it was locked. How could it be locked, unless—

The door flew open – her hand still on the knob – yanking her into the darkened room. There was a flash of light, and then a man over her, swinging something at her head.

Juliette fell onto her backside. A silver blur moved past her face, the crunch of a heavy wrench slamming into her shoulder, knocking her flat.

There was a high-pitched scream from the back of the room, drowning out Juliette's cry of pain. She swung the knife out in front of her, felt it hit the man's leg. The wrench clattered to the ground, more screams, people shouting. Juliette kicked away from the door and stood, clutching her shoulder. She was ready for the man to pounce, but her attacker was backing away, limping on one foot, a boy no more than fourteen, maybe fifteen.

'Stay where you are!' Juliette aimed the knife at him. The boy's eyes were wide with fear. A group of kids huddled against the back wall on a scattering of mattresses and blankets. They clung to one another, their wide eyes aimed at Juliette.

The confusion was overwhelming. She was seized by the sensation of wrongness. Where were the others? The adults? She could feel people with bad intentions sliding down the dark hallway behind her, ready to pounce. Here were their kids, locked away for safety. Soon, the mother rats would be back to punish her for disturbing their nest.

'Where are the others?' she asked, her hand trembling from the cold, the confusion, the fear. She scanned the room and saw that the boy standing, the one who had attacked her, was the oldest. A girl in her teens sat frozen on the tangle of blankets, two young boys and a young girl clinging to her.

The eldest boy glanced down at his leg. A stain of blood was spreading across his green overalls.

'How many are there?' She took a step closer. These kids were obviously more afraid of her than she was of them.

'Leave us alone!' the older girl screamed. She clutched something to her chest. The young girl beside her pressed her face into the older girl's lap, trying to disappear. The two young boys glared like cornered dogs, but didn't move.

'How did you get here?' she asked them. She aimed the knife at the tall boy, but started to feel silly for wielding it. He looked at her in confusion, not comprehending the question, and Juliette knew. Of course. How would there be decades of fighting in this silo without that second human passion?

'You were born down here, weren't you?'

Nobody answered. The boy's face screwed up in confusion, as if the question were mad. She peeked back over her shoulder.

'Where are your parents? When will they be back? How long?'

'Never!' the girl screeched, her head straining forward from the effort. 'They're dead!' Her mouth remained open, her chin trembling. The tendons stood out on her young neck.

The older boy turned and glared at the girl, seemed to want her to remain quiet. Juliette was still trying to comprehend that these were mere kids. She knew they couldn't be alone. Someone had attacked Solo.

As if to answer, her eyes were drawn to the wrench on the decking. It was Solo's wrench. The rust stains were distinctive. How was that possible? Solo had said . . .

And Juliette remembered what he'd said. She realised these kids, this young man, was the same age that he still saw himself. The same age he'd been when he'd been left alone. Had the last survivors of the down deep perished in recent years, but not before leaving something behind?

'What's your name?' Juliette asked the boy. She lowered her knife and showed him her other palm. 'My name's Juliette,' she said. She wanted to add that she came from another silo, a saner world, but didn't want to confuse or freak them out.

'Rickson,' the boy snarled. He puffed out his chest. 'My father was Rick the plumber.'

'Rick the plumber.' Juliette nodded. She saw along one wall, at the end of a tall dune of supplies and scavenges, the gear bag they'd stolen. Her change of clothes spilled out the gaping mouth of the bag. Her towel would be in there. She slid towards the bag, an eye on the kids huddled together on the makeshift bed, the group nest, wary of the older boy.

'Well, Rickson, I want you to gather your things.' Kneeling by her bag, she dug inside and searched for the towel. She found it, pulled it out and rubbed it over her damp hair, an indescribable luxury. There was no way she was leaving them here, these kids. She turned to face the other children, the towel draped across the back of her neck, their eyes all locked on hers.

'Go ahead,' she said. 'Get your things together. You're not going to live like this—'

'Just leave us,' the older girl said. The two boys had moved off the bed, though, and were going through piles of things. They looked to the girl, then to Juliette, unsure.

'Go back to where you're from,' Rickson said. The two eldest children seemed to be gaining strength from each other. 'Take your noisy machines and go.'

That's what this was about. Juliette remembered the sight of the compressor on its side, more heavily attacked maybe than Solo had been. She nodded to the two smaller boys, had their ages pegged for ten or eleven. 'Go on,' she told them. 'You're gonna help me and my friend get home. We have good food there. Real electricity. Hot water. Get your things—'

The youngest girl cried out at this, a horrible peal, the same cry Juliette had heard from the dark hallway. Rickson paced back and forth, eyeing her and the wrench on the floor. Juliette slid away from him and towards the bed to comfort the young girl, when she realised it wasn't her squealing.

Something moved in the older girl's arms.

Juliette froze at the edge of the bed.

'No,' she whispered.

Rickson took a step towards her.

'Stay!' She aimed the point of the knife at him. He glanced down at the wound on his leg, thought better of it. The two boys froze in the act of stuffing their bags. Nothing in the room moved save the baby squealing and fidgeting in the girl's arms.

'Is that a child?'

The girl turned her shoulders. It was a motherly gesture, but the girl couldn't be more than fifteen. Juliette didn't know that was possible. She wondered if that was why the implants went in so early. Her hand slid towards her hip almost as if to touch the place, to rub the bump beneath her skin.

'Just go,' the teenager whimpered. 'We've been fine without you.'

Juliette put down the knife. It felt strange to relinquish it but more wrong to have it in her hand as she approached the bed. 'I can help you,' she said. She turned and made sure the boy heard her. 'I used to work in a place that cared for newborns. Let me . . .' She reached out her hands. The girl turned further towards the wall, shielding the child from her.

'Okay.' Juliette held up her hands, showed her palms. 'But you're not going to live like this any more.' She nodded to the young boys, turned to Rickson, who hadn't moved. 'None of you are. This isn't how anyone should have to live their days, not even their last ones.'

She nodded to herself, her mind made up. 'Rickson? Get your things together. Only the necessities. We'll come back for anything else.' She dipped her chin at the younger boys, saw how their overalls had been chopped at the knees, their legs covered in grime from the farms. They took it as permission to return to packing. These two seemed eager to have someone else in charge, maybe anybody other than their brother, if that's who he was.

'Tell me your name.' Juliette sat down on the bed with the two girls while the others rummaged through their things. She fought to remain calm, not to succumb to the nausea of kids having kids.

The baby let out a hungry cry.

'I'm here to help you,' Juliette told the girl. 'Can I see? Is it a girl or a boy?'

The young mother relaxed her arms. A blanket was folded away, revealing the squinting eyes and pursed red lips of a baby no more than a few months old. A tiny arm waved at its mother.

'Girl,' she said softly.

The younger girl clinging to her side peeked around the mother's ribs at Juliette.

'Have you given her a name?'

She shook her head. 'Not yet.'

Rickson said something behind her to the two boys, trying to get them not to fight over something.

'My name's Elise,' the younger girl said, her head emerging from behind the other girl's side. Elise pointed at her mouth. 'I have a loose tooth.'

Juliette laughed. 'I can help you with that if you like.' She took a chance and reached out to squeeze the young girl's arm. Flashes of her childhood in her father's nursery flooded back, the memories of worried parents, of precious children, of all the hopes and dreams created and dashed around that lottery. Juliette's thoughts swerved to her brother, the one who was not meant to be, and she felt the tears well up in her eyes. What had these kids been through? Solo at least had normal experiences from before. He knew what it meant to live in a world where one could be safe. What had these five kids, six, grown up in? Seen? She felt such intense pity for them. Pity that verged on the sick, wrong, sad desire for none of them to have ever been born . . . which was just as soon washed over with a wave of guilt for even considering it.

'We're going to get you out of here,' she told the two girls. 'Gather your things.'

One of the young boys came over and dropped her bag nearby. He was putting things back into it, apologising to her, when Juliette heard another strange squeak.

What now?

She dabbed her mouth on the towel, watching as the girls reluctantly did an adult's bidding, finding their things and eyeing one another to make sure this was okay. Juliette heard a rustling in her gear bag. She used the handle to separate the zippered mouth, wary of what could be living in the rat's nest these kids had created, when she heard a tiny voice.

Calling her name.

She dropped the towel and clawed through the bag, past tools and bottles of water, under her spare overalls and loose socks, until she found the radio. She wondered how Solo could possibly be calling her. The other set had been ruined in her suit—

'—please say something,' the radio hissed. 'Juliette, are you there? It's Walker. Please, for God's sake, answer me—'

• Silo 18 •

'What happened? Why aren't they responding?' Courtnee looked from Walker to Shirly, as if either of them could know.

'Is it broken?' Shirly picked up the small dial with the painted marks and tried to tell if it had accidentally moved. 'Walk, did we break it?'

'No, it's still on,' he said. He held the headphones up by his cheek, his eyes drifting over the various components.

'Guys, I don't know how much longer we have.' Courtnee was watching the scene in the generator room through the observation window. Shirly stood up and peered out over the control panel towards the main entrance. Jenkins and some of his men were inside, rifles pinned against their shoulders, yelling at the others. The soundproofing made it impossible to hear what was going on.

'Hello?' A voice crackled from Walker's hands. The words seemed to tumble through his fingers.

'Who's there?' he called, flicking the switch. 'Who is this?'

Shirly rushed to Walker's side. She wrapped her hands around his arm, disbelieving. 'Juliette!' she screamed.

Walker held up his hand, tried to quieten her and Courtnee both. His hands were trembling as he fumbled with the detonator and finally clicked the red switch.

'Jules?' His old voice cracked. Shirly squeezed his arm. 'Is that you?'

There was a pause, and then a cry from the speakers, a sob. 'Walk? Walk, is that you? What's going on? Where are you? I thought . . .'

'Where is she?' Shirly whispered.

Courtnee watched them both, her cheeks in her palms, mouth open.

Walker hit the switch. 'Jules, where are you?'

A deep sigh hissed through the tiny speakers. Her voice was tiny and far away. 'Walk, I'm in *another silo*. There's more of them. You wouldn't believe . . .'

Her voice drifted off to static. Shirly leaned against Walker while Courtnee paced in front of them, looking from the radio to the window.

'We know about the others,' Walker said, holding the mic below his beard. 'We can hear them, Jules. *All* of them.'

He let go of the switch. Juliette's voice returned.

'How are you – Mechanical? I heard about the fighting. Are you in the middle of that?' Before she signed off, Juliette said something to someone else, her voice barely audible.

Walker raised his eyebrows at the mention of the fighting.

'How would she have heard?' Shirly asked.

'I wish she were here,' Courtnee said. 'Jules would know what to do.'

'Tell her about the exhaust. About the plan.' Shirly waved for the microphone. 'Here, let me.'

Walker nodded. He handed Shirly the headset and the detonator.

Shirly worked the switch. It was stiffer than she thought it'd be. 'Jules? Can you hear me? It's Shirly.'

'Shirly . . .' Juliette's voice wavered. 'Hey, you. You hanging in there?'

The emotion in her friend's voice brought tears to Shirly's eyes. 'Yeah—' She bobbed her head and swallowed. 'Hey, listen, some of the others are routing the exhaust feed to IT's cooling vents. But remember that time we lost back pressure? I'm worried the motor might—'

'No.' Juliette cut her off. 'You have to stop them. Shirly, can you hear me? You have to stop them. It won't do anything. The cooling is for the *servers*. The only people up there who—' She cleared her throat. 'Listen to me. Make them stop—'

Shirly fumbled with the red switch. Walker reached over as if to help, but she finally got the device under control. 'Wait,' she transmitted. 'How do you know where the vents lead?'

'I just do. This place is laid out the same. Goddammit, let me talk to them. You can't let them—'

Shirly hit the switch again. There was a blast of sound from the generator room as Courtnee threw open the door and ran outside. 'Courtnee's going,' she said. 'She's going right now. Jules – how did you . . . ? Who are you with? Can they help us? It's not looking good over here.'

The tiny speakers crackled again. Shirly could hear Juliette take a deep breath, could hear other voices in the background, heard her give commands or orders to some other person. Shirly thought her friend sounded exhausted. Weary. Sad.

'There's nothing I can do,' Juliette said. 'There's no one here. One man. Some kids. Everyone's gone. The people who lived here, they couldn't even help themselves.' The line went silent, and then she clicked through again. 'You have to stop the fighting,' she said. 'Whatever it takes. Please . . . don't let it be because of me. Please stop—'

The door opened again, Courtnee returning. Shirly heard shouts in the generator room. Gunfire.

'What is that?' Juliette asked. 'Where are you guys?'

'In the control room.' Shirly looked up at Courtnee, whose eyes were wide with fear. 'Jules, I don't think we have much time. I—' There was so much she wanted to say. She wanted to tell her about Marck. She needed more time. 'They're coming for us,' was all she could think to relate. 'I'm glad you're okay.'

The radio crackled. 'Oh God, make them stop. No more fighting! Shirly, listen to me—'

'It doesn't matter,' Shirly said, holding the button and wiping her cheeks. 'They won't stop.' The gunfire was getting closer, the pops audible through the thick door. Her people were dying while she cowered in the control room, talking to a ghost. Her people were dying.

'You take care of yourself,' Shirly said.

'Wait!'

Shirly handed the headset to Walker. She joined Courtnee by the window and watched the crush of people cower on the other side of the generator, the flash and shudder of barrels leaning against the railing, someone in the blue of Mechanical lying still on the ground. More faded pops. More distant and muted rattles.

'Jules!' Walker fumbled with the radio. He shouted her name, was still trying to talk to her.

'Let me talk to them!' Juliette yelled, her voice impossibly far away. 'Walk, why can I hear you and not them? I need to talk to the deputies, to Peter and Hank. Walk, how did you call me? I need to talk to them!'

Walker blubbered about soldering irons, about his magnifiers. The old man was crying, cradling his boards and wires and electrics as if they were a broken child, whispering to them and rocking back and forth, saltwater dripping dangerously onto this thing he'd built.

He babbled to Juliette while more men in blue fell, arms draped over railings, inadequate rifles dropping noiselessly to the ground. The men they had lived in terror of for a month were inside. It was over. Shirly groped for Courtnee, their arms entangling, while they watched, helpless. Behind them, the sobs and mad ravings of old Walk mixed with the jitter of deadened gunfire, a popping noise like the grumble of a machine losing its balance, sliding out of control . . .

Lukas teetered on the upturned trash can, the toes of his boots denting the soft plastic, feeling as if it could go flying out from under him or collapse under his weight at any moment. He steadied himself by holding the top of server twelve, the thick layer of dust up there telling him it had been years since anyone had been to clean with a ladder and a rag. He pressed his nose up to the air-conditioning vent and took another whiff.

The nearby door beeped, the locks clanking as they withdrew into the jamb. With a soft squeal, the massive hinges budged and the heavy door swung inward.

Lukas nearly lost his grip on the dusty server top as Bernard pushed his way inside. The head of IT looked up at him quizzically.

'You'll never fit,' Bernard said. He laughed as he turned to push the door shut. The locking pins clunked, the panel beeped, and a red light resumed its watch over the room.

Lukas pushed away from the dusty server and leaped from the trash can, the plastic bucket flipping over and scooting across the floor. He wiped his hands together, brushed them on the seat of his pants, and forced a laugh.

'I thought I smelled something,' he explained. 'Does it look smoky in here to you?'

Bernard squinted at the air. 'It always seems hazy in here to me. And I don't smell anything. Just hot servers.' He reached into his breast pocket and brought out a few folded pieces of paper. 'Here. Letters from your mother. I told her to porter them to me and I'd pass them along.'

Lukas smiled, embarrassed, and accepted them. 'I still think you should ask about . . .' He glanced up at the air-conditioning vent and realised there was no one in Mechanical to ask. The last that he'd heard from the radio below was that Sims and the others were mopping up. Dozens were dead. Three to four times that many were in custody. Apartment wings were being prepped in the mids to hold them all. It sounded like there would be enough people to clean for years.

'I'll have one of the replacement mechanics look into it,' Bernard promised. 'Which reminds me, I'd like to go over some of that with you. There's going to be a massive shift from green to blue as we push farmers into Mechanical. I was wondering what you'd think of Sammi heading up the entire division down there.'

Lukas nodded as he skimmed one of the letters from his mother. 'Sammi as head of Mechanical? I think he's overqualified but perfect. I've learned a lot from him.' He glanced up as Bernard opened the filing cabinet by the door and flipped through work orders. 'He's a great teacher, but would it be permanent?'

'Nothing's permanent.' Bernard found what he was looking for and tucked it into his breast pocket. 'You need anything else?' He pressed his glasses up his nose. Lukas thought he looked older from the past month. Older and worn down. 'Dinner'll be sent over in a few hours . . .'

Lukas did have something he wanted. He wanted to say that he was ready, that he had sufficiently absorbed the horror of his future job, had learned what he needed without going insane. And now could he please go home?

But that wasn't the way out of there. Lukas had sorted this out for himself.

'Well,' he said. 'I wouldn't mind some more reading material—'

The things he had discovered in server eighteen burned in his brain. He feared Bernard would be able to read them there. Lukas thought he knew, but he needed to ask for that folder in order to be sure.

Bernard smiled. 'Don't you have enough to read?'

Lukas fanned the letters from his mother. 'These? They'll keep me busy for the walk to the *ladder*—'

'I meant what you have below. The Order. Your studies.' Bernard tilted his head.

Lukas let out a sigh. 'Yeah, I do, but I can't be expected to read that twelve hours a day. I'm talking about something less dense.' He shook his head. 'Hey, forget it. If you can't—'

'What do you need?' Bernard said. 'I'm just giving you a hard time.' He leaned against the filing cabinet and interlocked his fingers across his belly. He peered at Lukas through the bottom of his glasses.

'Well, this might sound weird, but it's this case. An *old* case. The server says it's filed away in your office with all the closed investigations—'

'An *investigation?*' Bernard's voice rose quizzically.

Lukas nodded. 'Yeah. A friend of a friend thing. I'm just curious how it was resolved. There aren't any digital copies on the serv—'

'This isn't about Holston, is it?'

'*Who?* Oh, the old sheriff? No, no. Why?'

Bernard waved his hand to dismiss the thought.

'The file is under Wilkins,' Lukas said, watching Bernard closely. 'George Wilkins.'

Bernard's face hardened. His moustache dropped down over his lips like a lowered curtain.

Lukas cleared his throat. What he'd seen on Bernard's face was nearly enough. 'George died a few years ago down in Mech—' he started to say.

'I know how he died.' Bernard dipped his chin. 'Why would you want to see that file?'

'Just curious. I have a friend who—'

'What's this friend's name?' Bernard's small hands slid off his belly and he tucked them into his overalls. He moved away from the filing cabinet and took a step closer.

'What?'

'This friend, was he involved with George in any way? How close a friend was he?'

'No. Not that I know of. Look, if it's a big deal, don't worry about—' Lukas wanted simply to ask, to ask why he'd done it. But Bernard seemed intent on telling him with no prompting at all.

'It's a very big deal,' Bernard said. 'George Wilkins was a dangerous man. A man of *ideas*. The kind we catch in whispers, the kind who poisons the people around him—'

'What? What do you mean?'

'Section thirteen of the Order. Study it. All insurrections would start *right there* if we let them, start with men like him.'

Bernard's chin had lowered to his chest, his eyes peering over the rims of his glasses, the truth coming freely without all the deceit Lukas had planned.

Lukas never needed that folder; he had found the travel logs that coincided with George's death, the dozens of wires asking Holston to wrap things up. There was no shame in Bernard. George Wilkins hadn't died; he'd been murdered. And Bernard was willing to tell him why.

'What did he do?' Lukas asked quietly.

'I'll tell you what he did. He was a mechanic, a greaser. We started hearing chatter from the porters about these plans circulating, ideas for expanding the mine, doing a lateral dig. As you know, lateral digs are forbidden—'

'Yeah, obviously.' Lukas had a mental image of miners from silo eighteen pushing through and meeting miners from silo nineteen. It would be awkward, to say the least.

'A long chat with the old head of Mechanical put an end to that nonsense, and then George Wilkins came up with the idea of expanding *downward*. He and some others drew up schematics for a level one-fifty. And then a level one-sixty.'

'*Sixteen* more levels?'

'To begin with. That was the talk, anyway. Just whispers and sketches. But some of these whispers landed in a porter's ear, and then *ours* perked up.'

'So you killed him?'

'Someone did, yes. It doesn't matter who.' Bernard adjusted his glasses with one hand. The other stayed in the belly of his overalls. 'You'll have to do these things one day, son. You know that, don't you?'

'Yeah, but—'

'No buts.' Bernard shook his head slowly. 'Some men are like a virus. Unless you want to see a plague break out, you inoculate the silo against them. You remove them.'

Lukas remained silent.

'We've removed fourteen threats this year, Lukas. Do you have any idea what the average life expectancy would be if we weren't proactive about these things?'

'But the cleanings—'

'Useful for dealing with the people who want *out*. Who dream of a better world. This uprising we're having right now is full of people like that, but it's just one sort of sickness we deal with. The cleaning is one sort of cure. I'm not sure if someone with a different illness would even clean if we sent them out there. They have to want to *see* what we show them for it to work.'

This reminded Lukas of what he'd learned of the helmets, the visors. He had assumed this was the only kind of sickness there was. He was beginning to wish he'd read more of the Order and less of the Legacy.

'You've heard this latest outbreak on the radio. All of this could have been prevented if we'd caught the sickness earlier. Tell me that wouldn't have been better.'

Lukas looked down at his boots. The trash can lay nearby, on its side. It looked sad like that. No longer useful for holding things.

'Ideas are contagious, Lukas. This is basic Order material. You know this stuff.'

He nodded. He thought of Juliette, wondered why she hadn't called in what felt like for ever. She was one of these viruses Bernard was talking about, her words creeping in his mind and infecting him with outlandish dreams. He felt his entire body flush with heat as he realised he'd caught some of it too. He wanted to touch his breast pocket, feel the lumps of her personal effects there, the watch, the ring, the ID. He had taken them to remember her in death, but they had become even more precious knowing that she was still alive.

'This uprising hasn't been nearly as bad as the last one,' Bernard told him. 'And even after *that* one, things were eventually smoothed over, the damage welded back together, the people made to forget. The same thing will happen here. Are we clear?'

'Yessir.'

'Excellent. Now, was that all you wished to know from this folder?'

Lukas nodded.

'Good. It sounds like you need to be reading something else, anyway.' His moustache twitched with half a smile. Bernard turned to go.

'It was you, wasn't it?'

Bernard stopped, but didn't turn to face him.

'Who killed George Wilkins. It was you, right?'

'Does it matter?'

'Yeah. It matters to . . . to me . . . It means—'

'Or to your *friend*?' Bernard turned to face him. Lukas felt the temperature in the room go up yet another notch.

'Are you having second thoughts, son? About this job? Was I wrong about you? Because I've been wrong before.'

Lukas swallowed. 'I just want to know if it's something I'd ever have to . . . I mean, since I'm shadowing for . . .'

Bernard took a few steps towards him. Lukas felt himself back up half a step in response.

'I didn't think I was wrong about you. But I was, wasn't I?' Bernard shook his head. He looked disgusted. 'Goddammit,' he spat.

'Nossir. You weren't. I think I've just been in here too long.' Lukas brushed his hair off his forehead. His scalp was itchy. He needed to use the bathroom. 'Maybe I just need some air, you know? Go home for a while? Sleep in my bed. What's it been, a month? How long do I need—?'

'You want out of here?'

Lukas nodded.

Bernard peered down at his boots and seemed to consider this a while. When he looked up, there was sadness in his face, in the droop of his moustache, across the wet film of his eyes.

'Is that what you want? To get out of here?'

He adjusted his hands inside his overalls.

'Yessir.' Lukas nodded.

'Say it.'

'I want out of here.' Lukas glanced at the heavy steel door behind Bernard. 'Please. I want you to let me out.'

'Out.'

Lukas bobbed his head, exasperated, sweat tickling his cheek as it followed the line of his jaw. He was suddenly very afraid of this man, this man who all of a sudden reminded him even more of his father.

'Please,' Lukas said. 'It's just . . . I'm starting to feel cooped up. Please let me out.'

Bernard nodded. His cheeks twitched. He looked as if he were about to cry. Lukas had never seen this expression on the man's face.

'Sheriff Billings, are you there?'

His small hand emerged from his overalls and raised the radio to his sad, quivering moustache.

Peter's voice crackled back. 'I'm here, sir.'

Bernard clicked the transmitter. 'You heard the man,' he said, tears welling up in his eyes. 'Lukas Kyle, IT engineer first class, says he wants *out* . . .'

• Silo 17 •

'Hello? Walk? Shirly?'

Juliette shouted into the radio, the orphans and Solo watching her from several steps below. She had hurried the kids through the farms, made hasty introductions, checking the radio all the while. Several levels had gone by, the others trudging up behind her, and still no word from them, nothing since she'd been cut off, the sound of gunfire sprinkled among Walker's words. She kept thinking if she just got higher, if she tried one more time. She checked the light by the power knob and made sure the battery wasn't dead, turned the volume up until she could hear the static, knew that the thing was working.

She clicked the button. The static fell silent, the radio waiting for her to speak. 'Please say something, guys. This is Juliette. Can you hear me? Say anything.'

She looked to Solo, who was being supported by the very man who had dazed him. 'We need to go higher, I think. C'mon. Double-time.'

There were groans; these poor refugees of silo seventeen acted like she was the one who'd lost her mind. But they stomped up the stairs after her, their pace dictated by Solo, who had seemed to rally with some fruit and water but had slowed as the levels wore on.

'Where are these friends of yours we talked to?' Rickson asked. 'Can they come help?' He grunted as Solo lurched to one side. 'He's heavy.'

'They aren't coming to help us,' Juliette said. 'There's no getting from there to here.' *Or vice versa*, she told herself.

Her stomach lurched with worry. She needed to get to IT and call Lukas, find out what was going on. She needed to tell him how horribly awry her plans had gone, how she was failing at every turn. There was no going back, she realised. No saving her friends. No saving this silo. She glanced back over her shoulder. Her life was now going to be one of a mother to these orphaned children, kids who had survived merely because the people who had been left, who had been committing the violence on each other, didn't have the stomach to kill them. Or the *heart*, she thought.

And now it would fall to her. And to Solo, but to a lesser degree. He would probably be just one more child for her to attend to.

They made their gradual way up another flight, Solo seeming to regain his senses a little, progress being made. But still a long way to go.

They stopped in the mids for bathroom breaks, filling more empty toilets that wouldn't flush. Juliette helped the young ones. They didn't like going like this, preferred to do it in the dirt. She told them that was right, that they only did this when they were on the move. She didn't tell them about the years Solo had spent destroying entire levels of apartments. She didn't tell them about the clouds of flies she'd seen.

The last of their food was consumed, but they had plenty of water. Juliette wanted to get to the hydroponics on fifty-six before they stopped for the night. There was enough food and water there for the rest of the trip. She tried the radio repeatedly, aware that she was running down the battery. There was no reply. She didn't understand how she'd heard them to begin with; all the silos must use something different, some way of not hearing each other. It had to be Walker, something he'd engineered. When she got back to IT, would she be able to figure it out? Would she be able to contact him or Shirly? She wasn't sure, and Lukas had no way of talking to Mechanical from where he was, no way of patching her through. She'd asked a dozen times.

Lukas . . .

And Juliette *remembered*.

The radio in Solo's hovel. What had Lukas said one night? They were talking late and he'd said he wished they could chat from down below where it was more comfortable. Wasn't that where he was getting his updates about the uprising? It was over the radio. Just like the one in Solo's place, beneath the servers, locked behind that steel cage for which he'd never found the key.

Juliette turned and faced the group; they stopped climbing and gripped the rails, stared up at her. Helena, the young mother who didn't even know her own age, tried to comfort her baby as it began to squeal. The nameless infant preferred the sway of the climb.

'I need to go up,' she told them. She looked to Solo. 'How're you feeling?'

'Me? I'm fine.'

He didn't look fine.

'Can you get them up?' She nodded to Rickson. 'Are you okay?'

The boy dipped his chin. His resistance had seemed to crumble during the climb, especially during the bathroom break. The younger children, meanwhile, had been nothing but excited to see new parts of the silo, to feel that they could raise their voices without terrible things happening to them. They were coming to grips with there being only two adults left, and neither seemed all that bad.

'There's food on fifty-six,' she said.

'Numbers—' Rickson shook his head. 'I don't—'

Of course. Why would he need to count numbers he'd never live to see, and in more ways than one?

'Solo will show you where,' she told him. 'We've stayed there before. Good food. Canned stuff as well. Solo?' She waited until he looked up at her, the glazed expression partly melting away. 'I have to get back to your place. I have people I need to call, okay? My friends. I need to find out if they're okay.'

He nodded.

'You guys will be fine?' She hated to leave them but needed to. 'I'll try to make it back down to you tomorrow. Take your time getting all the way up, okay? No need to rush home.'

Home. Was she already resigned to that?

There were nods in the group. One of the young boys pulled

a water bottle out of the other's bag and unscrewed the cap. Juliette turned and began taking the stairs two at a time, her legs begging her not to.

Juliette was in the forties when it occurred to her that she might not make it. The sweat she'd worked up was chilling her skin; her legs were beyond the ache, beyond the pain: they were numb with fatigue. She found her arms doing a lot of the work as she lunged ahead, gripped the railing with clammy hands and hauled herself up another two steps.

Her breathing was ragged; it had been for half a dozen levels. She wondered if she'd done damage to her lungs from the underwater ordeal. Was that even possible? Her father would know. She thought of spending the rest of her life without a doctor, of teeth as yellow as Solo's, of caring for a growing child and the challenge of seeing that more weren't made, not until the children were older.

At the next landing, she again touched her hip where her birth control rode under her skin. Such things made more sense in light of silo seventeen. So *much* about her previous life made sense. Things that had once seemed twisted now had a sort of pattern, a logic about them. The expense of sending a wire, the spacing of the levels, the single and cramped stairway, the bright colours for particular jobs, dividing the silo into sections, breeding mistrust . . . it was all designed. She'd seen hints of this before, but never knew why. Now this empty silo told her, the presence of these kids told her. It turned out that some crooked things looked even worse when straightened. Some tangled knots only made sense once unravelled.

Her mind wandered while she climbed, wandered in order to avoid the aches in her muscles, to escape the day's ordeals. When she finally hit the thirties it gave her, if not an end to the suffering, a renewed focus. She stopped trying the portable radio as often. The static never changed, and she had a different idea for contacting Walker, something she should have pieced together sooner, a way to bypass the servers and communicate with other silos. It was there all along, staring her and Solo in the face. There was a small sliver of doubt that she might be wrong, but why else lock up a radio that was already locked up two other ways? It only made sense if that device was supremely dangerous. Which is what she hoped it would be.

She stomped up to thirty-five dead on her feet. Her body had never been pushed this hard, not even while plumbing the small pump, not during her trek through the outside. Will alone helped her lift each foot, plant it, straighten her leg, pull with her arm, lunge forward for another grab. One step at a time now. Her toe banged on the next step: she could barely lift her boot high enough. The green emergency lights gave her no sense of the passing of time, no idea if night had come, when morning would be. She desperately missed her watch. All she had these days was her knife. She laughed at the switch, at having gone from counting the seconds in her life to fending for each and every one of them.

Thirty-four. It was tempting to collapse to the steel grating, to sleep, to curl up like her first night in that place, just thankful to be alive. Instead, she pulled the door open, amazed at the effort this required, and stepped back into civilisation. Light. Power. Heat.

She staggered down the hallway with her vision so constricted it was as if she could only see through a straw at her centre, everything else out of focus and spinning.

Her shoulder brushed the wall. Walking required effort. All she wanted was to call Lukas, to hear his voice. She imagined falling asleep behind that server, warm air blowing over her from its fans, the headphones tight against her ears. He could murmur to her about the faraway stars while she slept for days and days . . .

But Lukas would wait. Lukas was locked up and safe. She had all the time in the world to call him.

She turned instead into the Suit Lab, shuffled towards the tool wall, didn't dare look at her cot. A glance at her cot, and she'd wake up the next day. Whatever day that was.

Grabbing the bolt cutters, she was about to leave, but went back for the small sledge as well. The tools were heavy, but they felt good in her hands, one tool in each, pulling down on her arms, stretching her muscles and grounding her, keeping her stable.

At the end of the hall, she pressed her shoulder against the heavy door to the server room. She leaned until it squeaked open.

Just a crack. Just wide enough for her. Juliette hurried as much as her numb muscles would allow towards the ladder.

Shuffling. Fast as she could go.

The grate was in place; she tugged it out of the way and dropped the tools down. Big noise. She didn't care – they couldn't break. Down she went, hands slick, chin catching a rung, floor coming up faster than she'd anticipated.

Juliette sank to the floor, sprawled out, shin banging the sledge. It took a force of will, an act of God, to get up. But she did.

Down the hall and past the small desk. There was a steel cage there, a radio, a big one. She remembered her days as sheriff. They had a radio just like it in her office, used it to call Marnes when he was on patrol, to call Hank and Deputy Marsh. But this one was different.

She set the sledge down and pinched the jaws of the cutter on one of the hinges. Squeezing was too hard. Her arms shook. They trembled.

Juliette adjusted herself, put one of the handles against her neck, cradled it with her collarbone and shoulder. She grabbed the other handle with both hands and pulled towards herself, hugging the cutters. Squeezing. She felt them move.

There was a loud crack, the twang of splitting steel. She moved to the other hinge and did it again. Her collarbone hurt where the handle dug in, felt like it might be the thing to crack, not the hinge.

Another violent burst of metal.

Juliette grabbed the steel cage and pulled. The hinges came away from the mounting plate. She tore hungrily at the box, trying to get to the prize inside, thinking of Walker and all her family, all her friends, the sound of people screaming in the background. She had to get them to stop fighting. Get everyone to stop fighting.

Once she had enough gap between the bent steel and the wall, she wrapped her fingers around this and tugged, bending the protective cage on its front edge, tilting the box away from the wall, the shelf, revealing the entire radio unit beneath. Who needed keys? Screw the keys. She wrenched the cage flat, then bent her weight on it, making a new hinge of its front, warping it out of the way.

The dial on the front seemed familiar. She turned it to power the unit on and found that it clicked instead of spinning. Juliette knelt down, panting and exhausted, sweat running down her neck. There was another switch for power; she turned this one instead, static rising in the speakers, a buzz filling the room.

The other knob. This was what she wanted, what she expected to find. She thought it might be patch cables like the back of the server, or dip switches like a pump control, but it was tiny numbers arranged around the edge of a knob. Juliette smiled, exhausted, and turned the pointer to '18'. Home. She grabbed the mic and squeezed the button.

'Walker? Are you there?'

Juliette slumped down to the ground and rested her back against the desk. With her eyes shut, mic by her face, she could imagine going to sleep like that. She saw what Lukas meant. This was comfortable.

She squeezed again. 'Walk? Shirly? Please answer me.'

The radio crackled to life.

Juliette opened her eyes. She stared up at the unit, her hands trembling.

A voice: 'Is this who I think it is?'

The voice was too high to be Walker. She knew this voice. Where did she know it from? She was tired and confused. She squeezed the button on the mic.

'This is Juliette. Who is this?'

Was it Hank? She thought it might be Hank. He had a radio. Maybe she had the wrong silo completely. Maybe she'd screwed up.

'I need radio silence,' the voice demanded. 'All of them off. Now.'

Was this directed at her? Juliette's mind spun in circles. A handful of voices chimed in, one after the other. There were pops of static. Was she supposed to say something? She was confused.

'You shouldn't be transmitting on this frequency,' the voice said. 'You should be put to cleaning for such things.'

Juliette's hand fell to her lap. She slumped against the wooden desk, dejected. She recognised the voice.

Bernard.

For weeks, she had been hoping to speak to this man, had been silently begging for him to answer. But not now. Now, she had nothing to say. She wanted to talk to her friends, to make things okay.

She squeezed the radio.

'No more fighting,' she said. All the will was drained from her. All desire for vengeance. She just wanted the world to quieten itself, for people to live and grow old and feed the roots one day—

'Speaking of cleanings,' the voice squeaked. 'Tomorrow will be the first of many more to come. Your friends are lined up and ready to go. And I believe you know the lucky one who's going first.'

There was a click, followed by the hiss and crinkle of static. Juliette didn't move. She felt dead. Numb. The will was drained from her body.

'Imagine my surprise,' the voice said. 'Imagine when I found out a decent man, a man I trusted, had been poisoned by you.'

She clicked the microphone with her fist but didn't raise it to her mouth. She simply raised her voice instead.

'You'll burn in hell,' she told him.

'Undoubtedly,' Bernard said. 'Until then, I'm holding some things in my hand that I think belong to you. An ID with your picture on it, a pretty little bracelet, and this wedding ring that doesn't look official at all. I wonder about that . . .'

Juliette groaned. She couldn't feel any part of her body. She could barely hear her thoughts. She managed to squeeze the mic, but it required every ounce of effort that she had left.

'What are you going on about, you twisted fuck?'

She spat the last, her head drifting to the side, her body craving sleep.

'I'm talking about Lukas, who betrayed me. We found some of your things on him just now. Exactly how long has he been talking to you? Well before the servers, right? Well, guess what? I'm sending him your way. And I finally figured out what you did last time, what those idiots in Supply helped you do, and I want you to be assured, be very assured, that your friend won't have the same help. I'm going to build his suit personally. Me. I'll stay up all night if I have to. So when he goes out in the morning, I can be sure that he gets nowhere *near* those blasted hills.'

A group of kids thundered down the staircase as Lukas was escorted to his death. One of them squealed in delighted horror as if being chased. They spiralled closer, coming into view, and Lukas and Peter had to squeeze to one side to let them pass.

Peter played the sheriff role and yelled at the kids to slow down, to be careful. They giggled and continued their mad descent. School was out for the day; no more listening to adults.

While Lukas was pressed against the outer railing, he took a moment to consider the temptation. Freedom was just a jump away. A death of his own choosing, one he had considered in the past when moods turned dark.

Peter pulled him along, hand on his elbow, before Lukas could act. He was left admiring that graceful bar of steel, watching the way it curved and curved, always spinning the same amount, never ending. He pictured it corkscrewing through the earth, could sense its vibrations like some cosmic string, like a single strand of DNA at the silo's core with all of life clinging to it.

Thoughts like these swirled as they gained another level on his death. He watched the welds go by, some of them neater than others. A few were puckered up like scars; several had been polished so smoothly he almost missed them. Each was a signature by its creator: a work of pride here, a rushed job at the end of a long day there, a shadow learning for the first time, a seasoned pro with decades of practice making it look all too easy.

He brushed his shackled hands over the rough paint, the bumps and wrinkles, the missing chips that revealed centuries of layers, of colours that changed with the times or with the supply of dyes or cost of paint. The layers reminded him of the wooden desk he'd stared down at for almost a month. Each little groove marked the passage of time, just as each name scratched into its surface marked a man's mad desire to have *more* of it, to not let that time whisk his poor soul away.

For a long while they marched in silence, a porter passing with a bulky load, a young couple looking guilty. Exiting the server vault had not been the stroll to freedom Lukas had longed for the past weeks. It had been an ambush, a march of shame, faces in doorways, faces on landings, faces on the stairway. Blank, unblinking faces. Faces of friends wondering if he was their enemy.

And maybe he was.

They would say he had broken down and uttered the fateful taboo, but Lukas now knew why people were put out. He was the virus. If he sneezed the wrong words, it would kill everyone he knew. This was the path Juliette had walked and for the same absence of reason. He believed her, always had, always knew she'd done nothing wrong, but now he *really* understood. She was like him in so many ways. Except he would not survive, he knew that. Bernard had told him so.

They were ten levels up from IT when Peter's radio buzzed with chatter. He took his hand off Lukas's elbow to turn up the volume, see if it was for him.

'This is Juliette. Who is this?'

That voice.

Lukas's heart leaped up a little before plummeting a very long way. He fixed his gaze on the railing and listened.

Bernard responded, asked for silence. Peter reached for his radio, turned it down but not off. The voices climbed with them, back and forth. Each step and each word ground down on Lukas, chipped away at him. He studied the railing and again considered *true* freedom.

A grab and a short leap up; a long flight.

He could feel himself going through the motions, bending his knees, throwing his feet over.

The voices in the radio argued. They said forbidden things.

They were sloppy with secrets, thinking other ears couldn't hear.

Lukas watched his death play out over and over. His fate awaited him over that rail. The visual was so powerful, it wrecked his climbing pace, it affected his legs.

He slowed, Peter slowing with him. Each of them began to falter, to waver in the conviction of their climb as they listened to Juliette and Bernard argue. The strength in Lukas drained away, and he decided not to jump.

Both men were having second thoughts.

Juliette woke up on a floor, someone shaking her. A man with a beard. It was Solo, and she was passed out in his room, by his desk.

'We made it,' he said, flashing his yellow teeth. He looked better than she remembered him looking. More alive. She felt as though she were dead.

Dead.

'What time is it?' she asked. 'What day?'

She tried to sit up. Every muscle felt torn in half, disconnected, floating beneath her skin.

Solo went to the computer and turned on the monitor. 'The others are picking out rooms and then going to the upper farms.' He turned to look at her. Juliette rubbed her temples. 'There are *others*,' he said solemnly, like this was still news.

Juliette nodded. There was only one other that she could think of right then. Dreams came back to her, dreams of Lukas, of all her friends in holding cells, a room of suits being prepped for each of them, no care for whether they cleaned or not. It would be a mass slaughter, a symbol to those who remained. She thought of all the bodies outside of *this* silo, silo seventeen. It was easy to imagine what came next.

'Friday,' Solo said, looking at the computer. 'Or Thursday night, depending on how you like it. Two in the morning.' He scratched his beard. 'Felt like we slept longer than that.'

'What day was it yesterday?' She shook her head. That didn't make sense.

'What day did I dive down? With the compressor?' Her brain wasn't working.

Solo looked at her like he was having similar thoughts. 'The dive was Thursday. Today is tomorrow.' He rubbed his head. 'Let's start over . . .'

'No time.' Juliette groaned and tried to stand up. Solo rushed to her and put his hands under her arms, helped lift her. 'Suit Lab,' she said. He nodded. She could tell he was exhausted, maybe half as much as she was, but he was still willing to do anything for her. It made her sad, someone being this loyal to her.

She led him down the narrow passage, and the climb up the ladder brought back a legion of aches. Juliette crawled out to the server-room floor; Solo followed up the ladder and helped her to her feet. They made their way to the Suit Lab together.

'I need all the heat tape we've got,' she told him, prepping him while he escorted her. She staggered through the servers, bumped into one of them. 'It needs to be the kind on the yellow spool, the stuff from Supply. Not the red kind.'

He nodded. 'The good kind. Like we used on the compressor.'

'Right.'

They left the server room and shuffled down the hallway. Juliette could hear the kids shouting excitedly around the bend, the patter of their feet. It was a strange sound, like the echoes of ghosts. But something normal. Something normal had returned to silo seventeen.

In the Suit Lab, she got Solo busy with the tape. He stretched out long strips on one of the workbenches, overlapping the edges, using the torch to cauterise and seal the joints.

'At least an inch of overlap,' she told him, when it looked like he was being shy with the stuff. He nodded. Juliette glanced at her cot and considered collapsing into it. But there was no time. She grabbed the smallest suit in the room, one with a collar she knew might be a tight fit. She remembered the difficult squeeze to get into silo seventeen and didn't want to repeat it.

'I'm not gonna have time to make another switch for the suit, so I won't have a radio.' She went through the cleaning outfit, piece by piece, pulling out the parts engineered to fail and hunting through

her hauls from Supply for a better version of each. Some she'd have
to seal over with the good tape. The suit wouldn't look as neat and
tidy as the one Walker had helped arrange, but it would be a world
away from what Lukas was getting. She grabbed all the parts she'd
spent weeks puzzling over, marvelling at the engineering it took to
make something weaker than it appeared. She tested a gasket from
a pile she wasn't sure about by pinching her fingernails together.
The gasket parted easily. She dug for another.

'How long?' Solo asked, noisily stretching another piece of
tape out. 'You'll be gone a day? A week?'

Juliette looked up from her workbench to the one Solo was
working over. She didn't want to tell him she might not make it.
This was a dark thought she would keep to herself. 'We'll figure
out a way to come for you,' she said. 'First, I have to try and save
someone.' It felt like a lie. She wanted to tell him she might be
gone for good.

'With this?' Solo rustled the blanket of heat tape.

She nodded. 'The doors to my home never open,' she told
him. 'Not unless they are sending someone to clean.'

Solo nodded. 'It was the same here, back when this place was
crazy.'

Juliette looked up at him, puzzled, and saw that he was smiling.
Solo had told a joke. She laughed, even though she didn't feel
like it, and then found that it helped.

'We've got six or seven hours until those doors open,' she told
him. 'And when they do, I want to be there.'

'And then what?' Solo shut down the torch and inspected his
work. He looked up at her.

'Then I want to see how they explain my being alive. I think'
– she changed out a seal and flipped the suit around to get to the
other sleeve – 'I think my friends are fighting on one side of this
fence, and the people who sent me here are fighting on the other.
Everyone else is watching, the vast majority of my people. They are
too scared to take sides, which basically means they've checked out.'

She paused while she used one of the small extractors to
remove the seal that linked the wrist to the glove. Once she had
it out, she reached for a good one.

'You think this will change that? Saving your friend?'

Juliette looked up and studied Solo, who was almost done with the tape.

'Saving my friend is all about saving my friend,' she said. 'What I think will happen, when all those people on that fence see that a cleaner has come home, I think it'll make them come down on the right side of things, and with that much support, the guns and the fighting are meaningless.'

Solo nodded. He began to fold up the blanket without even being asked. This bit of initiative, of knowing what needed to happen next, filled Juliette with hope. Maybe he needed these kids, needed someone to take care of. He seemed to have aged a dozen years already.

'I'll come back for you and the others,' she told him.

He dipped his head, kept his eyes on her a while, his brain seeming to whir. He came to her workbench and set the neatly folded blanket down, patted it twice. A quick smile flashed in his beard, and then he had to turn away, had to scratch his cheek as if he had an itch there.

He was still a teenager like that, Juliette saw. Still ashamed to cry.

Nearly four of Lukas's final hours were burned hiking the heavy gear up to level three. The kids had helped, but she made them stop one level down, worried about the air up top. Solo assisted her in suiting up for the second time in as many days. He studied her sombrely.

'You're sure about this?'

She nodded and accepted the blanket of heat tape. Rickson could be heard a level below, commanding one of the boys to settle down.

'Try not to worry,' she told him. 'What happens, happens. But I have to try.'

Solo frowned and scratched his chin. He nodded. 'You're used to being around your people,' he said. 'Probably happier there anyway.'

Juliette reached out and squeezed his arm with one of her

thick gloves. 'It's not that I would be miserable here, it's that I would be miserable knowing I let him go out without trying something.'

'And I was just starting to get used to having you here.' He turned his head to the side, bent over and grabbed her helmet from the decking.

Juliette checked her gloves, made sure everything was wrapped tightly, and looked up. The climb to the top would be brutal with the suit on. She dreaded it. And then navigating the remains of all those people in the sheriff's office and getting through the airlock doors. She accepted the helmet, scared of what she was about to do despite her convictions.

'Thanks for everything,' she said. She felt like she was doing more than saying goodbye. She knew there was a very good chance that she was doing willingly what Bernard had attempted so many weeks ago. Her cleaning had been delayed, but now she was going back to it.

Solo nodded and stepped around her to check her back. He patted the Velcro, tugged on her collar. 'You're good,' he said, his voice cracking.

'You take care of yourself, Solo.' She reached out and patted his shoulder. She had decided to carry the helmet one more flight up before putting it on, just to conserve her air.

'Jimmy,' he said. 'I think I'm going back to being called Jimmy, now.'

He smiled at Juliette. Shook his head sadly, but smiled.

'I'm not going to be alone any more,' he told her.

80

Juliette made her way through the airlock doors and up the ramp, ignoring the dead around her, just focusing on each step, and the hardest part was over. The rest was open space and the scattered remains she wished she could pretend were boulders. Finding her way was easy. She simply turned her back on that crumbling metropolis in the distance, the one she had set off for so very long ago, and began to walk away from it.

As she picked her way across the landscape, the sight of the occasional dead seemed sadder now than during that previous hike, more tragic for having shared their home for a while. Juliette was careful not to disturb them, passed them with the solemnity they deserved, wishing she could do more than feel sorry for them.

Eventually, they thinned, and she and the landscape were left alone. Trudging up that windswept hill, the sound of fine soil peppering her helmet became oddly familiar and strangely comforting. *This* was the world in which she lived, in which they all lived. Through the clear dome of her helmet, she saw it all as clearly as it could be seen. The speeding clouds hung angry and grey; sheets of dust whipped sideways and low to the ground; jagged rocks looked like they'd been sheared from some larger piece, perhaps by the machines that had crafted these hills.

When she reached the crest, she paused to take in the vista around her. The wind was fierce up there, her body exposed. She planted her boots wide so she wouldn't topple over and peered down into the inverted dome before her, at the flattened roof of her home. There was a mix of excitement and dread. The low sun had only barely cleared the distant hills, and the sensor tower below was still in shadow, still in night-time. She would make it. But before she started down the hill, she found herself gazing, amazed, at the scattering of depressions marching towards the horizon. They were just like the silo schematic, evenly spaced depressions, fifty of them.

And it occurred to her, suddenly and with a violent force, that countless others were going about their days nearby. People *alive*. More silos than just hers and Solo's. Silos unaware, packed with people waking up for work, going to school, maybe even to cleaning.

She turned in place and took it all in, wondering if maybe there was someone else out on that landscape at the exact same time as her wearing a similar suit, a completely different set of fears racing through their mind. If she could call out to them, she would. If she could wave to all the hidden sensors, she would.

The world took on a different scope, a new scale from this height. Her life had been cast away weeks ago, likely should have ended – if not on the slope of that hill in front of her home, then surely in the flooded deeps of silo seventeen. But it hadn't ended like that. It would probably end here, instead, this morning with Lukas. They might burn in that airlock together if her hunch was wrong. Or they could lie in the crook of that hill and waste away as a couple, a couple whose kinship had been formed by desperate talks lingering into the night, an intense bond between two stranded souls that was never spoken or admitted to.

Juliette had promised herself never to love in secret again, never to love at all. And somehow this time was worse: she had kept it a secret even from him. Even from *herself*.

Maybe it was the proximity of death talking, the reaper buffeting her clear helmet with sand and toxins. What did any of it matter, seeing how wide and full the world was? Her silo would probably go on. Other silos surely would.

A mighty gust of wind struck her, nearly ripping the folded blanket out of her hands. Juliette steadied herself, gathered her wits, and began the much easier descent toward her home. She ducked down below the crest with its sobering views and saddening heights, out of the harsh and caustic winds. She followed that crook where two hills met, winding her way towards the sad sight of a couple buried in plain view, who marked her fateful, desperate, and weary way home.

She arrived at the ramp early. There was no one on the landscape, the sun still hidden behind the hills. As she hurried down the slope, she wondered what anyone would think if they saw her on the sensors, stumbling towards the silo.

At the bottom of the ramp, she stood close to the heavy steel doors and waited. She checked the heat-tape blanket, ran through the procedure in her mind. Every scenario had been thought of during her climb, in her mad dreams, or during the walk through the wild outside. This would work, she told herself. The mechanics were sound. The only reason no one survived a cleaning was because they never had help; they couldn't bring tools or resources. But she had.

Time seemed to pass not at all. It was like her delicate and precious watch when she forgot to wind it. The trapped soil along the edge of the ramp shifted about impatiently with her, and Juliette wondered if maybe the cleaning had been called off, if she would die alone. That would be better, she told herself. She took a deep breath, wishing she had brought more air, enough for a return trip, just in case. But she had been too worried about the cleaning actually happening to consider that it might not. After a long wait, her nerves swelling and heart racing, she heard a noise inside, a metallic scraping of gears.

Juliette tensed, her arms rippling with chills, her throat constricting. This was it. She shifted in place, listening to the great grind of those heavy doors as they prepared to disgorge poor Lukas. She unfolded part of the heat blanket and waited. It would all go so quickly. She knew. But she would be in control. No one could come in and stop her.

With a terrible screech, the doors to silo eighteen parted, and a hiss of argon blasted out at her. Juliette leaned into it. The fog consumed her. She pushed blindly forward, groping ahead of herself, the blanket flapping noisily against her chest. She expected to run into him, to find herself wrestling a startled and frightened man, had prepared herself to hold him down, get him wrapped up tightly in the blanket – but there was no one in the doorway, no body struggling to get out, to get away from the coming purge of flames.

Juliette practically fell into the airlock; her body expected resistance like a boot at the top of a darkened stairway and found empty space instead.

As the argon cleared and the door began to grind shut, she had a brief hope, a tiny fantasy, that there was no cleaning. That the doors had simply been opened for her, welcoming her back. Maybe someone had seen her on the hillside and had taken a chance, had forgiven her, and all would be okay . . .

But as soon as she could see through the billowing gas, she saw that this was not the case. A man in a cleaning suit was kneeling in the centre of the airlock, hands on his thighs, facing the inner door.

Lukas.

Juliette raced to him as a halo of light bloomed in the room, the fire nozzles spitting on and reflecting off the shimmering plastic. The door thunked shut behind her, locking them both inside.

Juliette shook the blanket loose and shuffled around so he could see her, so he would know he wasn't alone.

The suit couldn't hide the shock. Lukas startled, his arms leaping up in alarm, even as the flames began to lance out.

She nodded, knowing he could see her through her clear dome, even if she couldn't see him. With a sweeping twirl she had practised in her mind a thousand times, she spread the blanket over his head and knelt down swiftly, covering herself as well.

It was dark under the heat tape. The temperature outside was rising. She tried to shout to Lukas that it was going to be okay, but her voice sounded muffled even inside her own helmet. Tucking the edges of the blanket down beneath her knees and feet, she wiggled until it was tightly pinned. She reached forward and tried to tuck the material under him as well, making sure his back was fully protected.

Lukas seemed to know what she was doing. His gloved hands

fell to her arms and rested there. She could feel how still he was, how calm. She couldn't believe he was going to wait, had chosen to burn rather than clean. She couldn't remember anyone ever making that choice. This worried her as they huddled together in the darkness, everything growing warm.

The flames licked against the heat tape, striking the blanket with enough force to be felt, like a buffeting wind. The temperature shot up, sweat leaping out on her lip and forehead, even with all the superior lining of her suit. The blanket wouldn't be enough. It wouldn't keep Lukas alive in his suit. The fear in her heart was only for him, even as her skin began to heat up.

Her panic seemed to leach into him, or maybe he was feeling the burns even worse. His hands trembled against her. And then she literally felt him go mad, felt him change his mind, begin to burn, *something*.

Lukas pushed her away from himself. Bright light entered their protective dome as he began to crawl out from under it, kicking away.

Juliette screamed for him to stop. She scrambled after him, clutching his arm, his leg, his boot, but he kicked out at her, beat her with his fists, frantically tried to get away.

The blanket fell off her head, and the light nearly blinded her. She felt the intense heat, could hear her dome pop and make noises, saw the clear bubble dip in above her and warp. She couldn't see Lukas, couldn't feel him, just saw blinding light and felt searing heat, scorching her wherever her suit crinkled against her body. She screamed in pain and yanked the blanket back over her head, covering the clear plastic.

And the flames raged on.

She couldn't feel him. Couldn't see him. There would be no way to find him. A thousand burns erupted across her body like so many knives gouging her flesh. Juliette sat alone under that thin film of protection, burning up, enduring the raging flames, and wept hot tears. Her body convulsed with sobs and anger, cursing the fire, the pain, the silo, the entire world.

Until eventually – she had no more tears and the fuel ran its course. The boiling temperature dropped to a mere scalding, and

Juliette could safely shrug off the steaming blanket. Her skin felt as if it were on fire. It burned wherever it touched the interior of her suit. She looked for Lukas and found she didn't have to look far.

He was lying against the door, his suit charred and flaking in the few places it remained intact. His helmet was still in place, saving her the horror of seeing his young face, but it had melted and warped far worse than hers. She crawled closer, aware that the door behind her was opening, that they were coming for her, that it was all over. She had failed.

Juliette whimpered when she saw the places his body had been exposed, the suit and charcoal liners burned away. There was his arm, charred black. His stomach, oddly distended. His tiny hands, so small and thin and burned to a—

No.

She didn't understand. She wept anew. She threw her gloved and steaming hands against her bubbled dome and cried out in shock, in a mix of anger and blessed relief.

This was not Lukas dead before her.

This was a man who deserved none of her tears.

81

• Silo 18 •

Awareness, like sporadic jolts of pain from her burns, came and went.

Juliette remembered a billowing fog, boots stomping all around her, lying on her side in the oven of an airlock. She watched the way the world warped out of shape as her helmet, a viscous thing, continued to sag towards her, melting. A bright silver star hovered in her vision, waving as it settled beyond her dome. Peter Billings peered through her helmet at her, shook her scalded shoulders, cried out to the people marching around, telling them to help.

They lifted her up and out of that steaming place, sweat dripping from faces, a melted suit cut from her body.

Juliette floated through her old office like a ghost. Flat on her back, the squeal of a fussy wheel below her, past the rows and rows of steel bars, an empty bench in an empty cell.

They carried her in circles.

Down.

She woke to the beeping of her heart, these machines checking in on her, a man dressed like her father.

He was the first to notice that she was awake. His eyebrows lifted, a smile, a nod to someone over her shoulder.

And Lukas was there, his face – so familiar, so strange – was in her blurry vision. She felt his hand in hers. She knew that hand had been there a while, that he had been there a while. He was crying and laughing, brushing her cheek. Jules wanted to know what was so funny. What was so sad. He just shook his head as she drifted back to sleep.

*

It wasn't just that the burns were bad; it was that they were everywhere.

The days of recovery were spent sliding in and out of painkiller fogs.

Every time she saw Lukas, she apologised. Everyone was making a fuss. Peter came. There were piles of notes from down deep, but nobody was allowed up. Nobody else could see her but the man dressed like her father and women who reminded her of her mother.

Her head cleared quickly once they let it.

Juliette came out of what felt like a deep dream, weeks of haze, nightmares of drowning and burning, of being outside, of dozens of silos just like hers. The drugs had kept the pain at bay – but had dulled her consciousness, too. She didn't mind the stings and aches if it meant winning back her mind. It was an easy trade.

'Hey.'

She flopped her head to the side – and Lukas was there. Was he ever not? A blanket fell from his chest as he leaned forward, held her hand. He smiled.

'You're looking better.'

Juliette licked her lips. Her mouth was dry.

'Where am I?'

'The infirmary on thirty-three. Just take it easy. Do you want me to get you anything?'

She shook her head. It felt amazing to be able to move, to respond to words. She tried to squeeze his hand.

'I'm sore,' she said weakly.

Lukas laughed. He looked relieved to hear this. 'I bet.'

She blinked and looked at him. 'There's an infirmary on thirty-three?' His words were on a delay.

He nodded gravely. 'I'm sorry, but it's the best in the silo. And we could keep you safe. But forget that. Rest. I'll go grab the nurse.'

He stood, a thick book spilling from his lap and tumbling into the chair, burying itself in the blanket and pillows.

'Do you think you can eat?'

She nodded, turned her head back to face the ceiling and the bright lights, everything coming back to her, memories popping up like the tingle of pain on her skin.

She read folded notes for days and cried. Lukas sat by her side, collecting the ones that spilled to the floor like paper planes tossed from landings. He apologised over and over, blubbering like he was the one who'd done it. Juliette read all of them a dozen times, trying to keep straight who was gone and who was still signing their names. She couldn't believe the terrible news about Knox. Some things seemed immutable, like the great stairway. She wept for him and for Marck, wanted desperately to see Shirly, was told that she couldn't.

Ghosts visited her when the lights were out. Juliette would wake up, eyes crusted over, pillow wet, Lukas rubbing her forehead and telling her it would be okay.

Peter came often. Juliette thanked him over and over. It was all Peter, all Peter. He had made the choice. Lukas told her of the stairway, his march to cleaning, hearing her voice on Peter's radio, the implications of her being alive.

Peter had taken the risk, had listened. That had led to him and Lukas talking. Lukas had said forbidden things, was in no danger of being sent any place worse, said something that confused her about being a bad virus, a catching cold. The radio barked with reports from Mechanical of people surrendering. Bernard sentenced them to death anyway.

And Peter had a decision to make. Was he the final law, or did he owe something to those who put him in place? Did he do what was right, or what was expected of him? It was so easy to do the latter, but Peter Billings was a good man. Lukas told him so on that stairwell. He told him that this was where they'd been put by fate, but what they did going forward defined them. That was who they were.

He told Peter that Bernard had killed a man. That he had proof. Lukas had done nothing to deserve this.

Peter pointed out that every ounce of IT security was a hundred levels away. There was only one gun up top. Only one law.

His.

82

Weeks Later
• Silo 18 •

The three of them sat around the conference table, Juliette adjusting the gauze bandage on her hand to cover the raised lace of scar tissue peeking out. The overalls they'd given her were loose to minimise the pain, but the undershirt itched everywhere it touched. She sat in one of the plush chairs and rolled back and forth with the push of her toes, impatient, ready to get out of there. But Lukas and Peter had things to discuss. They had escorted her this close to the exit, this close to the great stairwell, only to sit her down in that room. To get some *privacy*, they had said. The looks on their faces made her nervous.

Nobody said anything for a while. Peter used the excuse of sending a tech for some water, but when the pitcher came and the glasses were filled, nobody reached for a drink. Lukas and Peter exchanged nervous glances. Juliette grew tired of waiting.

'What is it?' she asked. 'Can I go? I feel like you've been delaying this for days.' She glanced at her watch, wiggled her arm so it would fall from the bandage on her wrist and she could see the tiny face. She stared across the table at Lukas and had to laugh at the worry on his face. 'Are you trying to keep me here for ever? Because I told everyone in the deep that I'd be seeing them tomorrow tonight.'

Lukas turned to Peter.

'C'mon, guys. Spit it out. What's troubling you? The doc said I was fine for the trip down and I told you I'd check in with Marsh and Hank if I had any problems. I'm gonna be late enough as it is if I don't get a move on.'

'Okay,' Lukas said, letting out a sigh. It was as though he'd given up on Peter being the one. 'It's been a few weeks—'

'And you two've made it feel like months.' She twisted the dial on the side of her watch, an ancient tic returning like it had never left.

'It's just that' – Lukas coughed into his fist, clearing his throat – 'we couldn't give you *all* the notes that were sent to you.' He frowned at her, looked guilty.

Juliette's heart dropped. She sagged forward, waiting for it. More names would be coming to move from one sad list to another—

Lukas held up his palms. 'Nothing like that,' he said quickly, recognising the worry on her face. 'God, sorry, nothing like that—'

'*Good* news,' Peter said. 'Congratulatory notes.'

Lukas shot him a look that told Juliette she might think otherwise.

'Well . . . it is *news*.' He looked across the table at her. His hands were folded in front of him, resting on the marred wood, just like hers. It felt as though they might both move them several inches until they met, until fingers interlocked. It would be so natural after weeks of practice. But that was something worried friends did in hospitals, right? Juliette pondered this while Lukas and Peter went on about elections.

'Wait. What?' She blinked and looked up from his hands, the last part coming back to her.

'It was the *timing*,' Lukas explained.

'You were all anyone was talking about,' Peter said.

'Go back,' she said. '*What* did you say?'

Lukas took a deep breath. 'Bernard was running unopposed. When we sent him out to cleaning, the election was called off. But then news got around about your miraculous return, and people showed up to vote anyway—'

'A *lot* of people,' Peter added.

Lukas nodded. 'It was quite a turnout. More than half the silo.'

'Yeah, but . . . *mayor?*' She laughed and looked around the scratched conference table, bare except for the untouched glasses of water. 'Isn't there something I need to sign? Some official way to turn this nonsense down?'

The two men exchanged glances.

'That's sorta the thing,' Peter said.

Lukas shook his head. 'I *told* you—'

'We were hoping you'd accept.'

'Me? *Mayor?*' Juliette crossed her arms and sat back, painfully, against the chair. She laughed. 'You've gotta be kidding. I wouldn't know the first thing about—'

'You wouldn't have to,' Peter said, leaning forward. 'You have an office, you shake some hands, sign some things, make people feel better—'

Lukas tapped him on the arm and shook his head. Juliette felt a flush of heat across her skin, which just made her scars and wounds itch more.

'Here's the thing,' Lukas said as Peter sat back in his chair. 'We *need* you. There's a power vacuum at the top. Peter's been in his post longer than anyone, and you know how long that's been.'

She was listening.

'Remember our conversations all those nights? Remember you telling me what that other silo was like? Do you understand how close to that we got?'

She chewed her lip, reached for one of the glasses, and took a long drink of water. Peering over the lip of the glass, she waited for him to continue.

'We have a chance, Jules. To hold this place together. To put it *back* to—'

She set the glass down and lifted her palm for him to stop.

'If we were to do this,' she told them coolly, looking from one of their expectant faces to the other. '*If* we do it, we do it my way.'

Peter frowned.

'No more lying,' she said. 'We give truth a chance.'

Lukas laughed nervously. Peter shook his head.

'Now listen to me,' she said. 'This isn't crazy. It's not the first time I've thought this through. Hell, I've had weeks of nothing *but* thinking.'

'The truth?' Peter asked.

She nodded. 'I know what you two are thinking. You think we need lies, fear—'

Peter nodded.

'But what could we invent that's scarier than what's *really out there?*' She pointed towards the roof and waited for that to sink in.

'When these places were built, the idea was that we were all in this together. Together but separate, ignorant of one another, so we didn't infect the others if one of us got sick. But I don't *want* to play for that team. I don't agree with their cause. I refuse.'

Lukas tilted his head. 'Yeah, but—'

'So it's us against them. And not the people in the silos, not the people working day to day who don't know, but those at the top who *do*. Silo eighteen will be different. Full of knowledge, of *purpose*. Think about it. Instead of manipulating people, why not *empower* them? Let them know what we're up against. And have *that* drive our collective will.'

Lukas raised his eyebrows. Peter ran his hands up through his hair.

'You guys should think about it.' She pushed herself away from the table. 'Take your time. I'm going to go see my family and friends. But either I'm in, or I'll be working against you. I'll be spreading the truth one way or the other.'

She smiled at Lukas. It was a dare, but he would know she wasn't joking.

Peter stood and showed her his palms. 'Can we at least agree not to do anything rash until we meet again?'

Juliette crossed her arms. She dipped her chin.

'Good,' Peter said, letting out his breath and dropping his arms.

She turned to Lukas. He was studying her, his lips pursed, and she could tell he knew. There was only one way this was going forward, and it scared the hell out of him.

Peter turned and opened the door. He looked back at Lukas.

'Can you give us a second?' Lukas asked, standing up and walking towards the door.

Peter nodded. He turned and shook Juliette's hand as she thanked him for the millionth time. He checked his star, which hung askew on his chest, and then left the conference room.

Lukas crossed out of sight of the window, grabbed Juliette's hand and pulled her towards the door.

'Are you kidding me?' she asked. 'Did you really think I would just accept that job and . . . ?'

Lukas pressed his palm against the door and forced it shut. Juliette faced him, confused, then felt his arms slide gently around her waist, mindful of her wounds.

'You were right,' he whispered. He leaned close, put his head by her shoulder. 'I'm stalling. I don't want you to go.'

His breath was warm against her neck. Juliette relaxed. She forgot what she was about to say. She wrapped an arm around his back, held his neck with her other hand. 'It's okay,' she said, relieved to hear him say it, to finally admit it. And she could feel him trembling, could hear his broken and stuttered exhalations.

'It's okay,' she whispered again, pressing her cheek against his, trying to comfort him. 'I'm not going anywhere for good—'

Lukas pulled away to look at her. She felt him searching her face, tears welling up in his eyes. His body had started shaking. She could feel it in his arms, his back.

And then she realised, as he pulled her close and pressed his lips against hers, that it wasn't fear or panic she was sensing in him. It was *nerves*.

She whimpered into their kiss, the rush to her head better than the doctor's drugs. It washed away any pain caused by his hands clutching her back. She couldn't remember the last time she'd felt lips move against her own. She kissed him back, and it was over too soon. He stepped away and held her hands, glanced nervously at the window.

'It's a . . . uh . . .'

'That was nice,' she told him, squeezing his hands.

'We should probably . . .' He jerked his chin towards the door.

Juliette smiled. 'Yeah. Probably so.'

He walked her through the entrance hall of IT and to the

landing. A tech was waiting with her shoulder bag. Juliette saw that Lukas had padded the strap with rags, worried about her wounds.

'And you're sure you don't need an escort?'

'I'll be fine,' she said, tucking her hair behind her ears. She shrugged the bag higher up her neck. 'I'll see you in a week or so.'

'You can radio me,' he told her.

Juliette laughed. 'I know.'

She grabbed his hand and gave it a squeeze, then turned to the great stairwell. Someone in the passing crowd nodded at her. She was sure she didn't know him, but nodded back. Other chins were turning to follow her. She walked past them and grabbed that great curved bar of steel that wound its way through the heart of things, that held those pouting and worn treads together as life after life was ground away on them. And Juliette lifted her boot to that first step on a journey far too long in coming—

'Hey!'

Lukas called after her. He ran across the landing, his brows lowered in confusion. 'I thought you were heading *down*, going to see your friends.'

Juliette smiled at him. A porter passed by, loaded down with his burdens. Juliette thought of how many of her own had recently slipped away.

'Family first,' she told Lukas. She glanced up that great shaft in the centre of the humming silo and lifted her boot to the next tread. 'I've got to go see my father, first.'

Epilogue
• Silo 17 •

'Thirty-two!'

Elise danced up the steps of the down deep, her breath trailing in long curls of steam behind her, the clumsy feet of youth making a racket with their heavy boots on the wet steel.

'Thirty-two steps, Mr Solo!'

She made it back up to the landing, tripped over the last step, and caught herself on her hands and knees. Elise stayed there a minute, head down, probably deciding if she would cry or be okay.

Solo waited for her to cry.

Instead, she looked up at him, a wide smile telling him she was fine. There was a gap in that smile where a loose tooth had come out and not yet been replaced.

'It's going *down*,' she said. She wiped her hands on her new overalls and ran over to him. 'The water's going down!'

Solo grunted as she threw herself into his hip and hugged his waist. He draped an arm across her back while she squeezed him.

'Everything's gonna be great!'

Solo held the railing with one hand and looked down past the rust-coloured stain of old blood beneath his feet, looked past that memory and into the receding waters far below. He reached for the radio on his hip. Juliette would be the most excited to know.

'I think you're right,' he told little Elise, pulling his radio free. 'I think everything's gonna be just fine . . .'

Q&A With Author Hugh Howey

Q: Is this really the end?!

A: To quote every one of my favourite top-ten kung-fu movies: *Every end is a new beginning.* There are many more stories to tell. Not just the rest of silo eighteen's story, but the future of silo seventeen, which is about to change. And then there are all the *other* silos crowding in around them. You won't *believe* what's going on in silo forty!

Q: Where did you get the idea for *Wool*?

A: My paranoid optimism. I fear, above all else, that the world beyond my sight isn't half as marvellous and brilliant as I believe it to be. *Wool* is an exploration of that cheery dread. It asks whether we can know the world by staring at a single screen or if we're better off going for a look-see.

Q: What inspires you to write?

A: I long to entertain people. I can't sing. I can't dance. If you point a camera at me, I break out in sweats. And I'm only funny on a stage if you enjoy watching blokes wet themselves. All that remained was making stuff up for a living, which I'm practised at.

Q: Which character in *Wool* would you compare yourself to?

A: Solo. He's unkempt and he won't grow up. If not for my wife, I'd probably poop around the house as well.

Q: What's next for Hugh Howey?

A: More books. *Wool* is just the first of a three-act story. In the next book, *Shift*, we explore the nefarious (and sometimes not) men and women of silo one. After that, we pull the two groups of players onto the same raucous stage for *Dust*, which concludes our less-than-merry tale.

Q: How can I keep up with your writing?
A: That's an awfully convenient question! Thanks for asking.
You can follow me on Twitter: @hughhowey.
You can visit my website regularly: www.hughhowey.com
And you can email me: hughhowey@gmail.com
I try to respond to all emails, and I love receiving them. Don't be shy!

Q: Tell the truth: did you come up with these questions yourself?
A: Yes.

Reading Group Questions on *Wool*

- The population must now live in the silos because of the toxic air, and therefore a degree of order must be maintained to ensure survival. How would you change Bernard's way of running the silo?

- Holston suggests that Allison was happier before she found the information which drove her outside. Do you believe that ignorance is bliss? Or would you want to know the truth?

- Both Holston and Marnes lose people very dear to them, which leads them both to drastic actions. Are there any other similarities between the two of them?

- Juliette gets to experience both life in Mechanical and life as the sheriff. If you had to choose a sector of the silo to work in, which one would it be?

- Juliette is the first person to not clean the cameras when she leaves the silo. Would you have wanted to clean the cameras if you had gone outside and seen the landscape through the visor?

- Juliette fares better than anyone once she steps outside thanks to certain people in the lower layers of the silo. Is it ultimately this network of relationships that ensures Juliette's survival when she returns?

- Bernard clearly believes in the Order and the Legacy. Do you think he is evil or just brainwashed by the system?

- In Part 5, Juliette and Lukas are in very different situations. Who do you think would feel more isolated?

- Solo believes he is alone in his silo. What would you do if you thought you were the only survivor of your world?

- Juliette is viewed as a symbol of the uprising. Do you think an uprising would have occurred without her? Who else could have been a figurehead for it?

- Peter realises that he has a choice between doing what is expected of him and doing what is right. Can you relate this decision to any other situation in the book?

- Juliette is an inspirational female character in the novel. What other strong women appear in the story and how do they gain or use their power?

Read on for a sneak preview of *Shift*,
Hugh Howey's new novel, out now in
hardback and e-book.

SHIFT

HUGH
HOWEY

In 2007, the Centre for Automation in Nanobiotech (CAN) outlined the hardware and software platforms that would one day allow robots smaller than human cells to make medical diagnoses, conduct repairs, and even self-propagate.

That same year, CBS re-aired a programme about the effects of propranolol on sufferers of extreme trauma. A simple pill, it had been discovered, could wipe out the memory of any traumatic event.

At almost the same moment in humanity's broad history, mankind had discovered the means for bringing about its utter downfall. And the ability to forget it ever happened.

Prologue

Troy returned to the living and found himself inside a tomb. He awoke to a world of confinement, a thick sheet of frosted glass pressed near to his face.

Dark shapes stirred on the other side of the icy murk. He tried to lift his arms, to beat on the glass, but his muscles were too weak. He attempted to scream – but could only cough. The taste in his mouth was foul. His ears rang with the clank of heavy locks opening, the hiss of air, the squeak of hinges long unused.

The lights overhead were bright, the hands on him warm. They helped him sit while he continued to cough, his breath clouding the chill air. Someone had water. Pills to take. The water was cool, the pills bitter. Troy fought down a few gulps. He was unable to hold the glass without help, hands trembling, memories flooding back, scenes from long nightmares. The feeling of deep time and yesterdays mingled. He shivered. The pills hit his gut, and his grip on the memories seemed to loosen.

A paper gown. The sting of tape removed. A tug on his arm, a tube pulled from his groin. Two men dressed in white helped him out of the coffin. Steam rose all around him, air condensing and dispersing like dreams upon waking.

His legs were like that of a foal, working at birth but not well. Blinking against the glare, exercising lids long shut, Troy saw the rows of coffins full of the living that stretched towards the distant and curved walls. The ceiling felt low; there was the suffocating press of dirt stacked high above. All that dirt and the dead, stacked high. And the years. So many years had passed. Anyone he cared about would be gone.

Everything was gone.

The pills were bitter in Troy's throat. He tried to swallow. The memories were fading. He was going to lose anything bad he'd ever known.

He collapsed – but the men in the white overalls saw this coming. They caught him and lowered him to the ground, a paper gown rustling on shivering skin.

Memories flooded back before fading; recollections rained down like bombs and then were gone. Awareness came – however fleeting.

The pills could only do so much. It took time to destroy the past. Until then, the nightmares were vivid and with him.

Troy sobbed into his palms, a sympathetic hand resting on his head. The two men in white gifted him with quiet and calm. They didn't rush the process. Here was a courtesy passed from one waking soul to the next, something all the men sleeping in their coffins would one day rise to discover.

And eventually … forget.

2049 · Washington, D.C. ·

The tall glass trophy cabinets had once served as bookshelves. There were hints. Little things like hardware on the shelves that dated back centuries, while the hinges and the tiny locks went back mere decades. There was the clash of wood: the framing around the glass was cherry, but the cases had been built of oak. Someone had attempted to remedy this with a few coats of stain, but the grain didn't match. The colour wasn't perfect. To trained eyes, details such as these were glaring.

Congressman Donald Keene gathered these clues without meaning to. He simply saw that long ago there had been a great purge, a making of space. At some point in the past, the Senator's waiting room had been stripped of its obligatory law books until only a handful remained. These beleaguered survivors sat silently in the dim corners of the glass cabinets. They were shut-in, their spines laced with cracks, old leather flaking off like sunburnt skin.

The rest of the books – all the survivors' kin – were gone. In their place stood a collection of mementos from the Senator's two lifetimes of service.

Congressman Keene could see, reflected in the glass, a handful of his fellow freshmen pacing and stirring, their terms of service newly begun. Like Donald, they were young and still hopelessly optimistic. They were bringing change to Capitol Hill. And this time, somehow, they hoped to deliver where their similarly naive predecessors had not.

While they waited their turns to meet with the great Senator Thurman from their home state of Georgia, they chatted nervously amongst themselves. They were a gaggle of priests, Donald thought, all lined up to meet the Pope, to kiss his ring. He let out a heavy breath and focused on the contents of the case, losing himself in the treasures behind the glass while a fellow representative from Georgia prattled on about his district's Centres for Disease Control and Prevention.

'—and they have this detailed guide on their website, this response and readiness manual in case of, okay, get this, a zombie invasion! Can you believe that? Zombies. Like even the CDC thinks something could go wrong and suddenly we're all *eating* each other—'

Donald stifled a smile, fearful it would be spied in the glass. He looked over a collection of photographs, one each of the Senator with the last four presidents. It was the same pose and handshake in each shot, the same staged background of windless flags and fancy oversized seals. The Senator seemed hardly to change as the presidents came and went. His hair started white and it stayed white; he seemed perfectly unfazed by the passing of decades, as if this was how he'd always been.

Seeing the photographs side by side devalued each of them somehow. They looked staged. Phoney. It was as if the world's most powerful men had begged their mommies to take their picture while they stood and posed with this cardboard cut-out, this imposing plastic statue, like some roadside attraction.

Donald laughed, and the congressman from Atlanta joined him.

'I know, right? Zombies. It's hilarious. But think about it, okay? Why would the CDC even *have* this field manual unless—?'

Donald wanted to correct his fellow freshman, to show him what he'd really been laughing about. Look at the smiles, he wanted to say. They were on the faces of the *presidents*. The Senator looked like he'd rather be anyplace else. It was as if each in this succession of commanders-in-chief knew who the more powerful man was, who would be there long after they had come and gone.

'—it's advice, like everyone should have a baseball bat with their flashlights and candles, right? Just in case. You know, for bashing brains.'

Donald pulled out his phone and checked the time. He glanced at the door leading off the waiting room and wondered how much longer he'd have to wait. Putting the phone away, he studied a shelf where a military uniform had been carefully arranged like a delicate work of origami. The left breast of the jacket featured a Lego-brick wall of medals; the sleeves were folded over and pinned to highlight the gold braids sewn along the cuffs. In front of the uniform, a collection of decorative coins rested in a custom wooden rack, tokens of appreciation from the men and women still serving.

The two arrangements spoke volumes – this uniform from the past and these coins from those currently deployed. They were bookends on a pair of wars. One that the Senator had fought in as a youth, the other a war he had battled to prevent as a grown and wiser man.

'—yeah, it sounds crazy, I know, but do you know what rabies does to a dog? I mean, what it *really* does, the biological—'

Donald leaned close to his reflection and studied the decorative coins. The number and slogan on each one represented a deployed group. Or was it a battalion? He couldn't remember. His sister Charlotte would know. She was over there somewhere.

Before Donald could consider the long odds, he scanned a collection of framed photographs for her, a wall of pictures in the back of the glass cabinet featuring servicemen and servicewomen huddled around the Senator. He searched the faces among the sand-coloured fatigues, all those smiles a long way from home.

'—you think the CDC knows something we don't? I mean, forget weaponised anthrax, imagine legions of *biters* breaking out all over the place—'

Most were Army photographs. And, of course, Charlotte wasn't in them. Donald studied one from the Navy. The Senator was standing on the deck of a ship with a crowd of men and women in neatly pressed uniforms. More smiles on warring faces. The ship may have been underway. The Senator's feet were planted wide, a breeze lifting his white hair, giving him a fierce mohawk – or maybe the comical tuft of a cockatiel. Above the group, stencilled in white paint on gunmetal grey: *USS The Sullivans*.

'Hey, aren't you even a little nervous about this?'

Donald realised he'd been asked a question. His focus drifted from the collection of photographs to the reflection of the chatty congressman in the glass. The man looked to be in his mid-thirties, probably Donald's age.

'Am I nervous about zombies?' He laughed. "No. Can't say that I am.'

The congressman stepped closer, his eyes drifting towards the imposing uniform that stood propped up as if a warrior's chest remained inside. 'No,' the man said. 'About meeting *him*.'

The door to the reception area opened, bleeps from the phones on the other side leaking out.

'Congressman Keene?'

Donald turned away from one last display: a piece of shrapnel, a Purple Heart, a note from a wounded soldier expressing his undying thanks. An elderly receptionist stood in the doorway, her white blouse and black skirt highlighting a thin and athletic frame.

'Senator Thurman will see you now,' she said.

Donald patted the congressman from Atlanta on the shoulder as he stepped past.

'Hey, good luck,' the gentleman stammered after him.

Donald smiled. He fought the temptation to turn and tell the man that he knew the Senator well enough, that he had been bounced on his knee back when he was but a child. Only, Donald was too busy concealing his own nerves to bother. This was different. He stepped through the deeply panelled door of rich hardwoods and entered the Senator's noisy inner sanctum. This wasn't like passing through a foyer to pick up a man's daughter for a date. This was the pressure of meeting as colleagues when Donald still felt like that same toddler from his bronco-knee days.

'Through here,' the receptionist said. She guided Donald between pairs of wide and busy desks, a dozen phones chirping in short bursts that sounded more medical than senatorial. Young men and women in suits and crisp blouses double-fisted receivers while somehow remaining calm. Their bored expressions suggested that this was a normal workload for a weekday morning. It wasn't as if the world was coming to an end, or anything.

Donald reached out a hand as he passed one of the desks, brushing the wood with his fingertips. Mahogany. The aides here had desks nicer than his own. And the decor: the plush carpet, the broad and ancient crown molding, the antique tile ceiling, the dangling light fixtures that may have been actual crystal. Everything was noticeably more opulent in the Dirksen Senate building. It was the House of Lords compared to Rayburn across the street, Donald's own House of Commons.

At the end of the buzzing and bleeping room, a panelled door opened and disgorged Congressman Mick Webb, just finished with his meeting. Mick didn't notice Donald, he was too absorbed by the open Manilla folder he held in front of him.

Donald stopped and waited for his colleague and old college acquaintance to approach. 'So,' he asked Mick. 'How did it go?'

Mick looked up and snapped the folder shut. He tucked it under his arm and nodded. 'Yeah, yeah. It went great.' He smiled. 'Sorry if we ran long. The old man couldn't get enough of me.'

Donald laughed. 'No problem.' He jabbed a thumb over his shoulder. 'I was making new friends.'

Mick smiled. 'I bet.'

'Yeah, well, I'll see you back at Rayburn.'

'Sure thing.' Mick slapped him on the arm with the folder and headed for the exit. Donald caught the impatient glare from the Senator's receptionist and hurried over. She waved him through the old door and into the dimly lit office before shutting it tight against the bleeping phones.

'Congressman Keene.'

Senator Paul Thurman stood from behind his desk and stretched out a hand. He flashed a familiar smile, one Donald had come to recognise as much from photos and TV as from his childhood. Despite Thurman's age – he had to be pushing seventy if he wasn't already there – the Senator was trim and fit. His oxford shirt hugged a military frame; a thick neck bulged out of his knotted tie; his white hair remained as crisp and orderly as an enlisted man's.

Donald crossed the dark room and accepted the hand that had clasped that of so many presidents.

'Good to see you, sir.'

As his fist was pumped up and down, he imagined flash bulbs

popping and expensive cameras clicking wildly. He almost turned to the side and adopted a frozen and smiling pose, thinking the Senator would get the joke at once. Fortunately, the urge passed. Donald reminded himself that he wasn't there to date the Senator's daughter but to serve alongside him.

'Please, sit.' Thurman released Donald's hand and gestured to one of the chairs across from his desk. Donald turned and lowered himself into the bright red leather, the gold grommets along the arm like sturdy rivets in a steel beam.

'How's Helen?'

'Helen?' Donald straightened his tie. 'She's great. She's back in Savannah. She really enjoyed seeing you at the reception.'

'She's a beautiful woman, your wife.'

'Thank you, sir.' Donald fought to relax, which didn't help. The office had the pall of dusk, even with the overhead lights on. The clouds outside had turned nasty – low and dark. If it rained, he would have to take the tunnel back to his office. He hated the tunnel. They could carpet it and hang those little chandeliers at intervals, but he could still tell he was belowground. The tunnels in Washington made him feel like a rat scurrying through a sewer. It always seemed like the roof was about to cave in.

'How's the job treating you so far?'

Donald shifted his gaze away from the clouds. 'The job's good,' he said. 'It's busy, but good.'

He started to ask the Senator how Anna was doing, but the door behind him opened before he could. The discordant cries of the busy phones disturbed the quiet as the thin receptionist entered and delivered two bottles of water. Donald thanked her, twisted the cap off, and saw that it had been pre-opened. Just like at that fancy steakhouse the lobbyist from the PAGW had taken him to.

'I hope you're not too busy to work on something for me.' Senator Thurman raised an eyebrow. Donald took a sip of water and wondered if that was a skill one could master, that eyebrow lift. It was effective as hell. It made him want to jump to attention and salute.

'Oh, I can make the time,' he said. 'After all the stumping you did for me? I doubt I would've made it past the primaries.'

He held the water bottle in his lap. When he crossed his legs, he became self-conscious of his brown socks and black pants. He lowered his foot back to the ground and wished Helen had stayed in D.C. longer.

'You and Mick Webb go back, right? Both Bulldogs.'

It took Donald a moment to realise the Senator was referring to their college mascot. He hadn't spent a lot of time at Georgia following sports. 'Yessir. Go Dawgs.'

He hoped that was right.

The Senator smiled. He leaned forward so that his face caught the soft light raining down on his desk. Donald watched as shadows caught in wrinkles otherwise easy to miss. Thurman's lean face and square chin made him look younger straight-on than he probably did from the side. Here was a man who got places by approaching others directly rather than in ambush.

'You studied architecture at Georgia.'

Donald nodded. It was easy to forget that he knew Thurman better than the Senator knew him. One of them grabbed far more newspaper headlines than the other.

'That's right. For my undergrad. I went into planning for my master's. I figured I could do more good governing people than I could drawing boxes to put them in.'

He winced to hear himself deliver the line. It was a pat phrase from grad school, something he should've left behind with crushing beer cans on his forehead and ogling asses in skirts. He wondered for the dozenth time why he and the other congressional newcomers had been summoned. When he first got the invite, he figured it was a social visit. Then Mick bragged about his own appointment, and Donald figured it was some kind of formality or tradition. But now he wondered if this was a power play, a chance to butter up the Reps from Georgia for those times when Thurman would need a particular vote in the lower and *lesser* house.

'Tell me, Donny—' The Senator reached for his bottle of water, glanced up. 'How good are you at keeping secrets?'

Donald's blood ran cold. He forced himself to laugh off the sudden flush of nerves.

'I got elected, didn't I?'

Senator Thurman smiled. 'And so you probably learned the best lesson there is about secrets.' He raised his plastic bottle in salute. '*Denial*.'

Donald nodded and took a sip of his own water. He wasn't sure where this was going, but he already felt uneasy. He sensed some of the backroom dealings coming on that he'd promised his constituents he'd root out if elected.

The Senator leaned back in his chair.

'Denial is the secret sauce in this town,' he said. 'It's the flavour that holds all the other ingredients together. Here's what I tell the newly elected: the truth is gonna get out – it always does – but it's gonna blend in with all the *lies*.' The Senator twirled a hand in the air. 'You have to deny each lie and every truth with the same vinegar. Let those websites and blowhards who bitch about cover-ups confuse the public *for* you.'

'Uh, yessir.' Donald didn't know what else to say. This seemed like a strange conversation to be having. He took another gulp of water.

The Senator lifted an eyebrow again. He remained frozen for a pause, and then asked, out of nowhere: 'Do you believe in aliens, Donny?'

Donald nearly lost the water out of his nose. He covered his mouth with his hand, coughed, had to wipe his chin. The Senator didn't budge.

'Aliens?' Donald shook his head and wiped his wet palm on his thigh. 'Nossir. I mean, not the abducting kind. Why?'

He wondered if this was some kind of debriefing. Why had the Senator asked him if he could keep a secret? Was this a security initiation? The Senator remained silent.

'They're not real,' Donald finally said. He watched for any twitch or hint. 'Are they?'

The old man cracked a smile. 'That's the thing,' he said. 'If they are or they aren't, the chatter out there would be the exact same. Would you be surprised if I told you they're very much real?'

'Hell, yeah, I'd be surprised.'

'Good.' The Senator slid a folder across the desk. Donald eyed it and held up a hand.

'Wait. Are they real or aren't they? What're you trying to tell me?'

Senator Thurman laughed. 'Of course they're not real. Are you kidding?' He took his hand off the folder and propped his elbows on the desk. 'Have you seen how much NASA wants from us so they can fly to Mars and back? No way we're getting to another star. Ever. And no one's coming here. Hell, why would they?'

Donald didn't know *what* to think, which was a far cry from how he'd felt less than a minute ago. He saw what the Senator meant, how truth and lies seemed black and white, but mixed together they made everything grey and confusing. He glanced down at the folder. It looked similar to the one Mick had been carrying and reminded him of the government's fondness for all things outdated.

'This is denial, right?' He studied the Senator. 'That's what you're doing right now. You're trying to throw me off.'

'No. This is me telling you to stop watching so many science fiction flicks. In fact, why do you think those eggheads are always dreaming of colonising some other planet? You have any idea what would be involved? It's ludicrous. Not cost-effective.'

Donald shrugged. He didn't think it was ludicrous. He twisted the cap back onto his water. 'It's in our nature to dream of open space,' he said. 'To find room to spread out in. Isn't that how we ended up here?'

'Here? In America?' The Senator laughed. 'We didn't come here and find open space. We got a bunch of people sick, killed them, and *made* space.' Thurman pointed at the folder. 'Which brings me to this. I've got something I'd like you to work on.'

Donald leaned forward and placed his bottle on the leather inlay of the formidable desk. He took the folder.

'Is this something coming through committee?'

He tried to temper his hopes. It was alluring to think of co-authoring a bill his first year in office. He opened the folder and tilted it towards the window, where storms were gathering.

'No, nothing like that. This is about CAD-FAC.'

Donald nodded. *Of course.* The preamble about secrets and conspiracies suddenly made perfect sense, as did the gathering of Georgia congressmen outside. This was about the Containment and Disposal Facility at the heart of the Senator's new energy bill, the complex that would one day house most of the world's spent nuclear fuel. Or, according to the websites Thurman had alluded to, it was going to be the next Area 51, or the site where a new-and-improved superbomb was being built, or a place where mad scientists would tunnel to the centre of the earth to prevent the core from melting down, or a secure holding facility for Libertarians who had purchased one too many guns at Walmart. Take your pick. There was enough noise out there to hide *any* truth.

'Yeah,' Donald said, deflated. 'I've been getting some entertaining calls from my district.' He didn't dare mention the one about the Lizard People, or the one that had to do with magnetic poles flipping. 'I want you to know, sir, that privately I'm behind the facility one hundred percent.' He looked up at the Senator. 'I'm glad I didn't have to vote on it publicly, of course, but it was about time *someone* offered up their backyard, right?'

'Precisely. For the common good.' Senator Thurman took a long pull from his water, and Donald noticed for the first time that his office didn't reek of old cigar smoke, wasn't infused with the stench of pipe tobacco, aged leather, expensive whiskey, and the other deal-making scents he constantly nosed back at Rayburn. Hell, despite Helen's aromatic electric candles, his own office still stank like the eight-term Representative he'd ousted in the primaries – the one who *had* voted on the energy bill.

Thurman leaned back in his chair and cleared his throat. 'You're a sharp young man, Donny. Not everyone sees what a boon to our state this'll be. A real life-saver.' He smiled. 'I'm sorry, you *are* still going by Donny, right? Or is it Donald, now?'

'Either's fine,' Donald lied. He no longer enjoyed being called Donny, but changing names in the middle of one's life was practically impossible. He returned to the folder and flipped the cover letter over. There was a drawing underneath, a drawing that struck him as being out of place. It was ... too familiar. Familiar, and yet it didn't belong there – it was from another life. It was as if he'd woken up and found in his bed some object he'd clutched in a dream.

'Have you seen the economic reports?' Thurman asked. 'Do you know how many jobs this bill created overnight?' He snapped his fingers. 'Forty thousand, just like that. And that's only from Georgia. A lot will be from your district, a lot of shipping, a lot of stevedores. Of course, now that it's passed, our less nimble colleagues are grumbling that *they* should've had a chance to bid—'

'I drew this,' Donald interrupted, pulling out the sheet of paper. He showed it to Thurman as if the Senator would be surprised to see it had snuck into the folder. Donald wondered if this was the Senator's daughter's doing, some kind of a joke or hello-and-wink from Anna.

Thurman nodded. 'Yes, well, it needs more detail, wouldn't you say?'

Donald studied the architectural illustration and wondered what sort of test this was. He remembered the drawing. It was a last-minute project for his biotecture class his senior year. There was nothing unusual or amazing about it. His professor had given him a B, the red ink still tinged purple from where it had bled into the overlapping streaks of blue sky.

With an impartial eye, Donald would give the project a C+. It was spare where his classmates had been bold, utilitarian where he could've taken risks. Green tufts jutted up from the flat roof, a horrible cliché. Half the building was cut away to reveal the interspersed levels for housing, working and shopping.

In sum, it was drab and boring. Donald couldn't imagine a design so bare rising from the deserts of Dubai alongside the great new breed of self-sustaining skyscrapers. He certainly couldn't see what the Senator wanted him to do with it, other than maybe burn it.

'More detail,' he murmured, repeating the Senator's words. He flipped through the rest of the folder, looking for hints, for context.

'Hm.' Thurman sipped from his water bottle.

'Wait.' Donald studied a list of requirements written up as if by a prospective client. 'This looks like a design proposal.' Words he had forgotten he'd ever learned caught his eye: *interior traffic flow, block plan, HVAC, hydroponics—*

'You'll have to lose the sunlight.' Senator Thurman's chair squeaked as he leaned over his desk. He moved Donald's sweating bottle to a coaster and wiped the leather dry with his palm.

'I'm sorry?'

'It's nothing. Forget about it.' Thurman waved his hand, obviously meaning the circle of moisture left by Donald's bottle.

'No, you said sunlight.' Donald held the folder up. 'What exactly are you wanting me to do?'

'I would suggest something like those lights my wife uses.' He cupped his hand into a tiny circle and pointed at the centre. 'She gets these tiny seeds to sprout in the winter, uses bulbs that cost me a goddamned fortune.'

'You mean grow lights.'

Thurman snapped his fingers. 'And don't worry about the cost. Whatever you need. I'm also going to get you some help with the mechanical stuff. An engineer. An entire team.'

Donald flipped through more of the folder. 'What is this *for?* And why me?'

'This is what we call a *just-in-case* building. Probably'll never get used, but they won't let us store the fuel rods out there unless we put this bugger nearby. It's like this window in my basement I had to lower before our house could pass inspection. It was for ... what do you call it—?'

'Egress,' Donald said, the word flowing back unaided.

Thurman snapped his fingers. 'Right. Egress.' He pointed to the folder. 'This building is like that window, something we've gotta build so the rest'll pass inspection. This'll be where – in the unlikely event of an attack or a leak – where facility employees can go. You know, like a shelter. And it needs to be *perfect* or this project'll be shut down faster than a tick's wink. Just because our bill passed and got signed doesn't mean we're home-free, Donny. There was that project out west that got okayed decades ago, scored funding. Eventually, it fell through.'

Donald knew the one he was talking about. A containment facility buried under a mountain. The buzz on the Hill was that the Georgia project had the same chances of success. The folder suddenly tripled in weight as he considered this. He was being asked to be a part of this future failure. He would be staking his newly won office on it.

'I've got Mick Webb working on something related. Logistics and planning, really. You two will need to collaborate on a few things. And Anna is taking leave from her post at MIT to lend a hand.'

'*Anna?*' Donald fumbled for his water, his hand shaking.

'Of course. She'll be your lead engineer on this project. There are details in there on what she'll need, space-wise.'

Donald took a gulp of water and forced himself to swallow.

'There are a lot of other people I could call in, sure, but this project can't fail, you understand? It needs to be like *family*. People I can trust.' Senator Thurman interlocked his fingers. 'If this is the only thing you were elected to do, I want you to do it right. It's why I stumped for you in the first place.'

'Of course.' Donald bobbed his head to hide his confusion. He had worried during the election that the Senator's endorsement stemmed from old family ties. This was somehow worse. Donald hadn't been using the Senator at all; it was the *other way around*. Studying the drawing in his lap, the newly elected congressman felt one job he was inadequately trained for melt away – only to be replaced by a *different* job that seemed equally daunting.

'Wait,' he said. 'I still don't get it.' He studied the old drawing. 'Why the grow lights?'

Senator Thurman reached for his bottle and polished off his water, the empty plastic crinkling in his fist. He smacked his lips and turned to toss the bottle into a blue recycling bin. His profile, Donald saw, was every bit as chiselled and handsome as the face he presented to the cameras. He had barely changed in all the years Donald had known him.

'Because, Donny—' He turned and smiled. 'This building I want you to design for me – it's going to go *below* ground.'

Hugh Howey spent eight years living on boats and working as a yacht captain for the rich and famous. It wasn't until the love of his life carried him away from these vagabond ways that he began to pursue literary adventures, rather than literal ones. Hugh wrote and self-published his first young adult novel, *Molly Fyde and the Parsona Rescue*. The Molly Fyde series won rave reviews and praise from readers but it was the release of *Wool* that made his career take off.